A Night with Damien Spur

A Night
with
Damien
Spur

Nina Saville

The Book Guild Ltd

First published in Great Britain in 2024 by
The Book Guild Ltd
Unit E2 Airfield Business Park,
Harrison Road, Market Harborough,
Leicestershire. LE16 7UL
Tel: 0116 2792299
www.bookguild.co.uk
Email: info@bookguild.co.uk
X: @bookguild

Typeset in 11pt Minion Pro

Printed and bound in Great Britain by 4edge Limited

ISBN 978 1835740 804

British Library Cataloguing in Publication Data.
A catalogue record for this book is available from the British Library.

To my beloved husband, legendary film and television director Philip Saville, who passed away December 22nd 2016. He mentored me for 36 years and taught me the essence of telling a story. The lows and the highs, the opera of life. How to weave the falls and crescendos from the darkness to the light.

Chapter 1

Damien Spur wasn't afraid of being on the edge of a precipice. He usually took a deep breath and jumped.

Sometimes he wondered how he'd lived so long, what with his desire to flood himself with every wicked pleasure, which would probably speed him along to an early death.

But tonight there was no danger. He'd kept his nose clean. He was Damien Spur, the star novelist, who had written another brilliant thriller.

It was a warm summer's evening in early June and Central London was a happy bustle of tourists and after-hours office workers enjoying glasses of chilled wine and alfresco dining in the street cafes, pubs and restaurants. Not quite the seasonal mass migration to Mediterranean climes yet, and so a perfect opportunity for book promotions and parties.

Time to celebrate, said the Voice in his head, as Damien stepped out of the limousine his publisher had sent for him.

'Leave me alone,' growled Damien. 'I can do this on my own.'

But, despite being an extraordinary writer with many successes behind him, he didn't believe that. Not really.

Apart from his literary gift he was also dangerously attractive. His eyes, an arresting navy blue, fixed a gaze that allowed no secrets, which some people found unsettling. But that warm smile, which reached his eyes and came unexpectedly, was a formidable weapon.

Especially when it came to women.

So tonight, impeccably dressed in a relaxed navy linen suit and white shirt, he ignored the Voice laughing quietly at him and stepped into the magnificent room overlooking Hyde Park, without any need to make his presence known.

Everyone was waiting for him; an electric thrill sparked through the crowded room.

He swooped a drink from a passing tray and was instantly surrounded, strangers throwing compliments at him like confetti.

'Love it, Damien, love it! You've done it again. Great reviews. *Writing in the Sand*, a page-turner, a sixties-mood thriller. Ernest Hemingway meets Raymond Chandler.'

Though it had been said before, his smile lit up his face. Hemingway. Chandler. His literary heroes.

And then someone asked the inevitable question. 'What next?' Which was fine. There was always another novel in the pipeline, or a film deal.

Most of the time, the stories just came to him. Sometimes, he would wake in the middle of the night and the words flowed like a burst dam. At other times, he'd wait. Let the characters talk to him, lead him, and he would follow.

The Empress, his first novel, written in his early twenties, had been a huge success. That was swiftly followed by his next book, *Legends Never Die*, another winner. And so his prolific output had continued, which had kept his agent, Angus McManus, happy for over fifteen years.

Damien Spur, star of the stable, always raced through his bestsellers, keeping pace with his readers' insatiable appetite for his books, while Angus cracked the whip.

'Come on,' he said when Damien slowed down. 'Get that brain into gear. Spin those yarns.'

It suited Damien, spurred him on.

He loved being famous, making huge amounts of money from the gift the good Lord had given him. He thrived in the limelight.

Yes, but nobody knows you like I do, said the Voice in Damien's head.

Oh, shut up, thought Damien, catching sight of a dazzling blonde standing tall amidst the usual dull literary flotsam.

Please, please, for once, just leave me alone. The blonde looked fresh and confident. Wide-eyed with a glittering smile, surrounded by a group of men eager to joust for her attention.

He wound his way towards his target. En route, he grabbed Elsa, a sexy ex, and paused to slip a smile at the lens of his favourite pap.

'Damien, you bastard, great to see you,' she whispered, and gave his ear a sharp nip. He winced at the camera. She smiled sweetly.

Click, click.

'Hey, George, make sure you send me the images before you print.'

'Yuh, boss!' he said.

'Thanks for that, Elsa.' He rubbed his battered earlobe.

'My pleasure, Damien.'

'You're such a bitch,' he said.

'Best in show. My bite's always worse than my bark,' she replied, and turned away. He moved on.

The blonde beauty was talking to his agent.

'Ah, Damien!' Angus said. 'Our star. Let me introduce you to the charming Sophie Fox.'

'I fully intended to introduce myself, but thank you,' he said.

'Oh, by the way, we need to discuss the film rights,' Angus said as a parting shot.

Sophie Fox was even better close up.

The breeze from the open French window brought with it the faint sounds of picnic conversations, cyclists, children laughing, birdsong.

But Damien was not to be distracted.

Sophie's red silk sleeveless dress flattered her slim, graceful body, falling just short of her knees. His eyes slipped down to her ankles, encased in delicate leather-strapped high-heeled sandals, which showed off her pretty feet and bright red toenails.

'*Writing in the Sand* is an intriguing title,' she said. 'Who wrote the message? Who sees it before it's washed away? A stranger? Or someone the writer knows?'

A good opener. And he liked her voice. Low and throaty. Soothing, like a hot toddy on a cold night. He swallowed. He could see at a glance that it wasn't going to be easy. She wasn't the type to fall for a quick pitch.

I like her, said the Voice, startling Damien.

'Y-yes,' replied Damien. 'Good titles create a platform for intelligent readers to project a storyline even before reading the book.'

He watched her face. Was she still interested? Yes, she was focused.

'And that's why I don't like spoilers from the critics. Before today's launch, the story has been kept strictly under wraps.'

For heaven's sake, cut to the chase, said the Voice.

'Must say, the reviews were fascinating, very mysterious. Couldn't have asked for better publicity.'

Nearly there.

'And with this title I've never pre-sold so many.'

Boom! Now, Damien, now... said the Voice. *Switch gear. Enough about you. What about her?*

'So, are you very mysterious, Sophie?'

'Let's put it this way, I'm not going to tell my life story to a stranger.'

Not the sort of answer he was looking for. He'd have to try harder.

'That's fair,' he said, 'but a little bit of history makes a conversation more compelling, don't you think?'

'Okay, so what would you like to ask me?'

'Are you married?'

'Not anymore.'

'Single?'

'Sometimes.'

'Sometimes?'

'When I feel I need a break,' she said.

'Mmm… That seems a good cue to me for your next hiatus. Why don't I call your mobile and you'll have my number if you feel like company,' he said.

'Didn't bring it with me.'

'Okay. Don't have a piece of paper, but give me your arm.' He took a sleek gold monogrammed fountain pen from the inside pocket of his jacket.

Sophie giggled as the tip tickled the inside of her arm.

He gave her a smile, and she blinked, her laughter fading. 'The romance of a good fountain pen,' said Damien. 'Such a pleasure to control the flow of ink. Do you have a tissue?'

She took one from her satin evening bag. Softly, he blotted her smooth skin.

'Now then, better not wash it away until you write it down. Unless, of course, you have no interest in keeping it.'

'Why not? Always good to add entertaining people to my guest list. Do you always like to brand women like cattle?'

'Only if they become my chattel.'

'Hold your horses! We've only just met, and you're already giving me the caveman chat.'

'But I've already made up my mind – you're definitely the one.'

'Well, I like your enthusiasm, but I'm a slow burner.'

'That's fine. I can wait. Better than a quick-fire romance,' he said.

It was the way he said it that made Sophie laugh. As if he were playing the smitten lover.

A wry grin spread across his face, as if to say, "How was I?"

You were great, Damien. Not too intense. But you're really keen, aren't you? Admit it. Like I always say, nobody knows you like I do, said the Voice.

George the pap whisked around.

Damien kept his grin as the photographer snapped. And that's when he blew it.

Plucking a pistachio from the porcelain dish, he tried to prise the stubborn shell open with his finger, but the gap was too narrow, and his nail got stuck. He yanked it out and popped the nut in his mouth and, clamping the edge of the shell with his teeth, split his incisor.

A needle of pain shot through his mouth and into his head. He clapped his hand to his lips, his eyes squeezing shut.

That's really blown your cool, hasn't it? sighed the Voice.

Sophie's laughter stopped abruptly. 'Damien?' she said, frowning, her hand gripping his forearm. 'Are you okay? You've gone as white as a sheet.'

'My tooth,' mumbled Damien.

What a klutz! said the Voice. *Just don't make a fuss. Say goodbye and go*, but Damien was already raising his hand in a polite farewell to Sophie, and heading for the door.

Chapter 2

Anna Rose examined her top lip. She hadn't seen those fine vertical lines before.

Her mother had warned her. *Don't scowl, don't pucker – and no big smiles. It will give you early wrinkles and crow's feet.*

Mirror, mirror, stay away. The years slip by. Stuck with her ex-husband, who has nowhere to go.

'Please, Anna,' he said, 'I'll pay the bills. Can't help being ill. I'll find a place. But, for now, please let me stay with you. I don't feel safe by myself.'

Anna felt sorry for him. And, to tell the truth, she needed the extra money.

Especially if she wanted to stay pretty. Find another fella. Give up being a dogsbody. But nearly four years down the line the ex still hadn't left.

Never mind. David Rose was her penance and duty. All those years when he pursued her, wooed her, looked after her.

David Rose, the once famous Mayfair restaurateur – patron of the legendary Valentino's, which he'd named after the eponymous lothario – had lived for romance.

Handsome waiters dressed in white shirts and velvet waistcoats served impeccable dishes and an excellent wine list.

And if music be the food of love, to encourage proposals,

a beautiful couple sang romantic ballads, reclining on a chaise lounge atop a rostrum strewn with flowers in the centre of the room, accompanied by a pianist.

Very soon, Valentino's became the go-to proposal restaurant. But money and fame had given David a taste for playing the tables. It started well enough. Sparked by his wins at roulette and blackjack he continued his nightly visits to the casino until Lady Luck turned her back, his gambling addiction took hold of him and he lost everything to chance.

After a quick shower, Anna returned to her dressing table. She peered at her face again.

Be brave, Anna! A lovely face. Almost doll-like, save for the landscape of fine lines etched around her sparkling almond-shaped eyes.

No time to waste. Swiftly applying mascara, tinted moisturiser, and her "kiss me" lip gloss, she gave her long dark hair a curt brush.

Next, she slipped on a simple, shift dress in a soft shade of powder blue, hastily clipped on delicate pearl earrings, and tucked her dainty little feet into cream leather kitten heels.

Audrey Hepburn style, her heroine, ever since she'd seen *Breakfast at Tiffany's.*

No need to think about her life, just get on with the day. And tonight, after she had made the dinner, she would close her bedroom door and write. Keep the demons at bay. Escape into her beautiful world of hope, where everything turned rosy pink and there were no dark angels.

The children's stories she told in her nursery-school days had always captivated the little boys and girls. What a gift she had. Such a bitter twist that David and she hadn't been able to have kids of their own. A low sperm count, the doctor had said. They had tried IVF for two years with no happy ending.

But for now Anna had taken a job as a medical receptionist. Despite her talent as a teacher, the nursery schools were taking younger women – they were cheaper. Anna's magic with children wasn't considered at a premium.

Down she went, swooping past her ex, whose extended temporary residence was in the guest bedroom.

She held her breath, and waited for his daily request.

'Anna, make me a cup of tea,' he wailed from his bed. 'Please, Anna…'

'No! I'm going to be late.'

Resigned, kettle boiled, she brought him a white mug of pale grey liquid. She crept into the darkened room and turned on the light.

'Oh, it's hurting my eyes! Please turn it off.'

'For goodness' sake.' She opened the curtains. 'I'm going to be late. I need this job.'

'I once was a man. Don't make me feel like a loser. You've had a good life, Anna. I've done my best.'

He glanced at the tea. 'You could have let it brew for longer.'

'Don't push your luck.'

She gulped down an instant coffee with a dash of milk, grabbed her coat and off to Planet Earth she went to the medical practice in Harley Street.

There were no seats on the packed bus to Baker Street. Steadying herself on the handhold, her legs braced stiffly apart, Anna stared in disgust at a young man with a mop of blond hair and full, girlish lips who sat with his backpack in a designated place for the disabled and elderly. He was too busy texting to notice her. She felt giddy. The heaving bodies squeezed her bones.

Next stop, backpack man got up and, pushing past Anna, roughly nudged her shoulder with his bulbous bag.

'What are you doing? Bloody rucksack! You just hit me. Shouldn't be allowed on a crowded bus.'

'I am so sorry. I didn't see you,' he said in a clipped foreign accent.

'Of course not! You blind fool! You're a teenager. You don't see anyone over the age of twenty-five. Yes, yes! Typical! You're German, aren't you? We know what you lot are like. Ruthless! Bagging mattresses around hotel pools at 6 a.m., while the rest of the guests are asleep.'

Anna stopped short. That's exactly what her mother would have said. It just popped out of her mouth as if it were nothing to do with her.

Maybe she'd become bipolar? Could it be depression? David Rose had worn her down. How dare he make her suffer. It wasn't as if she was his wife anymore.

Damn him!

The young man scuttled off the bus, shamed.

The next stop was Anna's.

She ran along the pavement like an untethered emu. Arriving at the Edwardian building, she flung herself up the stone steps and rang the bell.

'Hi, Sam! So sorry I'm late, had a terrible time on the bus,' she said into the intercom. The porter buzzed her in.

'Morning, Anna.' The old Scotsman handed her the daily schedule and looked at his watch. 'You're fifteen minutes late, and it's going to be busy today. Luckily, Nurse Aileen isn't here yet. And you know what she's like. A hard-working woman and a stickler for time.' He had kind eyes, with a glimmer of good humour, despite his outwardly dour demeanour. Anna liked him.

'Thanks, Sam. I'll get to it. Just hope we don't have any more problems with Dr Patel's clients. His secretary fits them in like sardines in a can. And he always keeps them waiting. The women look normal going up and when they come down their lips look like... like... pork sausages!'

'Anna, please speak quietly. Dr Patel is in the downstairs bathroom because there's something wrong with the loo on his floor. The walls have ears,' he said.

'Okay,' Anna moved closer to Sam and whispered conspiratorially, 'But what about that Mrs Cougar, shouting and screaming at me the other day!' You were off duty, but I'm sure you heard about it. Every five minutes, she said, "Call him again! Call him again! Call him again!" Like a broken record, and no "please"! As if it's my fault she waited half an hour to see him. So, I said, "Please, there's no need to shout – this isn't a fish market!". And that was it – she went crazy. Said she would report me for insulting her. 'Anna, your tongue is running away with you. Calm down.' The porter looked askance, as Dr Patel appeared.

Anna paused as the dapper doctor bounced up the stairs. Then, making sure that he was out of earshot, she grasped Sam's arm and moved closer to him to whisper, 'So, anyway, it gets worse. Then the other woman waiting to see the doctor started, said she was first. It got very vindictive. Well, what was I to do except tell them to keep their voices down? And then, can you imagine, they both turned on me.'

'Anna! You are not the UN peacekeeping force. Don't interfere with other people's business. And it's not your place to criticise Dr Patel. You'll get fired if he hears you've been gossiping about him. Not that it would come from me. Now get on with your work.' He patted her arm. 'The first patient is due in five minutes.'

Happy to be ensconced in the peaceful reception room with its inviting brown velvet sofa, leather armchairs and polished walnut table displaying a tempting array of glossy magazines, Anna settled herself at the grand Edwardian mahogany desk and glanced at the appointment list, ready and waiting to activate her charm for patients.

Anna greeted an impeccably groomed, tall red-headed woman with a polite smile. 'Hello, Mrs Askew. You've come to see Dr Lederman.'

'Yes.'

'Would you like to sit down? He shouldn't be long.'

Mrs Askew gave Anna a cursory glance, picked up a magazine from the waiting-room table and settled herself in the leather armchair.

Not even a hello? How rude of you, Anna thought. *No doubt your life is enviably neat. A house in the country, a flat in town. A wealthy husband who deals with financials, while you arrange perfect dinner parties between eating out at top restaurants, visits to the theatre and swanky holidays.*

Christmas in Barbados? No, probably at the country estate with the family and then to the Caribbean or Mexico for New Year.

Skiing in Feb, Gstaad or Courchevel? June in Sardinia or Santorini?

September to Kenya, South Africa, Zanzibar, not to forget weekends in Paris, Rome or New York.

That's where I used to go.

We have more in common than you know. Probably stayed in the same hotels and no doubt you ate at my husband's restaurant.

So perhaps you might be a little more polite next time. A nod would be fine.

Never mind, one day your husband will tire of your sour face, find a lovely young calf and put you out to pasture.

A steady stream of patients diverted her from vengeful thoughts.

Anna chivvied the kiddies waiting to be seen by the doctors for twitches and this and that.

In between the comings and goings, she popped a boiled sweet in her mouth from a stash she kept in a drawer and checked her mobile for emails.

There were the usual missives from travel firms selling cut-price holidays to exotic places that she couldn't afford but to which she subscribed just in case she had a windfall. She deleted those – but clicked the link in the message from her favourite online store, Eve's Lingerie Boutique, which had announced a mega sale. Searching through the underwear sets, she chose a pretty lavender lace bra with pink rosebuds and matching briefs for £20 and saved it in her basket.

She felt safe in the refined elegant room. Calm. Not like home, where emotions were stripped bare.

Fewer patients than the early morning rush allowed her a cup of instant coffee that she made in the little kitchen, and a ginger nut biscuit.

Back at her desk, she flicked through the glossy magazine she kept hidden in her drawer.

Holidays, divorces, weddings and glamorous celebrity parties. Anna was in flight mode, sipping a pina colada in Barbados with Brad Pitt when the doorbell buzzed.

'Your name, please?' Anna asked politely.

'Damien Spur. I haven't got an appointment, but I've chipped a tooth. I spoke with Dr Lacey this morning. He said he would squeeze me in between sessions.'

'That's fine. Please come in.'

Anna looked at his wildly handsome face and felt a rush of pleasure that made her blush.

She dropped her eyes and scanned the diary. 'I'm sure he won't be long, Mr Spur. I can see there's been a cancellation at midday.'

'I will probably need a couple of visits, but I might make it three.' He gave her a roguish smile.

She noticed his chipped incisor. She imagined him biting her neck.

'You're the thriller writer, aren't you?' Anna asked. 'I'm ashamed to say I haven't read your books. I mostly read historical novels. But I'm always seeing your photo in magazines.'

'What's your name?'

'Anna. Anna Rose.'

'Ah! A rose by any other name would smell as sweet. Now, can you find out what time Dr Lacey can see me?'

'Oh, of course, Mr Spur.' She buzzed up. 'He'll see you in fifteen minutes.'

'That's good,' he said, scanning back and forth from her lashy brown eyes to her cute little breasts… and back again.

'May I just say, funnily enough, I've written a children's book.' She gave him a flirty smile.

Here was a man who could change her life – and she must seize the opportunity. Carpe diem, do or die. She took courage.

'I know you're a terribly famous writer but I'm wondering, if you have the time, perhaps you could read my story. I would love to know your thoughts.'

Damien, please, said the Voice. *She's cute, but don't get carried away. Children's stories aren't your bag – and what happens if she can't write?*

He smiled. 'Well, okay. If it has potential, I'm happy to give you suggestions to improve it. But, if not, I'll tell you the truth.'

'Of course, I expect you to say what you think. It's kind of you to read it. Thank you so much.'

'What's it called?'

'*The Dog That Lost Its Bark*.'

'Good title,' he said.

'Thanks. Pleased you like it.'

'Yes, I do. Titles are very important. The first glimpse of what the reader sees on the bookshelf. Either it can pique their curiosity, entice them to open the door and see what's inside, or, if it's boring, they'll skim right past it. Take *War and Peace*, Tolstoy's legendary novel – those three little words cover the whole scope of human history.'

Yes, Anna thought as she listened to him talk, *I'm going to sleep with you.*

'And then there are the great books with just a character as the title. *Oliver Twist*, *Rebecca*, *Jane Eyre*, etc. They plant questions in the reader's mind. Who are they? What is their journey?'

'I do hope you like my story,' she said. 'I can tell you'll be a good teacher. Can I give you a hard copy? If you like, I could drop it round after work if you give me your address.'

Watch it, Damien. It's getting a bit too cosy. Keep it professional, at least until you've read it.

'Hard copy is fine, but don't worry – I'll pick it up at my next appointment. And maybe after I've read it, we can discuss it over coffee.' He gave her a generous smile.

A timely buzz. 'Dr Lacey is ready for you,' said Anna, returning Damien's smile as he disappeared up the stairs. 'And so am I,' Anna added to herself, clicking BUY on her Lingerie Boutique basket.

Chapter 3

Prompted by the seeds of promise that Damien Spur had sown, Anna sat back in the comfortable leather chair ready to let her thoughts fly.

In her mind's eye, she is on television reading *The Dog That Lost Its Bark* to a forum of children who sit enthralled on the television-studio floor.

She is wearing a pink-and-white-check prairie dress with puffed sleeves and a full skirt, her tiny waist cinched in a slim silver belt with matching ballerina pumps. She's near to the end of her tale, an allegory of Dickensian heights about a very rich but mean man called Iver Fortune, who learnt to love the world through a sweet servant girl and his once fierce dog.

Face to camera, Anna reads the final passage.

A presenter walks on to the stage floor.

'Thank you so much, Anna, for reading your beautiful story. And now I think you have some very exciting news for us.'

'Yes. My tale has been bought by Disney and I shall be writing the screenplay.'

'Anna, wake up! Where are you?' The efficient Irish practice nurse vigorously shook her shoulder. 'The patient has been buzzing for the last five minutes. She had to ring the practice to say there was no one to let her in. This is not the first time you've been up in your head playing with the fairies.'

'Oh no! I'm so sorry, Aileen!' Anna slapped her hand ferociously on the intercom.

'Too late for that, my girl. I let her in. She was already late for Dr Faith and so she went straight up.'

Anna reddened. 'Oh, I really don't know what to say. Please don't report me. Mrs Cougar has already lodged a complaint about me.'

'I'm sorry, but the truth of the matter is you just aren't doing your job. It's not enough to have a posh voice and nice little dresses. Your fluffy behaviour isn't suited to a top Harley Street practice.'

If only Anna could say what she really thought.

You're a nasty piece of work. I bet you're jealous of my pretty face and good legs. And there's you with your beady eyes and pinched lips without a trace of make-up, thick tights and flat black lace-up shoes, which make you look old and frumpy.

But Anna couldn't afford an argument, so she looked at the floor like a naughty child and let Aileen carry on scolding her.

Until Damien came down to say goodbye.

Anna flushed with embarrassment.

She needed to compose herself. Act with grace and dignity.

She smiled at Aileen and said sweetly, 'I'm sorry. It won't happen again.'

'Better not,' the nurse replied. 'You're here to do your job. The first thing the clients see is you. And if you're sitting at your desk half asleep, or eating sweets, it doesn't make a good impression.'

'What's this?' Damien interrupted. 'Are we having a spot of bother?'

'Not at all – everything's fine,' Anna replied.

'Good,' he said quietly. He turned to the nurse. 'Now then, I suggest that you go somewhere private if you want to tell your receptionist off. Very unprofessional.'

'I'm sorry. There was no one else in the waiting room and I didn't hear you come down the stairs.'

'Just as your receptionist didn't hear the buzzer.'

'Point taken. Right then, Anna. I'll leave you to it.' Aileen turned on her heels and walked away.

That was great, Damien, said the Voice. *What a hero.*

'Thank you so much,' Anna said. Her eyes shone with undisguised admiration.

Better watch out she doesn't corner you. Just read her story and proceed with caution.

'Goodbye, Anna. I'm booked in for next Tuesday morning. Until then,' he said, and left. Anna shut her eyes and took a deep breath. She was alive again.

***

Damien was tired. It was hard keeping up a facade.

He hailed a taxi. Sat in the back of the cab, rubbed his cheek. His gum felt numb. He'd take a painkiller when he arrived home. Maybe it was best that he was alone. He had all those women ready and willing, but all they wanted was Damien Spur, the sexy, charismatic writer. Why couldn't he be like most men? Fall in love with a one and only who loved him even when he was a raging nutter.

Because you're a must-have-can't-have man, said the Voice. *You don't really want a kind, caring angel; you need the sting in the tail or you're not interested.*

***

It was 2 p.m. when he arrived home. He opened the green door of his elegant town house. The place smelt of polish.

Marta, his Portuguese cleaner, had been.

He liked Marta. She was discreet. Turned a blind eye to his recreational habits.

He'd come home the night before and drunk half a bottle of whisky and smoked a couple of joints. The empty shot glasses and cigarette papers had been cleared from the glass table in the living room.

He went into the kitchen. Pristine, with no evidence of last night's debauchery.

In his ravenous stupor, he'd cooked a seafood pasta, but unfortunately, he'd been so plastered that he'd spilt it all over the tiled floor.

He'd keep the kitchen tidy this evening. Order a takeaway. Or maybe go to the Italian round the corner.

He switched on the TV. He loved watching old films in the afternoon. Especially the children's channel.

Bambi! You've got to be kidding, said the Voice. *You're already feeling sorry for yourself. Don't you remember what happened the last time when Bambi's mummy got shot? Boxing Day, two years ago. You couldn't stop crying in front of that Austrian model Clara Voss and her sister, Lena. Swore you'd never go hunting again.*

Damien poured himself a couple of shots and rolled a joint.

Bang goes Bambi, said the Voice.

***

Anna came home to find David slouched in an armchair watching the news.

'Oh, you're here,' she said. 'I thought you were going out with Stevie tonight.' She'd looked forward to an evening on her own.

'He's got the flu and I don't want to catch it. Haven't I got enough wrong with me? Had another blackout today. Lucky I was already on the sofa.'

'Where else would you be?' Anna said. She narrowed her eyes at him. 'Anyway, you seem okay now.'

'Yes, I bought a roast chicken and some salad. Lucky I didn't pass out in Waitrose or we wouldn't have had anything to eat this evening, would we?'

'Oh, for goodness' sake, David! You're at home all day and it takes you ten minutes to walk to the shops. The man next door is eighty-six and walks with a stick and he still manages to go out and buy the groceries. And you make such a big thing of it.'

Anna gave him a cursory look and, grabbing the remote from the side table next to his chair, switched off the TV.

'What are you doing?' David whined. 'Turn it on.'

'No, I've got a headache.'

'Yes, sure. Come on, you just want to make my life a misery. Why can't you let me be?'

'Poor you, sitting on your backside all day doing nothing, complaining how ill you are and yet you can still go down to the bookies and place your bets.'

'That's the only pleasure I get!' he said. 'I'd like to see how you'd cope with a dicky heart and chronic asthma to boot. You're a bloody ball-breaker, you are!' he shouted, his voice collapsing in a breathy wheeze. 'Look at me.' He clutched his chest. 'I'm a bloody wreck. Why don't you get a gun and shoot me? I'd be better off dead.'

'Oh, shut up!' Anna screamed back. 'I'm tired of your histrionics. Four years of hell. I'm fed up with your insults. Ball-breaker! How can you say that to me, you revolting man? You should have married a fishwife. At least you would have talked the same language. I'm going upstairs for a rest.'

She was exhausted. Lucky he didn't ask her for a cup of tea, or she would have thrown it at him. It was as if she wasn't a woman anymore. To think how he once had adored her. Called her his angel.

Said he would die for her.

Sometimes she thought if only he would. No more visceral slanging matches cutting each other to pieces, always ready for the next bout.

She slammed the bedroom door, kicked off her shoes and

20

threw herself onto the mattress. Propping a pillow behind her head, she googled "Damien Spur wife".

Divorced, that's good. No need for him to lie to her.

Impressive glittering accolades and reviews made him a worthy suitor. Her mother would certainly approve.

She allowed herself a fantasy. A wish. A future where she did more than just exist from day to day, locked in, hands tied, with a man who made her feel lonely.

Things happen when you dream. Damien Spur had flirted with her. He was going to read her book. Why not?

They would be great together.

She, the writer of enchanting fairy tales, and he, the glamorous literary legend, author of iconic political thrillers and darling of the glitterati, whose novels rocked the bestseller list every time.

Anna opened the bedside drawer and took out a notepad. Write it down, plot the story. Make it happen.

She shut her eyes and visualised her plan.

Number 1. She gives him the manuscript. He strokes her hand. 'Thank you, Anna. I'll read it as soon as I can,' he says.

Number 2. Damien sits next to her at Antoine's coffee shop wearing a blue silk shirt that matches his sapphire eyes.

'Anna,' he says, 'what a wonderful surprise. You have a great gift. There is no doubt in my mind that *The Dog That Lost Its Bark* will become a fable that is passed down through generations of children. A true classic. Let's work on it together.'

Number 3… Back to her place.

'Oh, Damien, what pretty flowers.' She kisses his cheek. He holds her. They linger, the chemistry is strong.

She pulls away from him and laughs. He's still holding her waist. 'Story first,' she says.

She knows he wants her. Let him wait.

Anna flies high in her fantasy land as she lies on her bed,

arms spread like a bird's wings, floating in dreams of what could be, what should be.

Damien sits next to her, focused, ready to light the fuse, fire her imagination. His voice is soft and gentle, coaxing her creativity...

Her delicious reverie was shattered by David Rose rasping up the stairs like a scratchy violin. 'Anna, Anna, pick up the bloody phone! Your mother's on the line.'

She heard, but waited for David to repeat himself. Just to annoy him.

'Anna, I said pick up the phone. Why can't you ask her to ring your mobile? I'm trying to watch the news!'

'Didn't hear you – the television was so loud.' Anna stretched out her arm and grasped the extension on the bedside table.

'Hello, Mother. Yes, I can take you for your blood test... I'll pick you up at ten. Brunch, oh, that would be nice... We could go to Antoine's, and I can drive straight on to work and you can get a taxi home... Yuh, I'm okay. Not the life I hoped for, but things can change. Thank goodness I have my little job. I meet some very interesting people... Okay, Mummy, see you tomorrow.'

***

Evelyn felt guilty that Anna's life had taken a dip. David Rose. Who could have predicted his demise?

But then again, looking back to those heady days in the south of France, their frequent visits to the casino should have been a clue.

Silly fool, she was. Impressed by the largesse of the house. All that complimentary vintage champagne and copious amounts of caviar. It had suited Evelyn very well. She loved drinking. Why bother to kick the habit?

But this morning she sat with her daughter at Antoine's, both perfectly suited and coiffed, sipping orange pekoe tea.

The good-looking Indian gent at a neighbouring table turned to stare at Anna.

Happy to be noticed, Anna gave him a coy little smile.

Evelyn shifted closer. 'You see! You've still got it. How can you waste your life with a man who offers you nothing anymore? When is he leaving? Ridiculous, living with your ex! What a turn-off for any male.' Evelyn lanced the top of her boiled egg with a vicious flick of the wrist. 'I mean it, darling. You are ruining your life. You need someone to look after you. Neither a nurse nor a purse should you be.'

Anna patted a flake of croissant from her plate and licked it from her finger with her pink little tongue.

The Indian gent was mesmerised.

She glanced at her mother, who sat with a silly smile on her face, pretending not to notice that the man was ready to make a pitch.

I don't want this, Mother. You've done all right, but I want more. I want to be like Claudia. Rock bottom she was after her failed marriage, and look at her now – a world-class tarot-card reader. Busy morning till night with A-list film stars, artists, bankers, entrepreneurs, doctors and even royalty.

***

Damien had woken up with a searing headache. His mobile was ringing. Who the hell would call at 11 p.m.?

He grabbed the phone and put it on loudspeaker.

'Damien, where are you?'

Damien winced. 'Oh shit, Aidan. I forgot we were meeting.'

'We said 11 p.m. at the Haunt. I brought you the fish-scale cocaine. This is the purest you can get, Damien, my good fellow. A couple of lines goes a long way. It's more expensive than the normal blow, but worth the high... Only don't worry if you can't make it – there are plenty of punters here who would be more than happy to buy the stuff instead.' Aidan's voice had a slippery edge that Damien hated.

'No, it's mine. No fill-ins. I'm coming now.' He hung up with a sigh and got out of bed.

You're really not all there, Damien. Just look at yourself, said the Voice. *If you don't get clean, you're going to end up with a heart attack.*

Damien winked at himself in the hall mirror. 'Come on, it's not that bad. Just a few lines tonight and a bit of keep-fit with the girls.'

***

The Haunt was full of illicit delights. An exclusive members' club in Mayfair for those special punters who had passed the exacting criteria. Money, power, charisma and discretion.

A private place where public figures could lay down their armour and surrender to their secret passions and fantasies and know that each and every one of them had been sworn to a confidential oath never to reveal their fellow guests.

The punishment of indiscretion? A serious accident.

And in return politicians, heads of state, judges, royalty, aristocracy, entrepreneurs, each could be whoever they chose.

Damien had seen the Speaker of the House of Commons dressed as Dolly Parton, a judge wearing prison garb, members of the clergy clad in leather and chains, saints and devils, teddy bears and puppy dogs, all welcome to enjoy their peccadilloes.

The club was owned by a guy known only as Lazarus. Damien had met him at a party in Paris, held in the private mansion of the fabulously wealthy Countess Clotilde Duchamp, who had "mentored" Damien when he was a young man.

Lazarus had watched as the handsome buck had enthusiastically "attached" himself to a striking lioness with a main of tumbling auburn hair, wild green eyes and long muscly legs in one of the antechambers.

And here was Damien twenty years later standing outside the discreet black door. Ready for the night ride.

The facial recognition lock clicked and he was in.

Aidan was waiting in the hallway. A scrawny, leather-clad grinning ghoul with a bald head and bad teeth.

'Look, mate, I've another two stops to make so can we be quick?' He took out a plastic ziplock bag from his pocket. 'Five grams, fish scale, pure as the Virgin Mary, 700 quid.'

Damien said nothing. Just pulled out his wallet, gave Aidan the money and took the coke.

'Thanks, mate,' the dealer said.

'My pleasure. But can you do me a favour? Don't call me mate. I'm not your friend.'

'Maybe not but the coke is,' said Aidan. 'Oh, and by the way, if you like I've got some new little beauties that will let you go all night without any downside.' He gave him a leery grin.

'Not my problem.' Damien brushed him aside.

Cheeky little bastard, said the Voice.

Damien keyed in the code to the second door, his index finger firmly on the numbers, but a red light flashed.

An automated voice announced, 'Code incorrect. Please try again.'

'Shit.' Damien banged the keypad with his fist. 'What the hell?' He tried again.

It still didn't work.

'Come on, you bugger, let me in,' he yelled at the machine. 'Why isn't there a bloody intercom?'

He pulled out the bag and sniffed a line of coke.

'1973 – it's got to be right,' he muttered to himself.

No, you fool, that's your credit-card pin, said the Voice. *Try 2791.*

He entered the new passcode. A green light flashed and the door opened. 'Yes!' He punched the air.

There you are, said the Voice. *What would you do without me?*

Damien passed through the dimly lit corridor and stepped into a candlelit boudoir, all gilt and mirrors, scattered with writhing twosomes and threesomes playing with each other.

A beautiful female lay moaning on a velvet throw, wearing nothing but a pair of Jimmy Choos, while a man and a woman caressed her.

Damien moved on, hardly glancing at the bodies, until he came to a golden cage.

And there sitting on two swings were his Belarusian twins, Kristina and Alina, wearing velvet masks and feathered wings.

'We waited all night for you to come,' Alina said in her soft smoky voice. 'Naughty Damien – we haven't seen you for a whole month.'

'We want to play with you,' Kristina cooed.

Damien took out a card and keyed in the code, placing his index finger on the sensor.

The cage door opened.

He looked up at the girls and smiled.

'Good to see you looking so chirpy.'

You really are flying tonight, said the Voice.

'Come on, tweeties, hop off your perches.'

Great, Damien, even better, said the Voice.

The women held hands and stepped out of the cage.

Alina veiled his eyes with a black satin scarf. 'So, let's go to the playroom,' she said.

This is a bit strange… What's with the mask? said the Voice.

'Make sure you've turned off your mobile,' said Kristina. 'We don't want any interruptions, and no peeking. Just behave and we won't smack you.'

'Well, here we are.' Alina removed the scarf.

Damien hadn't seen the room before.

The garish red-silk walls, high domed stained-glass windows, bronze lamps with burgundy shades and a bed swathed in purple velvet and gold satin pillows made the room seem more like a seedy Soho dive than an exclusive Mayfair sex club.

'Isn't this cosy?' Alina undid his shirt and slid her finger down his chest while Kristina unzipped his trousers. Damien looked at the round mattress flanked by four leather straps as the twins undressed him.

Damien, what the fuck? said the Voice.

Then the girls grabbed each of his arms and flung him on the mattress.

'Oh no,' groaned Damien. 'Stop. No, no, *no.*'

'No?' Alina said. 'But the reception said when you rang that you booked the special.'

'Well, I didn't request it,' Damien replied. 'I couldn't understand what was being offered. I thought the woman said something about Thai.'

'Yes. Tie Me Up, Tie Me Down,' the twins chorused.

'Oh my Lord, this is crazy!' Damien said. 'I must have been high as a kite when I said yes.'

The women took off their velvet masks and pouted their red pillowy lips.

Damien wished he'd taken Aidan up on the Viagra.

Okay, Mr Smoothy, said the Voice. *No way you're going to get a boner. Your best boy's in a coma! How are you going to get out of this one?*

'Thank you,' Damien said. 'You girls are wonderful.' He kissed them slowly. 'I'm sorry, but I need to leave.'

Damien drove his Jag back to his home in Cheyne Walk, crawled up the stairs and slumped on his bed.

'Horrible,' he groaned. 'Just horrible.'

Indeed, said the Voice. *Absolutely horrible. I don't mean to be cruel but your performance tonight was a flop.*

As he sank into a slumber Sophie Fox fluttered elusively across his mind.

Chapter 4

Early morning, and Damien found himself fully dressed lying on the bathroom floor.

He always woke at the same time no matter what state he was in. It must have been his boarding-school drill.

7 a.m., eyes wide open, brush teeth, a cold shower, dressed and ready for porridge at 8 a.m.

'Good training,' his mother had said. 'Rigorous discipline will keep you on track.'

If only she knew.

Come on, pull yourself together, said the Voice.

Damien lifted himself up and staggered to the basin.

Brush teeth.

Damien glanced at his face in the mirror.

He noticed that his left cheek was swollen.

He couldn't recall having a fight. Then it came to him. He had woken up at 4 a.m. and had gone to the bathroom feeling dizzy and nauseous.

He must have fainted, banged his face on the black and white tiled floor.

Shower next. Cold.

And then breakfast.

Earl Grey tea with a spoon of acacia honey, porridge made with water, followed by apricot jam on toast.

He switched on the radio. *Sunday Worship*, BBC 4.

Morning has broken, like the first morning. Blackbird has spoken, like the first bird... Damien loved to sing along with the choir.

Better now? said the Voice. *You see, Mummy was right. A strict morning routine sets you up for the day. Such a pity it all goes to pot at night.*

'Aren't you funny? Quick as a whippet.'

Angus called. The ringtone jangled Damien's nerves. 'Are you coming this evening?'

'Where to?' Damien poured himself another cup of tea.

'The Olga Krilova exhibition at the White Space.'

'Oh! I forgot about it.'

'Don't you keep a diary?'

'Yes. But only for things I need to remember.'

Damien took a sip of tea. 'And to be honest I'm not really keen on the artist. I've seen her work in a gallery in Paris.'

Watch it. Don't say anything you might regret, said the Voice. *Bad karma.*

Damien didn't care. He was ready to let rip.

'I find her art miserable and nihilistic.' He stabbed the butter and spread it on a second piece of toast. 'She could make you lose the will to live. Absolutely depressing! How could anyone want to live with those grim paintings? I can't understand for the life of me why she's so famous.'

'Well, that was venomous!' Angus said. 'Apparently, she's read all your books and is a great fan. Asked the PR to invite you.'

'You're lying.'

'Yes I am.'

'Okay, so I won't be coming.'

'Fine, but maybe I can change your mind.' Angus paused...

'Well?'

'Well, I just happen to know that Sophie Fox is going.'

'I'll have a think. Let me ring you back.'

Go on, Damien, you need a bit of circuit training, said the Voice. *You're networking in the wrong places. Last night was such a waste of time. Cost you a fortune and for what? You couldn't even get it up. Had to go home with your tail between your legs. Not good for your street cred.*

'Oh, button up with your lectures.'

All right. If you don't want my advice, just do what you want. But you're a mess. And I'm the only one who can sort you out.

'Okay,' Damien sighed. 'I'll tell Angus that I'm going.'

Good. That's the spirit. Visits to whore houses are not the place to find a soulmate.

'I didn't go there looking for a soulmate,' replied Damien, reaching into the back of the freezer for an ice pack to nurse his swollen cheek.

Clear your head and keep off the ganja, said the Voice. *You know that after a couple of spliffs you talk gibberish.*

***

It was late afternoon when Damien left his house. He trod carefully down the stone steps and unlocked his car, mercifully parked outside.

He arrived at the White Space at 6 p.m.

The flat pedestrian concrete building in Bermondsey had that cold, edgy look that was popular with the new guard.

Damien preferred the welcoming architectural glory of the RA, the National Portrait Gallery and Tate Britain.

It was the contrast that excited him.

The old with the new.

'Damien Spur,' he said to the woman who stood at the entrance with a clipboard and pen.

'Ah yes, here you are.' She scrolled down the list and ticked him off with a flourish. 'It's good that you could come. I really enjoyed *Writing in the Sand*.'

'Thank you.' He gave her a friendly smile. He was used to being recognised but it always gave him a buzz.

'It's a pity I hadn't seen the guest list before today or I would have brought my book in for you to sign.'

'Never mind, maybe another time,' he replied.

He liked her face. Big intelligent eyes, a sweet smile – and that lilting Jamaican voice.

Too young for you, said the Voice.

Damien walked through the open door.

The vast white room hummed with clusters of people dressed in minimalist gear milling around with glasses of champagne, picking at the trays of sushi and edamame beans offered by young waiting staff dressed in black T-shirts and trousers, topped by purple aprons.

Damien read the graffiti splashed on the first wall in big black shiny letters.

My art is subjective. No questions, no answers. Olga Krilova is me, and me is my art.

The next wall read:

Let your mind flow. Choose what you want to see. But don't ask me what I think or what I know.

Well, that's a conversation stopper, said the Voice.

Damien scanned the crowd. There she was, across the room – with a man.

Keep your cool, said the Voice. *Don't jump to conclusions. If she catches your eye, give her a casual wave. But take your time to amble over. Don't want to seem too eager.*

Damien nodded to himself, but his attention was quickly diverted by Angus, talking to a pale-skinned guy with long grey hair and large, black-framed glasses. Even from a distance he recognised him. It was Lazarus.

Better steer clear. Just in case Angus had been to the Haunt. Probably not. He was far too mean to spend a £1,000 for a night in the sack.

Damien started to amble his way towards Sophie. A painting caught his eye – a black square on a grey canvas and a girl in a white dress holding a bleeding heart on a cushion, titled *Sacrifice to Unrequited Love.*

Poor woman, said the Voice, *she definitely needs cheering up.*

He moved on to the next painting. A man with a gun to his head and a woman lying on the floor, covered in cockroaches.

Death of Love

Damien stared at the picture open-mouthed.

'Outrageous,' he muttered.

An incendiary rage coursed through his body like a hand grenade. 'What kind of world do we live in when this vile piece of rubbish is considered art?'

Steady now, said the Voice, *or the security men will throw you out.*

Luckily most of the guests had moved on to the next room, save for a Japanese couple who ignored him.

You really need to calm yourself, said the Voice. *CAN YOU HEAR ME?*

'Yes! You don't need to shout,' Damien whispered.

You're very embarrassing, the Voice hissed. *Just because you can't look further than Picasso or Matisse, doesn't mean that everyone else has to agree with you when it comes to other artists' work.*

'Just tell me why anybody would want to buy this depressing piece of ugliness.'

Damien had fired his last shot when a tiny woman with owlish eyes and thin lips suddenly appeared next to him.

'Someone already has,' she said in a thick Russian accent. 'The little red dot means sold in case you didn't know. By the way, I'm Olga,' she added casually.

Touché. Serves you right. Now apologise! said the Voice.

'And who are you?' she said.

'I'm Damien. Damien Spur.' He held out his hand.

Olga patted his fingers. 'Why would I shake hands with somebody who has just stabbed me in the back?' she said, all softly sweet.

She's good, Damien. A light touch with a deadly blow.

'So sorry I insulted you,' Damien said, his voice oily with regret. 'Please forgive me.'

Very good, Uriah Heep, crooned the Voice.

'Actually, it's okay,' she replied. 'I couldn't give a damn who likes my work.'

'Quite right. Art for art's sake. But can I ask you one question?'

'As long as you don't ask anything that makes me think,' she replied. 'What I do know is that when tonight is over, I will be happy to go back to Moscow. All this bullshit about art. I paint from the heart and I don't need the critics to tell me what I mean.'

'I get that. And now may I ask the question... please?' Damien said.

'If you must,' she said.

'Do you hate having fun?'

'I love being miserable.'

'A true Russian,' Damien said without any irony.

Olga proudly lifted her chin and stalked into the main room.

'LISTEN,' she commanded.

The guests fell silent.

'How can I see the light when there is so much pain? Democracy is dead. Leaders talk about freedom, but the truth is it's all lies. We are not in control of our lives. Money rules us. Today life without profit is worthless. We are slaves to the cash machine. We are living in dark times. Lost souls, all of us.'

Wow! said the Voice. *Step away from this little lady's toxic aura, Damien. Step away.*

He noticed Sophie leaving with her man. She looked back and waved at him.

Too late, said the Voice.

A touch on his shoulder. He turned abruptly.

'Hello,' a woman said. 'I can see you've had enough of the Krilova charm. You look as if you need a drink.' She handed him a glass of wine. 'I'm Claudia Madden.' She smiled. And something in the directness of her gaze made him pause. Those ice-blue eyes.

'Thank you,' said Damien, accepting the glass. 'I'm Damien Spur,' he said.

'The thriller writer.'

'Yes, the very same. So, what do you think?' he asked, gesturing with the wine glass to the miserable walls.

'About the paintings? Not a single one here that I would choose,' Claudia replied.

'To be honest,' Damien said, 'I can't imagine how she lives with herself.'

'That's very judgemental.' Claudia gave him a challenging glance. 'How do you know what she's really like?'

Claudia's right. There you go again, said the Voice. *Why assassinate the artist's character? You've only just met her.*

'Actually, I think it's part of her brand.' Claudia took a sushi roll from a passing tray. 'Depression paintings sell. Maybe it's a case of "There but for the grace of God go I" or perhaps people buy the work because it expresses how they feel inside.'

'Not my bag either way,' Damien said. 'So, Claudia, let me guess what you do…' he said.

'All right!' she replied with a secretive smile. 'You have one chance.'

'Well, you talk so freely and I can see that you really connect with people, so maybe you're a therapist?'

'Not quite,' she replied, 'but close. I read tarot.'

And so the conversation continued, and Damien forgot the paintings and the angry woman.

Clever Claudia edited her thoughts, allowing only a tiny chink of light to tempt him. Her talk of tarot was just enough to fascinate him.

'Is there such a thing as free will?' he asked. 'Can the cards really change the destiny of hapless souls buffeted by the wind?'

'Do you see yourself as a hapless soul?' she asked.

Didn't expect that direct response, did you? said the Voice. *Well, are you a hapless soul? Better make sure you think before you speak, cos this tigress is going to pick you up on anything you say and file it in her mind.*

'Depends in what context,' Damien replied. 'I know where I'm going in my novels, driving my characters and story through red herrings and minefields, and steering back on course to a satisfying denouement. But me? My personal life seems to have no particular direction. And far too many delicious deviations.'

'So, Damien, what are you frightened of?'

'What exactly do you mean by that?'

'Well, usually anybody who comes up with your questions, my first response would be, do you really want to know the answer? And do you really know what you're searching for?'

'Well, I know what I'm searching for in my work, but I don't necessarily know what I'm searching for in my life.'

'Ah, well, the art of tarot is all in the questions asked. So my only question to you would be, what would you like to ask the tarot?'

Claudia read him well. His suave disguise hid the truth.

'Okay, let's put the theory into practice,' Damien said. 'I would love you to read my cards. When I was a young man, I was interested in Aleister Crowley. Used to dabble in the black arts at Oxford. In fact, I still have a pack of his tarot cards.'

'My preferred deck is Ryder Waite. Far more subtle and informative.' Claudia was back in the jousting arena.

'Well, you're the expert.' He saluted her. 'But I liked the drama. Still do.'

'Yes,' she said, 'I can see you might have been the "sex, drugs and rock 'n' roll" type. Addiction and obsession are dangerous bedfellows. It sounds to me like you need to find some answers. Let me know when you'd like to come. Appointments are from 8.15 a.m. to 7 p.m. Monday to Friday. Here's my card.'

Damien slipped it in his pocket. He'd forgotten about Sophie and Angus.

He was drawn to this fascinating woman, who was both direct and ironic at the same time. She seemed to know, and be smiling, at his dark side.

Chapter 5

Friday morning, 7 a.m., Claudia was up and dressed, emails read, having breakfast with Peter in the kitchen of their elegant house in Holland Park, when Anna rang.

'Sorry to call you so early, but can you give me a reading in the next couple of days?'

'Hello, Anna. Why the urgency?'

'I've met a gorgeous man, and he's going to help me with my book, and I want to see if there's more to it than that.'

'You'll have to wait until next week. I've been invited to read at a hen party in Rome.'

'I just need to know when you're leaving?' Anna asked.

'Later this afternoon. I'll be back Wednesday.'

'Too late. He's coming into the practice on Tuesday.'

'Look, why don't you Skype me in ten minutes and I'll pull a card for you.'

'Okay, thanks. Sorry again, Claudia. I didn't mean to interrupt your breakfast.'

'Then why do it? I've told you before – text me first. When you phone me this early, I think it's an emergency.'

'Okay, next time, I promise I will. Thanks so much! Speak in ten.'

Claudia took her iPad and moved into the dining room. She picked up the tarot cards, shuffled them and spread them across the table.

Anna's face came up on the screen. She wasn't dressed and looked ghostly pale.

'Aren't you going to work?' Claudia said.

'Yes, but I didn't sleep well last night. Had a dream about that bully, Nurse Aileen. She was poking my gums in the dental chair. Kept on calling me a dirty girl. She hurt me. It was horrible. She bullies me every day! I wish I could give this all up.'

'Okay, Anna, we can deal with that when I get back. So, what would you like to ask the cards?'

'Will there be a romantic future with the man I met who said he was going to help me with my story?'

'What's his name?' Claudia replied.

'I'd rather not say. He's very well known, and if it doesn't work out I'll feel foolish.'

'Come on, I'm not going to tell anyone.'

'Okay. His name is Damien Spur. You know, the novelist.'

'Certainly do.' *Better not say too much. Keep Anna on track.* She pulled the card.

'Well,' she said, 'the Knight of Wands. A man who charges fearlessly into many relationships and often out again. Loving the challenge and excitement, living in the moment, but not easy to tame. There will be fire, but not necessarily love and security.'

'Oh dear. Sounds as if he'll break my heart,' Anna said.

'Probably. If you're easy prey. He's a must-have-can't-have man. Enjoys the challenge. Look, let's do a spread when I come back from Italy, to allow a wider perspective.'

'Okay. Just have to keep my cool on Tuesday, then. At least he's going to read my story.'

'Well, that's good. He's a terrific writer. I'm sure he'll give you excellent advice. Just don't throw your body at him!'

***

When Damien arrived at the practice, Anna made sure she was standing by the printing machine.

She wanted him to see her legs. Especially as she was wearing black patent high heels that showed off her neat ankles and shapely calves.

'Can I make you a cup of tea, Mr Spur? Or perhaps you'd prefer coffee?'

Great pair of pins, said the Voice, *but keep it professional. If she can't write, it's best not to encourage her.*

'No thanks, Anna. Just your story.'

'Here you are.' She took out a brown Manila envelope from a plastic bag under her desk and, with a covert glance around the waiting room to make sure no one was watching, slipped it to him.

He leant forward to take it. His neck smelt of soap and Vétiver. Anna's nose twitched. So sensual, so manly. If only.

Pity I can't kiss you. The electric current sizzled through her body.

'Contact number?' Damien said. 'It's not on the back.'

'It's inside,' she said.

'I'll give it a read when I have time. It might not be till the end of next week.'

'So lovely of you to do this,' she replied.

Nurse Aileen, who was talking to the porter, had seen the exchange.

'Ah, Mr Spur,' she said, approaching the desk, 'Dr Lacey's ready for you.'

She noticed a bag of boiled sweets on the desk.

'Anna!' The nurse grabbed the packet. 'Not a good advert for a dental practice.'

'May I have them back, please?'

You nasty bitch. How dare you embarrass me in front of Damien Spur.

Damien plucked the bag from the nurse's hand and gave them back to Anna.

'You're lucky to have such a lovely receptionist,' he said. 'She deserves better treatment, and if you don't stop bullying her, I'll speak to your supervisor.'

He turned to Anna. 'I'll be in touch next week.'

He swept past the nurse and headed up the stairs.

***

Anna couldn't wait to tell Sophie, her younger sister, about Damien.

She phoned her every day. Just to say hi, make sure she was all right.

The beautiful and lonely widow had lost her husband, Daniel, and son, Mikey, in a tragic accident six years ago off the coast of Mallorca.

The little boy had been swept off the rocks by a tidal wave. His father had dived in to try to rescue him. Both had drowned.

But now she'd made a dangerous friendship with Nicholas, a married man.

'How are you, Sophie?' Anna asked.

'I'm okay. I really wish you wouldn't ask me that every day.'

'I just think you're barking up the wrong tree. Why can't you find someone single?'

'Here you go again. Please stop treating me like a baby. I'm perfectly capable of leading my own life.'

'Has Nicholas told his wife about you? Surely, she must know what's going on. All the things you tell me and she doesn't seem to care where he is? I think she wants him to have an affair.'

'Anna, please. You're jumping to conclusions. Our relationship is platonic.'

'Platonic! But for how long? It's your life, Sophie. Just be careful that you don't fall for a man who's already taken.'

'Actually, I have met a very interesting single man, but I'm not sure he's my type.'

'Where?'

'At a book launch.'

'That's great!' Anna had a feeling that maybe her sister was going to tell her something she didn't want to hear.

'I met him last week at the launch party of his new thriller, *Writing in the Sand*. Good company,' Sophie said. 'Charming and funny, but I think he's quite a handful.'

'I can't believe it. You're talking about Damien Spur.' Anna's cheeks burned. Her throat was dry. *Her damn sister always got there first.*

'And funnily enough,' Sophie said, 'last week he popped up at a gallery opening of an amazing painter, Olga Krilova. Claudia was there, too.'

Anna tried to keep her voice steady. 'Well, that's uncanny, because I also met him! He came into the practice, said he would help me with my book. So, are you keen, Sophie?' Anna tried to keep her voice light.

'Not really. I told you, he's not my usual sort of guy. You know I'm a bit of a masochist.'

Anna sighed. 'Well, I have to say that makes me feel better. To be honest, Sophie, I really like him. And what's this about Claudia?'

Anna's paranoia had got the better of her. Claudia was hypnotic. She knew how to make men fall in love with her.

'She didn't tell me she'd met Damien,' Anna said. 'When I asked her to pull a card on a future relationship with him, she said she knew who he was, and that was all. So, you saw them together last week?'

'Yes. I definitely saw them chatting.'

'For a long time?'

'I don't know,' Sophie said flippantly. 'There were so many people there and, frankly, I was more interested in looking at the work... and, of course, the Russians. What a glamorous lot.'

'Well,' Anna persisted, 'maybe they were talking about the art. They probably didn't exchange names.'

'Really, I can't tell you any more. Besides, Claudia adores her husband. She wouldn't jeopardise her marriage for another man.'

'Okay, let's leave it at that,' Anna said. 'Anyway, I'm glad that we don't share the same taste in guys. But you really need to find someone else. Nicholas isn't good for you. Do you want to spend your best years being a well-kept secret?'

That's exactly what Evelyn would say. But, although she paid lip service to their mother's words, a tiny part of Anna was glad to see her sister wasting her life with a married man who would never leave his wife.

Perhaps this time Anna could be first to the finishing post.

Chapter 6

Despite having a "perfect" wife and two bright, attractive teenagers, Nicholas Morley found life in Bournemouth unimaginably dull. Thus, weekly business trips to London to buy and sell antiques, visits to auctions, valuations and occasional dealings with Philip Green, a reliable fence with an eclectic collection of booty, kept him occupied and well supplied to wheel and deal with a healthy profit margin.

But he wanted more. And more he got when he met the desirable widow, Sophie Fox, at Fortes Auction House.

Sophie selling, Nicholas bidding – for an exquisite nineteenth-century bronze horse. Bang – it was his and she gave him a grateful hug and he took her for tea.

But what of Nicholas's wife, Kate, a special-needs teacher?

Nicholas professed to Sophie that she was stunning and perfect, also adding that he would never transgress the invisible line from chaste companionship to divine communion with another woman.

So Nicholas and Sophie continued their trysts, without sex being the currency of their relationship. The strength of their friendship – an easy compliance with each other, a breezy affinity, mutual joy in the romance of life. Innocent meetings, greeting and parting with a kiss on the cheek and a friendly hug.

And yet... Sophie, this lovely woman, married at twenty-two and widowed at thirty, when he looked at her ravishing face, her languorous sea green eyes, her gentle Cupid smile, her generous breasts and slim hips, her English-filly coltish legs, his thoughts wandered into darker waters.

As time slid by, Nicholas struggled to keep his vow of chastity, but he held on, knowing that the complications of intimacy would make his life uncomfortable. And now that he had his easy parallel life, the boring gaps in his marriage were filled.

In truth, Sophie and he shared the same passions, whereas Kate and he had nothing in common. He loved books, music, art and Mediterranean luxury holidays. She liked TV – mostly cooking programmes – cleaning, gardening and big nighties.

Selfless with her vulnerable pupils, but when it came to her husband she would not surrender to his pleasures and nor would he to hers. Theirs was a sex-free marriage and, try as he might, she wasn't interested in his conjugal rights anymore.

And so it was London life with his new frisson of excitement, the delightful and alluring Sophie, that kept his marriage ticking.

He waived his chaste relationship like a badge of honour to Kate, who was happy to let him have his fun.

'She trusts me,' Nicholas told Sophie. 'She knows that I would never betray her... never have, never will, but,' he added, just to keep things rolling in Sophie's court, 'if I were single, I would marry you tomorrow.'

Lovely to be spoilt without a price tag, Sophie was happy to be entertained. Visits to galleries, dinners in elegant restaurants, flowers and walks in the park and in turn she liked to play wifey at her pretty house in Holland Park, cooking and baking, making him comfy beside her on the sofa with cups of tea served with home-made feather-light biscuits. Silky Sophie, fragrant and sexy, touched his cheek in a motherly way, pleased to see him enjoying her little pleasures.

But, when she found herself falling into dangerous lusty dreams, she played the wise owl, wished him well in his future life and kissed him goodbye.

***

A visit to her friend Claudia gave Sophie little comfort.

Even a marvellous summer garden swathed with fragrant jasmine and climbing roses couldn't distract her from her misery.

'I just don't understand why he doesn't leave her. He talks as if there's nothing to keep them together… I'm so fed up.'

She poured herself a second glass of Chablis. It would cool her brain.

Sunday afternoon and Nicholas was probably having lunch in the local pub with his dogs, while his wife was watching TV, eating a pizza from the freezer. What's to leave?

'I'm not surprised,' Claudia replied, 'but you chose to be in a relationship with a married man. Of course it's going to be problematic.'

'I told him I wasn't going to see him again, but I didn't really believe it myself.'

'And how did he react?'

'He's not leaving her.'

'Well, at least he's truthful.'

'Why are you defending him? You're meant to be helping me.' She leant down and stroked the cat.

'Sophie, he could have lied to you, like so many married men do. There are probably many reasons why he might feel he can't leave. For instance, you told me he said the children would never speak to him again. And that's just one.'

'Yes, but they're grown-ups, and anyway one day they'll be gone. And what then? He's left with his boring wife who doesn't make him happy. Can you imagine, she cooks for the kids but never for Nicholas?'

'Really?' Claudia raised a quizzical brow. 'You're so naive, Sophie. I've heard the same story from clients over and over again. He says he doesn't sleep with her, she doesn't cook for him, they have nothing to say to each other... That's Nicholas's story. He's telling you what you want to hear. I'm sure much of it is genuine, but he isn't leaving in the near future unless there's a change in the family dynamic. It's a co-dependency built over many years of unhappy marriage.'

'Thank God I haven't slept with him. That's to protect me, not her. It's the only shred of self-esteem I have left.' Sophie drained her glass.

'Yes, very wise. The power of an emotional relationship with you without sex is more powerful than consummation. There's anticipation, excitement and forbidden fruit.'

'Please, Claudia. I'm struggling. I don't know why I've fallen in love with Nicholas. He's not my sort of guy at all. Very shy and polite. Doesn't make waves. He's just there. And although he says he loves me he's adamant he doesn't want an affair.'

She leant forward and whispered her confession.

'He makes me feel like I'm the predator. And in a strange way I enjoy it. I think I'm going crazy... lusting after a married man. So what do I do?' Sophie's face was flushed and her eyes glazed. Half disgusted with herself and the other half ignited. The wine and the thought of ravishing Nicholas had brought flames to her cheeks.

Claudia looked at her dear friend and said in her calm, impartial way, 'I honestly think it's important to create some space between you. Let him miss you. All you're doing is facilitating his marital relationship.'

'But it's so lonely being on my own. Why can't he just get a flat in London? He says he hardly sees her anyway. I know it's true because he's up here most of the time and he's with me at least three times a week, and on Friday evenings he's out playing poker with his cronies. What sort of marriage is that?' The words flew from her lips.

'It's a typical twenty-year marriage of people who don't work at their relationship. Why not enjoy a bit of glamour and fun with a beautiful woman and then back to the wife and dog walks? Would you like to pull a card on his wife?' Claudia suggested gently.

'Okay. I know he loves me, but I just can't go on in a relationship that's going nowhere.'

Sophie pulled one from the deck. 'The Empress?' she said.

'Yes,' Claudia replied, 'the Empress Demeter, Mother Earth. The Major Arcana card of femininity and motherhood. She sits on her throne. A symbol of female fertility, creativity and stability. Giving birth and nurturing, giving and receiving unconditional love.'

'How interesting,' Sophie said. 'Did you know that Damien wrote a book called *The Empress*? It's about a wealthy woman who rescues Brazilian teenagers sold into prostitution and takes them to live with her.'

'I did,' Claudia replied. 'He really knows how to write about women. Not the usual one-dimensional females you get in thrillers written by men.'

'In fact, the lady has some of Demeter's qualities,' Sophie mused. 'Down to earth, gives the kids discipline with a fair hand. Loves them all, even the kid who attacks her with a knife. It's a brilliant novel, don't you think? Such an intriguing story. I would never have guessed the ending.'

'Sophie, please keep on track,' Claudia said. 'We haven't got all day. Just try and focus.' But in truth Damien had played on her mind. He was handsome, dynamic and passionate. She looked forward to reading his cards, finding out what made him tick.

Passion was something that Peter lacked. But he was kind and warm and she knew he would never betray her.

Not like her first husband, Adam, who'd had an affair with Lala, a Southern belle married to a Russian billionaire called Boris Smirnov.

Claudia had caught them together having erotic sex. Lala was lying on the kitchen table, while Adam was licking her breasts, which were covered with honey.

Sophie glanced at the card. 'Is that really meant to be his wife?' she asked. 'Because I certainly don't think she's creative. According to Nicholas, she hates the arts.'

'Whatever you say, I am sure she's been a good mother, maybe too good. Her children might find it hard to fly the nest. He also may well have become her son, if there isn't sex – after all, she's had the children. What's the point!'

'That's spot on.' Sophie nodded vigorously. 'They're at home way past the time they should be, and he said the sex stopped after the children. Can I pull a card on whether he will leave her?'

'Only if you're prepared to accept the truth,' Claudia said.

Sophie pulled the card. 'Three of Swords!' She clutched her breast. 'That's so horrible, three swords through a heart. Please tell me... do you see death?'

'Don't be so dramatic,' replied Claudia. 'There's no blood.'

'So what will happen?' Sophie asked.

'He won't be leaving any time soon. Absence, delay and separation, putting things on hold for logical reasons... It could be three years.'

'Well, I am not waiting!' Sophie raised her voice. 'It's not fair. How can he be so weak? She's just a convenience and he thinks I'm prepared to be his bestie without benefits.'

Someone coughed from over the next-door fence.

'Sophie,' Claudia said, 'please keep your voice down and do stop airing your dirty laundry in my back garden.'

'Dirty laundry in my back garden. Funny, funny pun.'

Sophie shook her head and giggled... and then she cried and wailed like an air-raid siren until the new neighbour, a literary sort in a Panama hat, popped his head above the fence and said, 'Sorry to disturb you, but I'm trying to write and it's very hard to concentrate with all the noise.'

'No, no, it's we who should apologise,' Claudia replied. 'We're just going inside.'

Sophie's eyes lit up, despite the rivulets of black mascara running down her cheeks.

'Are you writing a book?' she said, all cocktail-party chatty. 'What's it about? You look academic. Let me guess. Is it hysterical?' She gripped the arms of the wicker chair and, rocking back and forth, levered herself to her feet.

'I mean historical… silly me!' She teetered towards the fence. 'Mind you, it could be a funny book, couldn't it?'

He was a handsome man in a writerly sort of way. An intelligent, refined face with defined features and a smooth jawline.

Sophie wondered if he was single and, tilting her chin just a little, gave him a coquettish smile, half shy, half come-hither.

'You got it right first time. I am a historian.' He looked at this divine woman who, even in a dishevelled state, her white linen dress creased, her messy hair and sweaty face – a damsel in distress – appealed to his chivalry.

But just as he was ready to progress the tête-à-tête, a woman shouted from the window.

'Claude, shall we eat alfresco?'

'Oh.' Sophie sighed. 'Claude! What a lovely name and of course that must be Mrs Claude?'

'Well…'

'Well yes,' Sophie said. 'The world is full of married men.' She blew him a kiss and turned away.

Claudia took her by the arm and guided her back through the French doors. 'Please, Sophie, pull yourself together. How much did you drink before you came?'

'Just enough to give me courage. Because, Claudia, I had a feeling it wouldn't be good news. And the Empress proved it. Because that's not me, it's her. What a shame. Can I pull another card?'

Claudia handed her a glass of water.

'Sophie, stop trying to change the outcome!'

Chapter 7

How many men whose marriages have run their course stay because they are unchallenged?

It's a satisfactory arrangement: the boredom of domestic life without waves, a dull pulse that saves his pocket from divorce and an affair where he rides a thrilling storm.

'Please, Sophie… my life is such fun with you – I need you. I think all this self-denial is creating more chemistry. I am in agony. Maybe we should make love once and I can get you out of my system. View it as a kindness.'

'Better not.' Sophie removed his hand from her knee. As Claudia said, forbidden fruit would keep his interest.

But in reality, furtive hugs and timid touches were not enough to satisfy her lusty nature.

'So text him,' Claudia said. 'You know what you want. Sound him out. Find out what he wants.'

Hello Nicholas x

Hello Sophie x

Dearest lover… yes, we are lovers, in mind and heart. After much reflection, I think the sensible way forward for us is for me to become your mistress. It's clear we cannot separate emotionally, so why not seal our relationship?

I await your response. Yours, Sophie
xxx

                                                Speechless! xxx

Not a sufficient response! X

Find your voice, man! Girls like me don't come
around that often x

                               Once in a lifetime. And what a relief!!
                                       love and hugs!!

So what, my love, are you going
to do about relief?

                                   Mend a gold charm bracelet? xx

I don't think we are on the same page.
For relief, a charm bracelet? I mean, please!

                                     I've missed you, Sophie.

That's good to hear.

So, when do I become your mistress?
My original question.
Dinner first?! xx

                           Eternally platonic, then, just so that I'm clear? x

Eternally platonic – with dinner, walks in the park, trips to
the theatre and fun in the sun! xx

                    Understood. I love you no less and can't wait to see you
                                very soon. Until then Sophie xxx

There are times when you are the loveliest woman in the world xxx

What do you mean, times? Please elaborate?

Okay! All the time! xx

Dinner chez moi?

Lovely! xx

When?

I'm going to an auction in Chiswick on Thursday?

Perfect. Come at 7.30. S xxx

***

When Anna rang, Sophie was at the hairdressers.

'It's all right, Tom, carry on,' she said. 'It's my sister. I'll ring her later.'

But Anna called again. And again.

Sophie shouldn't have told her that Nicholas was coming to dinner. She knew that it would aggravate her.

But something in her wanted that.

At the back of her mind, she remembered that when she was six Anna had cut off her pigtail, jealous of her fair hair. Sophie had cried and cried.

Evelyn, their mother, laughed at all the spiteful things Anna did to her little sister. She hadn't wanted another girl.

Worse was when Sophie was sixteen and Anna stole her first boyfriend, Matthew, and did things with him that Sophie wouldn't do.

And so it continued until Anna got married. At last she was hitched and Sophie was happily out of harm's way.

Sophie's phone rang again. 'For goodness' sake, Anna, can't it wait? My hair's wet.' She signalled to Tom to switch on the dryer. 'Now then, if you've anything to tell me, call later.'

But Anna was determined to have her say. 'Why, Sophie, why? You're in your prime – you could have anyone.'

'Please don't go on,' Sophie replied.

'You're wasting your life. He will never leave his wife.'

***

Thursday 7.15 p.m., Nicholas had arrived early. He had brought her a box of hand-made chocolates, a gift from a client that he'd saved for a special occasion.

He wouldn't ring the bell just yet. She could be getting dressed. He sat on the doorstep and waited.

Nicholas wasn't sure what to expect when Sophie opened the door. Nor was he quite sure what to do. He felt guilty. He'd told Kate that he would be late home as he had a second valuation in Kensington. He shouldn't have lied, but then again what could he have said? That he was visiting a drop-dead gorgeous woman who had filled his head night and day ever since he'd met her?

Sophie had prepared rocket and Parmesan salad followed by lasagne al forno, and for dessert, raspberry panna cotta.

She served him like a geisha. Let him have the pleasure of a woman who adores him, wants to please him, spoil him.

'More lasagne?' she asked.

'It's so delicious, just a little.'

Panna cotta next. He took a spoonful of the luscious, quivering cream and slipped it in his mouth.

'Sublime,' he said. 'You are superb. The most beautiful woman I have ever met.'

And that was when Sophie got up from the table, leaving her dessert unfinished, and did what she did best.

'So why be shy?' She pulled him towards her. 'Nicholas, I'm not sure I can just be your friend. Please kiss me.'

He gave her a dry little peck like a budgerigar.

'No, properly… like this…' She teased his mouth open with the tip of her finger and sucked his bottom lip. After which she plunged her tongue into his mouth and played with his.

Nicholas, helpless with lust, thrust his hips against hers. 'You are hot as hell,' he said.

He felt such love and now he couldn't escape. That was it. A fatal touch of lips that changed everything.

'Do you realise what you're doing to me? I've gone twenty years without having an affair and then you come along with your passionate kisses and sweet breath, and now it's such an effort to keep strong.'

She took his hand in hers. 'Come on,' she said, her voice husky with wine and desire. 'Let's go to bed. We don't have to do anything… compromising. We could just, you know, have a cuddle.'

Nicholas was in a dream state. And when she dropped her dress to reveal her naked beauty he could hardly breathe.

'I want you so much,' he said.

'I want you too,' she said. They huffed and puffed, moaned and groaned and still, despite a thrilling ride, Nicholas – at the point of entry – held fire.

'No! I cannot take you,' he cried.

'What? Why?' Sophie shoved him back against the pillows. 'You really think that just because we haven't actually had sex, you're not having an affair?'

'In my mind, yes. I just know that if I did go all the way I'd have a meltdown. I'd feel so guilty. Probably have to tell my wife and she'd literally kill me.' The thought of her made Nicholas's penis shrivel. 'Sophie, I have to go,' he said, flustered, bundling sheets round his middle. 'I don't want to hurt anyone.'

Nicholas left, hurrying to his car, already picturing the loving conversation he'd have to his wife on the phone. How he'd describe his day of work to her.

I am a good man, he thought virtuously. *I am a very good man. I didn't cross the line.*

***

Claudia hatched a plan for Sophie.

'Viagra,' Claudia said. 'You can get the tablets over the counter now. Make him minestrone and drop one in his soup.'

Sophie liked the idea.

But the pharmacist at Boots said she couldn't buy it.

Sophie called Claudia. 'I thought it wouldn't be that simple. In order to buy the pills, the man has to come in and have a consultation...'

'Well... we could ask Bryan, my gardener,' Claudia said. 'I'm sure he'd do it if we offered him twenty quid... I'll try him out when he comes next week.'

Bryan was good with plants, but the problem was he was a compulsive talker, which really irritated Claudia, but if she was going to ask him for a favour, best to be friendly.

Not easy. He'd already annoyed her by arriving Thursday morning at 8.50 a.m., when he wasn't due till nine o'clock.

'You're ten minutes early,' Claudia said icily.

'Yes, trying to squeeze in two more jobs today so I thought I'd give myself a head start. Hope you don't mind.'

'Well, luckily my 8 a.m. reading was cancelled. It's best that you ask me first in future.'

'Yeah, I will... promise.' He stood at the door, his knobbly arms and legs sticking out like gnarled branches from the sleeves of his black T-shirt and khaki combat shorts.

'Anyway…' Claudia clapped her hands together. 'Would you like a cup of tea, Bryan?'

'Thank you.' He was surprised. She didn't normally offer him tea before he started gardening.

He followed her into the kitchen. 'Didn't have time this morning,' he said. 'Too busy packing for tomorrow. Going to Tenerife with my girlfriend. Going to climb up part of the Tiède. She's a bit worried in case she gets dizzy. Had a few turns in the last couple of weeks. I dunno, maybe she's pregnant?'

Claudia yawned. Perhaps she should just wave the twenty quid in front of him and forget the small talk and the tea. No, it would be better to keep him sweet.

He looked so chuffed, as if the Queen had invited him into Buckingham Palace for a cuppa.

He had a huge crush on Claudia.

'Bryan, just come and sit down for a minute. I want to ask you to do something. You can say no, but I'll make it worth your while.' Claudia placed a white ceramic mug on the table.

Bryan's milky green eyes slid sideways.

'Oh yes? I'm all ears. Uh, but… I wonder… you wouldn't have a biscuit, would you? Had nothing in my mouth since last night.'

'Of course.' Claudia plopped a couple of digestives on a plate.

He eyed the fruit bowl.

'Wouldn't mind a banana,' he said. 'That's if you can spare one.'

'Sure. Perhaps you'd like a tangerine as well?'

Bryan didn't understand irony.

'No thanks. Bad for my acid reflux. I'm taking pills, but it's still causing me problems. Shame, really. I love tangerines and oranges… and kiwis and pineapples, but they make my tongue swell. I can eat apples, though…' His eyes flicked back and forth to the bowl. He waited.

She'd had enough.

'Down to business, Bryan.' Claudia sat. 'Now then, I'm sure you've heard of Viagra.'

'Yes, of course.' Bryan took a bite of his banana. 'Keeps you up and at it. Haven't tried it myself. Luckily no problem down under. Doesn't take a lot for me to go up north. Mind you, I think that gardening helps... Keeps a man "earthed", so to speak.' Bryan smirked at his pun. 'Anyway, why so?' He eyeballed her and took another bite of the banana.

'Well, you used to be able only to get it on prescription, but now you can buy it over the counter. And, well... I... I thought you might...'

Bryan's eyes glistened. He couldn't believe it. Mrs M was finally making a move. The story in his head was actually happening...

It was a hot summer's day. Bryan was pruning the roses. He had taken off his T-shirt. He could feel her watching him.

'Would you like some pink lemonade, Bryan?' Her voice wafted across the lawn. He turned round. She was standing on the terrace barefoot, wearing a black bikini top, flaunting her long, tanned legs in snug denim shorts.

'Thank you, Mrs M, my throat's parched.'

And there she was beside him, holding the glass to his lips.

'No need for a free hand, Bryan. You just keep on pruning...'

Her beautiful soft hand slid down his back and she said, 'Your shoulders are burning. Let me get you some lotion.'

And now here he was, living the dream.

Bryan leant forward and circled his lips with his tongue. 'You don't have to say it, Mrs M... I understand.'

'You do?'

'Your hubby.'

'What about him?'

'Well, he probably works all hours God sends him.'

'Yes, he does work hard.'

'And you…' Brian winked. 'Viagra… I get it.'

'Get what?'

'You know… roses need water otherwise the petals dry up.' He placed the banana skin on the plate and leered at Claudia with his toady eyes.

'What are you talking about?'

'Well then, you don't have to pay me. You know I'd do it for free.'

'Of course I have to pay you, Bryan!' She ignored the innuendo and yanked the conversation back on track.

'The pharmacist will ask you questions, so you have to pretend that you have a problem.'

'No, no… I don't need Viagra anyway. I can go for hours.'

'What are you talking about? It's not for you – it's for a friend.'

'Oh.' He swallowed hard. 'Oh well.' He shook his head. 'Now I see. I thought you meant you… and me… but…' Bryan stuck out his chin and crossed his arms. 'But if it's for another fella, why can't he ask himself?'

'It's for a girlfriend.'

'Why would a girl need Viagra?'

'Oh, never mind. I really don't have time for this.' Claudia snatched her bag and took out her wallet. 'Here's twenty pounds plus another twenty for the Viagra. No more questions. Will you just do it? Today? After you've done the gardening, bring me the pills this afternoon. Okay?'

'Done deal, Mrs M.' He plucked the notes from her delicate fingers.

Claudia looked at his filthy nails and wondered how any woman could let him touch her.

'Well then, best be getting on, Mrs M. I'll sort out the garden, go straight to the chemist and be back around 3 p.m.'

'Good.' She gave him a dry smile and opened her iPad.

***

Bryan proved reliable and returned that afternoon.

'Abracadabra, here's the Viagra.' He waved a packet of four little pills in the air. 'It was easy peasy, Mrs M.' He gave her a cocky grin. 'I was expecting the pharmacist to ask me about my todger, but he didn't. Just questions on my general health and whether I was taking any other medication. In a way, it was a pity, because I was quite looking forward to telling him a cock and bull story. Well, that one just popped out,' he said.

Claudia didn't smile.

'Geddit, Mrs M, cock and bull?' His eyebrows jiggled up and down. He motored on. 'I said how depressed I was because my dad had died a few weeks ago and every time I tried to get it up, I thought of the coffin being lowered into the ground and my mum crying. Oh dear, I can feel the tears welling up.' He took out a dirty handkerchief and blew his nose.

Claudia looked the other way.

'Well… then that's that. Thanks for your help.' She snatched the packet of Viagra and hustled him out of the kitchen door. 'I've a reading in ten minutes, so off you go.'

'Oh… maybe you could read my cards? See if I should marry my Mary.'

Claudia slammed her back against the door and raised her eyes to heaven.

She'd wait before she locked the garden gate, just to make sure he'd gone.

***

Anna was on the bus when Damien rang.

'I like your story, but you need to make the read less complex and the narrative more fluid,' he said. 'Would you like me to tweak it? We could meet this weekend. Sunday?'

Tweak it! Damien Spur tweaking it. Anna blushed. Just the thought of it made her nipples stiffen. Yes, he could tweak her any time.

'Sunday's fine. Come to me – I'll make you lunch,' she said.

'How about dinner? We can do the work first in the afternoon.'

The woman sitting next to Anna nudged her. 'Turn the volume down, please. What's it to me what you're doing at the weekend?'

Anna nudged the woman back. 'Well, I am certainly not inviting *you* to lunch,' she retorted. Then, 'Yes, Damien, that will be fine,' she said, lowering her voice.

'Anna,' he said, 'I can't hear you.'

'I said that's fine. Two o'clock?' She raised her voice again. 'You've got my address on the manuscript. See you then. Byeee.'

The woman beside her got up and pushed past her. 'You're so bloody rude. If you want to shout on the phone, why don't you take a taxi?'

Anna ignored her.

At last her life was flowing. It was such a joy not to be locked in her imagination. To have things actually happen. She had been numb from the waist down for years. A closed shop. Told herself that she didn't miss it. But now she felt that tingle again, that rush of pleasure. She was absolutely ready to give this man anything he wanted.

That night, happy Anna dreamt of flying.

***

In the morning, Anna drew the curtains with a flourish and smiled at herself in the pretty heart-shaped mirror that David had given her as a Valentine gift, with a card that said:

Darling, Anna,
You'll always be beautiful. Look at your reflection
and see the greatest love of my life.

When he took her to the edge with his incessant moaning, the mirror reminded her of the romantic man he once was.

And today Anna wanted to please him. After she'd washed and dressed, she went into the kitchen and took out the loose-leaf Earl Grey from the larder instead of the usual builder's teabag. She swilled the teapot with the boiled water and let the tea brew for three minutes, straining it into a porcelain cup resting on a saucer.

Just how he liked it. Then she made him some toast with lots of butter and raspberry jam, his favourite, and brought it up to him on a silver-plated tray.

'Well, this is a surprise,' David said. 'And it isn't even my birthday.'

'Just thought, as I took the time off work today, I'd make breakfast.'

'Thank you, Anna,' he said. 'You look very pretty.'

'I feel it,' she said. 'I'll see you later.' And off she went to Claudia for her tarot reading. Even if this wasn't going to be an easy ride, her friend always gave her good advice.

When Anna arrived, she pressed the buzzer. No answer. She buzzed again.

After a few minutes, Claudia opened the door.

'Oh good,' Anna said brightly. 'I thought you'd forgotten I was coming.'

'Come in,' she whispered. 'But we have to be quiet – Peter's here.'

'What's the matter? You look worried,' Anna said.

'It's okay. He's just not feeling too well.'

'What happened?'

'He lost a patient during an operation yesterday. He was very upset. Didn't sleep all night.'

'It must be terribly hard,' Anna said.

'Yes, but fortunately for him it's very rare.'

Claudia sat down at the dining room table, Anna opposite her, and gave Anna the cards.

'I can understand why Peter might think this is trivial,' said Anna, shuffling the cards.

'Boundaries, Anna,' snapped Claudia. 'It's really not your business what Peter thinks. And he would never use the word "trivial" about what I do, even if that's what he believes.'

'Sorry, Claudia, that was tactless of me.' Anna had always been frightened of her friend's temper. Claudia never raised her voice, even when she was angry. 'I really didn't mean to be intrusive, but whenever he's around he seems in a mood. And last time you said...'

'Now then, let's change the subject and get back on course.' Claudia spread the cards on the table. 'What would you like to ask?'

'The same question as last time. You said it would be a good idea to get a wider perspective. Will Damien and I have a romantic future together?'

'So, why don't you pull three cards on it?'

Anna's finger hovered over the deck.

Maybe she shouldn't have asked the question. Perhaps all her fantasies would be shot to pieces...

Come on, just get on with it. He's still going to help you with your book.

Claudia wasn't surprised. The first card was just as she thought. 'Well, Anna. The Knight of Wands and the Devil – it's unlikely any single female can give him what he wants and keep him interested. He's a man who craves the sensuality and excitement of many women.'

'Oh dear. I'm not sure I want to be part of a harem.'

'But with the Nine of Cups you could have fun. It's the hedonist card. Take it as it comes. Enjoy it, relax, don't be heavy or he will run for the hills. If you can do that and not be disappointed when he disappears as quickly as he appeared, it could be what the doctor ordered.' Claudia gestured towards the cards. 'Why not ask if this is what you need?'

'Okay, here goes.'

'The Chariot, that's great. Focus on a heroic goal. Work hard, be organised. Keep the two sides of your life apart. Don't mix business with pleasure. Focus on your book with him. The main course, no flirting. Save the sex for dessert. By harnessing the power of both, you achieve your ambition.'

Chapter 8

Early morning and Sophie was having second thoughts. Reading the list of side effects of Viagra had made her feel queasy.

What if I kill him? He could have a heart attack! No, surely not.

Strong as an ox, he said he was. Only been to hospital to visit friends and relatives.

But all the other possibilities? Blindness, nausea, headache, backache…

It was Claudia's fault. She had fired her imagination and now she would be up all night, grappling with her conscience.

She called Damien first. After the art show she'd phoned him and they'd spent some time together. They enjoyed each other's company, going to lunch, going to the theatre, having coffee.

She really liked him.

He had a generous spirit. He'd become a good friend on whom she could depend to give her wise advice when she needed it, from a man's point of view.

'For goodness' sake, Sophie, what's the matter?' he said. 'It's 7 a.m.'

'Have you ever taken Viagra?'

'Why?'

'Not why. Just tell me.'

'Calm down. Once in LA. Four women in one day. Needed the staying power.'

'And you were okay?'

'Fine. But why do you—'

'No side effects? Nausea, headaches, upset stomach?'

'No. No, no. Can I go now?'

'Yes. And thank you.'

Next, Sophie called Claudia.

'I know you're still in bed, but I need your moral support.'

'What for?'

'I'm scared… the side effects.'

'Of what?'

'Tonight. The Viagra minestrone.'

'Every medication can have side effects,' Claudia said. 'Did you check to see whether Nicholas had any underlying conditions, like I told you?'

'Yes, I did.'

'And?'

'Only one – not having the courage to leave his boring wife.'

'Well then, I don't think Viagra will change that. But if you're prepared to settle for an affair, seeing as you say he doesn't have any serious medical history, it could be worth the risk. But it's your call. I don't want to be responsible if things go wrong.'

How could anything go wrong?

Nicholas needed help. She would free him of his guilt. Emancipate his soul.

Go, Sophie, go. A quick cup of coffee first, a shower and then to work.

No, not the black ceramic cooking pot; too much like a cauldron. Yes, the large two-handled stockpot. Everyday and reassuring.

She sliced and diced the vegetables. A dash of olive oil in the saucepan. Sautéed the onions until soft and pale yellow.

Then, one by one, she dropped in the carrots, celery, potatoes, green beans, courgette, cabbage. Next, a tin of Italian tomatoes and then, after pouring in rich beef stock, she added the rind of a piece of Parmesan, saving the cannellini beans for later.

Bring to the boil and let it simmer.

And how should she play her role tonight?

The siren dressed to kill, ready to devour her man?

The pussycat ready to serve her man? Something softer, less obvious… more romantic.

Yes, that's it. A softer approach.

Nicholas needed to be gently coaxed. Teased out of his comfort zone.

***

It was late afternoon. Sophie smiled at her reflection in the mirror and raised her glass of champagne.

'And here is Sophie, freshly bathed…' she mouthed the words like a commentator on a TV cookery show, '… swathed in an oyster silk slip dress and, underneath, just a pair of gossamer lace panties. For the perfume? She is wearing Miss Dior – subtle, chic, not too overpowering. A perfect dish, moist and tender, ready to be served on a bed of crisp white linen. And the winner is…' Sophie giggled. 'Oh, Nicholas, if you only knew.'

Nicholas arrived with a bunch of yellow roses from Waitrose, a bottle of Rioja and some superglue from Tyler's DIY to mend the handle of a treasured bright red ceramic jug that the cleaner had broken.

The jug was a memento from her favourite hotel, La Colombe d'Or in St Paul de Vence, a reminder of happy summers spent with her beloved husband, Daniel, at the charming auberge. Picasso nestled in one corner, Matisse in the other. Miró, Chagall, Bonnard, Kandinsky casually hung in the bedrooms, hallways, the rustic dining room.

How she missed her Daniel. The romance of it all. Even when little Mikey came along it didn't spoil the fun. His father taught him to swim in the pool and sometimes in the afternoon they would all go to the Café de la Place and play boules.

Her family. Lost.

And here she was, about to seduce a married man by spiking his soup.

'Sophie?' asked Nicholas. 'You okay? When do you want me to mend the jug? I can do it now if you like.'

'Oh, I'm fine,' said Sophie hastily, back to real time. 'Don't worry about the jug. You can do it tomorrow.'

'Tomorrow? That might not be possible.'

'But you said…'

No, Sophie, no. Don't go there. Let the evening unfold naturally. Don't make him feel uncomfortable. Relax him. Wait and see what happens after the Viagra.

'Anyway, darling,' Sophie wrapped her arms around his waist, 'can you open the champagne?'

'Of course, darling.' He kissed her neck, ever so softly. 'You smell wonderful,' he let his nose linger on her fragrant skin.

And then he thought of Kate.

It's okay, Nicholas, don't worry. Just have a good wash before you go home. And surely Sophie's got some antiseptic in her bathroom cabinet. Dab it on. That'll mask the scent.

The guilt had made Nicholas sweat.

Timing, Sophie. Too soon.

He's not ready yet.

'I'll be back in a minute.' She gently pushed him away. 'Need to check the dinner.'

Drop the cannellini beans into the soup and cook for fifteen minutes. That leaves just enough time for a cuddle on the sofa. Get him in the mood.

'Chin-chin.' *Look deep into his eyes. Hold his gaze and just a little smile. Now talk to him, flatter him, tell him how much you missed him.*

Play with his finger, stroke his hair. That's it. Tease him... then give him a gentle kiss. That's enough. Keep him wanting more.

'Sophie...' he called from the living room.

'Yes?' she said.

'Can I use your loo?'

Sophie gave a dry laugh. 'Why do you have to ask? Really, Nicholas, every time you visit me it's the same question. As if I were a stranger. It's almost an insult.'

Sophie, keep your temper.

'Force of habit. Sorry, darling,' he said.

'That's okay. Just want you to feel at home.'

'I do, I do. Especially when you cook... Smells delicious. Let me guess – minestrone, isn't it?'

'Yes,' Sophie said. 'I remember you saying your mother used to make it.'

'My very favourite. Can't wait,' he said. 'I'll just be a tick.'

Sophie shut the kitchen door.

She took the porcelain teddy bear mug out of the cupboard and shook it. Yes, the pill was there.

She removed the rind from the soup and stirred in the grated parmesan. Soup in the bowl, bread in a basket, salmon in the fridge, just in case the pill took longer than expected to work its magic.

The good girl said, *Oh, Sophie, how could you! An innocent soul like Nicholas. Who knows what could happen? He could have a meltdown. Totally immoral. And absolutely illegal. You're worse than any man.*

And the bad girl said, *Come on, Sophie. Don't take any notice. He'll love it, once he does it. All that foreplay and nowhere to go... frustrating for both of you.*

'Yes, it is. But...'

No buts, Sophie. Just get on with it.

If he finds out, he'll never trust you again, said the good girl.

How would he know, unless you tell him? He'll just be so proud he can go all night, said the bad girl.

'Okay. You win,' Sophie muttered.

'Gosh, that looks fantastic.' Nicholas had crept up behind her and peered over her shoulder.

Sophie swung round with the ladle in her hand. 'You gave me a shock!'

'I'm sorry. What's the matter? You're not usually so jumpy.'

Sophie, you're going to blow it. Calm down. Be nice.

'Nothing.' She brushed his cheek with a kiss. 'You just surprised me, that's all. Now go and sit down.'

Breathe, Sophie, breathe.

She handed him the basket of French bread. 'Here, take this in.'

'I'll open the Rioja. Where's the corkscrew?'

'In the top drawer. Please, I need some space. You know what I'm like when I'm cooking.'

'Just like looking at you, so sure of yourself,' he said. 'Kate's such a ditherer. She's probably out of practice. Mind you, she used to cook when I first married her.'

'Oh, look at that cute little mug,' Nicholas picked it up. 'You're such a complicated woman. One minute a sophisticated diva with your silk and pearls and the next you collect things like this.' He waved it in the air. 'Oh, there's something inside.'

'Just give it back, please,' she said calmly. 'It's very delicate, just like me.' She grasped the mug and cradled it in both hands. 'Now then.' She sighed gently.

For heaven's sake, get him out of here! the bad girl said.

'Come on, Nicholas. Just leave me to it and open the wine.'

'Job done,' Nicholas said. The steamy kitchen had made his cheeks red. He gave her a shy smile. 'I'm so happy to be with you tonight.'

Alone at last, Sophie set about her task.

She ladled the soup into Nicholas's bowl and tipped in the little blue pill. She waited for it to dissolve and tasted the soup. Slightly bitter.

A little honey? She took a taste – better – and added more Parmesan. Don't want to stir it too much, just in case he leaves some at the bottom.

Such a cosy dining room with its floor-to-ceiling shuttered windows. The pale oak table was elegantly dressed with Georgian silver, fine linen napkins, and the roses that Nicholas had brought her arranged in an exquisite lead-crystal vase.

He took his first spoonful.

Sophie waited. Her eyes glittered in the candlelight. Her mouth quivered. Underneath the table she crossed her fingers.

'You like?' she said.

'Lovely,' he said, 'but a little sweet. Just needs a pinch of salt and maybe another sprinkle of cheese and then it'll be perfect.'

Nicholas, always polite, known for his manners, tweaked the minestrone and Sophie followed suit.

Sit on his lap... and nibble his ear; he loves that.

'Ah.' He sighed. 'Oh my Lord, what have you done to me?'

'Do you want me to stop?'

'No, but…'

'But what?'

He paused. A quick check-in with his moral barometer.

Here I am, Nicholas Morley from Bournemouth, a wife and two kids, with a steaming diva who wants me, adores me, cooks for me. Begs me to make love to her. Oh, what the hell, I'm hard as a rock! Let's go for it!

The Tarzan fantasy was one of his favourites. He lifted her up and slung her over his shoulder. His Jane.

For what we are about to receive… Sophie, his gift, was compliant, yielding. He wanted to please her – make her sizzle…

He played with her. He stalled.

'You tease,' she said.

He started again.

'You're such a good lover,' she whispered.

Come on, Nicholas, now or never. Find yourself... lose yourself in the moment. No wife, no kids, no guilt. Take the plunge, dive in, shame the Devil.

'Ahhh,' he moaned.

'At last,' she cried. 'Don't stop, just carry on forever!'

It was glorious. He was cruising on the highway, keeping an even pace. His battered conscience had made it through. And the reward for his bravery? The drive of the century.

The difference between a Ford Fiesta and a Ferrari. Entwined like vines, her legs coiled round his waist.

Nicholas surprised himself. He was going strong. Full throttle, piston pumping. Longer than he could ever have imagined.

And Sophie? The foreplay was fun, but now she was aching. 'Please, slow down... I never want it to end,' she lied.

'No problemo. Couldn't stop if I tried.'

Don't worry, Sophie, good that you kick-started the engine. You can fine-tune the performance later.

A couple more circuits, and then just flag him over the finish line...

'NOW!' she cried. Sophie bit his neck and scratched his back. Her nails left a fiery track down to his buttocks.

'Ah,' he moaned.

Poor Nicholas was out of his depth.

Teach him to swim, the good girl said. *Save him from his boring life. He's yours now.*

Yes. He's yours now, the bad girl said.

Chapter 9

Lunchtime. Damien and Sophie were sitting in a booth at Lemonia, in Primrose Hill, his favourite Greek restaurant.

'We'll have some starters,' he said to the waiter. 'Hummus, taramasalata, calamari and pitta bread. Anything else for you, Sophie?'

'No thank you, that's perfect.'

Sophie was on her best behaviour. She hadn't started drinking the Pinot Grigio till midday.

'And for the main,' Damien said, 'I'll have the kleftiko.'

'I'll have the baby chicken, please.'

'Wine?' he said.

Of course, said the Voice.

'Yes, please,' she said, plucking an olive from a little china saucer.

Damien glanced at the menu. 'We'll have the Sancerre 2018.'

Not sure a bottle is a good idea at lunchtime, said the Voice. *But, then again, it might make it easier for her to express her feelings about Nicholas. Must say it's a pity the conversation isn't about you. Would have been much more interesting.*

'Okay, Sophie,' Damien said when the waiter had gone, 'you've spiked the man's soup with Viagra and had your way with him, which I might say was a heinous thing to do. So what's next?'

'Who knows?' she replied. 'For the moment I'll take life as it comes. At least there's no going back now.'

Damien couldn't admit he had a vested interest. That he was nuts about her. He needed to be political. Tell her his honest opinion. What a waste of space Nicholas was.

'I don't really want to play the agony aunt,' he said. 'But why are you so attracted to this guy? I can guarantee if he did leave his wife and come and live with you, you'd go potty. You'd be bored after a week.'

But Sophie had her own thoughts.

'It wouldn't be like that. I don't want someone who wants to discuss the you-ness, the me-ness, the us-ness. Nicholas is happy to be practical. He can fix anything. Plumbing, electrics, mending things. He's not predatory. There's an innocence about him. And I can tell you it feels very sexy being the seducer.' She lowered her voice and looked up at Damien, her eyes soft and dreamy.

There you go! said the Voice. *So now you know what turns her on, next time drop your alpha-male side and show her your inner child. But, for now, carry on with the therapy bit.*

'I think you've got a real problem, Sophie,' Damien said, pouring her another glass of wine. 'Why are you punishing yourself? You're an amazing woman. How could you fall for such an ordinary man?'

The starters had arrived. Damien dipped a radish in the taramasalata and popped it in his mouth. Sophie just played with a celery stick, swirling it around and around the hummus.

'Please, Damien, you don't understand,' Sophie replied. 'When Nicholas came along, it was a godsend to meet someone who was happy to take on a weeping widow. I was a wreck after Daniel and Mikey died. To tell you the truth, I didn't want to live.' Sophie picked up her napkin and hid her eyes. 'Just give me a second,' she said tearfully.

'You really don't have to talk about it any more.' Damien stroked her hand.

Let her, said the Voice. *She's obviously still in love with her husband. Misses him terribly. Nicholas is just a sticking plaster.*

Who knows, maybe she thinks a guy like you would be too dangerous for her.

Damien reached for Sophie's napkin and gently wiped away her tears.

Well, that's a start, said the Voice.

She gave him a wan smile. 'Nicholas rescued me. He was so kind. Always a phone call away if I needed anything. And he's still around five years later.'

'Why wouldn't he be?' Damien said. 'Nothing to lose for him. Comes up to London, has a bit of glamour and then back to his dull life in Bournemouth.'

'I suppose that's true.' Sophie chewed pensively on a calamari ring. 'Maybe I just fill in the gaps. Do all the things that his wife never does. Cook for him, go with him to art galleries and the theatre, watch old movies. Apparently, she hates anything to do with culture. They seem to have absolutely nothing in common.'

Yes, they do, said the Voice. *Two children, a couple of dogs and twenty years of marriage.*

'He's a romantic. I know it gives him pleasure to bring me flowers and presents. He says she's more excited by a chainsaw than a piece of jewellery.'

'Don't tell me, he also told you that they haven't had sex for years.'

'As a matter of fact, yes. And when they did, it was mechanical. No passion.'

What a loyal chap, said the Voice.

'So at last we're finally lovers.' Sophie sighed. 'I'm glad I gave him Viagra. He would never have succumbed normally. Too disciplined. Likes to give himself a hard time.'

The mains had arrived. Damien was hungry. All that talk about Nicholas had made him feel insecure. Why couldn't she let herself love him? Damien Spur: handsome, world-class writer, legend in the sack.

He took a bite of kleftiko. 'Food's always good here. Shall I order some more wine?'

Sophie picked at her chicken. *Damien, you're a gorgeous man. What's wrong with me?*

'Anyway, maybe now he'll see the light and leave her.'

'I'm not sure about that.'

'Just tell me what you think,' she said.

'About what?'

'Nicholas,' she said. 'Do you think it a dead end?'

Here goes, said the Voice. *Your chance to wean her away from Mr Creepy.*

Damien put his knife and fork down and looked her in the eyes.

'If you want to know my honest opinion, Nicholas is a con man. He's flattering you to keep you on the hook. He wants you, but he won't leave his wife. Why? Because you're trouble. Far too sophisticated for him. A little of you goes a long way. And then he can go back to his wife and fantasise about you at night.'

Clever Damien.

Chapter 10

Indeed, Nicholas was having the time of his life.

It was exciting to have a clandestine affair with a delicious woman who fed his desire, ego and stomach.

Every time he came to London for a meeting, Sophie was ready to receive him with open arms. He seldom stayed overnight, but when he did Sophie made sure he was happy.

He was in a permanent state of arousal. His mind was full of her.

While Kate watched her soaps, Sophie was embedded in his thoughts. Her legs round his waist, graceful, gliding, rising with Nicholas in perfect unison until they reached the state of nirvana.

But stolen nights and hurried sex sandwiched between his clients were not enough to satisfy their hunger for each other. Thus Nicholas planned to take his Sophie on a trip to Venice.

A business trip, he told his wife, to meet a client who wished to sell a Renaissance bronze.

Kate bought the story, happily unaware that Nicholas was having an affair, despite his trips to London extending to weekends.

Or so he thought...

For Kate was not as innocent as she appeared. A good soul who gave herself to those in need, looked after the kids with a close eye despite her lack of culinary skills, did the gardening, while her husband sighed between another woman's thighs.

The truth was that she was also cheating with a man she'd met in a garden centre named Rick, and he was rich. Their passions wed with love of organic compost, hibiscus, lilies, clematis, roses and a mutual hatred of kinks in garden hoses.

Rick ravished Kate at his baronial estate every Thursday – what her family knew as "bridge night".

But he wanted more… so Tuesday, too. But what to do? For Kate looked tired of late. The cleaning, weeding and the needy children had sapped her lust, and Rick insisted that she mustn't be a martyr.

'Come and live with me, my darling Kate, and you'll fornicate in luxury.'

'Look,' she said. 'My husband leaves on Saturday, for a buying trip to Italy. He's going for a week and luckily, it's half-term so there's no school for me.'

'Then shall we have a trial run?'

'That'll be fun. I'll tell the kids I'm going on a gardening course.'

So Nicholas and Sophie went to Italy while Kate joined Rick at his estate in Dorset.

Chapter 11

'When are you going?' Anna asked David.

'Why?'

'Because I don't want you here when Damien arrives.'

'I'm sorry, but I'm not meeting Stevie till after lunch.'

'Well, if you thing that you're going to hang around here you've got another thing coming. We are working this afternoon.'

'Okay, I won't queer your pitch. I'll go to the pub.'

'You do that!'

'Funny to think we were married. You treat me as if I'm a leper,' David said.

'Just don't ruin it for me, please. Damien Spur is one of the best writers of the decade and he likes my work. I am so lucky. He's going to help me.'

'Okay, okay. There's no need to go on about it.'

But David took his time. When the intercom buzzed at 2 p.m., he still hadn't left.

Anna was in the bedroom fiddling with her make-up.

Damien rang the bell again.

'Shall I let him in?' David shouted up the stairs.

'Yes,' she shouted back, 'but for goodness' sake, just say hello and go.' Anna knew that David wasn't going to make it easy. He still loved her.

So here was David, face to face with the urbane, successful Damien Spur. And who was he? A has-been restaurateur who'd pissed away his life on the gambling tables.

'Hello,' Damien said. 'You must be David.'

'Yes, for my sins.'

'Anna's told me about you.'

'Probably given you all the bad bits.' David gave a bitter laugh.

'Not at all. She said you were a terrific restaurateur – and I must tell you that I remember your fabulous restaurant very well. When I was a young man, my stepfather took me to Valentino's. Such a glamorous place. And I can't forget the lobster with port wine sauce and the fabulous roasted duck breast with spring rolls.'

'Ah! Those were the two dishes that put us on the map,' David said. 'That, and the fact that we were a favourite haunt of all the high-class hookers in Mayfair who insisted that they ate with their clients first and the sex came later. And in the main room every night there were at least three geezers who were ready to go down on bended knees.'

'Well then, I'm sure you might remember my stepfather. His name was Teddy McDermott. In fact, I think he proposed to my mother at your restaurant.'

'Of course I remember Teddy!'

David's face lit up. He looked alive again. He had the keen expression of a man who had woken up to the days when his life mattered. David Rose, the great bon viveur.

'And I remember your mother, Virginia, too.'

'Funny to hear her name,' Damien said. 'I always called her Mummy, which didn't suit her at all. Couldn't stand the maternal stuff.'

'Maybe I saw her in a different light,' David replied. 'She was gorgeous, like a film star, very Rita Hayworth with that silky auburn hair and those flirty brown eyes. So elegant and charming. When he proposed to her, everybody stood up and clapped and then Teddy sang "It Had to Be You". It was beautiful.'

'Teddy was so romantic,' Damien said. 'I really adored my stepfather.'

'They were regulars after they married. Sometimes they would ask me to sit at their table. Teddy had a great sense of humour. Made me and your mother laugh with his funny quips.'

Anna appeared. She stood watching the two men who were fired up by their exchange and, for the first time since the demise of her marriage, she saw the David that she'd married. As if the memory of Teddy and Damien's mother had suffused him with fresh blood, recharged him.

Here was the David who had charmed her.

'Well,' she said, 'what a coincidence! But we have work to do. And you don't want to keep your friend waiting, do you, David?' She gave him a tight little smile.

'Sorry, but that was such a great surprise. Thank you, Damien. You brought back fond memories.'

'Good to meet you too, and if you can dig up some of the recipes, I'd really appreciate it if you would send them to me. I love cooking. It's my passion.'

'And I'd love to hear more about your adventures,' Damien said.

Anna was losing ground. Eyes narrowed, she threw David a killer glance.

They were both ignoring her. Maybe Damien was more interested in her ex than her story. Never mind, best to be charming.

'Perhaps you can come over to dinner one night,' she suggested politely. 'I'm sure David would be delighted to tell you all about his life. But not now,' she added somewhat sharply.

'Love to,' Damien replied.

'Well, I'd better go, before she throws me out.' David picked up his overnight bag and turned to Anna. 'See you Monday,' he said with a twinkle in his eye. 'Goodbye.'

Anna blushed as he left. Why did he have to say that? *See you Monday.*

And there was no mistaking the sly look he'd given her. She could see that Damien had clocked it.

'Your husband's an interesting man,' Damien said.

'Ex,' she replied. 'He's living with me at the moment until he finds a new place. Anyway, let's get on with the story.'

Damien took the manuscript out of its envelope and they sat on the sofa.

'Take away the wordiness and drive the text with feeling,' he said. 'Keep the sentences simple. Remember, you are writing for children.'

Anna loved the way he treated her. He gave her courage. Inspired her with his thoughtful comments.

She looked at his face as he studied the pages, and wondered how he could be so serious. It was, after all, a children's story.

But he knew how to make words come alive. 'Show, don't tell,' he said. 'More dialogue, breathe life into your characters. Forget the pretty words and frilly sentences. Even younger readers want to know who the characters are, what they think, what they feel. Dig deep.'

Anna was dying to kiss him.

Better to wait till the end of the session.

'Don't mix business with pleasure,' Claudia had said. 'Don't throw your body at him.'

But it was Damien who held fire. Doing his thing. Pacing himself. Giving her the drill.

When they'd finished the chapter, he looked at her with thrilling intimacy and said, 'Well, Anna, I think that's enough for today.'

Make her wait. Start slow.

He curled his lips as if he was going to kiss her, but no, he hovered just close enough so she could feel his breath.

Her legs were shaking.

Oh my goodness, he hasn't even touched me and I'm already wet!

The thought had made her tremble. It was delicious. Full of promise. He certainly knew what he was doing. Agitating her. Making her want him.

He gently grazed her lips with his and waited for her response. Anna was ravenous.

She gave a deep sigh. Here she was in the moment. Her past forgotten. The years of nothingness disappeared. She was beautiful again.

And then he moved away. Held her face.

'Why don't we have a walk? Clear our heads after the work? It's a lovely day.'

Come on, Anna. It's your call. Forget Claudia. Here's your chance. Be brave. Nothing to stop you.

'I've a better idea,' she said.

Anna took his hand and led him upstairs to the bedroom. He didn't resist.

As she passed the heart-shaped mirror, she winked at herself.

You, Anna Rose, are a very skilled seductress.

She'd sprayed the bedroom with Oud, bought from a Moroccan shop in Portobello.

Damien sneezed. It smelt stale, made his eyes water. Reminded him of the souk in Marrakesh where a thief had stolen his wallet.

He scanned the lavender silk curtains and the shabby-chic dressing table. It was not a room in which he was comfortable. Too many frills and pictures of flowers on the wall.

He wanted to leave, but Anna was so keen that he didn't want to disappoint her.

'Let's have a shower first,' he said.

Come on, Casanova, get on with it. She's chomping at the bit! said the Voice.

He unzipped her dress and slid his finger down her spine; twanged the edge of her silky panties.

Full speed ahead, the Voice said. *Don't do the number. You want this done and dusted by six if she's going to cook you dinner.*

She was beautiful undressed. Her lovely breasts stood to attention like proud soldiers. Her tummy flat, her legs slender and graceful.

Damien was glad he'd stayed.

'You're perfect,' he said.

'And so are you.' She sighed, her eyes wide, feasting on his beautiful torso, fine muscles and golden unblemished skin.

And so the ritual began. Damien's tried-and-tested thriller. He lathered her with soap and water.

'Oh my God,' she moaned. 'Please, Damien, take me to bed. I don't think I can stand this much longer.'

Their bodies entwined, she nuzzled his neck and lifted her legs round his waist. He carried her to the bedroom.

She made weird animalistic sounds as he caressed her. Purred like a cheetah, growled like a tiger, hissed like a snake.

Damien stifled a giggle.

Come on. Don't be mean. She's having a good time, said the Voice.

Even Damien, who was used to endless marathons, found Anna's gymnastics exhausting.

She changed positions frequently.

You need a breather, said the Voice. *Lie back and enjoy it.*

He rolled over and now she was on top, astride him, riding her stallion at a furious pace.

'Yes, yes!' she panted. 'This is just what I needed. You're the best. I could go on forever.'

Oh no! said the Voice. *You wanted to leave at 10.30. By the time she cooks dinner, you won't be finished till midnight! If you want to get home this evening, you'll have to chivvy things along. Come on, don't fall asleep on the job. Show her who's boss.*

Damien grabbed Anna's arms and rolled her over. Now he was on top. A few master strokes and she was on her way.

Surfing the waves, her back arched, she squeezed Damien's buttocks hard and gave one final animal cry. A howl so plaintive that the neighbour next door rang her intercom.

At first Anna ignored it. But the buzzing carried on.

'Oh, for goodness' sake,' she said. 'I'd better answer it.'

Damien gave her a sweet smile. 'That's a shame.'

Who are you trying to kid? said the Voice. *You're relieved, admit it. Back on schedule.*

Anna jumped out of bed, went downstairs and picked up the receiver.

'Sorry to disturb you,' her neighbour said, 'but I heard a very strange noise. Didn't know you had a dog, but it sounded in pain. Is everything all right?'

'Yes, fine,' Anna said. 'No need to call the RSPCA. I was watching a documentary about wolves. I'll turn the TV down.'

Meanwhile, Damien had slipped into the shower again. He needed to think.

Let me help you, said the Voice. *You could just get dressed and leave. Or maybe you should stay. She's interesting. Strange, but kind of sexy, in an unbridled sort of way.*

When Damien came out of the bathroom, Anna was sitting on the edge of the bed, crying. She looked up at him, her eyes smudged with mascara.

'I'm so sorry,' she said. 'I don't know what came over me.'

'What do you mean?' Damien said.

'Those noises I was making – I've never done that before.'

'What's wrong with that? You were just enjoying yourself.'

'Yes, but how embarrassing that my nosy neighbour heard me. She's always interfering. Thought I was hitting a dog. Was going to call the RSPCA. Can you imagine?'

So bizarre. Damien burst out laughing. And that's when he knew he would see her again.

Yes, she was a strange creature, though he somewhat enjoyed her eccentric behaviour. There was something about her that was appealing. A mix of steely determination where her ambition was concerned, yet she was also amusing and childishly enthusiastic.

Plus she was an excellent cook. That evening, she made him osso bucco, which he loved, followed by tiramisu.

She'd been charming and light during dinner. After a few glasses of wine, Damien decided to stay the night.

They made love again, and this time Anna was calmer, more attentive to his needs.

'Anna,' he sighed, 'you're a very gifted woman.'

***

Monday afternoon. Anna had come home from work elated. Damien had called her, urged by the Voice. Another date. His place this time.

But where was David? He'd said he would be back in the morning. Not that she minded.

Peace and quiet, no squabbling. He was probably still playing snooker at the local in Harrow.

Whereas Damien Spur was surely more interested in cultural pursuits. Filling his playtime with visits to the theatre and dining in fine restaurants.

Yes, he was definitely on the A-list. And then she stopped herself.

Remembered how David used to take her to the smartest places. He especially loved the opera. They would go all the time until his life fell apart. Couldn't afford it anymore. Listened to his CDs instead.

When her ex finally came home, he greeted her with a kiss on the cheek.

'Sorry I'm late,' he said. 'These are for you.' He presented her with a fancy red carrier bag.

'How lovely,' she replied. 'Most unexpected.' She gave him a charming smile.

This was a new David. Was he wooing her? Did he feel threatened by Damien?

'Surprise number one.' His face was flushed with excitement.

She pulled out a gold box. 'My favourite chocolates! Thank you, David.' She patted his cheek.

'And now, number two. Do you want to sit down? It's big news.'

Anna laughed. 'It's okay. I can assure you I won't keel over, whatever it is.'

'No, come and sit. For once, don't fight me.' He took her hand and sat her on the ivory chintz sofa that Evelyn had given her.

'Well, I know it hasn't been easy having me around,' he said slowly. 'And now I've met your new friend Damien, who seems a lovely guy, I might add, I think you need some space. So...'

Yes... Come on, David, spit it out.

'Stevie's asked me to come and share his flat. What do you think?'

'Well, it seems a good idea, but how will I...'

He finished her sentence. '...make ends meet?'

'Yes.'

'Don't worry about the money. I'll still help you with the bills.'

'But how can you afford it?'

'Because – here comes the big one – surprise number three. I'm going to manage a gastropub.'

'Well, I certainly didn't expect that. What wonderful news! So then, when are you leaving?'

'At the end of the week,' he replied. 'And I start my new job next Monday.'

He whisked a bottle of champagne from his case. 'Ready chilled. Let's celebrate!'

Damien was half asleep when the doorbell rang. He looked at his watch. It was 6 p.m. Anna was early.

He opened the door in his dressing gown. She looked bemused.

'Oh, have I got the wrong day?'

'No. But you're a little premature. We said six thirty, didn't we? I like to have a snooze between five and six, if I can.'

'Oh dear, my mistake. So sorry. I can come back later if you like?'

'Of course not. Do come in.' Anna noticed he was barefoot. He had beautiful toes. Perfectly formed.

'Would you like a drink while I get dressed?' he said.

What a pity. He looks so sexy in his ivory, damask silk robe. Why bother to get dressed when he's only going to have to take it off again?

'Yes, please,' she said.

He took out a bottle of wine from the fridge and poured her a glass of excellent white burgundy. 'I'll just be a tick,' he said, and disappeared.

Anna looked at the elegant art deco light, the impeccable satinwood desk, the ruby-red Persian carpet, and imagined herself settled in the blue velvet armchair in a cream silk peignoir. Damien Spur's girlfriend, the novelist Anna Rose. Twenty minutes later, he appeared again.

'Now then, let's continue.'

They sat at his desk, side by side. Anna stole a quick glance at his handsome profile. Forehead, eyes, nose, lips, chin in perfect symmetry.

Just like a Greek god. Oh dear, you've got it bad, Anna. You lovestruck fool. Stop staring at him. Concentrate on the work or you'll lose his respect.

It was hard. They were sitting so close to each other. His neck smelt of lemons. Everything about him was sensual.

'Good, really good,' Damien said. 'So much better. The writing really flows now. You've worked very hard. Taken the notes and given me back more than I expected. A few more sessions and I think we'll have a book.'

And that's what Anna feared. But she knew not to ask him questions. Just take what she could. Enjoy it while it lasted.

'Thank you, Damien. You're a wonderful teacher.' She gave him a coy look.

And then, she had the wave. That rush of heat rising between her legs, up through her body, burning her cheeks. She was sizzling again. Taken over by the need to touch him, kiss him.

'I've made you dinner,' Damien said. 'Then we can go to bed.'

And so the sessions continued. Her place or his. Work, dinner, sex – and goodbye in the morning.

Until the day he set sail.

They lay in post-coital bliss while Damien tenderly stroked her hair. 'Anna, what am I to do with you?'

'I don't know, Damien. What do you want to do with me?'

'Well, I don't want to hurt you,' he said. 'I've loved being your mentor. The story is wonderful and really works now. I am happy to send it to my agent, but…'

'But what? It's been more than just the book, hasn't it?'

'Well, yes.'

Here it comes, the goodbye line. Keep it fresh, Damien.

'It's not your fault, it's mine,' he said. 'But I just can't be with one woman, Anna. I'm an adventurer. You need a man who loves just you.'

'Please don't tell me what I need. I'm grateful that you've helped me with my book, but I don't see why we can't carry on seeing each other. Are you bored with me?'

'You should never ask that question.'

Anna sighed and turned away. Maybe it was for the best. Keep the work separate. Stay friends.

After he'd left, she rang Claudia.

'It's over. Damien will help me with the book, but he doesn't want a relationship.'

'So, was he good in bed?'

'Claudia! What are you saying?'

'I heard he has a five-star rating.'

Anna shouldn't have called. There was a side to Claudia that she found cruel. She didn't need the cards to tell her that he slept around.

'Who did you hear that from?'

'Never mind. Just giving you a reality check. I told you. He's not a man who has long-term relationships. And he doesn't go for women that fall in love with him.'

'How do you know?'

'Trust me. Get on with your life and let him help you with your book. Much more useful than having your heart broken.'

Chapter 12

What Claudia didn't say was that after she had read Damien's cards, he'd confided in her. Said that he'd never been in love since his wife, Laura, took her life.

They'd met at Oxford: Damien had read English and she, history. A glass of wine together and Damien was caught. He was intoxicated by Laura's brilliant mind, and she with his. He had pursued, wooed and won her, and after university they were married. This was followed by a honeymoon in Capri, which was not as it should have been.

That first night, after dinner, they sat on the vast terrace of their suite, gazing at the magenta starlit sky, with the moon illuminating the Mediterranean below. The gentle waves washed in and out of the shoreline with a whispering sound, like the sweep of mermaids' tails.

'Laura,' Damien said softly. He traced her profile with his finger. 'I love your sweet nose. What are you thinking?'

'Please, just give me a moment.' The beauty of the night had eluded her.

Her mind was somewhere else.

He waited and then she turned to him.

'I'm ready now,' she said.

Damien swept her up in his arms and carried her into the bedroom.

He slid the straps of her oyster satin dress down her shoulders and kissed her neck. Brushing aside the gossamer curtain that veiled the baroque four-poster bed, he lay her on the silky sheets.

Here he was with the love of his life – his virgin bride. He was about to bless their marriage with a sacred consummation.

He tried so hard to please her but as soon as he became aroused, she pushed him away as if he were a stranger.

'No, Damien – stop! I need more time,' she said.

But time didn't change her.

Yes, in the months that followed, she placated him. Gave him as little as she could to appease him. Allowed him a swift thrust that she accepted and endured which left him lonely and confused.

'Laura,' he said one night as she lay beside him, her face implacable, eyes glazed, far away. 'Where are you?'

And she looked at him and sighed. 'Damien, why do you love me? I don't deserve you.'

Until one day she gave him a platonic hug and said, 'You love me too much. I'm sorry I can't give you what you need.'

Damien looked at her pale, tortured face and wondered why she'd married him.

'This is crazy, Laura. I thought that we were soulmates. But you're ice cold in bed.'

'I can't help it,' she said. 'I'm locked in my head. I do love you. But my body just shuts off. I feel physically numb.'

She looked up at him and for a moment he saw something else. An arrogance. As if to say, 'You don't know how to please me.'

There were no more conversations. Damien stopped trying. It hurt less.

Frustrated that his manly needs were unrequited, he sought other willing beauties who were simply delighted to oblige.

The sensational response to his debut novel, *The Empress*, had prompted his publishers to send him on a book tour to the States: LA, Miami and New York.

'I was in full throttle, Claudia,' he said. 'I just couldn't stop. Laura made me so angry. Every time I had sex with another woman, I wanted her to know. I was glad the paparazzi took pics of me with gorgeous actresses and models. I wanted to hurt her – to humiliate her, like she did me. And why not? She didn't want my body, she just wanted my soul. What kind of marriage is that! So I was happy to go on tour and have my ego stroked by my adoring fans. Laura cried when I said goodbye.'

'Well then, she must have cared about you,' Claudia said.

'Don't think so. More like crocodile tears.'

Claudia passed him a glass of water. He took a sip.

'I had lost the sense of who I was with her,' he continued. 'She made me feel useless – a failure. But, luckily, on the plane to LA I met a gorgeous girl called Lilly, sitting in a first-class seat next to me. I was back in the game.'

'And what was her story?' Claudia asked.

'Well, she was getting married to a wealthy Greek man, twice divorced and pushing sixty.'

'How old was she?' asked Claudia.

'Twenty-three. It was a huge age gap. I asked her whether she was happy with that. Lilly said that at the time it didn't cross her mind. He just swept her off her feet. She said that they'd met in Paris a year ago when he came to a fashion show. She was on the catwalk modelling Givenchy and afterwards he waited for her. And every day for a month he sent her flowers and took her to the finest restaurants. He treated her beautifully and didn't ask to sleep with her. Until he took her for a weekend to St Tropez.'

Now he had pushed Laura out of his mind, Damien coasted along. He enjoyed talking about his exploits.

'We were both getting a bit tipsy by then. I asked her whether her husband was a good lover. She said he was good technically, but he was selfish, and that once he'd had his fun, he fell asleep. And that's when I knew I had her. We needed each other. We were both fired up. It was so erotic playing under the blanket while the other passengers were asleep. And that rush…'

Damien looked at Claudia, his eyes drawing her in. 'Feeling each other's heartbeat rise.' Just thinking about it, Damien was up there with the gods flying.

'And then the calm,' he said. 'We held each other and kissed. Intimate strangers who would probably never meet again.'

In LA he said the starlets had clamoured for his glamour. An endless queue of pretty misses were ready and willing to allow him any pleasure he wished, and basking in their adoration he'd had no hesitation in taking all he could. TV chat shows, meetings with moguls eager to option the book, movie-star parties. Damien loved the glitz.

'What better than to be an Englishman abroad? Especially in America, Claudia,' he said.

Next there had been a quickie in Miami. He made small talk and signed books in the day and in the evening after dinner, to satisfy his appetite further, Damien paid a visit to the 10 Den, his favourite haunt. It was a downtown dive where the girls rocked and rolled on poles, fake breasts harnessed in leather straps, shimmying their perky-thonged bottoms in the air and inviting guests who sat on the periphery to flutter banknotes on their favourite body parts.

Sweaty men laughed and leered while their women, some dressed like Arkansas housewives, wearing high-necked frilly milkmaid frocks with their hair held neatly with plastic barrettes, patted the girls' bottoms with the green notes, in exchange for a cheap thrill.

Damien, among the diverse clusters of night owls milling and drinking, spotted a pretty girl who took his fancy. Yes, she was ready for his pleasure.

Then he went to New York, where there was a more serious affair. A Manhattan party in the Museum of Modern Art.

A cool brunette with her hair slicked back in a ponytail, wearing a black polo neck and jeans, slid up to him.

She looked like a fifties beatnik. Damien liked her style.

'It's such a pleasure to read a thriller that digs deeper into the characters,' she said. 'I find your empathy with the somewhat deviant villain very refreshing. Exploring the grey areas always draws me in.'

'I find it more interesting than writing stereotypes.' Damien noticed she had a serpent wrapped round a rose tattooed on her index finger.

'The symbol of temptation?' he said. 'But you look so sweet.'

'Yes, we all have our dark sides,' she replied, and gave him an impish look. 'Anyway, I would love you to sign my book.'

'Of course. Your name?' He took out his gold pen.

'Desiree.'

'Beautiful.'

'…and perhaps after the party you might like to come to a nightclub in the village.' She was enjoyable. He'd go.

When they arrived, the smell of dope hit him. They sat and smoked a spliff and danced close, and afterwards she took him back to her place. She was great, and for once Damien was happy for her to take charge.

'My reputation as a lover almost matched that of writer,' he said to Claudia with just a hint of conceit. 'When I arrived back in London, Laura was beside herself. Everybody seemed to know about my peccadilloes. I said I was sorry, that I knew I'd been a bastard but… did she expect me to live like a monk? And that's when she told me we both needed therapy. And I said, "Why *we*? There's nothing wrong with me." She begged me. "Maybe," I said to placate her, but I knew I wasn't going to go. I spent nights and days away from her. Lied to her. My capacity for deception was immense. I slept with a different woman every day. Sometimes two or three.'

***

Sadly, the long weekend in Venice that Nicholas had planned was a washout.

He'd booked a suite at the Cipriani Hotel and, as luck would have it, that first night whilst he and Sophie were sitting on the terrace sipping aperitifs, entwined, her head on his shoulder, his arm round her neck, they were observed.

Charles Lane, an art dealer whom Nicholas had known for years, came and sat at the table next to them. A few moments later he was joined by a beautiful young woman with long, dark hair and honey-brown eyes. She wasn't his wife, either.

The two men smiled at each other, but neither spoke.

'Who's that?' Sophie asked as she sipped her Bellini. 'He looks dangerously attractive.'

'Someone I've met a few times at auctions. Now just drink up and let's go.' He swigged his whisky down and caught the waiter's eye.

'The bill,' he said without his usual smile.

Sophie hadn't seen this side of Nicholas before. The silky charmer had disappeared, replaced by a stony-faced stranger.

He didn't even look at her. He drummed his fingers on the table and stared at her glass.

'Aren't you going to finish your champagne?' he asked.

'Why?' she replied. 'There's plenty of time. I thought you said you booked the table for nine? It's only seven thirty.'

Sophie knew what was going on. Nicholas was stewing about being caught in this *compromising position*. She watched him look askance at the good-looking man, who was far more relaxed than he was.

What's your problem, Nicholas Morley? Why would a sophisticated player like Charles Lane be the least bit interested in the love life of a small-time antiques dealer from Bournemouth whose big night before he met Sophie was playing poker with the boys?

Sophie could see him thinking that even though he and Lane were in the same boat, someone else he knew could turn up.

He sneakily edged his chair away from Sophie.

She looked at Nicholas and felt sorry for him.

He wasn't the sort of guy who took an affair in his stride.

Go easy on him, Sophie. You knew the score when you seduced him. A married man would never be an easy catch.

'No need to pretend, Nicholas. I get you,' she said. 'Spotted with the mistress; how unfortunate. Well then, let's put you out of your misery, Mr Morley. I'm going to the loo while you pay the bill, and off we go.'

As Sophie passed the art dealer, she winked at him. He winked back.

After that evening, they didn't see him again, but it was fair warning. For the rest of their stay, Nicholas made sure that he didn't hold Sophie's hand in public. Any lovers' gestures remained strictly under cover.

And so it continued back in England – grabbing days and nights here and there, midweek visits and the occasional weekend together when he went to an art fair in the country.

Nicholas and she had been going strong for six months, but when it came to the crunch, he didn't want to leave his wife.

Sophie was becoming increasingly impatient. The more she saw him, the lonelier she became when he left.

A mistress's life just didn't satisfy her. She yearned for domestic bliss.

It was on Valentine's Day that things finally came to a head. Nicholas had managed to slip away from Kate to spend the night with Sophie. He bought her red roses and a pretty diamond necklace, and she made him his favourite: lobster zucchini noodles.

She loved watching him eat. The way he sighed when he forked the juicy lobster meat and slipped it in his mouth.

'Oh, Sophie. This is sublime.'

'More wine?' she said.

'Yes, please,' he said.

She brushed his shoulder with her breast as she poured him another glass.

He slipped his hand under the straps of her red silk dress.

'Not now.' She gently moved his hand away. 'I want you to wait.'

That's it! Make him so hot that he forgets he has a wife. Get him to the point where he can't live without you. Give him the time of his life and then withdraw.

'How do you want me?' she asked, teasing his mouth open with a strawberry dipped in Chantilly cream. 'In bed or on the sofa?'

She undid his shirt and rubbed her palm against his nipple.

'Oh my Lord, here we go again.' Nicholas could hardy speak. 'Bed's good, but I'm bursting for a piddle.'

Damn him. Why was she besotted with this man-boy? What did he want from her? He didn't even care if they had sex. And yet he was such a wonderful lover. He was so controlled. Heated her up to boiling point and then cooled her down. Watched her as he got her all steamed up again and just as she was ready to blow a fuse he melted her.

She could hear Evelyn's voice.

'Sophie, keep a man dangling. Don't let him know what you're thinking. And only when he's worked for it, give him what he wants. And then it's important you retreat, pull the rug out from under his feet, until he's on his knees begging you to be with him forever.'

But after they made love Sophie just couldn't help herself. Instead of being mysterious and cool she immediately persisted with her post-coital nag.

'Nicholas, we're going nowhere,' she said. 'I'm fed up with being a secret.'

He crossed his arms and stared at the ceiling. 'What do you expect me to do? Just up and go? Kate's given me no reason to leave her.'

'Thanks very much. Where does that leave me?'

'Sophie, you were the one who turned me on. I was happy to keep it platonic.'

'I thought you loved me. You said that you'd never felt a connection with anyone as you did with me.'

Sophie hugged her silk pillow.

Nicholas hadn't signed up for this. Feisty was fine, but her childish whining made him wish he was back in Bournemouth, sitting on the sofa, the dogs at his feet, with a good book and a glass of wine, listening to Classic FM.

'I do.' He sighed. 'But you marry a life, not just a wife. And what about the dogs? Who will take them for walks every morning?'

'You're pathetic. Happy to settle for less than any husband expects. You pay for everything and she can't even be bothered to put a pizza in the oven when you get home. And, worse than that, now she won't even let you come near her. When was the last time you had sex?'

'Really, Sophie, I don't want to talk about it,' Nicholas said. 'It's late. Let's go to sleep. I made up a very elaborate fib to stay here tonight. Said I was looking after a friend's dog because he had to visit his dying mum in hospital and he was staying overnight.'

'What a wonderful guy you are to risk life and limb for li'l ol' me.'

She gazed at him with goo-goo eyes and gave him a syrupy smile.

'That's refreshing. At least now you recognise the risks I take to be with you.'

'You're joking, aren't you, Nicholas? I don't give a monkey's toss how you managed to get here and I don't care what you said. I want to talk about your boring marriage…'

'Talk away, Sophie dearest, but don't expect me to join in.'

'…and another thing, even if you've forgotten when you had sex with her, I remember.'

Go on – let him have it. The final slam-dunk.

'You told me about a year ago, and that was only because she was drunk. For heaven's sake, Nicholas, get real. You don't have to be Sherlock Holmes to work out that she's been having an affair. Suddenly, after years of not caring about how she looked, you said she started wearing make-up and going to the hairdresser. And what about the nights she didn't come home? Told you she was staying at friends, needed a break. But here's the strange bit, I think you're being followed. Which puzzles me, because you'd think she would be pleased to have you out of the way.'

Sophie swung her legs out of bed and opened the curtains. 'You see that black Fiesta on the opposite side of the road with the man at the wheel? It's been there all night. I spotted it when you arrived. Last week too, same car.'

'It could be your imagination, Sophie.'

He stared at the car outside the window tapping his forehead rapidly with his index finger. *Think, Nicholas, think. What are you going to say? Be clear. Give Sophie your best shot. Tell her what she wants to hear. Give her hope.*

'I can tell you one thing, Sophie, if she is having an affair that would be a different matter. I promise you, Sophie, if that happens, there'll be no way of stopping me. I'll be knocking at your door with my suitcase. But if she isn't, I am not going to jump ship. For one thing my children will never forgive me.'

'Children!' Sophie threw the silk pillow at him. 'That old chestnut. If they're old enough to smoke a spliff, they can mind their own business and let you get on with your life.'

***

The next time he came home late, Kate was waiting. For, despite her own betrayal with Rick, the prospect of confronting Nicholas with videos and photos of his comings and goings with Sophie gave her a venomous thrill.

Oh, to see Nicholas squirm, watching the telescopic details filmed through the chink in the curtain of him astride his filly, a glorious exultant ride to the finishing line.

'Actually, I was amazed,' Kate said. 'Didn't think you were up to it.' Her mouth slipped into a spiteful smile. 'So, what have you got to say for yourself?'

'What do you expect?' Nicholas replied. 'When was the last time that we slept together? Do you think I'm a fool?'

'What do you mean?' She stared at him defiantly.

'Come clean. You're a hypocrite! You think I haven't noticed silky knickers hanging out to dry on Friday after bridge night? So tell me, who is he?'

'Okay, I admit it. Yes, I have a wonderful lover. He's called Richard Delaney and for six months he's been my saviour. I met him in the garden centre. He woke me up! I never thought I'd be interested in sex again. So many years of pretending, frozen stiff, waiting for it to be over.'

'Then why don't you leave me?'

'I don't know. Maybe because you've been around so long that I don't have to pretend. I can be myself. Anyway, I suspected all along that you were also having a fling, but to be honest I didn't care. As long as Rick was happy, it suited me. But now that he wants more, I'm not sure. We've been a family so long…' Her voice trailed off. 'I didn't want to break us up.'

'Then why did you have me followed?'

'Because I could see how happy you were when you came home from your so-called business trips. And one day when you were up in London, I found a condom in your shaving kit. That's when I found the private eye.'

For the first time in a decade, Nicholas and Kate locked horns. No distractions. It was exciting. Kate's mask-like face was moving again. There was a glint of hope in her dull eyes. A vestige of life.

'Why didn't you confront me? You already had the evidence. I couldn't lie to you. And maybe we could have worked things out there and then. Instead of you going to a private dick? We could have had counselling.'

Trembling, she clenched her fists. Stealing herself. Ready to let rip. Secret thoughts, buried in the depth of her mind, locked away.

Pandora's box flew open.

'Because I wanted to know what you were like with another woman. You obviously did the trick. She was on another planet.'

'So what about Rick?' Nicholas asked.

'I can't think at the moment,' Kate replied. 'I'm very confused. Watching you making love with another woman turned me on. She was so sexy I wanted to make love to her too.' After an everlasting pause Kate said tearfully, 'Shall you and I try to make things work? I want the Nicholas in the video to ravish me like he does with his Sophie. I'll tell you what. If I stop seeing Rick, would you stop seeing her?'

'I would,' said Nick. 'We've lost each other over the years. Too much domestic stuff and not enough romance. Why don't we go to Paris for a weekend? We could take the Eurostar.'

'I'd love that,' she said, and kissed him on the cheek.

It would be a litmus test. A holiday with Kate. Just the two of them. After all those years of camping with the kids, would they get on?

***

The weekend wasn't great, but neither was it a tragedy. Kate complained about the bed in the little boutique hotel on the Left Bank. Said it was too soft, gave her backache, not like her orthopaedic mattress. But, still, she and Nicholas made love which was as it had always been – not exactly thrilling, but perfectly adequate.

Afterwards, the street lamp cast a light on Kate's face through the window and Nicholas saw a glimpse of the young bride that he'd married. Yes, he could see why Rick had wanted her. She had a sweet face when she wasn't being tortured by the weight of her responsibilities.

'So, Nicholas,' she said, 'how are we doing?'

'I think we're doing okay,' he replied. But what he really wished for was to stay with Kate and have Sophie on the side. Just to give his life some fizz.

A few hours later, they made love again with comfortable familiarity. But when they slept, Nicholas dreamed of Sophie, whilst Kate dreamed of Rick.

***

Months went by and Nicholas tried surviving his boring life at home by texting Sophie whenever he was alone.

However, his visits once a week were brief and seldom satisfying. Any fun they had was overshadowed by Sophie's demands. She was not prepared to spend her life waiting for him.

Tired of stolen moments governed by train timetables, Sophie booked a trip to an art retreat in Bordeaux.

'That's a very good idea,' Evelyn said over lunch at Romano's, the Italian restaurant she had frequented at least once a week for twenty years, save when she was abroad.

'I hope the break makes you realise that there's more to life than being a snack for a married man.' She dipped a piece of bread roll in her glass of Chianti and popped it in her mouth.

'Please, Mother, don't start. There's more to our relationship than that.'

'But it's not going anywhere! Can't you see? You're skipping down a blind alley. Eventually you'll crash into a wall.'

The waiter arrived with the dishes. Evelyn plunged her fork into a large portion of gooey lasagne, whilst Sophie pecked at her Caesar salad. How her mother, a tiny sparrow of a woman, could eat more than a burly man and still have an appetite for dessert had always amazed Sophie.

'Come on, eat up.' Evelyn swirled her fork in the air. 'What's happened to your appetite? You're not getting any younger. You need some flesh on your cheeks. In a way, Anna's luckier than you. Her face stays put because of her bone structure. But you have a round face, more like your father. So when you don't eat properly everything drops.'

'Really, Mother, I don't need this now.'

'Well, you're looking haggard,' Evelyn persisted. 'You need to find a man before it's too late. At least now you have more of a choice. Wait any longer and the field will narrow. Especially if you want children.'

'I can freeze my eggs if I want a child.'

'Have you gone mad? Why would you want to do that? Surely a beautiful woman like you can find a husband. I can assure you, if you hadn't wasted your time with that Nicholas man, you'd be married by now. What happened to that gorgeous writer Damien Spur? You seemed to spend a lot of time with him.'

'We're friends – it's just platonic.'

'But why aren't you interested?' Evelyn said. 'I saw that interview with him on *Night Owls*. Not only handsome as a god, but that deep, gravelly voice; so sexy.'

'Anna is crazy about him and I don't want to tread on her toes.'

'How noble of you! Fat chance she has. Too needy. Really, Sophie! It's time to take stock of your life, before it's too late. Who wouldn't want a man like Damien Spur? I can tell you one thing, if I were your age and single, there would be no stopping me. Don't be so protective. Just open yourself up to a new opportunity. What are you doing chasing a married man's trousers? It's time to take stock of your life, before it's too late.'

Sophie wanted to leave. Evelyn had a way of turning any conversation with her into a lecture.

'I really don't need you to pressure me. Maybe I don't want a family anymore.'

'Why not? Wouldn't you like to have company? Even when William was away on business, I had you two girls to keep me busy.'

'And I had Mikey.' Sophie pushed her plate away and got up from the table. 'Really, Mother, I can't take this anymore. Let me remind you that I had a wonderful husband and child and that I couldn't have had a happier life.'

'Oh dear! Sit down. I'm sorry.' Evelyn grabbed her daughter's wrist.

'No!' Sophie yanked away her arm. 'I want to pay the bill and go. I don't need your treats.' She flagged the waiter, who had diplomatically ignored the altercation.

Luckily, it was closing time and the only guests left were the Japanese couple at the next table, who were mesmerised by the warring females.

'Please don't make a scene,' Evelyn whispered. 'I won't go on any more. Please, Sophie, forgive me.'

At last a chink of light. Sophie usually had to fight to be heard. Very rarely did her mother listen to anyone but herself.

But Sophie had pulled her up this time. Stopped her short.

Little Mikey had been the apple of Evelyn's eye. Her grandchild. The only one. And she'd adored Daniel. He'd been a lovely man and a good father.

Sophie sat down. Better give her mother a chance to redeem herself. Essentially, she meant no harm, but why did she have to interfere with the very fabric of her life? Nicholas wasn't her business.

Evelyn fiddled with her pearl brooch. Of course she remembered Mikey and Daniel. And then, surprising Sophie, she burst into tears.

'Oh dear, oh dear, what a poppy show I'm making of myself.' Trying to be discreet, she took out her hanky and dabbed her eyes. 'I'm so sorry, darling. Please forgive me. I just don't want you to be lonely. It must be so terrible for you. One moment you have a wonderful husband and son and the next they're gone. I miss them so much too.' She took a shaky breath. 'But now you're punishing yourself with a married man who I'm sure if he left his wife, you wouldn't want anymore. It breaks my heart.'

Sophie held her mother's hand and at that moment the only thing that mattered was their love for Mikey and Daniel.

But ten minutes later, after she'd eaten tiramisu accompanied by a digestif, Evelyn had retrenched. 'May I just say one more thing? I don't think you should put your eggs into one basket. When you're in Bordeaux, just be open to meeting people. You're stunning. You've been married. Always a good thing when a man knows you've been loved.'

'I'll bear that in mind,' Sophie said. 'But don't you worry about me. I'm going to have a great time, with or without a man.'

***

When Nicholas rang, Sophie had just finished packing. 'Wanted to wish you a safe journey,' he said.

'Thank you.' *Why did she answer the phone?* She was meant to be moving on.

'...And...' he said.

There was always an "and". Just a little opener to start the ball rolling, keep the chat alive.

'...And I also wanted to say that there's no need for you to feel guilty.'

'I'm sorry? What do you mean?' she asked.

'I bit the apple, Sophie. My choice. After the drought, you came along and offered me so much...'

'Look, Nicholas, this isn't the time for a heart to heart. I'm leaving in a few minutes.' *Don't you churn me up again, with your flattery.* 'My flight's at ten thirty. Damien's taking me to the airport.'

'Oh. I would have taken you. Why didn't you ask?'

'Don't start that nonsense. I can hardly imagine you driving up to London just to give me a lift.'

'Maybe you're wrong.'

'Be a good chap – let's drop this one.'

'Why are you so angry with me, Sophie?'

'Because you're selfish. I'm a distraction when you need a boredom fix.' She opened the zip of her bag. Passport, keys, credit card, yes.

'How can you say that? I have always been there for you. Drove up from Bournemouth in the middle of the night when you burnt your hand. Took you to the hospital and didn't even bother to hide it from Kate.'

Sophie hesitated.

'True,' she replied almost apologetically. 'I was very surprised.'

But why should she be surprised? Isn't that what you'd normally expect from someone who's a dear friend? Next, he'll be totting up the presents he's given you.

She glanced at her face in the mirror. She looked so confident. On top of things.

Go on, Sophie, tell him what you really think.

She started well enough.

'Yes, you tipped up in an emergency,' she said. 'Nicholas to the rescue. That was very good of you. But here's the thing. You'll never be around on Christmas Day. Wild horses wouldn't drag you away from your family. Of course, that's how it should be.

But it's not good enough for me. Waiting for the holidays to be over, so I can see you again.'

She paused. *Oops! Too much information. Okay, stop now! You sound like the pathetic, self-pitying mistress you are.*

'Darling, please! I don't want to lose you. I need your friendship… I can talk to you. Say what I feel…'

'Great for you.' Her mouth was dry. It was getting late. She needed to go.

Just finish it. Now, Sophie, now!

'How did I ever get caught up in this half-cooked relationship? I know I'm culpable too, but it was up to you to stop it if you weren't going to leave your wife. Not keep me hanging on. The truth is that you're weak. Why bother to make waves? Better to stay in your comfort zone, especially if you can get your kicks from someone else without any consequences.'

There was a silence on the phone… She could hear him take a deep breath for the next round of blarney.

Oh no you don't. I won't let you reel me in.

'Anyway, I *really* have to leave, Nicholas. Please let me get on with my life.'

She didn't wait for him to say goodbye.

***

Damien arrived a few minutes later.

'It's really kind of you to take me to the airport. You really didn't have to,' she said.

'Don't be silly. Why not?' He wheeled her suitcase to the front door. 'That's what I'm here for.'

Bit smarmy, said the Voice.

'You're such a charmer,' said Sophie.

There you go – she liked it, Damien said to himself.

Okay, the Voice replied. *But you need to say something sensible. Make her feel comfortable and secure.*

Damien opened the boot of his navy-blue Jag and placed her case next to his sports kit and tennis racquet.

'Love tennis,' Sophie said. 'Would be great to have a game when I get back. Since I've been with Nicholas, I haven't really been playing that much.'

'Good idea. I'm looking for a mixed-doubles partner.' He shut the boot and, sweeping round to the passenger side, opened the door for her.

She sat on the seat and swung her legs inside. Damien stole a quick glance at her graceful limbs. She was wearing leopard-skin ballerina shoes.

Better not start.

'To be honest,' he said, 'it's a novelty for me to have a female friend who's not a lover. And I must say I enjoy it. There's a lot to be said for a platonic relationship between a man and a woman. No sexual tension. No jealousy.'

'I agree,' Sophie said. 'No expectations.'

It was Sunday and the traffic wasn't too bad. Damien kept an easy pace. No point in rushing. More time to chat.

'I really hope you have a great time in Bordeaux.' He patted her hand in a friendly sort of way. 'Get Nicholas out of your mind. Maybe meet someone else. You deserve it.'

That's a good one, the Voice said. *I didn't mean you to go that far. Who are you trying to kid? You know that Sophie Fox is just up your street.*

Damien wasn't sure how he was going to temper his feelings. But the noble part of him was ready to help her.

And she trusted him.

On the way to the airport, Sophie spilled the beans about Nicholas and Damien listened.

'He just manages to manoeuvre me. Brings out my lust. He's never had an affair before. Little innocent Nicholas, I'm the one who corrupted him. And then after we make love, he feels guilty. Talks to me about his wife as if I'm his therapist.

Says it does him good. Even offered to pay me! I think if I'd said yes, he would even have taken me up on it.'

Damien shot her a horrified glance. 'Sophie! Do you know how lovely you are? Why are you punishing yourself?'

'Because I'll never get over Daniel,' she said, and burst into tears.

'I'll stop at the next lay-by.'

'It's okay. I'll be all right. I need to get on with my life. Thank you for being so kind to me. You're such a good man.'

Damien paused. He gulped.

'No, I'm not. I was a bastard to my wife. My life's been such a mess. Laura's death, my addiction to the dark side.'

Damien looked at her black-rimmed eyes.

'You look like a panda,' he said. 'A very beautiful panda.'

Sophie laughed.

'There's a packet of tissues in the glove compartment,' he said, reaching over to open it.

She took one and dabbed the smudged mascara.

'I just hope Daniel isn't up there watching me make a fool of myself. How could I have fallen for such an ordinary man? Maybe I'm glad he won't leave his wife.'

'What are you trying to say?'

'Perhaps it's a way of me staying faithful to Daniel.'

'You deserve more than being locked into a hopeless relationship. Why don't you go and see an analyst?'

Or why don't we both get soused and see what happens? he thought.

∗∗∗

Sophie wasn't sure what life had in store for her, but her visit to Bordeaux might be refreshing.

Days spent painting the beautiful scenery, happy to be distracted. Relieved to be with strangers who didn't pry into her personal life.

And in the evenings, it would be peaceful to dine al fresco with her fellow guests and watch the setting sun fall into dusk.

When Nicholas rang on Wednesday morning, she didn't answer her phone. It was early, 7 a.m. The voicemail pinged a few seconds later.

Don't listen to it. He's doing his number, keeping you on the hook.

She drew the blue-and-white chintz curtains and stepped onto the balcony. Such majesty. The stone path, flanked on either side by smooth grass and perfectly manicured topiary, led down to a large lily pond.

The light was so gentle that it spread across the landscape, stroking nature's colours with a misty glow.

Time for breakfast in the courtyard with the other students, and then to paint.

'We're going to the meadow near Margaux today,' said Marie, the teacher and owner of the chateau.

Morning glory. The pastel field of wildflowers – pink, lavender, lemon peeping through the grass – and in the distance, a dark silhouette of cypress trees edging the horizon. Sophie was happy. Nature had lifted her spirit.

Marie guided her students, weaving in and out between their easels. 'That's good, Charles. Don't be so tentative with your brush strokes.'

'Rosie, keep the paints flowing. Let the colours bleed into each other.'

And so she continued quietly appraising each student.

Sophie had set up her easel far away from the others. She wanted to be alone. To listen to the air moving softly across the field. It was her meditation, her eyes free to wander across the beautiful tableau and create her own vision.

Marie stood behind her. For a moment she was silent, her eyes darting across the canvas.

'That is so lovely,' she said. 'You use your palette beautifully.

Your colours sing. And the sun, sending swathes of light across the fields, I really like that. And those cypress trees, tall and proud. Gives the impression that they are standing guard. Fine work, Sophie.'

***

'Any news?' Evelyn's voice crackled down the phone. 'Have you met anyone?'

'I can't hear you properly,' Sophie replied. 'It's very bad reception here. You're cutting in and out.' She moved out of the bedroom onto the terrace.

Evelyn raised her voice. 'I said are there any nice men? Can you hear me now?'

'Yes, Mother, loud and clear.'

'Well?'

'Is that all you rang to ask?' Sophie sighed. 'I'm here to paint. Not to find a husband.'

'But why not? Wouldn't it be nice to meet someone with the same interests?'

'Yes.'

'It's a perfect opportunity. I did a little search on the internet about the woman who is running the course. Her name's Marie Fournier, isn't it?' Evelyn didn't bother to wait for an answer. 'She's old money, owns the chateau. Her family tree is impeccable. She must know everyone.'

Come on, tell her. At least it will give her something to dream about.

'I think she does,' Sophie replied. 'In fact, if it makes you feel any better, just so you don't think the trip is wasted, she's invited me to a soirée at the neighbouring chateau this evening.'

Evelyn sounded as if she'd been gifted a diamond. 'That's wonderful, darling! Probably the word has got round that there's a pretty woman in the group. Or maybe a sighting at the local village? So they asked Marie if she could bring you to the party. I am so pleased. A good old-fashioned introduction to Bordeaux society. How exciting!' Evelyn raced on.

Sophie held the phone away from her ear.

'I'm sure there are lots of rich men who own the vineyards. I might even know the winery. Happy to do the research if you need me. Sophie? SOPHIE! Can you hear me?' she shouted.

'Mother, stop. It's not your life – it's mine. You're making me feel desperate.'

'Sorry, yes. But you know me. I'm a romantic. Want to see you fall in love again. Or at least find someone who can look after you. Okay, I'll let you go. I'm sure you'll want to get yourself scrubbed up for the party. Is there a hairdresser in the village?'

'I don't know. Haven't looked for one.'

'Well, do tell me what happens.'

'I will, Mum.'

'Thank goodness that you've left that other chap,' Evelyn said.

'Other chap presupposes I have a new man,' replied Sophie.

'I just know that someone is going to come into your life. I have always been psychic. So glad that you've finally come to your senses. Now you're free of him, you'll see how much better your life will be. No more hiding... like that Venice trip.'

Sophie looked at her watch: 6 p.m.! Her mother had been talking for an hour.

'I've really got to go. We're leaving at 7 p.m. and I'm not even dressed yet.'

'Would love you to give me a quick call after the party to tell me how it went.'

'No, Mother. Just let me have a break. I need to concentrate on my painting. I'll ring you when I'm back in London.'

'All right. Have a lovely time at the soirée, but remember don't drink too much wine. You know what you're like when you're tipsy.'

Sophie laughed. 'Runs in the family. Goodbye, Mother,' she said, and rang off before Evelyn could have the last word.

Chapter 13

Sophie slipped on a silvery dress and ivory satin shoes, and made her way downstairs.

'You look so lovely.' Marie plucked a pale pink rose from a crystal vase and placed it in her hair. 'It should be fun this evening. Mostly locals, but a few interesting people and someone in particular that I think you should meet.'

In truth, Sophie found it strange that her hostess had been so quick to play matchmaker. She hardly knew her and already she was being introduced to a new man.

Perhaps her mother was right. News travels fast in a small village.

Marie drove through the large wrought-iron gate and up the driveway to the delightful chateau, friendly to the eye with its wooden shutters, a pretty pale green, and roses creeping up the sepia stone walls.

A smart young man around twenty, wearing a dark evening suit, opened the door. He was holding a list in his hand.

'Good evening, Madame Fournier. And you are Mademoiselle Fox?' His eyes shone when he saw Sophie.

'Yes, I am indeed.'

'Good evening, Olivier,' Marie said.

He ticked their names. 'The guests are on the lawn.'

The two women walked through the lustrous salon.

So formal and graceful. Huge arched windows. Carved giltwood chairs upholstered in silk, a Louis XV walnut side table.

On the mantle above the marble fireplace were a pair of Ormolu-mounted Sèvres porcelain vases, each portraying a gallant kneeling to his maiden. And on the walls, ancestral portraits, landscapes and bare-breasted courtesans.

Sophie followed Marie out onto the terrace and down the stone stairs leading to the floodlit lawn.

Six years, Daniel. Let me dance. Free me.

Marie introduced her to the guests. A mix of glamorous bourgeoisie, local artists, musicians and the man who ran the cafe in the square.

'Another glass of wine?'

Why not? It wouldn't hurt. It would give her courage. Help her to be light and funny; flirty.

'Yes, please,' she said.

And for a while she was just how she wanted to be. The men clustered round her and Sophie, poised in her beautiful dress, threw back her head and laughed at their jokes, while their wives stole sour glances and cursed their husbands.

But Sophie didn't care.

Horatio de Beaumont stood spellbound, watching her.

A perfect plan. Marie already knew that she had found a match for the elegant, wealthy aristocrat. He was the owner of a vineyard famed for its Grand Cru Merlot.

Marie took her arm. 'Let me introduce you to the Count de Beaumont.' She led Sophie over to a tall man with an impenetrable gaze. He had a noble face with dark grey eyes, a strong aquiline nose and a mouth that had no doubt kissed the most difficult women into submission. 'And this, Horatio, is Sophie Fox.'

'Your reputation goes before you, Sophie,' he said. 'I even saw the painting you did of the fields near Margaux.'

'That was quick. I only finished it this morning.'

Just keep it cool, thought Sophie. *This man needs a firm hand.*

'Yes, well, I think Marie had already picked you out as someone I should meet, and when she saw that you were also gifted, she wanted to share it with me. I have an art gallery in Paris. Not that she was trying to interest me in buying it.'

'Can't say that I came here to sell anything,' Sophie replied. 'I'm just doing a course like the other students.' She watched the tray of drinks go past.

No, you've drunk too much already.

'I must say, the Merlot is excellent,' she remarked.

'Actually, it's from my vineyard,' Horatio said.

'Ah yes, Marie told me…'

Stop, thought Sophie. *Don't let him think that you knew about the set-up.*

'Provincial conversations bore me, Sophie. Let's talk about you.'

Ah, another line. Horatio the sweet-talker. I bet it works on most women. Well, I'm not going to fall for it.

Sophie summoned the waiter. 'May I have a glass of rosé?'

'Not a good idea to mix the two.'

'Thank you for your advice, but it's fine. I'm used to mixing my drinks. And to be honest I have already had two glasses of the Merlot and it's a very heady wine.'

Sophie was not on her best behaviour. She swayed a little, and saw Marie watching her, but she really couldn't give a damn what people thought about her.

And, certainly, she had marked her card with a pretty but older woman in a floral dress who approached the count.

'Horatio!' She flung her arms around his neck. 'I didn't expect to see you here. I thought you were still in Paris setting up the new exhibition. Anyway, I'm glad you're back. Missed you.' She turned to Sophie and looked her up and down. 'You're doing the art course?'

'Yes.'

'It's a nice break. And you get to meet new people like Horatio. He's always happy to add fresh blood to his stable. Aren't you, darling?' she said.

'Especially if he has old nags like you around,' Sophie replied. 'I think it's probably time to put you out to pasture.'

The woman turned on her heel and fled.

Sophie stood proud and gave Horatio a big smile. A waiter had arrived with a tray of canapés.

She took a bite of a Roquefort cheese and pear morsel. 'Delicious,' she said. 'The sweet with the savoury, such a great combination.'

Horatio laughed. 'What a wicked woman you are.'

Had she gone too far? She glanced back at the woman in the floral dress who was whispering to Marie.

'Oh dear, I hope she isn't cross with me.'

'Oh, I don't know. She likes a bit of drama,' Horatio replied. 'But I think we should go anyway before the good women of Bordeaux put you in the stocks and throw canapés at you.'

She laughed, but he'd made her feel uncomfortable. 'You make me feel like a Jezebel.'

'Too biblical,' he said. 'More medieval. Maybe a witch. They probably would have burnt you at the stake. I'll tell you what, there's a lovely restaurant near here.' He took her hand and guided her up the steps. 'We'll have dinner first and then I'll take you home.'

∗∗∗

Horatio drove them in his open-topped Mercedes to the village. The sultry air sobered Sophie up. She glanced at Horatio. His eyes were steady on the road.

It was a pretty brasserie. Diners sat outside under a canopy of vines. Laughing and drinking. An easy atmosphere. Maurice, the patron, showed them to a table in the corner away from the other guests where Horatio always sat.

'Here, Sophie.' Horatio poured her a large glass of ice water. 'This will clear your head.'

They ate white asparagus with béchamel sauce, followed by tender pigeon with sweet potato and parsnip, accompanied by two glasses of excellent Bordeaux and, to finish, canelés, delectable little pastries flavoured with rum and vanilla with a soft and tender custard centre and a dark, thick caramelised crust, followed by mint tea.

Sophie was happy. The water and delicious cuisine had calmed her. She felt safe with Horatio. He was witty and charming and disarmingly romantic.

There was music coming from the Cafe de la Place in the square: a group of musicians played a lilting melody and a female chanteuse sang slow French songs full of passion in her deep, fluid voice.

'Come, Sophie.' Horatio took her in his arms and they danced for hours until they were alone. Just the two of them, Sophie with her head nestled in Horatio's neck.

'You have fallen asleep. I think it's time to go home,' he whispered, waking her gently.

He gave the musicians 100 euros and, holding Sophie round her waist, he took her to his car.

They arrived in the early hours, the light illuminating the entrance. The stars still clear in the night sky.

Sophie lifted her head. The moonlight caught her profile as she leant against the oak double doors.

'Such a joy to meet you.' He kissed her hand, making no apology for his old-school manners.

'Thank you for a wonderful evening,' she said, and waited.

He held her face in both hands and brushed her lips with his.

Let yourself taste him, but don't give him too much. Don't pull away – you want this. A kiss full of promise.

Finally, he let her go.

'I'll call tomorrow. Two weeks is such a short time to get to know you.'

'Yes, and most days I'll be painting.'

That's it, Sophie – show him you're independent.

'Of course,' he replied. 'Maybe we can set up an easel in my grounds. The view is beautiful and it's a good reason for me to see you more often.'

'That's a lovely idea, but I think in the day I should stay with the group as I don't want to miss my tuition.'

***

Sophie was no easy prize and when Horatio took her to his vineyard the next day to taste the wines, she kept her head. Every evening he courted her with courteous self-restraint.

And yet…

Sophie found herself wishing he would pull the reins and tether her affections.

So one night, as they dined by candlelight on the splendid terrace of his chateau, she said, 'Horatio, I want you to know that I am not the delicate flower that you perceive me to be. I haven't exactly lived behind a widow's veil for the past six years.'

'I wouldn't expect a beautiful woman like you to waste herself in that way.'

The sweet scent of jasmine and the rich wine had gone to her head.

Was he going to reach for her, touch her cheek, kiss her neck? *No, he wants me to seduce him. Lead him to the edge.*

'Shall I tell you a bedtime story, Horatio?' she whispered.

'Please do,' he said.

He held her gaze while he poured her another glass of wine. Sophie took a sip and moved towards him.

'When I was a sweet thirteen-year-old, my parents took me to Cannes. We stayed at the Carlton Hotel. And in the foyer, there was a woman called Madame Molière who had a kiosk displaying cigarettes, sweets and magazines. But hidden in her little nook was a secret stash of erotic books conveniently covered in brown paper for guests to savour... Classics such as *Fanny Hill*, *Lady Chatterley's Lover* and *The Story of O*.'

'I know the kiosk well,' he said.

She paused and, giving him a naughty smile, lowered her eyes.

'And...' he said.

'And so I bought one, encouraged by my friend Emily, who was also staying at the hotel with her parents. She was older than me, sixteen, and had already been fondled by a boy she'd met at a disco in Juan Les Pins.'

'Tell me, Sophie, which book did you choose?'

'*Lady Chatterley's Lover*,' she replied. 'So exciting to read about sexual pleasures beneath the sheets. My parents were surprised when I insisted on having early nights! One evening, Emily came to my room and we read my precious book together. She was Mellor and I was Lady Chatterley. We kissed and touched, tenderly arousing each other. Such a gentle preparation for our adult years. Don't you think so, Horatio?'

'Mmmm. Two innocent beauties discovering forbidden fruits is surely better than some clumsy young male's first attempt.'

'And you?' Sophie asked. 'What was your first adventure?'

'When I was eighteen, a beautiful older woman called Ondine tutored me in the art of pleasing the fairer sex. Once a week for a year, she would visit and teach me the secrets of a woman's inner chambers, and if I came too quickly, she would whip me. But I have to admit she was so passionate that I loved it. She was a dedicated soul. Wanted me to be the best lover in Bordeaux, and I worked hard as her willing pupil to fill the role.'

Horatio had matched her story with his. They were seducing each other. Waiting to see who would surrender first.

He changed the subject to tease her. 'Sophie, how do you like the scallops?'

But Sophie was still on course. Almost as if her every word, every thought was to urge him to consume her. Satiate her.

'Delicious… so soft and moist.'

Come on. Kiss me. Can't you see that I want you?

But Horatio held his ground.

The entrée arrived, a succulent lobster Thermidor. Sophie broke the claws and sucked the meat. Her ravishing mouth shone with sauce as she looked at Horatio with limpid green eyes, inviting him.

'Sophie, are you ready for me?' he finally said. Lifting her dress beneath the table, he touched her.

'Oh yes,' she replied, and held his hand between her thighs.

'You're like a flower.' He sat her on his lap and played with her.

'Please, Horatio,' she moaned. 'I'm in agony. Make love to me.'

'Not yet,' he said as he scooped her up in his arms and swept her off to bed.

At last, he gave her what she wanted. She was open to him.

Afterwards, Horatio lay by Sophie's side and played with her breasts.

'Come and live with me,' he said impetuously.

'Darling Horatio,' she said, kissing his chest, 'we've only known each other a couple of weeks.'

'Sophie, I know you're the one.'

Handsome, rich and available. Think of the years you've wasted with a man who can't make up his mind. What's stopping you?

***

Nicholas was waiting for Sophie at the airport.

He wanted to surprise her. Show her how much he missed her.

Usually on Sunday, he had lunch with his family at the Captain Blighty Gastro Pub and then took the dogs for a run on the beach.

This time he told Kate that he was going to see a client in Knightsbridge who was flying to Milan on Monday morning.

'That's okay,' she said. 'Just make sure you take the rubbish out before you go.'

So here he was, staring at the noticeboard. Sophie's plane was delayed.

He went to the men's room, had a pee, washed his hands, combed his hair and checked his face in the mirror. Good thing he had. There was a piece of spinach stuck between his teeth.

He'd made himself a smoothie before he left. Spinach and carrot.

Kate had laughed. 'How could you drink that revolting mess? You're such a masochist.'

'Well, why don't you cook me bacon and eggs instead?' he said, pouring his juice into a Thermos flask.

'You're much better at fry-ups than I am,' she replied. 'And anyway, I don't have time in the morning. Have to be at school at 8 a.m. And you know I like to have a lie-in on weekends.'

Nicholas averted his eyes. She used to be so different when they first met. Even made him soufflés.

No point in trying. She wasn't going to change. 'Bye, Kate, don't wait up for me,' he said.

Nicholas was nervous. Sophie seemed so cool before she'd left for France. And for two weeks she had barely answered his texts.

At last the Bordeaux passengers were coming through arrivals.

And here was Sophie. She looked happy. Striding through the lounge with her trolley.

Nicholas stood between the waiting minicab drivers holding up their placards. 'Sophie,' he shouted, and waved at her. She didn't hear him.

He shouted again.

She turned round and saw him. He looked just as he always did. Bright eyed, smiling, wearing a white shirt and pale blue jeans.

Don't give in, Sophie. What's the point? You've made up your mind, now stick to it.

Sophie stood her ground as he made his way over to her.

'Well, this is a surprise. What are you doing here? It's Sunday,' she said.

'I missed you. There's no other reason I'm up in London. I just needed to see you.'

'It's nice of you to pick me up, but there's a minicab waiting for me.'

'Not a problem,' Nicholas said. 'I'll pay him the cost of the trip.'

***

Back at the flat, Nicholas made himself comfortable. He was used to Sophie looking after him. 'You don't have any nibbles, do you? I'm starving. Nuts will do. Or we could get a takeaway.'

'There's a jar of olives in the fridge,' she said, 'and I've brought back some wine. Can you open it, please?'

'Of course,' he said, taking the corkscrew from the kitchen drawer. He pulled out the cork. '2016, a good vintage Merlot. Best to let it breathe.'

They sat and chatted, very civilised. Almost as if they were strangers. Nicholas kept his distance.

Maybe best until the frost had melted.

'So then,' he said, popping an olive in his mouth, 'tell me all about the trip. Was it fun?'

'Wonderful. Lots of painting and a lovely teacher.'

'Meet anybody interesting?'

'Do you really want to know?'

'Of course!'

'Yes. I met a lovely man.'

'Did you?' Nicholas swallowed hard. 'What does he do?'

'Taste the wine.' She proffered a glass. 'It's from his vineyard, a family business, very successful. Do you like it?'

He swilled it round his mouth and paused.

'Very refined. Rich and plummy. But… a little too tannic.'

Change tack, Nicholas. Let her feel as if you're happy for her. That you don't mind if she's found another man. She'll want you more.

'I'm pleased for you, Sophie. I love you so much. You deserve so much more than I can give you. I can understand you wanting to move on. But I hope that we can still be friends. Platonically speaking.'

'Are you serious?'

'Yes. Why not?'

Sophie, don't do it. But she couldn't stop.

'Look, Nicholas, stop messing about. You know that we'll never be platonic! I'll give you one last chance. Do you want to be with me? Or shall I go to France?'

'How can I just up sticks and go? I need to work things out in my head. Maybe once the kids have left home.'

'Don't start that again. I won't have any more excuses. This time you have to make up your mind. I'll give you two weeks.'

Nicholas went back to Bournemouth. He thought and thought about leaving. He weighed up the pros and cons. Imagined himself sitting in bed with Sophie after they'd made love. Drinking a glass of wine and listening to Mozart. And in the morning, before he went to work, she'd make him breakfast. Scrambled egg with sausage, mushrooms and grilled tomatoes, French toast with maple syrup, and she'd squeeze him fresh orange juice, and make him fresh coffee with hot milk.

And in the evening, he'd take her out to dinner once a week

and the rest of the time she'd cook gourmet meals or they'd be invited to dinner parties with her snazzy friends and they would return the compliment.

Then, just as quickly, he pushed it out of his mind. It wasn't going to work. How could he leave his family? Nobody would speak to him again. He'd be known as the jerk of Bournemouth.

Divorce was out of the question. Kids, dogs, wife… a comfortable house, an easy life.

It didn't take him long. He didn't wait two weeks. Some flowers and a little note arrived at Sophie's door.

I can't do it. Forgive me.

Horatio had won his Sophie by default.

Chapter 14

Happy birthday, said the Voice. *Forty-three! Did you ever believe you'd live that long? Poor guy. So screwed up!*

It was true. Damien had wondered how he'd managed to carry on. So many years of pushing the boundaries almost without limitations.

He examined his face in the mirror.

You're quite extraordinary, said the Voice. *For all your shenanigans, you still look great. But we both know that if you continue to lead your dysfunctional life, sooner or later you'll land up in the snakepit.*

'It's my birthday – can't you leave me alone for once?'

Such a shame about Sophie. Just the kind of woman who would put you straight, said the Voice.

'What do you mean by such a shame?'

Oh, don't be delusional. She's fond of you. But it's bro time for her.

'Okay, just let it go.' Damien sighed. 'Can't you make me feel good for a change? Say something positive.'

Well, I'm sure she'll give you a birthday kiss this evening.

'You make me feel like an adolescent going out on his first date.'

Look, if she goes for your cheek, just whip your head round so you catch her lips.

***

The Barbican. Damien closed his eyes. *St Matthew Passion*. Bach's meditation on mortality, grief and redemption had always moved him, ever since his student days at Oxford. He had sat beside Laura in the church, holding hands, feeling so close to her.

The sublime aria *Aus Liebe* sung by the pure-voiced soprano had filled his heart.

'Laura,' he'd whispered then, 'I love you.' He'd known that one day she'd be his angel bride. What he hadn't known was that it wouldn't last.

So now here he was with Sophie who sat next to him, so composed in a chic black velvet dress. Her soft pale hands with red-painted nails neatly placed on her lap.

But when the soprano sang *Ause Liebe* Damien could only think of Laura and how at that moment in time he'd thought that no one could capture his soul like she had. And then he glanced at Sophie.

Where was she? Not here with Damien.

Eyes downcast, hands clasped as if in prayer.

Let her go, said the Voice. *She's thinking of Daniel and Mikey. Not of Nicholas, nor the man she met in Bordeaux. Pure music stirs the heart to remember true love that has passed.*

After the concert, dinner at Romano's. Sophie talked about Bordeaux and Horatio.

'Do you know, while Horatio made love to me, I never thought of Nicholas once?' Sophie sucked a piece of pasta back into her mouth. 'Horatio intrigues me. He's sophisticated and gracious. He owns a vineyard, and he's available. Nicholas isn't. Anyway, even if he did leave his wife, I'm sure I'd get bored. He'd probably moan about missing his kids and his solitary walks with the dogs.'

Damien looked at her mouth, red with tomato sauce, and her cheeks, rosy from the wine.

She's kidding herself, he thought. *While Daniel and Mikey are whizzing around the ether, no man has a chance.*

Ask her, said the Voice.

'At night when you dream, do you see them?' Damien asked.

'Who?'

'Your husband and son.'

She paused and looked away from Damien.

'I'm sorry, Sophie. I really didn't want to upset you.'

'It's okay,' she said. 'Yes, they're in my dreams, whenever I start to feel close to another man.' She picked up her napkin and wiped her lips. 'It's as if they know.'

Hmm, said the Voice. *She needs time. Take her home. And don't try your luck.*

Chapter 15

Nicholas still pined for Sophie, but trying to make amends, he took Kate to dinner at the Olive Branch, a romantic French bistro.

Over candlelight, champagne and a sweet bunch of pansies in a little glass jar, they stared at each other across the table.

'There's a flower festival in Poole tomorrow. Would you like to go?' Nicholas asked.

'Could do,' Kate replied. 'Isn't it a shame that Mark has failed his driving test again?'

'Well, he obviously isn't ready to be let loose on the road.'

'Beth passed first time.' Kate took a sip of wine. 'I wonder if girls have a better pass rate.'

'I don't know. Anyway…' Nicholas sank back into no man's land. 'Oh, I forgot to mention, poker night's been changed to Tuesday, just for this week. It's Pepe's birthday on our usual Friday and his wife has arranged a special treat.'

'Oh. What will you do instead?'

'I thought maybe you would like to go to the cinema or see a show.'

'Not really… Chicken's nice.'

'My steak's not bad. Bit overcooked, though. All these health and safety rules… Bet they don't have that problem in Argentina…' He plucked a green bean from his plate and popped it in his mouth. 'Well, what would you like to do?'

'Mmm, let me think.' Kate shut her eyes and strummed the table with her fingers.

'Ah!' she said. 'I know. Why don't I make a romantic dinner for two at home?'

'Fine! That would be lovely.' Nicholas patted her hand. She seemed so happy. He'd cracked through her shell. He hadn't seen her looking so well in ages.

Maybe we can make it work, he thought.

***

Tripping down the aisle with her trolley that Friday, Kate grabbed the Romantic Dinner for Two special: twelve quid with a bottle of wine thrown in.

Caesar salad, main chicken and leek cosy casserole and a side of mash, two lemon tartlets and a bottle of Rioja.

Late afternoon, Nicholas whistled up the garden path and called out a husbandly, 'Darling, I'm back,' to signal his arrival.

'I'm in the kitchen, Nick,' she shouted.

Kate, in navy tracks and a grey T-shirt, was arranging the ready-made Caesar salad on plates. 'I didn't expect you to come home so early. Was going to have dinner ready on the table and I'm not even dressed yet.'

She gave Nicholas a slither of a smile as he stood by the door with a black leather man bag on his shoulder and one hand behind his back.

'My second appointment in Cambridge was cancelled at the last moment,' he said, 'so I took the earlier train home. Had to buy a new ticket, as the one I'd bought was off-peak. Cost me another hundred and twenty pounds. Anyway – ta-da! – I bought you some flowers…' He proffered a bunch of tired-looking yellow and white carnations. 'I know they look sad, but not much left on a Friday afternoon… Best of the bunch, as it were,' he added apologetically.

'Can you put them in a vase?' Kate asked with a cursory glance.

Nick grabbed a blue pitcher, filled it with water and dropped them in.

Kate stared at the faded bouquet. 'They look how I feel, but thanks anyway. It's the thought that counts as they say… So, how was your day?' She opened the oven door and poked the chicken, which sat in a foil dish, with a fork.

'Mmmm, something smells good.' He gave her a peck on the cheek.

'Well, one of us has to save money. Dinner for two, twelve quid, you can't go wrong. Would you like a glass of wine? There's the Rioja that comes with the meal, but I've already got a bottle of white in the fridge. Opened it today for lunch.'

'Thanks.' He held up the bottle. 'Not much left. Anyway, it doesn't matter. I bought some red. I'll open that instead.'

'So, how was your day?' Kate asked again.

'My day was okay,' he said, 'but on the way back the train was crowded and I had this girl next to me who wouldn't stop shouting on her mobile.'

'Oh well.' Kate took the bottle of white from the fridge and poured the remainder into a tumbler.

'Can't you use a proper wine glass, Kate?'

'I don't like the stems. They always seem to get broken in the dishwasher, and it takes ages to wash them by hand, because they go all misty if you don't do them properly. Anyway, I'm going to have a shower now.'

She gulped down the wine. 'I'm a bit smelly. It was very muggy today and after the supermarket I did some DIY to the shed. There were a few wooden planks that needed fixing and it really made me sweat, plus I put some compost on the vegetable patch. I did wash my hands, but still it's hard to get rid of the pong.'

'Oh, I didn't notice,' he lied politely. 'I could only smell the casserole... Well, you'll just have to keep washing your hands like Lady Macbeth.' Nicholas laughed at his quip.

'I'm going up. Chicken should only take another forty minutes. Best to turn the gas off for now and start again when I come down,' Kate said.

'Okay. I'll lay the table while you're having a shower or... shall I go first, because I'll be quick and you'll probably want to put on some make-up?'

'Oh, for goodness' sake, always have to put yourself first, Mr Selfish. I'm going up now and that's it... Oh, and can you let the dogs in? I didn't want them sniffing around me in the kitchen. You know how they start whining when they smell food.'

She spooned some pet meat into two large bowls and plonked them on the kitchen floor. 'There. You can give them some fresh water.'

Nicholas did as he was told, then settled himself in the comfy beige leather chair by the living-room window and looked out at the lovely garden. He could see the dogs frolicking and the solar lights winking as the dusk fell. He dozed off, and woke with a start when she called him to the table.

She's a good woman, Nicholas thought, squashing down the realisation that time had eroded her enthusiasm for life and for him. Maybe he should try and read her a poem. Nothing too complicated. She loved flowers, so why not try Wordsworth now that the daffodils were in bloom. Or maybe not. She'd probably laugh at him.

'Not bad... the Caesar salad,' Kate said. 'Especially if you reckon to make it would cost at least £6.50. Three pounds for chicken breasts, £1 for the lettuce, a tin of anchovies £1.20 and don't forget the croutons, around £1.30. There you go, and that's just for the starter. I really don't know how they do it... I mean dinner for two with three courses – twelve quid. Ooh, I forgot the serviettes.' She went to the sideboard and, bending down, took two paper napkins from a packet in a drawer.

'Mmm, very good salad… You look nice, Kate.' He scanned her backside. 'New jeans?'

'Yuh. Bought them yesterday… at New Line, very comfy.'

'See any nice skirts?'

'Nicholas, you know I don't like skirts.'

'It's such a shame. You've got beautiful legs.' He poured them both a large glass of red. 'Do you remember when we first met at college? You walked into the canteen with the shortest black miniskirt. Stunning! To tell the truth, I fell in love with your legs before we even started chatting.'

'Oh… such a long time ago. What has happened to the years? Anyway, we did manage to bring up two good kids…'

'That's true. By the way, where are they?'

'Mark has gone to Glastonbury with his mates, camping overnight, and Beth is at a sleepover with her friend Lilly.'

'Well, that's good. We won't have any rude interruptions.' Nicholas topped up Kate's Rioja.

'But we do have these two little beauties.' Kate patted the lively spaniels who had bounced into the sitting room and, competing for attention, nuzzled her legs.

'Hello, Sally! Hello, Rocket! Ooh, look! Daddy's left a bit of chicken on his plate…' She threw a couple of pieces to the panting dogs, whisked the empty gravy boat away and walked briskly to the kitchen.

'Wish you wouldn't feed the dogs the scraps at the table,' Nicholas muttered. 'You know it encourages them to beg.'

He refilled his glass of wine.

'Heard that,' Kate called back. 'Can't you just chill for once?'

Exasperated, Nicholas sat back, staring stonily ahead. The Victorian watercolour on the opposite side of the wall seemed to taunt him. He had paid a fortune for it - a painting of a beautiful young maiden picking flowers in a field of bluebells.

He didn't care about the cost. He'd been smitten by the beauty of the girl.

Just like Kate. When he first saw her. The outside had been enough.

Ha! How not to marry, he thought. Husband and wife trying to make their way out of a cul-de-sac. Standing still, frozen habits, words for the sake of making conversation, a lonely play for attention and companionship.

Nicholas dreamt of his soulmate Sophie, while Kate didn't dream at all.

She came back with the gravy boat refilled.

He poured some on the potato and patted it in with his fork. 'Don't think much of the mash. Tastes a bit bland. It's better home-made. My mother made the best mash. She cracked two raw egg yolks into the potato, whisked it up with a pat of butter and a tad of milk... I miss her, you know,' Nicholas said.

'Yes, she was a lovely person. I was very fond of her.' What a porky! Kate had deeply resented his mother. She'd invaded their marriage, Nicholas always ready to jump at her command. To do his duty as a loving son.

'She certainly made good use of your DIY skills. You were like a yo-yo. Always back and forth from our house to hers fixing things. In fact, you were more there than here.' Kate slurred her words and this time poured her own wine.

'You really do get vindictive when you've had too much to drink.'

'Your fault! You shouldn't have bought the extra bottle.' Kate poked his chest with her index finger.

'Well, you shouldn't have drunk so much at lunch.' He pushed her finger aside.

'Stop ordering me around, Mr Headmaster.'

'Come on, Kate. Don't spoil things. It's our special night.'

'Well then, stop irritating me. It's meant to be our evening and all you talk about is how you miss your mother.'

'Well, I do.'

'But she's been dead ten years. And you know she never liked me…'

'She tried… You were the one who never made an effort. She always gave you a present on your birthday and you never even sent her a card.'

'That's because I always knew she didn't think I was good enough for you. Not cultured enough. You used to drag me with her to see those bloody Shakespeare plays. It's like a foreign language. And the stories are so complicated.'

'Well… you don't ever have to see one again.'

'No, I certainly won't. And as for those trips to art galleries; traipsing round with you both eyeballing painting after painting. I remember you and your mother used to sit on a bench and sometimes look at a picture for half an hour… What were you doing? What were you waiting for?'

'You didn't have to come.'

'Well, I did. To please you.' She hardly ever cried, and when the flood came it surprised them both.

'Oh, Kate, that was a nice thing to say. Please don't be upset.' He stroked her hair and wiped her tears with his napkin.

'And another thing, I don't like classical music – it sounds morbid. Give me Ed Sheeran any day. Anyway… you can't say I'm not honest.'

They both laughed…

They knew each other. No games, no intrigue, no bleeding hearts. A painless life together and sometimes, just sometimes, there was a spark of recognition. When they found each other.

Maybe, Nicholas thought, *there's hope for us yet.*

'Look,' she said, 'let's skip the lemon tarts and leave the washing up and then we can watch the last twenty minutes of my baking programme. It's the finals.'

'Can't you watch it on catch-up? I thought we were going to have a journey of rediscovery.'

'Sounds scary,' she said. 'Okay, we'll do it your way. Just hope the climax is as exciting as the competition's.'

In the sitting room, Kate sprawled on the sofa, legs apart, while Nicholas lit the fire.

'Alexa, play… Sinatra,' he said.

'I don't know that one,' Alexa replied.

He raised his voice. 'Alexa, play "Strangers in the Night" by Frank Sinatra.'

Nicholas danced over to the cocktail cabinet. 'Fancy a Cointreau?'

'Are you having one?'

'Mmm… No, I think I'm already over my limit… but you can have one.'

'Okay.'

'Such sublime songs… what a voice.'

His hand shook as he poured the liquor into a small crystal glass and passed it to her. He was nervous. Twenty years down the line and he was courting her again. Maybe he wasn't going to be able to perform… He needed Frank to help him out. Stir him up. He sat next to her and sank into the lyrics as the singer crooned his favourite song.

Kate stared ahead.

Nicholas tentatively made his first move… He slid his arm round her shoulder. 'It's funny, Kate – it's like being on our first date again. Come on, let's dance.'

He scooped her up and held her round her waist.

'Nicholas, you're being soppy. You know I'm not the romantic kind.'

'Come on, Kate. We haven't done this for years. Do you remember before we had the kids we loved to dance?'

'Okay,' she said.

He pulled her closer, swayed her back and forth, crooning in unison with his idol, but Kate was getting very dizzy.

'Stop… please! It's like being on a boat. I feel seasick… I can't dance any more. Come on, let's go to bed…'

Nicholas was quite happy to acquiesce and they went upstairs. Kate waited, fully dressed, lying on top of the floral duvet, relieved to have a breather while Nicholas undressed down to his spotted boxers and navy socks.

'Alexa, play "When a Man Loves a Woman"… Percy Sledge.'

Alexa complied.

'Good girl, Alexa.' Nicholas slipped onto the bed and, nestling against Kate, shifted his left leg over hers and moved in for a kiss.

'Oh, can we just cuddle for a bit more? You know how much I don't… you know… Kissing isn't my thing… It makes me feel queasy… Sorry.' Kate turned her face away.

'No worries.' Nicholas slid his hand down to her waist. 'Oh, Kate… Kate…' He sighed 'Where have we been…? It's time to reinvent ourselves. Please, Kate… I need you. I love you.'

He tugged at the zip of her jeans. He pulled and she wriggled, but it just wouldn't budge.

'Ow,' he yelped.

'What now?'

'I've nicked my finger… It's bleeding.'

'Oh no, please don't get it on the sheets. I only changed them yesterday.'

'Okay.' He rolled off her like a bale of hay. 'It's only a prick.' He sucked the tip.

'Well, put a plaster on it.'

'Will do… And while I'm about it I'll get some Vaseline to unstick the zip…'

'No, you'll get grease on my new jeans. Better to use soap. I can do it.' She bounced out of bed, all hope of a graceful seduction over.

Chapter 16

Friends' connections, online dating, cocktail and dinner parties, evening classes, yoga and pilates sessions and especially art exhibitions. Now that Damien had flown, Anna intended to explore them all.

She started with an early morning trip to the National Gallery before the crowds descended. Exquisite in a white lace dress, her long dark hair tied up in a black velvet bow, she sat on a bench, gazing at Goya's lush portrait of the actress Antonia Zarate.

And along came James, early fifties, just about sexy and still willing to have another shot after two divorces. Seeing the lovely Anna, he was ready to throw her a line and reel her in with an arty chat-up.

He settled himself next to her at a respectable distance and surreptitiously googled a quick critique of Goya's painting on his mobile.

'She's very pretty, isn't she?' he said in his soft Welsh accent.

Anna gave him a coy glance and a sweet smile. 'Are you talking to me?' she said.

He moved a little closer to his target.

'Yes, I am. I like to share my observations. Do you mind? Am I disturbing you?'

'No, no, please carry on,' she replied. He was quite attractive.

'You see there's something not quite right with her mouth.' He squinted his eyes and stared hard at the lips.

She looked back at the portrait, whilst he glanced at his mobile and extended his pitch. 'However, the eye's instinct to auto-correct makes it right, but if you override this reflex, you can see that her mouth is faintly odd, like a brilliantly repaired harelip.'

As she turned back to him, he deftly slipped the phone into his pocket.

Anna didn't understand a word of it, but was suitably impressed with his intellect.

'Yes, you're quite right. I would never have noticed if you hadn't pointed out her imperfection. However, I think the flaw makes her more interesting,' she said, and looked up at him with a hint of 'try me' eyes.

That's it! He sensed the little spark, which he then expertly kindled with perfect timing. Names were exchanged and a meeting arranged for Wednesday, 7 p.m., after work.

***

They met at a bar off Baker Street.

'What would you like to drink?' he asked.

'G&T for me, please,' she said, sitting primly on a stool in a little pink suit matched with a pair of silver slingbacks that she'd found in the Oxfam shop on Finchley Road.

He had a beer and they moved to a booth.

James talked about his terrible marriages, golf trips to Spain and the flats he owned in Cardiff, while she nodded.

'Bought them years ago with my business partner, Bob, who still lives there. Pain in the neck, really. The tenants aren't exactly house proud. There's always a flood in one of the bathrooms or an electricity short. But the properties were cheap and at least Bob can sort things out. Can't say I miss Wales.'

'I haven't been there myself,' she said, 'but I've heard that some parts are beautiful. And all those marvellous Welsh singers.'

But James didn't hear her. Just ploughed on as if she wasn't there.

'I was a bright lad,' he reminisced. 'I should have gone to university, but my dad wanted me to run the business – removals. We did a lot of top jobs. Transporting antiques and artwork from stately homes to London and abroad. Then Dad died and I was left to carry on. I married a couple of disasters on the way and finally, after running the business for another ten years, I jacked it all in. To tell you the truth, I was bored stiff.'

Not as bored as I am. Anna's hand had gone to sleep propping up her head.

'So I bought the properties and moved up to London,' he droned on.

When was he going to ask her if she wanted another G&T?

He paused and looked at her glass.

Oh good, she thought. *At last*.

But, no, he hadn't finished.

'Things are better now. I like living in London, got a flat in Bayswater, which is quite convenient for getting around. But I like to think if I had my chance again, I would have gone to art school. In fact, I sold a few of my paintings at local fairs... Anyway... how about you?' he finally asked.

His sudden interest jolted Anna out of her trance.

'Well, to be honest, there's not much to say about me.' She glanced at her watch. 'It's getting late and I really should be going.'

'Well, it was good to meet you,' he said. 'Do you want to visit the ladies first?'

'No, it's okay.'

'That's good, a bladder like a camel.' Couldn't he see that she was desperate to leave?

Maybe if she took a taxi, she'd be back in time to see her favourite show, *Someone Like Us*, a programme about ordinary people who had secret habits like shoplifting and stealing deliveries left outside houses.

'Sorry, I really have to go. I have a dinner appointment,' she said.

And on she went, eager to meet the man who would whisk her off to Sardinia and treat her like a precious jewel.

But no one came. Nothing changed.

Until that Monday…

Chapter 17

Anna's morning began as usual.

First: wake up, wash, make-up, dress.

Then: radio on, Magic FM and a quick cup of coffee.

Next: check the dating app.

Messages: yes.

Message: *We seem to be a good match, what do you think?*

A generic one-liner from Hopeful Dick, Essex.

Anna glanced at his picture and winced. He was hideous. A shiny bald head, tiny eyes, a ring in his nose and a thin, sadistic smile.

She scrolled down his profile page, a game she played just to see if the personality matched the face.

Occupation: *Ask me later*

Income: *Struggling*

Dating activities: *Cooking at home and walking. Favourite food Indian*

Anna disliked Indian food and there was no mention of restaurants, theatre *or* travelling.

Turn-ons: *Erotica, flirting, dancing, skinny dipping*

Her eyes flickered and her mouth twitched.

Personality traits: *Wild, thrill-seeking, adventurous, sexy*

Valued qualities in a partner: *Wild, thrill-seeking, adventurous, sexy*

Anna wondered how on earth she – a woman who had not only been bedded by celebrity writer Damien Spur, but who had been mentored by him – she, who had been the queen of the social scene, and indeed still mixed with some very chic people, could have been contacted by such a creep.

Her lovely profile photos, her sophisticated likes: *Fine dining, travel, theatre*

Her sort of man: *Handsome, wealthy, cultured, etc.*

A zero match.

Not a good start to the morning. She'd only posted her profile a couple of days ago. But so far, no good.

There were mostly men with pathetic nicknames like Lost Soul and Try Me, or who lived miles away, like Eddie from Esher.

Maybe give it another week. No shame in it. Difficult to meet people nowadays. And most of her single friends were fishing in the same pond.

But why hadn't Damien called? Surely he had sent her story to the agent as he'd promised.

She put on her shiny white raincoat and black velvet beret, ready to go out to the corner shop to buy some milk as she usually did at the beginning of the week.

It was a miserable morning. Dark grey sky and drizzling. But she liked where she lived. Thanked the good Lord every day that she had no mortgage to pay on her very nice Victorian house in Gondar Gardens. Next to civilised neighbours – a solicitor on her left with a very nice wife and two well-behaved children, and on her right, an anaesthetist, who wasn't married but lived with a friendly nurse called Margaret who'd invited Anna for coffee last week.

She clip-clopped down the hill and while she was waiting to cross the road, she saw the shop owner on the other side taking the newspapers in out of the rain. At that very moment, a new thought popped into her head.

She had been coming to the store for three years and yet she didn't know his name.

So this time when she went into the shop, she asked, 'I don't want to be intrusive, but what is your name?'

'Christos Georgalides,' replied the good-looking Greek with grey curly hair who always greeted her with a big smile.

'Mine is Anna Rose. Lovely to meet you.'

'Nice to meet you, too,' he said. 'It's funny, I see you more than I see my own sister and yet we've never had a chat. Well, now we've met, would you like an Easter biscuit? My wife made them.'

'Thank you.' She took one of the powdery crescents from the paper plate on the counter and popped it in her mouth. 'Mmm, scrumptious. So light and crumbly.'

She walked over to the fridge. 'You know what, Christos? I think I'll try the almond milk today for a change.'

'It's very good, and next week you can try my wife's baklava,' he said, putting the carton into a blue plastic bag.

Anna had a feeling on her way back to her house that today something special was going to happen. And it did.

As she came through the front door the phone rang.

'Anna,' Damien said, 'expect a call from my friend, Justin Baird. He runs a top literary agency that has a large children's division. He likes your book.'

She held her breath. 'Damien, I never thought… This is fantastic! A million kisses! Oh, thank you. Would you like to come for—'

He cut her short. 'My pleasure,' he said. 'Just be your sweet self. Got to go.'

Chapter 18

Justin Baird had invited Anna to lunch at the Ivy. Main chat: contracts, film deals and celebrity gossip.

She arrived fifteen minutes late, a tradition she had always kept, dressed in her fifties glamour: a sleek brown mink that Evelyn had given to her, a chic black dress, patent-leather high heels and a velvet pillbox hat.

'Mr Baird's table, please,' she said to the maître d'.

'May I take your jacket?' he asked.

'Thank you.' She dropped it from her shoulders and walked gracefully to the table.

'Hello, Anna.' Justin Baird stood up to greet her – a tall, good-looking guy with rugged features and dark hair, who wore an elegant navy suit with a silk tie.

Early fifties, she guessed. *A proper man: old school, Evelyn would say.*

Attractive, late thirties, he mused.

Justin Baird didn't waste time. '*The Dog That Lost Its Bark* is magical. The agency would love to represent you. I think we could tie the story up with a book and a movie deal. We'll pitch it to Disney.'

Just as she'd imagined.

'That's wonderful, Mr Baird,' she said.

'Do call me Justin.'

'Justin.' She was keen to complete the scenario she'd written in her head. 'I hope you won't think me pushy, but may I suggest that if all goes well with the publishing deal, I might read my story on *Tell Me a Tale*? It's a children's show at teatime on the BBC. Do you know it?'

'Yes, I do. We've had a few writers on the programme. I think you would be very good. As soon as we get a publishing deal, I'll phone the producers.'

'Thank you.' She gave him a sweet little kiss on the cheek. 'I'm delighted to have found you. I'm sure that I will be in very good hands.'

'So let's celebrate. Champagne?'

'Yes, please.'

'A bottle of Krug,' he said to the hovering waiter.

Krug, how sophisticated. 'Don't jump the gun,' she could hear her mother say, 'until you're absolutely sure you have him hook, line and sinker. And that means a ring on your finger.'

Anna laughed to herself. Her mother had lost the plot. Better to be naughty, now she was forty. Book first and then to bed. The ring on the finger came last.

Chapter 19

Claudia had rung Anna. 'I'm helping Elizabeth Maitland plan a charity ball to raise money to build a new special-needs school in Guildford,' she said.

'Oh yes?' said Anna.

'And we would love you to join the committee. Sophie has already said yes. Are you free to have lunch on Saturday?'

Why was it that her sister was always first in line? Anna paused. 'Give me a second and I will look at the diary.'

Anna stared out of the window and counted to five.

'Saturday lunchtime is fine. What time?'

'One.'

'Great. See you then.'

***

Saturday was not going to plan. Anna was late. She'd taken the underground to Holland Park, but when she came out of the station her kitten heel had got stuck in a crack in the pavement.

She managed to yank it out, but it had come away from the rest of the shoe.

Luckily, she found a mender on her mobile who was just round the corner. However, she had to hop on one foot, which took her ten minutes to get to the shop.

'Phew! Thank goodness I found you,' Anna said to the man behind the counter. She took a tissue out of her bag and mopped her brow.

'You look like you need to sit down,' he replied.

'Don't have time,' she panted. 'Here's the shoe. Please can you fix it quickly?'

He had thick black curly hair and gave her a toothy grin.

'Lucky I have customers like you. Nowadays, so many women wear trainers. Not good for business.'

Anna wasn't listening. She paid him and went.

When she arrived at Claudia's house, Sophie's shiny new red Audi A5 Cabriolet was parked outside the front.

Oh yes, my little princess. Aren't you the hot potato? Driving around in your sexy racer, while most of the time my clapped-out Mini is stuck outside my house, because I can't afford the parking and congestion charge.

'Hi there, Anna.' Her sister's sweet voice wafted through the intercom. 'Come in! We're in the living room.'

There she goes again, taking over. Why couldn't Claudia have let her in? Anna kicked off her kitten heels and padded across the parquet floor.

'Hi, girls.' She blew her sister a perfunctory kiss. 'Hello, Elizabeth. Sorry I'm late, had a mishap with my shoe. The heel came off.'

'You really should wear trainers or flatties for walking,' Sophie said. 'Those spiky things you wear all day are treacherous.'

Anna's mouth twitched involuntarily, which didn't suit her. Her sister had started again. Sitting pretty with a glass of wine, making her feel clumsy.

'Well, I think she looks gorgeous,' Elizabeth said. 'Very Audrey Hepburn.'

Anna blushed with pleasure. Such honeyed words. She looked gorgeous, very AUDREY HEPBURN. That would put her little sister in her place.

Anna patted the lapel of the pink woven suit, threaded with silver, that Evelyn had given her.

'Thank you, one of Mummy's.'

Oh no! Why did she tell Elizabeth that she was wearing her mother's hand-me-downs? How gauche!

'Where's Claudia?' she asked quickly.

'In the kitchen making lunch,' Sophie replied. 'Would you like a glass of wine?'

Anna gave a little half smile. *Now she's playing hostess. So easy breezy. Dear little Sophie just fitted in. Carefree. Work was fun, illustrating books. Banker Daniel had left her a wealthy widow.*

She stopped short.

Oh, don't be mean. It's terrible that Daniel and little Mikey died. Anna Rose, stop your nasty thoughts before they crinkle you up with bitter little wrinkles!

'Thank you, Sophie, I'd love a glass.'

Claudia had prepared a fabulous spread.

Baked organic asparagus, cherry tomatoes, black olives and capers. Grilled chicken salad with parmesan dressing, smoked salmon, crème fraiche and chive quiche, and a watermelon and feta salad.

Elizabeth tinkered with a small plate of the salad, while Sophie and Anna tucked into every dish.

'Oh my God, Claudia,' Anna said. 'You've done it again. The quiche is sublime – and as for the grilled chicken, please, I must have the recipe.'

'Gosh, I can't stop eating.' Sophie took another helping of the salad. 'I love lunches where you can pick and choose. You really are a wonder. These asparagus are just perfect.'

Claudia was disappointed.

All very well to have the sisters wax lyrical, but she so wanted to impress Elizabeth. Why was she surprised? Her friend had played hostess to so many swanky dinner parties and even then, she seldom ate more than a sparrow's portion.

'And now, if the girls have had their fill, let's discuss the charity ball over coffee,' Elizabeth said.

'What would you like us to do, Elizabeth?' Sophie asked.

'I would like you both to request donations for the auction. Sophie, you've met a gorgeous new man who lives in a sumptuous chateau and owns a vineyard in Bordeaux and thank goodness, he's single. That could be very useful for the auction. A weekend wine-tasting trip? And you don't mind me asking Nicholas? You're still friends, aren't you? He could donate a painting, or a bronze statuette.'

'Yes, what good ideas. I'll be happy to ask Horatio.'

'Lovely, Sophie. You look like a woman who knows how to pitch and can bring home the trophies,' Elizabeth said.

'And what about you?' Claudia turned to Anna.

'What about me? Haven't managed to land a prize yet. Had a date with a disaster a couple of weeks ago! I met him at the National Gallery. Then he asked me for a drink so we went to a bar and all he did was talk about himself. Definitely not my type. But at least you were right about my book. Damien was such a help introducing me to my agent, Justin Baird.'

'It was good of him to help you,' Claudia said. 'In fact, why don't you ask Damien Spur if the guests can bid for an evening with him? A handsome, celebrated thriller writer. No doubt his company would be very exciting!'

'I can vouch for that – and I think he would enjoy women bidding for him. Give him a thrill... Okay, I'll do it,' Anna said.

Elizabeth raised an elegant eyebrow. 'Excellent, Anna. Good that you found him entertaining. It will certainly add a little spice to the evening.'

'And Justin Baird, is he single?' asked Claudia.

'I think so,' Anna replied.

'Well, ask him to take you to the ball.'

'The Russians are coming as well,' Elizabeth said, 'including Boris and his wife, Lala.'

Claudia gave a wicked laugh. 'Adam is coming too. Which should be interesting, as I've seated Lala between them both. So we could have a dead body at the end of the evening if my dearest ex tries anything.'

'We've planned the date for Sunday, 28 June,' Elizabeth said. 'So please get to it with the auction requests.'

She blew Anna and Sophie a kiss and got up from the table. 'Now then, I'd better go. I have a meeting with a race-horse owner, who has promised to donate half his winnings if his mare Cleopatra wins at Cheltenham.'

Chapter 20

Damien had arrived.

Anna, dressed in black lace and pearls, opened the door and threw her chin back offering each cheek for a kiss.

She had prepared the evening with military precision.

For dinner, her speciality, boeuf bourguignon to be served with mashed potatoes and green beans, accompanied by a red burgundy.

Crystal glasses and silver candlesticks sparkled on the dining table, the centrepiece pale pink roses in a Lalique vase.

She liked to do things properly.

'Thank you, Damien, for all your help. I think that Justin Baird will be great for me... He's so enthusiastic about my book.'

'My pleasure,' he said.

'Would you like a whisky?'

'Yes, please.' He watched her trip this way and that. His drink first, and then into the kitchen to check the beans. Damien could hear her whistling.

How strange, he thought, *this delicate creature trilling like a nightingale.*

Back to the sofa she came and sat next to him, with her goo-goo eyes and pink flirty smile, her bare, pretty knees glued together.

Maybe just one more time. He stroked her leg with his little finger.

Once Damien had sunk his fork into the tender beef and tasted the sublime dish, Anna knew that he was hers for the evening.

She charmed and flattered, played with his ego, plied him with wine and moving closer said, 'Will you be a prize?'

'A prize?'

'Yes.'

'For what?'

'A charity auction ball raising money for a special-needs school. Claudia asked Sophie and me to join the committee, chaired by Lady Elizabeth Maitland. Do you know her?'

'No, I haven't met her.'

'Well, she knows who you are and she's very keen for you to donate your time.'

Damien ran his fingers through his hair and fixed her with a naughty-boy look. 'And how will you list me?' he asked.

'The main prize…' Anna improvised. 'A night with Damien Spur. The famed thriller writer, bon viveur and heart-throb, would love to entertain you.'

'Excellent, Anna. How could I say no? So, please tell your committee that I am delighted to say yes.'

'Thank you, Damien.' Anna leant forward and brushed his lips.

And yet… had he known that saying yes to her innocent request would send him plummeting into the depths of despair, he would have said no.

Chapter 21

Elizabeth stood at the top of the sweeping staircase leading down to the Grand Hall of the Ritz Hotel.

Radiant and magnificent in a pale grey silk gown, her swan's neck encased in a diamond choker, she greeted her glamorous guests, ready to open their hearts and their wallets.

She loved organising charity balls. It made it easier to live with herself. Assuaged her guilty conscience. Allowed her to justify her predatory need to possess and then destroy men who had fallen for her dark charisma.

'It's just in my nature,' she would say to her girlfriends. 'The sting in the tail. I suppose I'm a woman who can't be taken unless a man gives me a hard time.'

Damien was the last to arrive.

That afternoon, he'd slept with a girl whom he'd met at The London Library. She'd managed to keep him interested for longer than anticipated.

Afterwards, a little flustered, he'd showered and dressed.

'Your bow tie's crooked,' she said.

'Never mind, at least people will know it's not a clip-on.' He checked his hair in the mirror and turned to the girl lying on his bed and blew her a kiss. 'Well, I'm off now. You can stay as long as you like, just make sure the door's closed when you let yourself out.'

'How generous of you.' She gave him that look. The one he'd seen so many times: No need to pretend, Damien Spur. You've no intention of seeing me again. 'Don't worry,' she said. 'I'll be gone by the time you get back.'

Damien paid lip service to the end game. 'I'll call you,' he said, and left.

***

'Hello, Mr Spur.' Elizabeth held out her hand. 'So pleased you could make it.'

All those retouched images in magazines were arresting, but in the flesh, she was even more impressive. Copper hair, a refined face, amber wide-set eyes and her skin – glistening, pearl white.

'Very flattered that you asked me.' He kissed her hand. 'Sorry I'm a bit late.'

'That's okay. The auction hasn't started yet. Now then, shall we go down? But first, may I?' She straightened his bow tie with a confidence that already gave him a thrill.

At the foot of the stairs, celebrity auctioneer suave Danny Archer stood with Claudia scanning the list of donations.

'Well, Horatio de Beaumont's weekend at his chateau and a case of Premier Cru Merlot should fetch a pretty sum, Claudia,' he said. 'And I love the fine Russian icon from Nicholas Morley, which no doubt will interest your Slavic guests. But the star by far is the evening with Damien Spur. I am sure that there are plenty of chic divorcees here ready to bid for his undivided attention.'

At the Freesia table sat Horatio and Sophie, Adam next, then Lala with her husband, Boris, on her other side. To complete the circle, Elizabeth and Damien.

'A hen between two cockerels could be fun,' Elizabeth had said to Claudia when they were arranging the seating plan.

At the neighbouring Orchid table, Nicholas sat between wife, Kate, and dainty Anna, who sparkled in rose pink. Her agent, Justin Baird, seated opposite, smiled at her proudly. Anna's book, not only a literary hit, was set to be a Disney animation. Next to Justin sat Damien's agent, Angus McManus and his wife.

Claudia and husband, Peter, hosted the Rose table. Their guests were Vladimir Pushkin and a group of ritzy Russians.

Danny Archer stepped up onto the podium and started the bidding at £3,000 for the Russian icon.

So excited was Boris at the prospect of beating his enemy Vladimir Pushkin, who had raised his paddle, that he reached beneath the table to squeeze his favourite part of Lala's anatomy, only to find that Adam's hand was in the way.

Locking fingers, an undercover battle raged to win the lady's favour, but finally it was Boris's winning hand that aced with his queen in a royal flush. Thus, Lala's peak of pleasure was intact and, not only that, but Boris had, with his final bid of £30,000, beaten off his competition and won the special treasure.

And so the auction sped along with Danny Archer's skilful patter.

Going, going, gone: a fine pair of diamond earrings, a gold Rolex watch, an eighteenth-century rococo tall case clock, a vintage Hermès bag, the weekend at the chateau and the Premier Cru, Pushkin's prize for £15K and then the beautiful diamond ring that had taken Sophie's fancy.

Horatio waited as rapidly the bidding rose.

'Twelve thousand pounds, twelve and a half, thirteen, thirteen and a half, fourteen, fifteen thousand pounds... from the gentleman at the Freesia table,' Danny called.

Horatio patted Sophie's hand, and playfully wagged her engagement finger. Jealous Nicholas, eyes peeled, poured another large glass of wine.

'Do I see £16,000?' Danny scanned the room. 'Yes, £16,000 from the Daffodil table and here's £17,000 back at the Freesia table.'

Sophie smiled serenely at her beau.

At the Orchid table, Nicholas, trembling with rage and alcohol, flapped his paddle. '£20,000.'

'£25,000,' Horatio coolly trounced him.

Nicholas, all rational thought obliterated by the wine, rose from his seat and, swaying back and forth, yelled, '£40,000. Beat that, you pompous prat!'

'Why is this man so angry with me, Sophie? I've never even met him,' Horatio said.

Sophie lowered her eyes and played with her napkin. 'Please, Horatio, don't ask me now. I'll tell you later.'

But what was there to tell? That she had fallen for a married man. Seduced him and allowed herself the pleasure of his company when he had a space in his diary. Maybe best to keep it to herself.

'£50,000.' Boris waved his paddle from the Freesia table. Lala squeezed his thigh. 'Thank you, darling.'

'I'm enjoying myself.' He picked up his wine glass and toasted Horatio. 'But we're missing a player. Come on, Pushkin,' he boomed. 'Put your money where your mouth is.'

'£55,000, you crazy bastard,' Vladimir roared from the Rose table.

'£58,000,' Horatio countered.

Nicholas was in again, quick as a whippet. 'And £60,000.' Kate gripped his arm. 'Are you insane?'

'I'm upping Horatio's game. Pricking his vanity,' Nicholas whispered vindictively.

'£70,000!' Horatio shouted.

'Horatio, stop,' Sophie pleaded. 'Charity is one thing, but it's a ridiculous price to pay for the ring.'

'Don't you worry. I want to see how far the guy will go.'

'£75,000.' Nicholas challenged his rival with an arrogant stare.

'Do I hear £80,000?' Danny looked around the room. Silence.

'I'll buy you the ring from Asprey,' Horatio whispered to Sophie, and kissed her ear.

'That's it, Nicholas.' Kate kicked him under the table. 'Clear out the bank account, why don't you?'

'Do I hear £76,000?' Danny asked. Silence.

'Going… going… gone.' He banged the gavel. 'Sold for £75,000. Congratulations to Mr Nicholas Morley.'

'Oh God! What the fuck have I done?' muttered Nicholas with a clenched smile.

'You've just bought a ring you can't afford.' Kate picked up her glass of red wine and threw it at Nicholas's face. 'Why would you be so stupid? It's that Sophie, isn't it?' Kate was oblivious to the people around them, turning to stare. 'You said it was over. But you're still obsessed with her.'

'Stop,' Nicholas hissed. 'Everybody's staring at us.'

'I don't care. You deserve to be embarrassed.'

Kate jumped to her feet and shouted to her audience, 'Lords, ladies and gentlemen, let me introduce you to Nicholas Morley, arsehole of the century.'

The audience gasped.

'That's enough, Kate!' Nicholas grabbed her wrist. 'Time to go.'

The two of them walked through the stunned guests out of the hotel, Nicholas stiff-lipped, eyes straight ahead, and Kate belligerent, stony-faced.

'Item number six.' Danny Archer waved Damien up onto the podium.

'Let's see what price you'll bring,' Elizabeth said. 'Perhaps not as much as the ring, but I'm sure you'll be a lot of fun.' Damien arched an eyebrow at her.

'For a good cause,' she added, smiling.

He crossed the floor, mounted the platform and, turning to the guests, bowed. A tall, graceful figure with his rakish smile and sparkling eyes, he gave a wink that encompassed them all. The women in the audience giggled, and Danny stepped forward to open the bidding.

'So who will start the bidding with £1,000 for a very special night with Damien Spur, literary icon and, by all accounts, fascinating company.'

Damien smiled at Danny and took another bow.

The Voice was surprised. *Not bad for a starter. Can't say I'd pay a thousand quid to listen to your porkies.*

A pause. At the Tulip table, a spiky-haired blonde with tanned skin and bony, chiselled features raised her paddle, flashing an impossibly white smile.

Relieved, his ego intact, Damien gave her a charming nod.

'A thousand pounds from the foxy lady at the Tulip table. And do I hear fifteen hundred? Ah, good!'

'The Daffodil table at £1,500 from the redhead in the gold dress. Getting hotter, and so is Damien. Can we see two thousand...? Look at that! A gent at the Lilac table,' Danny said.

'For my soon-to-be ex-wife. A parting gift.' A rugged, slick, dark-haired man raised his glass. Damien had started to enjoy himself. Danny was fielding bids from all corners of the room.

'Two and a half thousand pounds? Yes! Foxy lady ups the game at the Tulip table. Three? Back to the gentleman at the Lilac table. Hopefully a generous divorce for the ex-to-be. Where to now? Come on, let's really play. Do I see four thousand?'

Vladimir Pushkin waved his paddle.

'Ah! Four thousand pounds from our Russian comrade at the Rose table.'

'Five thousand!' Boris shouted from the Freesia table. 'Damien Spur, you teach me how to write about a bald, ugly traitor, a business crook – all about you, Pushkin!'

'Boris, loser! You belong in one of your shipping containers in a black plastic bag,' Pushkin yelled.

'You vodka-swilling peasant,' Boris yelled back. 'You will never beat me on contracts. You're a pussy, a big fat peasant. Your poor wife. I pity her in your bed. She needs our new product, Venus Viagra. When a woman takes our Venus pills, she could fall in love with a donkey.'

The audience gave a round of applause.

'Come on, gentlemen, back to the bidding,' Danny said. 'This is no place to bicker. Remember we're raising money for a good cause.'

Damien straightened his tie and grabbed the microphone. 'I am happy to offer an extra night. Just not sure where I can allocate it in my schedule.'

'Thank you, Damien.' Danny whisked the mike back. 'But the way the bidding is going, one night will be just great. Now… where were we?'

'We are here.' Elizabeth's voice, clear and deep, resonated from the Freesia table. 'Let's double the last bid from our Russian friend to ten thousand pounds.'

Damien shifted his gaze to Elizabeth, who gave him a sanguine smile.

Blimey, said the Voice.

'Shhhh,' Damien hissed. 'Don't interrupt.'

The Voice carried on. *You're a good-looking chap, but I wonder what she expects for that? Hope you're up to it.*

Would you stop? Damien pushed the Voice to the back of his head.

'Any advance on ten thousand?' Danny asked. The room was silent. 'Yes, not a good idea to disappoint our lovely hostess… So, going… going… gone… Here we have one Damien Spur, for one night only, promised to Lady Elizabeth Maitland.'

Damien walked back to the table smiling left and right as the guests clapped. Justin grabbed his arm as he passed him.

'Well done, old boy,' he said, 'but watch your step. She's a sticky one.'

Damien sat down, ruffled his hair and undid his bow tie.

'Well, that was a very generous bid,' he said to Elizabeth.

'I hope you're worth it,' she replied, without smiling. 'My place, next Friday, 7.30 p.m.'

A handsome Chinese man wearing ceremonial dress appeared, as if by magic. He handed Damien Elizabeth's calling card.

'This is my man, Chang,' she said.

Amazing! said the Voice. *Looks like you're in for quite a night.*

Chapter 22

Nicholas and Kate staggered out of the taxi and plunged into the sensual embrace of the Madrigal Hotel.

The desk clerk scanned the tipsy couple's flushed faces and forced a lip-enhanced smile.

'Good evening. You are staying with us tonight?'

'Yuh.' Nicholas tapped his suitcase. 'Think so.'

'Can I take your names, please?'

'Mr and Mrs Morley… Emile,' replied Nicholas, noting the name badge. 'I believe that Lady Elizabeth Maitland has booked a room for us?'

'Just a moment, sir, while I check the reservation.'

Nicholas swivelled round and scanned the uber-glitzy couples who whispered and canoodled on luxurious chenille sofas. Paintings of scantily attired voluptuaries hung on the red silk walls.

On the black marble table in the centre of the lounge clusters of deep purple grapes trailed from a silver plate.

Nicholas groaned. 'This is going to cost us a bloody fortune. We're going to have to raid a bank, Kate,' he whispered.

'That's rich coming from someone who just bought a £75,000 ring,' she hissed.

'Look, I'll sort that out in the morning. Can you just shut it now and try to keep your asp venom to yourself?'

Emile glanced up from the computer. 'Yes, indeed. You're in suite 21.'

'A suite?' Nicholas coughed.

'Our best suite.'

'And the room rate?' Kate asked.

'Normally £1,000 a night inclusive of tax and service, but a discount has been arranged by Lady Maitland and it will be £750.'

'With breakfast?' Kate said.

'Breakfast is extra, madam. Thirty pounds per person for a full English and twenty for the continental buffet.'

'Good,' Nicholas said nonchalantly. 'I take it you have twenty-four-hour room service?'

'Of course, sir.'

'Fine. There you are, Kate. We can send down for some champagne and have our own party.' Nicholas was determined not to lose financial face.

'The porter will escort you to the room and bring your luggage. Perhaps, while you are waiting, you and your wife would like to sit down?'

'Why not?'

'Oh, come on, Nicholas. We don't need a porter. Just let's go upstairs. I've got a big bone to pick with you.'

'Ooh hoo. Mmmm. Could be fun! I'll pick your bone if you pick mine.'

Nicholas took the brass key and slalomed with his overnight bag towards the lift.

'What is wrong with you?' Kate said as she stumbled behind him and, hiking up the voluminous skirt of her frumpish evening dress, pushed him into the lift. 'You're so embarrassing.'

'And so are you! Fancy grilling the man about the rates. I thought at one point you were going to ask for a cheaper room. Oh, you with your bargains and two for one.'

'You were the one who started it. Talking about bank raids.'

'Quiet! People are trying to sleep.'

The doors opened and, wheeling their cases down the wide corridor, they arrived at suite 21.

For a moment, the unhappy couple moved out of their troubled world and stepped into a glamorous fantasy. An ice bucket holding a bottle of complimentary champagne, and a porcelain dish of dark chocolates greeted them.

'Well, that's a nice surprise.' He glanced at the label. 'Mmm, Bollinger, not vintage, but still a good year.'

Nicholas popped the cork, and poured the champagne into two glasses and proffered one to Kate.

'Not for me.' She moved over to the Nespresso machine. 'I want a coffee.'

'Well, that's fun! A party for one. Chin-chin to myself.' Nicholas clinked the two flutes together and took a sip from each.

He ambled into the bedroom, sat on the large, inviting bed with its duck-down pillows and crisp cotton sheets and ran his hand across the satin cover, imagining how it would be if he were with his delicious Sophie.

But here was Kate, cup in hand, who ripped into his tender thoughts.

'Yes, Nicholas, she's still in there, isn't she? In your head, your darling Sophie. I saw you looking at her all evening. Do you think I'm blind? Your eyes were blazing. Blazing with lust and love. You made me feel like I was nothing. Like I didn't exist.'

'I'm sorry. I'm sorry, Kate. I just couldn't help it.'

'What do you mean you couldn't help it? How'd you think I felt? Sitting at the table watching you ogling that woman. Knowing that you have touched every part of her body and that every night when we're in bed you're thinking of her. Making love to her.'

'But, Kate, the way you talk to me half the time, I don't think you give a damn. Let's face it. You don't even like me touching

165

you. It's been months since we've done it. I remember. The last time was on my birthday and even then, you were too bloody lazy to pretend you were enjoying yourself. And I'm not so sure that you're Miss Innocent! Why are you going to the gym twice a day? Twice a day! In the morning and in the afternoon. Before and after work. Come on. Tell me the truth. You're at it again! Who is it this time?'

'Stop changing the subject. Stop it! Stop it, Nicholas! You're a shit. You're a *big* shit. Who do you think you are to tell me what to do with my life? I'm fed up. You don't give me any emotional support whatsoever, nothing. If you really must know, I *have* met somebody. Yes! Yes!'

'Who?'

'I've met a woman.'

'Well, that's a bolt from the blue.' Nicholas stopped short. Caught his breath. 'Another woman. So what can I say? If that's what floats your boat, it's fine by me. You carry on. Do what you want. I don't give a damn anymore.'

'You shit, Nicholas.'

'Oh, stop calling me that disgusting name. You've become so bloody crude.'

'I'll call you anything I like. Bastard! Dog! I've had it.' Moving towards Nicholas, propelled by her fury, she threw the cup at his face.

He ducked and it smashed against the wall, spraying an ugly dash of brown liquid across the ivory paint.

Kate wept.

'I'll sleep on the sofa,' Nicholas said. 'And you take the bed.'

***

'Sophie, Nicholas is your friend. Please can you ring him and find out what's going on?' asked Claudia.

'Can't you do that?'

166

'I've tried. He doesn't answer his mobile. I've left numerous messages, called his home number, absolutely no response... This isn't going to go away. It was generous of him to donate the icon, but he still owes the charity £75,000 and that's that. I hope he's not thinking of backing out.'

'Look, I can't talk now,' Sophie said quietly. 'I'm taking Horatio to the airport. I'll ring him this afternoon. Claudia, please could you keep this to yourself? I don't want Horatio to know that I'm going to call Nicholas... Look, I must go.'

'What about Nicholas?' Horatio slid up behind her.

Sophie spun round, whippet fast. 'Horatio!'

'What's the matter with you, darling? You're so edgy. Why are you in such a bad mood? Is it because of the ring? I'll get you a beauty, don't worry. Or is there something else?'

'Please, Horatio, let's leave it.'

'You don't have to take me to the airport. So much easier for you if I take a cab.'

'Don't be silly. I want to take you.'

'Are you sure?'

'Please, Horatio, stop.'

'Oh, is this an argument?' he asked with an amused glint in his eye.

Sophie answered his wry smile with one of her own, and laughed. 'Not if you stop asking questions.'

***

Nicholas wished he hadn't behaved like a drunken fool that night in front of Sophie. What must she have thought of him, let alone what her smarmy Horatio had concluded.

The bastard really got him. Shot him in the balls. Horatio had called his bluff, and now Nicholas was stuck.

He'd phoned his bank – not enough leverage for a loan. Funny that. Never been in debt and yet he couldn't get credit.

'That's what happens when you pay in cash,' his friend Skid said. 'Start borrowing, Nick, and they'll know who you are.'

And that Claudia. Her phone messages had made him sweat.

'Nicholas, answer my call, please,' she had said in her sweet, breathy voice. It had a steel edge that cut through him like a knife.

Later that afternoon he called her.

'Please could you give me Boris's office number,' he said.

'Why haven't you answered my calls?' Claudia replied.

'I'm sorry. I was going to ring you earlier, but I just haven't had the chance,' he lied.

'Well, let's get to the point. How do you want to pay the £75,000 for the ring? Cheque or bank transfer?' she said.

'Just hold on. I'm not sure yet. I know I have to pay for the ring, but I wasn't myself last night. I was drunk. I… I don't want to talk about it… Look, Claudia, I need a little time to sort this out. You'll get the money…'

And that's when he called Boris.

'Alexa, play Mozart's *Requiem*.' Nicholas lay with his head propped on a cushion, eyes glazed, pale-faced waiting for Boris to return his calls. He'd rung twice so far. Nicholas knew that he must resist calling again, or Boris would sense that he was desperate. He must be cool, casual.

Nicholas ran a speech in his head.

Hello, Boris, a little prob last night with my winning bid for the diamond ring. I was a bit tipsy. You know, all the excitement of the game. So, don't want to dig into my funds at the mo. Markets are down and £75k makes a bit of a dent. Wondered if you might like to buy another icon or two… for a quick sale? Want to settle asap. Don't want to let the charity down – it's a question of honour.

He poured himself a whisky and a large glass of water.

'Come on, you bastard, ring me back.' He punched the cushion. 'Bet you're doing it on purpose. Probably know I'm drowning in my own sweat.'

Nicholas was in the bathroom when Boris finally rang.

He had left his mobile on the table. Struggling with his trousers, he hopped into the living room.

Kate had just returned from the garden centre. 'Shall I answer the call?' she said, more out of curiosity than kindness.

'Leave it, please,' he said, and snatched the phone. 'Hello, it's Nicholas Morley. I'm trying to speak to Mr Smirnov.'

'Hold, please,' said his secretary. 'I will put you straight through.'

'Hello, Nicholas. What's up?'

'Ah, Boris, we are ships that pass in the night.'

'Ships? What ships?'

'It's a saying. It means we are missing each other,' Nicholas said.

'You are very nice man, but I cannot say I miss you. But I'm flattered you miss me.'

'That's fine. It's just another expression.'

'I know. Only joking. What can I do for you?' Boris said.

Kate planted herself in front of him, arms crossed.

'Piss off,' he mouthed.

She stood her ground.

Nicholas cleared his throat and gave his speech. 'A little prob last night with my winning bid for the diamond ring,' he said. His mouth was dry. 'I… I… was tipsy and… all the excitement of the game… Anyway…' He suppressed a cough, grabbed a glass of water and took a large gulp… 'So I don't want to dig into my funds at the mo. Markets are down and £75k makes a bit of a dent… Anyway, I wondered if you might like to buy another icon or two. Good price for a quick sale. Want to settle with the charity asap.'

'I don't want more icons, thank you. I bought your one at auction because Lala said it reminded her of her mother.'

'Look, Boris, can't you think of something I can do for you?'

'Mmm, Nicholas, we don't need to play. I know you are in difficult position. So, I have idea. Wanna be a mule?'

'Was that a joke, Boris?' Nicholas said.

'Not at all. I want you to deliver an icon to a collector who lives in LA.'

'What's his name?'

'Clifford Stark.'

'That doesn't sound a problem.'

'No problem for you, if you keep cool.'

'What do you mean?'

'Just get through customs without a search.'

'And what if I am searched?'

'Just don't get searched,' Boris said.

'Okay, I'll do it.' Nicholas paced the floor and gestured to Kate to pour him another glass of whisky.

'When?'

'Tomorrow night you will stay at the Landmark Hotel. My secretary will book it for you. The icons will be delivered to your room in a suitcase. You will be given an envelope with instructions and money. Your flight will be booked for the day after. Please do not ring me again. I will contact you.' Boris hung up.

Ashen-faced, Nicholas stood stock still, his mouth wide open, his trousers still round his ankles. He stared at his mobile.

'What was that about?' Kate said. 'You look like one of those human statues in Covent Garden.'

'I'm a fool. This is a big one, Kate. What have I done?'

'What do you mean?'

Nicholas downed the whisky and slammed the glass on the table. 'My dull bloody life has just become a melodrama.'

To be honest, despite the debacle with the ring, there was a part of Nicholas that was excited. Who knows what might happen? Perhaps he could start a side hustle; covert smuggling of valuable items all over the world.

Maybe the ring disaster had inadvertently given him a new lease of life. Not just a bit-player from Bournemouth, but one of the big boys. Bugger Horatio, stealing his Sophie. He'd show him. She'd be begging to come back to him.

The adrenalin rush made him dizzy.

Chapter 23

Damien ran his hand over his sleek stomach, admiring his six-pack. He was in good shape. Randy, his trainer, had pushed him to cut down on the alcohol and lower the carbs, which had increased his energy and cleared his head. He was looking forward to spending the evening with Elizabeth Maitland.

He arrived at seven thirty on the dot and rang the bell of the magnificent stucco-fronted Belgravia town house at the corner of Chester Square.

Elizabeth answered the door. A Pre-Raphaelite beauty her amber eyes and copper hair, enhanced by a peacock-green velvet dress.

Wowser, said the Voice.

'Elizabeth.' Damien brushed her cheek with a feather-light kiss. He proffered a bouquet of satiny pink peonies.

'How kind of you, Damien,' she said. 'Do come in.'

Damien followed her up the stairs to the grand living room, which was furnished with exquisite taste. A large deep-seated navy velvet sofa was artfully covered with plump silk cushions in rich hues of burgundy and grey, on the walls hung two huge paintings, both depicting erotic images of love-making, and in the centre of the room, a magnificent bronze of a man and woman entwined in a Kama Sutra coupling was placed on an elegant grey marble table.

'What a beautiful piece... Must say I haven't tried that position,' Damien said, always ready to test the water.

'I have, with a handsome young Indian called Mitash, whom I met at Oxford. We were both studying chemistry. In our first year, we visited his father who lived in Mumbai. He had a fabulous gallery of erotica which aroused my desire to collect.'

Elizabeth ran her finger down the torso of the male figure. 'This is from one of the Khajuraho temples that were destroyed. It's my favourite piece. Utterly captivating. Carnal but at the same time refined.'

Just like the look she gave him.

Damien's pulse quickened. 'Elizabeth...' he began. She tilted her head to one side, and her lips curved in a questioning smile.

'Yes?' she said.

'I... I'm finding this quite strange,' he continued.

'Why strange?'

'Well, I'm not quite sure about the terms of the contract. I thought we were going to chat about art and literature over dinner.'

'Come on, Damien, I paid for the full monty. You were my prize. Ten thousand pounds for a night with Damien Spur.'

Just surrender, said the Voice. *Take it as a compliment; she's hot for you.*

'Aaah, had I known, I would have brought my toothbrush,' Damien replied.

'Don't worry, I have plenty to spare.'

There was a gentle tap at the door. 'Come in,' Elizabeth said.

Chang appeared in a black silk kimono. He gave her a courteous bow and Damien an inscrutable glance. 'Dinner will be served in twenty minutes.'

'Thank you, Chang,' said Elizabeth. 'Champagne, Damien?'

'I'd rather a Scotch.'

'Any preference?'

'Just a good malt, please.'

'A whisky for my guest, champagne for me.' Elizabeth settled herself on the sofa. 'Come sit next to me. Now then, Damien, tell me about yourself. Who are you?'

'Who am I?' Damien was not altogether comfortable with his grand inquisitor. 'That's a very interesting question, because I've never really asked myself who I am. I just am.'

That's good, said the Voice. *Not too much information. Avoid talking about your inner sanctum. Don't want to put her off. Make it all about her.*

'And who are you?' Damien said.

'I'm a creature who doesn't believe in habit. I like adventures, lots of them. When I was at university, I decided there and then that I wanted to do something that would take me to faraway places. Ride a magic carpet seeking the unique, whether it be art or exquisite sensory experiences. What I found the most captivating were the exotic smells of the East.

'Having read chemistry I had the skill to capture the essence of rarified fragrances. So that is what I am. I'm a perfumer, and I love it… And you, Damien, why did you start writing thrillers?'

That's better, said the Voice, *your turn at last.*

'Well, I studied English at Oxford and when MI5 wanted to recruit me as a spy I said yes, although I wasn't interested in a career in espionage. I was just intrigued to see what sort of games were played. Thus I went through the process and met some interesting people. Speaking Russian made me rather valuable. But I found bouncing back and forth between Russia and London tiresome and actually rather boring. So, finally I managed to extricate myself from the dark and murky world of stealing secrets by faking anxiety attacks. Basically I got a sick note from the doc. However, some of it was good fodder for my books, especially tales from my Russian counterparts, who after a few vodkas told me some terrific stories. I suppose I'm a writer because I like a good yarn, especially my own.'

After his initial discomfort, Damien had started to enjoy talking with Elizabeth. She avoided light conversational clichés. She was both interesting and interested.

You're doing fine, said the Voice. *I'm sure you won't mind if I leave you to it.*

'So, time for dinner.' Elizabeth took Damien's arm and guided him up a circular staircase into a domed turret, a secret, sensual space, lit by candles scented with jasmine and bergamot, which gave Damien's senses a pleasant, heady lift. By the window, a small round table had been formally dressed for dinner with a white linen cloth, monogrammed silver cutlery and fine crystal glasses.

'This is my Rapunzel room,' Elizabeth said.

Chang filled their glasses and placed two plates of large oysters on the table.

Elizabeth took one and deftly slipped it from the shell into her mouth. Damien paled, but did the same.

'I'm so sorry.' He started to choke. 'I really can't eat oysters. I never could, ever since I had food poisoning. Please could you ask Ching... I mean, Chang, to take them away?'

'Certainly, the apology is mine. I just assumed that when you said you loved seafood, that you would enjoy oysters.' Elizabeth buzzed the intercom.

'Please could you take Mr Spur's plate of oysters away? Would you like smoked salmon instead?' she asked, glancing at Damien's pale face.

He nodded weakly. 'Thank you. Perhaps some dry toast would be better for now.'

By the time the main course arrived – tender seared duck breast with roasted vegetables – he had recovered.

'This is divine. Chang is an excellent cook. Where did you find him?'

'In Hong Kong. It was the ambassador's party. The dinner was fabulous and I asked to meet the chef. I just had to steal him. So I took him back to London with me. And now it's time for dessert.' She rose from her seat and, taking his hand, led him to the bedroom.

***

'Well done,' she said. 'That was fun.'

'Elizabeth…' He took a breath.

'Now don't say anything you might regret. No lovey-dovey chat. I can't stand that.'

He kissed her neck.

'But can I say that I love the way you smell? Rose? Jasmine?' He inhaled deeply. 'And sandalwood. Like the sweet scent of an Indian palace garden where a princess sits in the early evening, dreaming of tender kisses from her secret lover.'

Not bad. The Voice was back. *She'll like that.*

'Very good,' she said. 'You have an excellent nose.'

'Thank you…' He paused, anxious to hold her interest. 'So, tell me, what makes a fragrance great?'

'Creating a wonderful fragrance is like composing a piece of music. Both have notes and chords. To make a beautiful scent the composition has to harmonise perfectly to intoxicate the senses.'

'Perfume, the only dress a lovely woman needs under the sheets.' He reached out his hand to stroke her breast.

Elizabeth's eyes flicked towards the bathroom. He was losing her.

'I'm going to have a shower. Feel free to leave if you like,' she said, sliding out of bed.

'Is this the cue for my exit?' Damien asked.

Oh no! said the Voice. *And you were doing so well. Mr Insecure again.*

'It's your choice,' she said. 'But let me be clear, if you want to stay, I don't like to chat in the morning.'

'I think that it's best that we call it a night,' he said. 'At least you got what you paid for.'

Good onya, added the Voice. *What a great comeback. Maybe if you stay till the morning, you can charge her overtime.*

'Have I offended you, Damien?' she said, standing naked by the bed.

'No,' he replied. 'But I suppose the intimacy of strangers making love at night might not stand up in the cold light of day. Especially before we brush our teeth.'

That was terrific, said the Voice. *So elegantly put.*

***

But, after that first night Damien was in free fall. Usually, he found that women got boring and weepy over time, but the more he saw Elizabeth the more he missed her. She was a thrilling lover, but impenetrable outside the bedroom, which fired his obsession.

'How could I not fall for Elizabeth?' Damien said to Sophie. They were having lunch at Dino's, a discreet Italian round the corner from his apartment.

'You mean she appeals to your masochistic tendencies?'

'Maybe. I just can't second guess her. She's such a contradiction.'

Sophie was keen to talk about her own relationship with Horatio, but Damien couldn't stop.

'We went to Antibes last week. Had a glorious time. Made love like angels and then, when we arrived back in London, she disappeared for three days. Wouldn't return my calls. When I finally spoke to her, she said that I needed to give her some space. It was so bloody random.'

'Damien, you've got to cool off if you want to keep Elizabeth's interest. Needy is not sexy.'

He flagged the waiter. 'Another bottle of the Merlot, please.'

'I don't want any more wine. Why don't you just order another glass?' she said.

'It's fine, Sophie.' He wanted to get back on track. To continue talking about Elizabeth.

The wine helped. Made his stream of consciousness more lucid. Or so he thought. But Sophie stopped the flow.

'You're rambling. Can we talk about me for a change?' She patted his hand and took a sip of water.

'Sorry.'

'It's not going to work with Horatio,' she said.

'Why the hell not? He's a catch and he loves you. Talk about me being a masochist.'

'It's not so simple.'

'Don't tell me he's married.'

'No, but he has a sixteen-year-old daughter with Isabel, the woman who runs the vineyard. The girl can't stand living with her mother and wants to come and live with him in London, which means with us.'

'So what's the fuss? You can't expect an attractive man like Horatio not to have a complicated history.'

'No, I understand that. However, what really worried me was that when I rang the chateau Isabel answered the phone, which I fully expected as he told me she lived in a wing of the chateau. But here's the rub: she didn't know anything about me, let alone that we were getting married.'

'He must have had his reasons. Maybe she's still in love with him and he was worried she'd cause trouble – throw the dishes at him. Anyway, at least he's not a loser like that idiot Nicholas. Look at the way he behaved at the auction with that ring business.'

'He honoured the debt,' Sophie said.

'So, you still see him?'

'Well… we speak.'

'And?'

She shrugged. 'Nothing to tell.'

Chapter 24

Justin Baird had rescued Anna from unrequited love.

She'd been consumed by Damien Spur. Even when he'd moved on, during the week she continued her pastime of ravishing her pillow at night imagining his smooth body enclosing her delicate frame, save for Saturdays, when Justin came to stay. He was attractive, kind and generous and so when he proposed she said yes.

And why not? She liked the way he treated her. He said he loved her and that she was beautiful and talented.

He brought her flowers and took her to the ballet and elegant restaurants. But what she loved most about him was that he believed in her.

Nurse Aileen did not. She perceived her as a posh, ditzy little dreamer.

Which she confirmed one day at precisely 2 p.m.

It was Tuesday and the practice had been busy, followed by a quiet period with only one patient left in the waiting area. Anna was enjoying the lull when Mr Green arrived with his six-year-old daughter, Kylie, who had a dental appointment.

'Good morning, Mr Green. Hello, Kylie. Dr Lacey is running a little late, but please take a seat. He won't be long,' Anna said.

'I don't want to sit down,' Kylie said.

The elderly patient in the waiting area with sleek grey hair and a stylish navy suit looked up from her magazine and tut-tutted.

'I can give you a colouring book, if you like,' Anna whispered, and glanced apologetically at the woman.

'I'm not a baby,' said Kylie.

'Well, you're acting like one.' Anna took out a book and some crayons from a drawer in her desk and slapped them on the table.

'I don't like your face. It's twitchy like a rabbit,' Kylie said.

And that was it. Anna flipped.

'Can't you control your nasty little daughter, Mr Green?' she said. 'What a charmless child she is. She needs to be locked up in her room for a week. Nothing wrong with washing her mouth out with a bar of soap, either. And what's the mother doing? No doubt letting her daughter run riot. And why is the girl wearing nail polish at six years old? This mother-sister thing is no good. No wonder she behaves like a spoilt brat. It always stems from the mother.'

Mr Green's face flushed red. 'Don't you talk about my wife and Kylie like that. Who do you think you are with your posh voice? You're only a receptionist, not bloody royalty.'

'I'd rather be a receptionist than someone like you!' retorted Anna.

'Don't you speak to my dad like that!' squeaked Kylie, and then she spat at Anna.

'Ugh! You disgusting little brat. How *dare* you!' Anna took a tissue from her bag and wiped her cheek.

'Is this a Harley Street practice or a fish market?' the woman with the grey hair said.

'I am so sorry, Lady Langton.' Anna moved from behind her desk, grabbed Mr Green by the lapels and pulled him towards her.

And that's when Aileen walked in.

'Anna, what are you doing? Take your hands off Mr Green,' she snapped. 'Come outside.'

Anna put her few small belongings in her bag, followed Aileen to the door and said, 'You don't need to patronise me with another one of your condescending speeches, you hideous virago. I'm resigning. And when my book is published next month, I won't bother sending you a signed copy.'

Chapter 25

Nobody stopped Nicholas going through customs, and flying
BA business class made a pleasant change from the usual
no-frills budget flights he was used to.

In Manhattan, Clifford Stark came and went taking the
icons with him, hardly giving Nicholas a glance.

It was all so easy.

The major change in his life was that when he returned to
England Kate had left him to go and live with her girlfriend. His
wish was fulfilled. And so, with his new-found confidence, he
was ready to fight for his queen.

Claudia had warmed to him since he'd paid for the ring, and
a few weeks later had dropped the hint that Sophie and Horatio
had hit a snag.

Time for Nicholas to stake his claim. He rang her.

'I've found my mojo, Sophie. Please let's get back together
again. You are the love of my life,' he said.

'Oh, so you've heard that the engagement's off?' she said.

'Well, I have, but I would have fought for you anyway. Fate
plays a strange game. My marriage is over, and I have the ring to
give to you as soon as I get a divorce, darling one.'

'Ah, so you've actually left her?'

'Well…'

'I know… Come on, Nicholas. It's all very convenient… It's
the other way round, isn't it? She's left you.'

'Well… yes. For a woman called Greta, whom she met at her gym. She's a personal trainer.'

Sophie giggled. 'Damien will love the twist.'

'Glad you think it's funny. Well, at least I stayed for the family's sake. But we both knew we were in a mess. She's a good woman and I like her. But it's you I love, Sophie. And what about Horatio?' he asked. 'What happened to change your mind?' Nicholas held the phone to his ear and moved to the kitchen. He opened the fridge door and scanned an open tin of sardines, a bottle of wine and a can of Budweiser. He took out the beer and flipped the tab. He looked forward to hearing the tale of Sophie's break-up. 'I'm all ears.' He moved back into the living room and stretched himself out on the sofa. 'So tell me what happened.'

'Let's just say when it's hot it's hot and when it's not it's not.'

Nicholas made his pitch. 'So does that mean you're free for dinner?' He reached for the can again and, holding it away from the phone, took a sip. 'Sophie, are you there?' he said.

'Yes,' she said. Should she return to graze on old pastures? She relented. 'Look, I'm having an engagement party for Justin and Anna. Why don't you come?'

He'd won. Nicholas was enchanted with himself and life.

Ah, kismet.

Chapter 26

Anna was excited. Everything had moved so fast. And all because of Damien. She missed his tuition. Wanted to thank him. A last hurrah before she became officially engaged to Justin. Just one more time… Even just a kiss and a cuddle or maybe more?

The needy phone calls in the middle of the night were exhausting, especially when he was "entertaining" another guest. Namely Elizabeth, who laughed.

The phone rang. 'I bet it's poor Anna,' she said and, rolling across Damien, grabbed the phone from its cradle. She pressed answer and thrust it into the palm of his hand. 'Say hello – it won't hurt you. Obsession is a painful thing.'

'How would you know?' Damien tossed the phone back on the bedside table. 'Have you ever really loved anyone?' He held her on top of him.

'I don't think it's time to start a heart to heart.' She wriggled out of his arms, and slid back on to her side of the bed. 'I always find such conversations suffocating. Now then, don't keep the poor girl waiting. She needs your undivided attention.'

'Hello, hello, can you hear me?' Anna was still on the line.

He stretched out his index finger and tapped the loudspeaker button. 'I can now.'

'Damien,' she said. 'Come for a drink. For old times' sake. I promise not to jump on you.'

Her voice sounded breezy. Like a woman who had moved on.

Which was a relief. She was difficult to wean after he had turned off the heat.

'So then?' she said. 'How about 7 p.m. tomorrow?'

'That's fine,' Damien replied. 'See you then,' and he hung up. What was the harm in it? He was proud of his prodigy.

'Good for you,' Elizabeth said, flicking his shoulder. 'One last fling before she marries Justin. Do give her your best shot.'

There she goes again. Treating you like a gigolo, said the Voice.

***

The next evening Damien was pleased to see Anna looking so carefree. Money suited her.

'Lovely to see you,' she said. No pink lipstick or frills. White linen shirt and bootcut blue jeans, tan sandals. Hair shiny and loose. He kissed her cheek. She smelt different. Fresh, not the cloying musky rose she used to wear.

He knew that scent; jasmine and bergamot. He lingered. Gave her an extra kiss. Shut his eyes.

'You smell nice.' He scanned the room, which was an extension of Anna's transformation. 'Out with the old, in with Conran,' he said, and flopped on the ivory linen sofa.

'Your usual?' Anna asked.

'A bit of a change. Red, please. Given up the whisky. Elizabeth says it makes me angry.'

'I don't think she's right for you, if you ask me.'

'I'm not.'

'But, Damien, I think you're barking up the wrong tree, if you don't mind me saying.'

'I do. Come on, Anna, pour me some wine and come and sit down. I want to hear how you are.'

She poured him a glass from a crystal decanter and one for herself. Handing him the wine, she perched next to him and daintily plucked an olive from the Murano glass bowl standing on the coffee table.

'Open wide,' she said. 'Don't worry, they're pitted,' she added with a cheeky grin, and popped it in his mouth.

'Very witty,' he said.

'But seriously, Damien…' She gazed prettily at him. 'Isn't it crazy to think that you chipping your tooth changed my life?'

'That's certainly true,' he said, and gave her hand a fatherly pat. 'I'm so glad that it worked out with your book and Justin.'

'Amazing, really…' She smiled. A confident grown-up smile. Not the one he knew – the usual coy little-girl, poor-me smile.

'What's amazing?' Damien asked.

'Well, I don't want to sound vain, but here's me at forty-three marrying a rich, handsome man who's seven years younger.'

He felt comfortable with her. Especially as she was getting married to someone else. Anna had suffocated him with her neediness. Always there. Ready and willing. No holds barred. Repeating herself every time she saw him: "Why can't we live together?" And then she'd met Justin Baird. Who was happy to surrender. And yet… Damien could see she was still thrilled by him.

'I can't thank you enough for all your help,' she said and, moving closer, gently stroked the back of his neck, which she knew he liked.

Best not to, said the Voice. *Not a good idea to get her going.*

'And so, Anna, when's the book signing?' He shifted away from her sleek little body.

'Next week at the children's book fair in Oxford – I'm doing a reading.' She shifted towards him again.

'Well then, that should be fun. Is Justin going too?'

'No. He has too much work.' She stroked his thigh. He lifted up her straying hand and kissed her little finger. 'I really must say goodbye, Anna. It's been lovely seeing you.'

She was adorable, but he wouldn't see her again until her engagement party.

Chapter 27

A nna had arrived early to help her sister before the party. Chang, courtesy of Elizabeth, was preparing the food in the kitchen with his sister, Mae.

'So lovely to dine out in the garden.' Anna had folded the last of the eight napkins into an origami water lily and placed it on the table bedecked with crystal, silver and flowers. 'Such pretty roses, Sophie, and they smell so sweet. It's a perfect summer night. I'm glad Justin has invited Harry and James. They're so interesting and funny.'

'I know,' said Sophie. 'And their new cookery book is terrific – *Dreams for Queens*. My favourite recipe is called "Trans-Siberian Experience". It's a chocolate train with a marzipan Putin figure standing on top wearing a rainbow utility kilt and waving a gay-pride flag. There are also some lovely little fairy-themed biccies and a special coming-out cake – six layers of pink frills scattered with silver stars.'

***

All the neighbours seemed to be dining alfresco that evening. Gentle chatter and intermittent laughter wafted through the balmy air from garden to garden as the clear night sky turned indigo, illuminated by the incandescent stars.

Sophie smiled at Nicholas as he sweet-talked her over watercress soup, while Damien played his jaunty self, teasing Anna about her petit-bourgeois prejudices.

'It isn't right, it just isn't right,' she said.

'Why isn't it right?' Damien asked. 'Scotsmen wear kilts, why shouldn't Harry wear a skirt? In ancient Egypt, the main garment worn by men was the skirt. And Roman males wore a skirt called a fustanella, similar to a kilt, for ceremonies and military occasions.'

'Actually, you would look good in a skirt.' Anna leant forward, her breasts tipping out of her pink lace dress. 'You have lovely legs,' she whispered.

Justin watched, aware of the frisson of sexual tension between them. Had they had an affair? he wondered.

Damien was being charming, but intermittently his eyes would dart to the end of the table where Elizabeth sat, to see whether she was watching him flirt with Anna. He turned to Claudia. 'Must book another tarot session. Not sure where I'm going,' he said under his breath. 'Probably hell if I carry on the way I am.'

Claudia could feel Damien's leg shaking under the table. Chang had offered him the soup, but he'd waved it away. 'Not keen on the colour green,' he said.

'Where's Peter?' he asked Claudia.

'In the operating theatre,' she replied.

'He's one of the good guys,' Damien sighed. 'Mending broken hearts, saving lives; a noble profession.' He glanced at Elizabeth again. She was deep in conversation with James, who was dressed in a sky-blue silk suit and Harry, who wore a pink silk chiffon skirt with a white sleeveless top and pearls.

They were discussing the merits of creating an edible massage oil.

'Well, Harry...' Elizabeth said.

'Oh, do call me Harriet. I am a "she" tonight and tomorrow morning I might be a "he", depending on how I feel.'

'Well, Harriet, I would love to collaborate with you both in creating a really erotic and unique edible oil that smells beautiful and tastes pleasant. Most, if not all, of the products on the market leave a horrific aftertaste.'

'Indeed!' said Harriet. 'Simply vile.'

'We shall be the three witches,' she said. 'The alchemists whose spell invokes the sublime fusion of the senses. The magic potion, a sweet and fragrant nectar, that brings all men and women together to reach the sublime.'

'How divine!' Harriet shrieked.

'We're in!' said James.

And so the start of a new adventure was born. Elizabeth sensed that their journeys would converge – what with her perfect nose and their culinary gifts – to create an amazing product.

'Mmm, stunning.' James slipped a morsel of the tender seared sea bass in his mouth, relishing the flavour of the lemon and herb butter with the creamed spinach and new potatoes.

'No one cooks fish better than Chang,' Elizabeth said.

James gazed up at the elegant man, dressed in black silk, as he swept past the guests gracefully holding a tray in the air, single-handed. 'Is he attached to anyone?' he said.

'Only to me,' she replied.

Nicholas felt at ease. Here he was sitting with Sophie, his Aphrodite, who promised him a life of endless pleasure, and they would dance the years away with glorious vacations in the Mediterranean, visits to the theatre, fine dining, galleries and concerts. And at home she would cook exquisite dinners for him and then they would sit together and he would hold his precious princess in his arms, her head resting peacefully against his chest.

'Sophie,' he said, 'I'll buy a flat in London. Come live with me.'

'If you really loved me, Nicholas, you would get a divorce and marry me.'

'Of course.' He stroked her wedding finger. 'I can't wait to make you my wife. You are my life, Sophie.'

The night was full of sweet promises... until the fracas began.

'You what? You bloody bastard, get off me! I want a divorce!' a woman shouted from the next-door garden.

'Shhh! Please, Jane,' a man's voice said.

'Why are you telling me this now?' asked Jane.

'I thought I'd better warn you,' the man replied. 'It was a joke. Mike posted my profile on the site. I didn't do it.'

'Oh yes! Sure, you knew nothing about it. Simon, you're a bloody liar.'

'It was just a one-night fling. I didn't know she was going to start sexting me.'

'So every time I go to visit my mother you think you have the right to dip your noodle into any tart who's willing?'

'Look, I won't do it ever again. How many times can I say I'm sorry?'

There was silence, underpinned by desperate sobbing.

'This is a magical script! Carry on, don't stop!' Damien called across the fence. 'On such a night as this even the man in the moon himself must be enjoying watching the action!'

'Who is that?' wailed Jane.

'What are you doing, Jane? Please don't start with the neighbours,' Simon pleaded.

She had staggered over to the fence holding a bottle of wine. 'Why not? At least I don't have to listen to you.' There was a rustle and a thud, and then, 'Hello, Sophie!' Jane said, peeking through the bushes. 'Lovely to see you. Can I join your party?' She lifted her arm and waved the bottle in the air.

'Well, I suppose...'

'Great stuff... Simon, pass me a chair,' she said.

'Jane, please.'

'*Now*, you skunk!' More rustling and commotion as Jane announced, 'I need someone to catch me on the other side.' She kicked off her shoes and climbed onto the seat. 'Right, which one of you lovely men will be so kind as to volunteer?'

'With the greatest of pleasure,' Damien said.

And over she flipped, wrapping both her legs round Damien's neck.

'Well, how do you do?' he said as he gently lowered her onto the grass.

'Bloody awful! Four years and already he's a bed-hopper. How do you explain that to a three-year-old kid?'

He sat her at the table and poured her a glass of wine. She had the good grace to sit quietly and listen to Damien talk about himself, grateful that she had escaped from Simon's company. Ironic that everyone at the table had heard the exchange. Strangers, and yet here they were, privy to her husband's pathetic confession.

Nicholas felt vindicated. His was a very different affair. Kate had chosen to leave him and didn't care that he was in love with Sophie. *Yes*, he thought, *you couldn't compare the situation.*

Kate was happy with Greta and now he was free to be with the love of his life.

He looked at Sophie's beautiful face and felt at that moment a sublime contentment.

He held her eyes with a tender, loving gaze and gently stroked her cheek.

'How did this happen, Sophie? You are a miracle.'

Well, then…

Chang brought out the dessert: rose-petal panna cotta with damson and lavender Viennese shortbread.

Sophie was happy. Nicholas was happy. Elizabeth, Harriet and James were happy. So were Justin, Anna and Claudia.

Damien and Jane were not.

'Hard for me to take the moral high ground.' Damien popped a rose petal in his mouth. 'I have always enjoyed a this and a that. Given a choice, I would always take both.'

'Can you translate, please?' said Jane.

'Duality. Two women. Split focus… until now.'

She still looked confused.

Oh, my goodness, the Voice piped up with an offended tone. *The woman's an airhead. Why would she understand your cryptic thoughts? What the hell! If you want to spill your heart out to some random stranger, be my guest.*

'The problem is,' he said, fiddling with his fork, 'I have fallen in love. Do you see that woman?' He glanced at Elizabeth. 'She is my nemesis.'

'I'm sorry, your what?' Jane looked at his untouched dessert. 'Are you going to eat your pudding?'

'No.' He shifted the plate towards her. 'I've lost my appetite. You can have it if you like.'

'Thank you so much. I do like puddings. They're my downfall.' She took a bite. 'Mmm, just right. Not too sweet.'

'When I'm unhappy, I just can't eat,' he said.

'You're lucky. I just can't stop, like now.'

Damien's eyelids were dropping. He had a habit of falling asleep when he was bored.

Jane didn't seem to notice until his chin fell on his chest and he started to snore. She prodded him hard with a forceful index finger.

Damien woke up from his cat-nap.

'You're an arrogant bugger, Mr Big-shot Writer,' Jane said. 'I might not be the most exciting company – but falling asleep…'

'Not my fault,' he replied. 'I was under attack with your mind-numbing chatter.' He tapped his forehead. 'You tasered my brain cells.'

Jane looked dismayed. Damien could see her mulling over his words. Was she really that dull? Perhaps that was why Simon had gone online.

'I'm going home,' she said. 'I hope your head feels better.' She took her chair and clambered back over the garden fence.

Excellent! said the Voice. *Now we can move on to the fun stuff.*

Damien, happy to be alone with his thoughts, gazed at Nicholas and Sophie, who were cooing like doves.

'Sophie, let's go away,' Nicholas was saying. 'I miss the sea. Why don't we go to Italy again, maybe Sardinia?'

'When?'

'Whenever you're free. Sooner rather than later would be best. I know a lovely hotel near Cagliari. Fabulous food, right on the beach, beautiful rooms... beginning of August?'

'Sounds lovely.' Sophie's eyes sparkled in the candlelight. 'I can't wait.'

In his mind's eye, Damien imagined the besotted couple making love. He dipped a finger in his wine glass and lightly circled the rim. The high-pitched sound hummed through the still night air.

Claudia gently nudged him. 'Damien... Damien?'

'What is it?'

'Are you serenading the two lovebirds?'

'Who?'

'Justin and Anna.'

'No, I'm not. Nicholas and Sophie are much more interesting, mainly because they're an unlikely pair.' He narrowed his eyes and focused on Nicholas's face. 'Look at the way he's gazing at Sophie, all goggle-eyed. He seems obsessed with her, totally consumed, but then look at his chin...'

Damien had stopped circling the glass.

'Yes, it's weak,' Claudia said. 'He's the sort of man who can be buffeted by the wind. Change his mind at any point of time. He's not a safe bet. But he's very charming. Sophie likes that.'

'He's a romantic, like me.' Damien had lassoed the conversation back to himself. 'That's why I'm always disappointed,' he said. 'The reality never matches up to my fantasies...' He winced at what he could guess was playing out beneath the linen tablecloth between Nicholas and Sophie.

'Oh, Sophie,' Nicholas said, 'you're very naughty.' She had slipped her hand under the table and placed it between his thighs.

Put on your social smiley face, Nicholas, thought Damien. *Don't just stare into space, and your mouth – stop gawping.*

Damien felt sorry for him. It was embarrassing. It was obvious that Nicholas was a novice and, in a way, it was cruel of Sophie to initiate him surrounded by acquaintances. Better to be in a restaurant, at a corner table, where the waiters ignored such intimacies.

Mind you, Sophie was an excellent player. A sophisticated mistress of the game with her demure smile as she dipped in and out of random conversations with her friends, and her insouciant laugh when someone made a witty remark.

Damien gave her a wink.

Sophie blew him a kiss with her free hand.

'Nicholas,' she whispered, 'isn't this fun?'

'If you like torture.'

'Oh, I'm sorry…' she said, 'shall we have a coffee break?'

***

In truth, Nicholas wasn't sure how he was going to handle the pay-off.

Sophie tiptoed her fingers down to his knee.

'No, don't stop, please…'

She trotted her fingers up again.

At last, Nicholas was heading for the home run. *Just stay cool, dude. You can do it. Keep that poker face. Nearly there.*

It was all going so well…

Until…

His mobile rang.

Sophie snatched her hand away and Nicholas, his nirvana broken, fumbled for his phone.

'Damn, should have put it on silent. Sod's law,' he said.

Sophie had forgotten how he had the ability to change tack as required.

'Bugger it.' The phone was stuck. He tussled with his trouser pocket.

'Sorry, everyone,' he announced to the guests. The loud marimba ringtone had cut through the muted conversation.

He moved away from the table.

Elizabeth looked profoundly irritated.

'I suggest,' she said, 'that you trot down to the bottom of the garden, if you are going to have a conversation.'

'Thank you,' he said, 'that's exactly what I was going to do.'

He knew that she had never liked him, which surprised Nicholas after his generous donation to her charity.

Well, everyone else seemed to like him. His Aunt Iris said that he had "a devilish charm".

Mind you, there were times when Kate had expressed a deep hatred for him, usually after a bottle of wine.

'You vain bastard,' she had said. 'Just because you flog a few antiques you think that makes you part of the posh set.' She criticised the very essence of his being, spewed her venomous spleen all over him. An abused husband, that's what he used to be.

He didn't miss her one bit.

By the time he'd yanked the phone from his pocket, the ringing had ceased.

He could have left it at that, turned off his mobile and gone back to the table to his fabulous Sophie. But he did not.

He checked the last call… It was Kate. She rang again.

Sophie had followed him to the end of the garden, and surprised Nicholas with a fierce grip on his arm. 'It's your damn wife, isn't it?'

He nodded. His face burned. He was back at the altar, nineteen years old, promising to love, honour and cherish a beautiful young woman.

197

'Nicholas,' Sophie said, 'if you give way this time, I promise you, we're finished.'

'I have to speak to her. It might be about the kids.'

'Well, off you go, then.' She waved him away and turned back towards the table.

Elizabeth caught Sophie's hand as she went back to her chair. 'Best get rid of him, or he'll play with you for the rest of your life.'

At the bottom of the garden, Nicholas plucked a dead leaf off a clematis and crumbled it in his hand. 'What are you talking about, Kate? Who's in hospital?... Greta?... I can't hear you... Stop crying and tell me what happened again... Who hit who?... Oh my goodness, how could you?

'Well, you broke her nose, Kate. Of course she's going to press charges. Why did you punch her?... Oh bloody hell, you mean the guy who fixed our Mac, the computer man?... When did Greta meet him?... Look, main thing is, are the kids okay?'

Nicholas hadn't noticed Sophie standing behind him.

'Give me the phone, you bastard. I want to speak to her.' Sophie fought like a feral cat. Biting and scratching, she wrenched the mobile from his hand.

'Hello, Kate...' she said.

'Who's this?'

'Sophie... your husband's lover...'

Nicholas plucked at the air, trying to retrieve the phone, while Sophie, dodging this way and that, dashed behind the rhododendron bush.

'Still there, Kate?' she said. '...Ah, good... This will only take a minute...'

'Don't.' Nicholas grasped her arm.

'Don't you dare touch me.' Sophie bit his wrist and gave him a swift kick between the legs. She stared at her lover bent over double, holding his groin. He wanted to say something, but all that came out was a gasp. How could she have ever been drawn to such a pathetic man-boy?

She was ready for her parting shot.

'Hi, Kate,' she said. '…No… you can speak to him in a minute… I just wanted to say that he's never going to leave you. He's a loyal hound. So even if you've screwed it up with Greta, he'll still be coming back to you…'

Sophie threw the phone at Nicholas.

'Go back to your wife, two kids and your dogs. You're a lucky man. All I have are your broken promises.'

'Look, I'm sorry. I know I'm a two-faced bastard but I just can't abandon a woman who I've been with for twenty years. She's in a terrible state.' Nicholas had already put the phone to his ear. 'Kate, are you there?… Yes… I'm coming home. No, don't worry, I'll speak to Greta… Yes, I'll try to make it better.'

He was a con artist and she had been caught. Sophie elbowed him out of the way and marched back to the other guests.

Eight faces looked up at her.

'Apologies for the fuss, everyone.' She kept her smiley mask in place and sat on the spare chair next to Damien. 'Nicholas has a domestic drama.'

'So then, after all that lovey-dovey stuff, no happy ending?' he said.

'Please, Damien, I really don't want to talk about it now. It's a party, not a wake.'

'Okay, we can compare notes later.' There was a tiny little bit of him that was pleased.

'How about a toast?' Damien announced to the table and raised his glass. 'To Justin and Anna, may your lives be full of love and happiness forever and a day.'

'To Justin and Anna,' the others chorused.

Damien glanced at Elizabeth. She caught his gaze and gave him a warm smile.

Damien was thrilled. He had a ringing sensation in his ears, which blotted out all sound, save for his rapid heartbeat, banging against his chest.

Don't play the sop, the Voice whispered.

Damien relaxed his face and, lifting his left eyebrow in a devil-may-care sort of way, let his mouth slip into his roguish smile.

Not bad. But try not to look so grateful, said the Voice. *Remember you're an alpha male, not some silly lovesick boy.*

Nicholas slunk past. 'Have to leave, an emergency.' He muttered his apology to Justin and Anna and with a meek goodbye to the other guests he left.

The Voice was tired. *Well, what are you waiting for? Take the lead, claim her. Women like that need a bit of welly.*

'Elizabeth, *andiamo!*' he said.

She laughed. 'Where?'

'To my house.'

'Do you have a spare toothbrush?'

'Oh yes, always a plentiful supply for house guests.'

***

Damien didn't speak as he drove Elizabeth back to his home in Cheyne Walk. He had taken his cue from her silence and let his mind fast-forward to the erotic journey that the night promised.

He was feeling sanguine. The air was sweet, he had his dream woman at his side ready to ride the waves… and so the sudden need to pee surprised him.

Why didn't you go and wee-wee before you left the party? said the Voice. *Remember what Mummy said: always go to the toilet before you travel and especially before you go to bed.*

Elizabeth frowned. 'Are you okay, Damien?'

'Why?'

'You look in distress.'

'No, no, I'm fine…' he lied. They'd arrived, but his neighbour Charlie's Harley-Davidson was parked outside his house.

Like a hunted animal, he drove round the block looking for another space.

No luck. Bugger Charlie's Harley. He swiped the bike with his bumper and knocked it sideways onto the pavement.

'Well, here we are.' He leapt out of the car and potty-danced to the door.

'Don't worry about me,' Elizabeth said. 'You just go and pee.'

Chapter 28

This was the first time she'd been to his place. He'd always been on her turf, save for the weekend at his house in Antibes.

Elizabeth seemed happy for Damien to take the lead. He took her into the living room and made her China tea.

How could she not be moved by the magnificent view from the tall window of the white moonlight casting a mesh of silvery streaks that glittered across the river?

She admired his collection of Pre-Raphaelite masters.

'I found the Millais at an auction in Ireland twenty years ago. *Lady Eden and Her Dog*. Bought it from the sale of my first book.'

He made his move.

'Elizabeth,' he said, devouring her with his eyes, 'how can any man resist you?'

No, Damien, no! You were doing so well. Not with Elizabeth. Stop! Not another of your usual clichés, said the Voice.

Blake's words tripped across his mind.

Never seek to tell thy love
Love that never told can be
For the gentle wind does move
Silently invisibly.

He pulled himself together.

Don't rush things. Change the subject. Make her wait.

'Would you like a game of chess?' he said.

'It's a bit late for that,' she said.

'Well, then...'

It was an easy segue into the bedroom.

He was pleased that his cleaner had changed the sheets that morning.

And yet...

Damien couldn't pretend that she was just another beauty who had fired his lust. He held back. Treated her with gentle respect.

He kissed the nape of her smooth neck, undid the zip of her black silk dress. He slipped it from her shoulders. She was naked, save for a pair of fine lace panties. He slid her onto the bed and kissed each breast, moving his lips down to her navel. But just as he was taking flight, she said, 'Damien, where is your protection?'

He stretched out his hand and fumbled in the bedside drawer.

One left; what a relief. He took the packet and ripped it open with his teeth.

It was an interesting night. Damien performed with sensual grace and expertise.

However, he noticed that Elizabeth seemed distracted.

'I'm sorry, am I boring you?' he said.

'Well, not really,' she replied. 'You're a good lover, but...'

'But what?'

'Have you heard of sexual Gong Fu?'

Damien paused. 'Can't say that I have...'

'It's the Taoist word for sexual mastery.'

'Well, you learn something new every day... Perhaps we should discuss it over a cup of tea?'

'Seriously,' she said, 'I would love to show you some tantric positions that I studied in Tibet.'

Elizabeth flipped him on his back and sat astride him.

'So. Let's start with Shakti Sky Dancing on a Column of Fire,' she said.

***

Sophie had not returned Nicholas's calls. He had tried everything to repair their severed relationship. He even sent a pair of diamond earrings from Asprey, delivered in a bouquet of red roses, which she'd returned to his home address, swapping cards and writing the message to Kate.

My darling, it read. *You are the love of my life. No other woman could replace you. You are my wife and despite my affair my life is with you. If they're not your cup of tea please feel free to give the earrings back to me and I can return them. Forever yours, Nicholas.*

***

Justin and Anna were busy planning their wedding. Not only had she found love again, but she had won the Sunflower Prize for best children's book of the year: a prize of £50,000 and a trip to Disneyland to unveil the newly erected statue of Iver Fortune.

A well-deserved gong, the reviewer from *The Times Literary Supplement* wrote. *"The Dog That Lost Its Bark" is a magical tale. Anna Rose has perfected the art of storytelling without patronising her young readers. The book is exquisitely written but never lets the beauty of the writing distract from the parable.*

Rose has created characters from another era and presents her novel as a period piece without succumbing to the cheap "fast food" writing that has become the norm for boys and girls whose minds have been invaded by aliens, namely Facebook, Twitter and Instagram.

"The Dog That Lost Its Bark" is a simple but beautiful allegory of redemption that serves young readers with a reminder that the hardest heart can be touched and moved to human kindness.

Chapter 29

Damien had sunk deeper into his labyrinthian obsession with Elizabeth. The last session in bed was exquisite. He couldn't think of anything else save for her undulating hips giving him the most thrilling ride since… he couldn't remember.

He ached for her company and in between their meetings to assuage the waves of melancholia he found it soothing to write poetry.

Against his better judgement he sent her…

Damien's Lament

Elizabeth, your goodbye was cool when we did part.
Shall I become an ice man to warm your heart?
A little chill to thrill you?
You have tired of my fire.
The burning coals of my desire
Have quenched your flame,
Leaving you free to roam again
Into your fragrant chamber where you are safe to dream.
And I, who once was your king, must let his passion cease.
But no, I will not throw myself into the hands of such a fate.
Damien will save his warmth
And make Elizabeth miss his soft kisses and sweet embrace.

…but he couldn't play that game. The more he saw her, the worse he became. In truth, he was no longer entertaining. His adoration had become irritating and Elizabeth's enthusiasm for his company had begun to wane.

He couldn't write, couldn't sleep, couldn't eat, hardly talked: "Yes, no, please, thanks."

He should never have asked Elizabeth that question. But after they had made love, the way she looked at him, so soft, with that wisp of a smile – that moment had sent him into a spin.

'The question is,' he'd said, 'what is it that makes people fall madly in love with each other? It's a mysterious process, isn't it? Not a calculated thing.'

You idiot, said the Voice. *You're asking for it. She's going to cut your balls off.*

'I've no idea. I've never been in love,' she said. Her thoughts wandered out of the bedroom.

There you go, said the Voice. *What did I tell you? Now, for God's sake, shut it!*

But Damien pushed on. 'Do you really mean that?' The words skidded out of his mouth.

That's it. Keep on digging your own grave, said the Voice.

'Mean what?' Elizabeth tossed the question back. Her skin crawled. What would he say next? How far would he go? Was he going to change the status quo from a casual, airy relationship, to a masochistic nightmare, where inevitably she held the whip, as she had always done, save for once? But that wasn't love – it was obsession. She buried that corpse deep in her memory.

'Did you really mean it that you've never been in love?' he said.

'Yes. I did.' Sometimes it was fun to hurt.

'So say it,' he said.

'Say what?'

'Just say you don't love me.'

'This is tedious, Damien. Stop.'

He seized her hands and held them to his cheek. 'I can't. I love you.'

Bingo! said the Voice. *You smashed it. Finally made a full-blown arsehole of yourself.*

Why did he take it further? He just couldn't stop. He was in free fall.

Elizabeth watched the emotions chase across Damien's face. Why had she given Chang the night off? She didn't feel safe. His unbridled overflow of emotion suffocated her. Made her feel nauseous. And this was what he called love.

'Say it,' he repeated, and squeezed her hands to his breast.

'I don't love you,' she said, 'but that doesn't mean I don't enjoy your company. It never worried you before. Did you ever love any of the women you slept with? I thought you and I were made of the same metal.'

'We are. That's why I want to marry you.'

Ooh, big mistake! groaned the Voice.

'Please, no. To spend a lifetime watching your partner decay is not for me.'

Damien had withdrawn his hands from hers and grasped his head in despair. A terrible mistake.

He was like all those women he'd caught in his net and thrown back in the sea because they had become needy, wanting more – and now, Sod's law, it was he who was drowning.

Mindful of his dangerous mood, she said, 'Come on, Damien, cool down. Let's have a nightcap,' and she slipped out of bed.

'Thanks,' he said.

Clever Elizabeth knew how to change his mood. Just in case love turned to hate, she slipped her mobile into the pocket of her dressing gown. Chang would be home soon and then she could send Damien on his way.

He looked at the floor, his eyes glazed.

'Elizabeth,' he said, 'can you forgive me?'

'For what?'

'For falling in love with you. For boring you. For being a romantic idiot.'

Elizabeth, high priestess, was taking his confessional.

It reminded him of the time he went to confession after Laura had died. He'd read the priest a list of names of the women he'd slept with while she was alive. It had cost him ten Hail Marys and a Glory Be to free him to sin again.

He had a dangerous look on his face. Elizabeth patted her mobile. He needed defusing.

She took two glasses and poured a tot of cognac in each. 'Yes, I forgive you. A toast to good friends with boundaries. Chin-chin.'

They clinked, her steely gaze holding his just long enough to give him no hope of ever being loved by her.

***

Next morning, Elizabeth called. 'Damien, I'm so sorry to let you down at the last moment, but I think it's best that I go with Javier to Anna's wedding.'

'Who's Javier?' Damien said.

Not clever, said the Voice. *You're digging your own grave. She's going to enjoy tormenting you.*

'A very close friend who understands me,' she replied.

'Elizabeth, is this because of last night?'

'Well, you were behaving very strangely. You just seem to have lost control. All that romantic drivel. You gave me indigestion with your love talk. I like a variety of dishes to excite my tastebuds. And you're just too rich for me…'

'I can change.'

'No, you can't.'

'Just give me a chance.'

'No. You're a self-serving love addict,' she said. 'And I don't want a man who needs me. Javier knows how to please me.'

'You're very cruel.'

'It's for your own good. No point in giving you false hope. Why don't you go to the wedding with Sophie?'

Damien ended the call. He couldn't breathe. His alcohol consumption had increased dramatically over the last few months. He poured the last tot of whisky left in the bottle to numb himself from the pain of unrequited love. He checked his watch. It was only 11 a.m.

Sophie rang.

'Hello, Damien, are we still on for tomorrow?'

'Oh dear, I'm so sorry. I've been in a bit of a rut. Completely forgot.'

'We were meeting for lunch at Lemonia at one.'

'Sophie, I don't really feel up to lunch. Can you come here for coffee instead?'

'What's wrong?'

'I'll tell you when I see you. Can you come around 11 a.m.?'

'Sure. See you then.'

Damien looked at the empty bottle and opened the drinks cabinet. No more whisky. He unlocked the drawer of his writing desk and took out the silver box with his engraved initials. Inside was a little white packet, a razor blade and a neatly rolled banknote.

He sniffed the last line of coke and called Aidan.

'This evening, my place. Five grams… Okay, four hundred quid, that's fine.'

Now come on, Damien, don't mess things up, said the Voice.

All those cat-and-mouse games and Elizabeth had finally shut him down. "Needy is not sexy," Sophie's words echoed in his head, and now he'd blown it.

Chapter 30

When Sophie arrived, Damien was still in his silk pyjamas. He was on the phone.

'Not enough. I want a bigger advance. Fuck you, Angus. I made you... I'll self-publish if you keep on selling me short. Now piss off and do your job.'

'Damien. What's wrong with you?' Sophie said. 'You look and sound possessed. Why are you screaming at your agent like that?'

'Sophie... don't interfere.' He shot her a blind, hateful glance. The blood rush turned his pale skin an angry purple.

Her eyes fell on the writing desk where the white powder was equally divided into ten lines.

'How much have you had, Damien?' she asked in a calm voice.

'Enough to fire my gun at that bitch Elizabeth,' he said, and moved towards the desk.

Sophie tried to pull him away, but he'd already taken the banknote and was about to sniff another line of coke when she pushed his arm aside and blew the white powder into a dust cloud that settled on the Persian carpet.

Damien fell to his knees. Nose to the ground, he moved across the rug like a hog searching for truffles.

'For goodness' sake, Damien – stop!' Sophie took hold of

his neck. 'If this is what love does to you, better to just screw around.'

Damien shook his head violently from side to side. 'Leave me alone! Don't tell me what to do. You're not my mother.'

Sophie held her grip. 'Thank goodness I'm not. But I'm your friend and I love you.'

'Don't give me all that lovey-dovey talk.' He crawled across the floor, dragging her with him.

'Damien, behave. I'm not letting you go. You need to cool down.'

He turned to face her.

'Why? What's it to you? You're not really interested in who I am. How do you think I feel always playing your therapist? Listening to your bullshit about a shitty little married man who sees you as a treat.'

'Well,' Sophie said. 'Carry on. You can slag him off all you want. To tell you the truth it makes me feel better.'

They lay on the rug beside each other. Damien closed his eyes. Coaxing his breath to centre him. He inhaled deeply and then blew his breath out with a whoosh.

Here I am again, said the Voice. *Have you missed me? It's been a while, but you've been in no fit state to listen to my words of wisdom.*

'So what's next for Nicholas and me?' she asked.

Damien paused and shut his eyes. 'Wait… it's coming to me. Okay,' he said, opening his eyes again. 'Here's the scenario. Mr Creep really yearned for some fiddle dee dee with Mistress Hanky Panky. There really wasn't much going on at home. Bedtimes were boring. Too many years of same-old, same-old. He tried a couple of new tricks Mistress Hanky Panky taught him, but his wife was more interested in going to sleep. So it was lights out at ten and time for Mr Creep's bedtime treat. He shut his eyes, fiddled with himself and thought of his beautiful Mistress Hanky Panky, conjuring up fond memories of those passionate nights… But of course he wants her back. Wants to stroke her smooth, silky flesh, taste her sweet, salty neck as they pleasure each other—'

Okay, Damien, slow down. Too many adjectives. Keep it clean. Keep calm, said the Voice.

Damien stopped short. 'Anyway, Nicholas has all the luck. I don't even have a fond memory. Elizabeth was always a bitch and now she's fucking someone else. Talk about being a stupid prick. That's me.' He prodded his chest hard.

'Come on,' sighed Sophie. 'You're getting all fired up again. You need a cold shower.'

She helped him to his feet and holding his hand guided him up the stairs and into the bathroom. She pulled off his pyjama top and pushed him into the shower.

He wanted to pull her in with him, but he didn't.

She switched on the cold water and he screamed.

'What the hell are you doing? Are you trying to give me hypothermia?'

Sophie was wet herself, but she was determined to get Damien back into the world.

'Calm down,' she said. 'You need this.'

'Sure, like a hole in the head.'

Damien banged his shoulder against the tiled wall of the cubicle and let the icy water waken him.

Sophie looked at the fallen angel. She wanted to save him. He was shaking.

'Can you turn off the water, Damien?' she asked, and he twisted the tap, his hands slipping.

She grabbed a towel and, wrapping it round him, rubbed him dry. They were very close. She patted his damp cheek.

'Why are we punishing ourselves?' he whispered. 'I've been shafted by Miss Ice Queen Elizabeth, who grabbed me by the balls, and you're still in love with Mr Creep. Admit it. You're wavering. One more wag of his finger and you're back.'

'Not true.'

'Come on, Sophie, admit it.'

'No. I've had enough. I'm moving on.'

'Lucky you. My problem is I'm still obsessed with Elizabeth.'

'Is it love or passion?' Sophie said.

'I don't know.' He looked at Sophie like a little boy, his eyes unfocused as she put his pyjama top back on him.

'I'm really ashamed, Sophie,' he said. 'I've behaved like a pillock. Letting her kick me in the balls.'

Sophie couldn't help but smile. 'Pillock! You really are hilarious, Damien. Come on now. You need to rest.'

Sophie took him to bed, tucked him in and kissed him on his forehead. His skin tasted damp and salty.

'You're still sweating.' She passed him the glass of water on the bedside table. 'Drink up.' He obediently gulped it down and she refilled his glass from the jug.

'So shall we call it a day?' she said.

Now don't get any ideas. You're in no shape to perform, warned the Voice.

'Yes. I don't think either of us is ready to begin again.'

Chapter 31

Evelyn rang Anna to tell her what she perceived as very good news.

'Sophie has been looking after Damien,' said Evelyn. 'But my intuition tells me there's more to it than that. They are each other's confidants. Damien and his obsession with that hard-hearted Elizabeth and Sophie's unspeakable relationship with that nasty little rat Nicholas will soon run their course and hopefully they will both see the light. They are made for each other. I just know it.'

Evelyn's monologue had thrown Anna into a state of confusion.

Sophie had usurped her. Not that Anna would have been a good nurse. But Damien turned her on: mind and body. She missed the sex and fun.

Fuelled by a burning curiosity about her relationship with Damien, Anna orchestrated a rendezvous with her sister.

***

They arranged to meet at the Chelsea Physic Garden. One of London's secret delights.

Its sheltered walls whispered tales of centuries past, bursting with medicinal herbs and edible wonders.

Anna and Sophie greeted each other with an awkward hug.

But after the initial chill, things warmed up as they walked through the peaceful grounds.

Caught up in another world, the vivid colours of summer flowers and sounds of birdsong were enough to distract them for a while.

Sophie caught herself thinking of Damien when they walked past the medicinal herbs.

It was one of his favourite places.

He had taken her there after one of their Sunday lunches, which were usually catch-ups about their respective doomed relationships.

'I never tire of standing in the midst of all these miracles that are so vital to modern medicine,' he had said. 'This is one of Elizabeth's treasured spots too. As a perfumer, she appreciates the magic of these plants. And she's as fascinated by their history as I am. Did you know that in Mesopotamia the written study of herbs and botanicals dates back over 5,000 years to the Sumerians, who created clay tablets with lists of hundreds of medicinal plants including myrrh and opium?'

Sophie's mind wandered back to Damien's drug-infused foray. She wondered how he was. Perhaps she'd call in later today.

Anna cut into her thoughts. 'Where are you, Sophie? What's on your mind? You seem so distracted.'

She shouldn't have asked. Why torture herself? And, yes, the answer came, just as expected.

'I'm worried about Damien,' Sophie said.

'Oh, so maybe there's more to your friendship than meets the eye.' Anna's mouth twitched involuntarily.

'I have to say I'm very drawn to him. He's such a firebrand. But there's also a vulnerability that brings out the mother in me. Maybe one day we'll find each other when we both wake up.'

'Good luck to you,' Anna said, tight-lipped. 'He's a great guy. Tell you one thing, though, he's a wonderful lover,' she added smugly.

'Good to know,' Sophie replied. She looked away.

'Anyway, at least he's free,' Anna said. 'Better than having your heart twisted in knots obsessed with somebody else's husband.'

You're waiting for me to bite back, Anna, but I won't, thought Sophie. *I'm not going to give you the pleasure of hurting me.*

They had walked out of the herb garden, past the climbers. Sophie focused on a butterfly that had attached itself to the ivy.

'Look. How pretty, Anna.'

'Seriously.' Anna's mouth twitched again. 'Have things moved on with you and Damien?'

'Why are you asking?'

'Because I don't want the pictures in my head.'

'But you're getting married. Aren't you in love with Justin?'

Anna looked askance at her sister. 'To be honest, I'm not sure I want to have this deep and meaningful chat just before I get hitched.'

But Sophie continued digging. 'Just that when you talk about him, I don't think you've ever used the word love.'

'Look, I'm very fond of him. Justin's a really good man and I respect him.'

'But is that enough?'

'Please, little sister, don't give me your romantic nonsense. The important thing is he adores me. Propelled me into becoming a leading children's writer, and what's more, I know that he would never, ever look at another woman.'

'I suppose we're made of different stuff. The earth has to move for me,' Sophie said. 'And from the way you're talking, he doesn't seem to steam you up.'

'What are you suggesting? That we don't have a good sex life?' Anna stuck out her chin and gave her sister a belligerent look. 'Are you trying to throw me off course before my marriage just because you've had a rough ride? Justin loves me and I feel a great affection for him. Surely that's better than being the sneaky bit on the side for a married man.' She punctuated her words with a thin, sarcastic smile.

Sophie wanted to leave. But instead she took Anna's arm and gently steered her towards the cafeteria.

'Come on, let's have a glass of wine. Just think – you're marrying a guy who is besotted with you. Remember Mummy's motto: "Always choose a man who loves you more than you love him and then you'll be a happy wife".'

Chapter 32

Maybe it would have been different if he hadn't been alone the night before the wedding. Maybe if Sophie had been there. But she had gone to her sister's hen party.

Damien was left with his thoughts for company. Bad thoughts. And in his misery, he had snorted six lines of cocaine and drunk a bottle of whisky.

Come the day, he was lying on the sofa with a nosebleed, dabbing his nostrils with a sheet of toilet paper, when Sophie rang.

'I'm not going to make it to the church, Sophie. Go without me,' he said.

'Thanks, Damien. I've been waiting for you for forty minutes and you didn't even have the good grace to tell me you weren't coming.'

'Sophie, just don't hassle me. I'll show up this evening. You know I've had a terrible week.'

He turned off his mobile and closed his eyes. He didn't want to listen to the increasingly vitriolic phone messages that his agent had left him over the last couple of days.

Damien had screwed up on the deal with Netflix, and he'd been so out of it for the last month that he'd forgotten to finish the screenplay of *Writing in the Sand*.

He'd finally drifted off to sleep when the insistent chime of the electric doorbell woke him.

'Okay… okay! I hear you.' He staggered to the entry phone, eyes half shut. 'Who is it?' he demanded. 'God help you if you're Bible pushers. I really don't care if Jesus is coming back. Although, on second thoughts, he could be quite useful if I run out of vino.'

'It's your agent, in case you've forgotten you have one,' Angus said.

'Well, how thoughtful of you to come and remind me.'

'Stop fooling around, Damien. Where's the bloody script?'

'In my head, Angus, don't worry. Just need another few weeks to write it down. I'm very busy at the moment. Can I call you later?'

'No,' Angus said firmly. 'I want to see you face to face.'

'Okay, okay… just a second. I'm coming.' He threw on his dressing gown, staggered down the stairs and flung open his front door. 'Here I am.' Damien stood barefoot in the doorway, squinting at the sunlight. 'How can I help you, Angus? What's the trouble?'

'You're the bloody trouble,' Angus replied, staring at the dried blood caked round the edges of Damien's nostrils and the grubby white piqué dressing gown. 'You look terrible. For goodness' sake, let me in.'

'Of course.' Damien bowed and waved him through with a flourish. 'Please excuse the mess… To be honest, I've been preoccupied with personal matters and my last cleaner has gone back to Ireland. I think she only came here to have an abortion. Went off without any warning.'

Angus stood gaping at the slices of chewed pepperoni pizza, which had migrated from the cardboard box directly onto the surface of the coffee table, the empty whisky bottle lying on its side, an open wallet, a credit card and three rolled-up banknotes.

'Oh, my God, you self-sabotaging fool, you need to get yourself sorted out.'

He scanned Damien's glazed, dark-rimmed, soulless eyes. 'What sort of psychodrama are you creating this time?'

'Elizabeth's the trigger. I know I've always been a mad muller, but this time the evil witch has pushed me right to the edge of the cliff and I'm about to fall off and to tell you the truth I don't give a damn. It's my karmic punishment. I swear to God, if Laura was still alive, I would treasure her and never touch another woman again. What a fool I was. I could have saved her. Instead, I screwed everything that moved, and she knew it.' Damien bit the back of his hand.

Angus grasped his arm. 'Don't do that!' He hated histrionics from anyone. And his star writer was losing his grip. 'Look, I feel sorry for you,' he said, 'but what gives you the right to screw up things for everyone else? If you don't deliver the screenplay by the end of next week, my reputation will be in the shit. They'll say I can't handle the horses in my stable. The deadline was yesterday. You've been given a huge advance – how could you be so irresponsible?'

'Money,' Damien said. 'Sometimes it gets in the way and obstructs the path of my existential angst, but essentially I know my journey is between me and God.'

'Don't give me that esoteric gibberish.' Angus waved at the table of powdery residue. 'What else have you been taking?'

'Just a touch of MDMA, Angus. You should try some. You'll feel all loved up and want to kissy cuddle everyone. Anyway, it's been a pleasure speaking with you, but I'm sorry, you'll have to go. I need to get dressed for a wedding reception.'

'I don't think you can pull back from this one, Damien. You've broken the clause in your contract. I only hope that you haven't sniffed all the advance up your nose, because I am certainly not bailing you out.' And he was gone.

Damien's nose had started bleeding again. He went to the bathroom, took another sheet of toilet paper and pushed it into his nostrils. He pressed his face to the bathroom mirror. 'Just between you and me,' he whispered, 'I think my time's up.' His hot breath clouded his reflection.

Pull yourself together, Damien Spur, you selfish bastard, and get dressed, the Voice said.

'I don't know where my clip-on dickie is.'

Next to the self-tie in the box on top of your dresser, the Voice said.

Damien smiled at himself. 'Clip-on dickie, best friend when you're high.'

Try not to make a fool of yourself, the Voice said.

'But it's going to hurt seeing Elizabeth with another man... Well then, see you later. Please don't give up on me.'

You need to listen to me, Damien. I know you better than anyone, the Voice said.

Damien showered and struggled into his clothes. Thank God his nose had stopped bleeding.

'Bloody hell! Where are all my cufflinks?' Damien had opened the left-hand drawer of his desk where he kept them in a small velvet pouch.

He fumbled around the inside of the drawer.

No luck; gone. And where was the Movado fob watch that his father had left him, and the little leather box with Laura's wedding band?

All gone. Save for Laura's love letters; her legacy. A punishment that served as a reminder of what a bastard he had been. He didn't need to read them. The words were etched in his head.

Every time you leave, my soul weeps.

I know that you love me,

but my mind is in the way, Damien.

My body won't let me say what I feel.

He pushed her to the back of his mind. At this rate he wouldn't even make the reception.

But who was the thief? Was it the temporary cleaner who stood in while Marta was away on holiday last week? Or was it

Yulia, the sexy Russian blonde he'd met at a nightclub in Regent Street the weekend before? Most likely it was her.

'Are you free this evening?' he'd asked transfixed. 'Can I buy you a drink?' Here she was in the flesh. The fantasy queen from his schoolboy days with her glossy voluptuous lips and large firm breasts accentuated by a tight red satin dress.

She had given him a playful smile. 'I am not free, but for you being so handsome, I will give you a special price, £800 for the whole night.'

So he'd brought her back to his flat, and had fallen asleep on the job.

In the morning when he woke, she'd gone and so had the £50 notes left in his wallet on the bedside table.

He cursed her and ripped off the smart silk shirt with French cuffs and put on a foppish chemise with a jabot and a black velvet suit.

'Randy Dandy, I am,' he said to the mirror. 'Fuck the bow tie.'

Calm down, said the Voice.

He waited in the road for the Uber. He needed some air. His own company had begun to frighten him, and he was relieved to see the elegant black Mercedes slow down in front of his house. He flung the door open and settled himself in the back on the black leather seat.

'Very nice car. I always go for the executive class. Those standard Priuses are such ugly buggers. Where are you from, driver?' he said.

'Guess.'

'Iran.'

'No. Try again.'

'Armenia?'

'That's right!'

'How long have you been living here?' Damien said.

'Ten years.'

'And where do you live?' Damien liked hearing the drivers' stories. It stopped him thinking about himself.

'Cricklewood,' he replied.

'Ah, very central. Are you married?'

'Yes.'

'Does your wife work?'

'No, she look after our two children.' The driver looked around thirty, his strong features softened by deep-set, gentle eyes. He wore a spotless, well-pressed shirt.

'And she cooks for all of you?'

'Of course. How else to eat?'

'What a lucky man you are,' Damien said. 'And what does she cook?'

'Everything,' he said. 'Lamb, dolma, beef and aubergine… and sometimes she make English food. Roast chicken, shepherd's pie and stew with dumplings.'

'Love to come to dinner,' Damien said, and gave the driver a smile.

The driver looked uncomfortable.

'Come on, I'm not serious.' He took a £10 note from his wallet.

'For your wife,' he said. 'She is fast becoming extinct.'

By the time the driver pulled up outside Quaglino's, he and Damien were talking like old friends. He waved Damien farewell, pocketing the tip, and Damien squared his shoulders, walking tall as he approached the doorman.

'Good evening, sir.'

Damien offered a mock salute. 'I'm here for the wedding… Spur… Damien Spur,' he said.

You're so bloody late, the Voice said. *Fancy arriving at ten for a reception that started at seven. Terribly rude.*

'Look, just leave me alone,' Damien muttered. 'You're embarrassing me.'

'I'm sorry, sir,' the doorman said. 'What did you say?'

'Nothing, just talking to myself. Open sesame, please. I'm dying for a pee.'

'Downstairs on the left, sir.'

In the quiet of the bathroom, Damien winked at himself in the mirror. 'No one here. Now, then.' He tweaked the frill of his white silk jabot. 'You look a bit pale, but apart from that, not bad for a nutter.'

You look great. Just be your amusing, erudite self, the Voice said.

'If you say so.' Damien slipped his hand in his trouser pocket. 'Just one for luck. Have to be the party me, now.'

Don't, you mad bugger, the Voice said.

'Why should I listen to you?' Damien said.

Because I'm the Voice of Reason – and you're out of line.

'Oh no I'm not.' Damien took a folded paper from his trouser pocket and waved it in the air. 'You stay outside,' he said to the Voice, and slammed the door of the cubicle.

***

Ten minutes later, Damien, wedged against the wall at the back of the room, unseen by anyone, watched the passionate couple dance the paso doble.

'Oh, Javier, you snake, that's great. Give the bitch what she wants,' he whispered to himself.

The handsome Argentinian swivelled his body this way and that while Elizabeth dipped and swayed, making beautiful shapes as she circled him.

Damien bit his lip. The jabot felt tight round his neck. A waiter was passing. He grabbed his arm.

'Bring me a glass of white, please.'

'Of course, sir. Where are you sitting?'

'I'm staying here. Don't you know it's bad manners to interrupt a performance? You stand at the back and wait till it's over.'

'Yes, sir.'

'Well, what do you think?'

'About what, sir?'

'The couple dancing.'

The waiter paused. 'I think they look in love,' he said.

'What the fuck? I didn't ask you that. He's the matador and she's the bloody cape. I was asking you whether you thought they caught the spirit of the dance. The story. You're from Spain, aren't you?'

'Yes, I'm from Cordoba.'

'Well then, surely you should know the paso doble.'

'Yes, but... I didn't understand what you meant. I just think they look hot for each other.'

'Do me a favour. Undo the button at the back of my neck.'

'Sir...'

'Do you want me to have a heart attack? Okay, okay, leave it.' He tugged at the jabot and pulled it apart. 'Anyway. Here's the question. Do you know what's missing?' Damien crossed his arms, his flushed face dripping with sweat.

'Where?'

'In the dance, you fool. You don't know shit. The bull... the bull. That's what's missing.' The waiter drew breath to speak, but Damien pushed past him. 'I've had it. Fuck the glass of wine.'

He made a swift beeline to the nearest table of guests. 'Good evening,' he said. 'I apologise for the interruption, but do you have a couple of spare forks?'

'That's a strange request,' said a woman with spiky blonde hair and large breasts.

Damien glanced beside her plate. 'Look, here's one. You only need to eat ice cream with a spoon, so there's no problem.' He took her fork, and scanned the table. 'And I'll take this one.' He plucked another resting next to a piece of chocolate cake.

'I haven't finished yet,' said a plump woman with a tiny mouth and curly dark hair.

'Well, if I were you,' Damien replied, 'I would have chosen the strawberries instead.'

He blew her a kiss and swivelled round to address the other astonished guests.

'These are my horns.' He placed a fork on each side of his head, puffed out his chest and charged, deftly weaving his way through the tables to the edge of the dance floor.

Don't, the Voice said. *You crazy fool. No point in going any further. The bull always loses.*

'Not me – you'll see,' Damien shouted.

Sophie, who had left her table to help her drunken mother find a cab, returned just in time to see Damien's extraordinary behaviour.

'What are you doing? Where have you been? You look terrible,' she said.

He turned to her and wiggled the forks. 'I'm feeling horny.'

'Please, Damien, let me take you home. You're not well. Your eyes, they're so red! And you're shaking. Please, let me help you.' Sophie took his arm.

'Leave me alone,' he said, and pushed her aside.

Damien dipped his head, flared his nostrils and pawed his foot. 'Stiffen the sinews, summon up the blood. Disguise fair nature with hard-favour'd rage.' He narrowed his eyes focusing on his enemy. 'God for Harry, England, and Saint George! Let's go!'

The lovesick rival charged.

'Javieeeeeeeer,' he roared.

Javier, who had previously been oblivious to all but the dance, seeing crazy Damien come for him armed with forks, nimbly ducked.

'Okay, let's play the game properly,' the Argentinian said, and with a flourish swiped a cloth from a nearby table.

Damien, who had sprinted past him, spun round and paused to stamp his foot, the forks still held to his head, ready to charge again.

Elizabeth smiled, thrilled to see two men fight, beguiled by her beauty.

If only they both had guns, she thought, *now that would be sport.*

There was a silence in the room. The bride and groom sat like king and queen, watching the horror unfold.

Damien was ready. It was exciting. 'Come on, the crowd is waiting,' he said to himself.

No, said the Voice, *you'll regret it.*

'Leave me alone. This is my show. Don't try and stop me. I'm super-charged. I can take on anybody.'

The thoughts pounded in his head.

He crouched down, eyes straight ahead.

The taunting matador brandishing the tablecloth struck the floor with his foot. Suavely, he pivoted and shuffled back as Damien rushed through the makeshift cape.

'*Olé*,' the guests chanted, swept up by the macabre dance.

Damien, incensed that he'd missed his target, charged again, but this time fell. The forks clattered across the floor as a rivulet of blood trickled from Damien's temple.

'Oh my goodness, is he dead?' Sophie cried.

'Don't be ridiculous.' Elizabeth laughed, and stepped over him.

'That's it, old boy.' Justin appeared. 'Thanks for the show, but now it's time to go home.'

Damien struggled to his feet and, smiling at the victor, bowed.

'Pride comes before a fall,' he said as the groom led him through the guests to the exit.

Justin hoisted Damien into the back of the taxi. He was a lot heavier than he looked. 'Come on, old boy, need a bit of compliance here.'

Damien tugged at the lapels of his friend's dinner jacket. 'Stay with me.'

The smell of his sweat made Justin queasy. 'Take him to 22 Cheyne Walk,' he said, and gave the driver a £20 note. 'And look after him.'

The car pulled into the traffic. Damien curled himself into a foetal position and wept. What had he become? A tragic disappointment of a man who had sunk into the abyss of unrequited love. Waves of nausea swept through his body. The throbbing in his head had fogged his brain, obscuring all reason. He wanted to die.

'Driver, let me out at the river. I need to walk. I need some air.'

'Whereabouts, mate?'

'Waterloo. Walk will do me good. Take me to the bridge.'

'Are you sure? Your mate asked me to keep an eye on you,' the driver said.

'Yes. I need to breathe. It's nearer than my house. Can't talk any more. Feel very sick.'

'Right, mate. Please don't throw up in my cab.' He sped down the empty streets, a brief ride to the bridge.

Damien clambered out of the taxi and fell onto the pavement. Grasping the open door, he pulled himself to his feet.

'Thank you, driver.' He fumbled in his pocket, took a five-pound note from his wallet and thrust it into the cab driver's hand. 'Buy yourself a drink, my man.'

'It's nearly midnight, mate. I'm going home to the wife.'

'You're a lucky chap, having a good woman waiting for you.'

The cabbie looked worried. 'Think I might have a coffee at the all-nighter round the corner. Shall I get you one?'

'No, thanks. You go home.' Damien gave him a hint of a smile. 'Give your wife a cuddle from me.'

The stillness of the river at night did not calm his dark thoughts.

He staggered past a grimy old man asleep in a cardboard box. At the entrance of the bridge, he focused on the ornate riverside lamp post a few feet ahead. He grasped the railings and pulled himself along. Reaching the metal post, he clamped his legs around the circumference and levered himself up the pole. Finally, at the top, he grasped the neck of the lamp and looked down at the glittering water.

'I am a king without a throne,' he shouted at the moon.

He held his breath and then, with a silent prayer, plunged into the river. The icy water flooded his eyes and mouth, and the powerful current dragged him along, miraculously propelling him to the edge of the bank.

He grabbed the safety chain and held on while the water gushed beneath his feet. His hands were frozen stiff and he was losing his grip. 'Oh God, please help me,' he pleaded.

'Hold on to my hand, mate,' a man's voice said.

'Who are you?' Damien said. 'Am I dreaming?'

'No.' A firm hand grasped his wrist. 'Now come on, mate, give me a bit of help.'

Damien grabbed the eyebolt with his other hand and found a foothold on the wall.

The man managed to lift him out of the water and Damien collapsed on the verge, his body covered in mud. His eyes half closed, he looked up at the man. 'Are you an angel?' he said.

'I'm the cabbie, mate. Thought you looked as if you were going to do yourself a damage, so I stuck around.'

'Don't have any money.'

'No worries, mate. I'm taking you to hospital.'

Chapter 33

Damien was flying to the moon on sedatives. He had the undivided attention of three other men in the Dolphin Ward at St Pancras Hospital, who were fascinated by his sonorous outbursts in Latin. The two glamorous women by his bedside added the eye candy.

'*Genua placet peullis.*' He lifted his hands and gently patted Sophie's and Claudia's heads.

'Can you please translate?' Sophie asked.

'Maidens, please kneel,' he said. 'You are strangers in a strange land.'

The women exchanged nods and knelt at either side of his bed.

'Feed me the grapes, please. When in Rome…'

Sophie plucked one from the bowl on the bedside table and popped it in his mouth.

'I'm waiting,' he said to Claudia.

'Oh, Caesar, I am your willing slave, but first I will peel the grape,' she said, carefully stripping the pale green skin. 'There.' She delicately slipped it between his lips.

'After you've finished with him, could you both come over to me?' asked the cheerful plumber in the adjacent bed.

Happy to provide the entertainment, even in his weakened state, Damien had managed to charm the nurses into giving him extra attention.

He was good at feigning pain. Clutching his head and moaning produced a couple of paracetamol, admittedly a poor substitute for the codeine, but what he really looked forward to at night were the sleeping pills.

Even in his weakened state, he had managed to sign the form giving Sophie full authority to discuss his medical condition.

'Just don't sell me down the river,' he had said to her. 'I don't want to find myself in some goddamn awful rehab in a padded cell doing cold turkey. I'm a man who needs weaning, Sophie.'

***

Four days later, Damien was ready to be released from the ward, and Sophie was summoned.

'The hospital has treated Mr Spur for hypothermia,' the psychiatrist said. 'But according to his mental status examination he needs intensive drug and alcohol addiction therapy before he can be given psychiatric help.'

'I understand,' Sophie said. 'So what would you suggest?'

'I'd like to give you this list of rehabilitation centres, some of which are covered by insurance. He would really benefit from a residential programme. If you wish me to do so, I would be happy to give Mr Spur a referral.' He handed her the sheet of paper.

Sophie slipped it into her bag. 'Thank you so much. I'll go through the list with him and try to sort things out as soon as possible.'

'That's good.' He gave her a serious nod. 'But meanwhile, and this is key, he shouldn't be left alone for any length of time. Will someone be staying with him?'

'I will,' she said. 'At least for a few days until we can sort out a rehab programme.'

***

Damien sat on the edge of the mattress, clutching a Waitrose bag with his belongings.

The plumber smiled at Sophie. 'Taking him home?' he said. 'Can't say I'm sorry. He's such a plonker, shouting and swearing all night.' He eyed the tangerines and a couple of bananas on Damien's bedside table. 'Anyway, if you don't want the fruit… can I have it? Shame for it to go to waste.'

Damien, the sexy intellectual, darling of countless women who would lay down their arms and gladly surrender to his advances, had been reduced to a plonker.

'No, you slimy little bastard. I wouldn't even give you my spit,' said Damien.

Sophie swept away Damien's hand as he tried to grab the fruit. She gave it to the man.

'Do you have a pen and paper?' the man asked Sophie.

'I've got a pen.' She took it out of her bag and handed it to him.

'Right then, give us your wrist,' he said.

Sophie looked at Damien and giggled.

She stretched out her arm.

'If you ever need your drain fixed, give me a call. Don't forget to write it down before you wash it off,' he said.

***

Sophie had tried to make sure that Damien was safe. She and Claudia had cleared his stash of tranquillizers and opiates, but his mind was still playing tricks.

He saw things at night. His mummy, standing by his bedside wagging her finger. 'Pull yourself together,' she said. 'You're a big boy now.'

But usually it was Nanny who came to him. She was kind. 'You're a clever chap. Just try to keep your nose clean.'

And one very special night his beloved father came to him.

'Remember, my son, the words of Confucius,' he said. '*Our greatest glory is not in never falling, but in rising every time we fall.*'

The next morning, Sophie's call had irritated the Voice.

Damien had been so excited about the visit from his father that he had forgotten to put his mobile on silent. The ring had woken him from his pleasant sleep.

Well, we know who that is, don't we? groaned the Voice. *Nurse Sophie. She really gets on my wick. Always interrupting our chats. Wouldn't mind if she was interested in you as a brilliant man rather than as a poor, wounded eunuch. That's the problem. She turns you on. She makes you grumpy, cos you want some rumpy-pumpy.*

Damien stretched out his arm. Blindly patting his hand on the bedside table, he knocked over a glass of water.

He picked up the dripping phone, flipped it on loudspeaker and threw it on the duvet cover.

'Damien, where are you?' Sophie asked.

'Dammit! I'm at home in bed! Where else would I be? And now I'm soaking wet. Knocked a glass of water over. Thanks, Sophie. Why do you have to keep on checking up on me?'

'I'm sorry. I just wanted to make sure you were okay.'

'I was – until you rang. Now I'm stuck. Haven't got the strength to get up. Can't change the sheets. Cleaner isn't coming.'

'That's all right. I was going to pop in anyway. I'll change your bedding.'

Sophie was outside the Italian deli. She had bought him some fresh pasta, a jar of pesto sauce and a slice of tiramisu.

When she arrived at Damien's house, she phoned him first.

'Hi, Damien, it's only me. I'm here.'

She let herself in with the spare set of keys he had given her.

He had to admit that it felt good. Made him feel secure. He trusted her.

He pretended that he had gone back to sleep. Let her wake him. He liked that.

'Damien,' she whispered. He could feel her warm breath on his neck. He wanted to turn round and kiss her, but he didn't.

Come on, old boy, go for it, said the Voice. *Aren't you fed up with the nursey bit?*

She gently shook his shoulder.

'I'll change the sheets,' she said.

Sophie calmed him nearly as much as the Voice did. Even when he'd been overcome by his demons, the boom-boom cocaine and enough whisky to sink a ship, she had somehow managed to cool his head. Talk him down.

Damien got out of bed. She deftly stripped the damp sheets and replaced them with fresh ones from the ottoman.

'You can stay forever if you like,' he said in a jokey-serious sort of way.

Sophie kissed his forehead. 'That's quite an invitation. But not necessarily the best timing. I can't see myself as a full-time nurse.'

Yes, but she's a good mummy. Probably why you're drawn to her. Poor, starving little lamb. You just want a bit of TLC.

He was seven years old again. Standing in the garden, watching his mother making small talk after the funeral while he tried to be a big boy. Trying not to cry. Daddy's dead. Be brave. Or Mummy will ignore you.

Come on, Damien, the past is done.

Sophie flitted about, served his lunch. Spent the day with him. Filled it with light chatter.

But the Voice was getting jumpy.

I need to talk to you, Damien. You should be getting on with your screenplay, but it's difficult with Sophie always being here. Best thing, why don't you send her shopping?

'She hates leaving me. Worries that I'll do something terrible.'

Go on, speak to her. Tell her that you fancy some edamame beans. And she could also buy you some orange pekoe tea! the Voice said.

It was Sunday afternoon. The Voice knew that the supermarkets closed early, but there was a rather smart delicatessen in World's End that stocked unusual items. It stayed open till 6 p.m.

At least, the Voice said, *we'll have an hour by ourselves.*

'Sophie,' Damien shouted from his bed. 'Can you come here, please?'

'Edamame beans?' she said, wide-eyed at his request.

'Yes, please. And the tea.'

'Well, I'll try. Not sure about the beans, though.'

'Thank you so much, Sophie,' Damien said. 'I really appreciate you looking after me. I'm sure you'll be able to get the tea, but if there's a problem with the edamame you could get a portion from the Japanese restaurant in Parsons Green.'

'I see. Okay!' she said brightly. 'Are you sure you'll be all right?'

'Of course, Sophie. I enjoy my own company.'

***

'Who am I?' When he was at last alone with the Voice, Damien looked at his reflection in the bathroom mirror. The face stared back with glassy fish eyes, ash-grey skin, a tight white mouth.

Look, you miserable fucker, pull yourself together, said the Voice.

'Can't,' Damien said. 'I'm gone, like *Writing in the Sand*, washed away.'

No, you're not. The cold water woke you up when you tried to top yourself, the Voice said. *Not worth dying for a woman who doesn't love you.*

'You're right. I need to fight my monsters, clear that witch Elizabeth out of my head,' Damien said.

The phone rang.

'Guess who?' Elizabeth crooned.

Would you believe it? said the Voice. *She's bloody psychic. You say her name and – bang – she's ready to torment you all over again. Now, Damien, don't get sucked in.*

'Why are you calling me?' he said.

'Claudia told me that you tried to kill yourself,' she said.

What's it to you? the Voice whispered in his head. *Go on, say it, say it.*

But the words didn't come.

'Damien… are you there?' Elizabeth said.

'Not all there.' He watched the man in the mirror shake his head. 'But I'm going to say something that you should hear. I just have to wait for good advice.'

'Who's there with you?'

'A friend who makes sure that I'm okay. My minder.'

'Shall I send Chang?' Elizabeth said. 'He can make sure you're all right.'

Why should she send her servant? She should come herself. Tell that cold fish to go to hell, said the Voice.

Damien smiled at himself in the mirror.

'Elizabeth, you icy bitch, go to hell.'

***

Damien opened his iPad and looked at the beginning of the screenplay. He scanned the words – but his mind was elsewhere.

He unlocked the drawer and took out Laura's letters. So many he had read when they'd first wed. So much love.

And then her pain, when he'd slept with Anne, Miranda, Rosie…

And here amongst the fragments of unhappiness, the debris of their lives, was the last letter, unopened, dated 11 September. The one he couldn't bear to read.

She had, in true Laura style, waited for a significant day to kill herself. A day that Damien would remember forever: their wedding anniversary.

Come on, the Voice said, *it's time to read the last chapter. All good thrillers must come to an end.*

Damien slid a paper knife across the edge of the envelope and opened the neatly folded page.

I have started this letter again and again. It's not easy for me to confess my deepest secret that no doubt will cause you pain. But maybe what I am going to say will in some way justify your dalliances. You have always said you loved my mind and indeed, if we were disembodied souls, I am sure that we would have lived and died together as faithful as swans. But you and I have ended in the trash heap. If only I had been honest, it might have been different. But you took all the blame and I feel so ashamed.

Damien paused.

Read on, the Voice said.

'Okay, stop nagging me.' Damien held the letter up to the light. 'It's hard to read. The ink has faded.'

But the truth is, Damien, you didn't desire me – *only my mind. I want a man to fire me, to free me of my thoughts. I wanted lust in the bedroom, not your worship.*

There you go, the Voice said. *Fragile little Laura just wanted a bit of the ol' rumpy-pumpy. Ready for some more?*

'Wait a second.' Damien went to the coat cupboard and took out the silver hip flask from his Barbour. 'Might be a spot left.' He unscrewed the top and gave it a shake. Not a drop.

Stop procrastinating. Get on with it, the Voice said.

'Okay! Don't hassle me. I'm not sure I want to know what's coming next.'

Remember when you were in LA – "playing" – and I went to Skiathos to stay with my girlfriend Raliya? Well, one night we went to a taverna. That's when I met Andreas. He was playing backgammon, tavli as the Greeks call it. He looked at me and smiled. A strong, handsome face, warm eyes. He asked me to sit and watch him play, and he won.

'You bring luck.' He kissed his fingers and patted my cheek. Then we chatted a little. He spoke bad English and I spoke bad Greek. All the better not to try and make polite conversation.

After a couple of glasses of wine, I was caught.

I can see your shocked face in my mind's eye, Damien. But it doesn't mean that I didn't love you. It's just that Andreas flipped my switch.

He was a farmer. Salt of the earth. When we made love, he took me. Claimed my body. Set me alight. I lost my mind. I didn't have to pretend, as I did with you.

I stayed with him for two months while you were away. I lied to you when I said that I had been offered a temporary position teaching history at the university in Athens.

I was pregnant, Damien. For two years we had tried and nothing happened. And yet with Andreas... fire and earth. The first night.

You just didn't turn her on, the Voice said. *No chemistry. Pray continue...*

I was going to have an abortion, but when I arrived back home, you refused to come with me to therapy and then you left for America again and I went back to Andreas.

I lied when I told you that the university had extended my position.

It seemed that there was nothing left to keep us together, so we agreed to divorce.

And then, it all started to go wrong with Andreas. Every night he went to the taverna and sometimes he didn't come home till dawn. One morning he came home blind drunk and woke me up. He shook me so hard that I thought he had dislocated my shoulder. He said he'd lost a lot of money playing tavli and that I had stopped bringing him luck. That I was a chain round his neck.

To tell the truth, I missed you, Damien.

I was six months gone. Andreas's family were kind. But I wasn't having an easy time. So I made a plan.

To have the baby and take the newborn back to England, even if we weren't going to be together. However, the best laid plans...

But then one night he came home drunk again. He was so cruel. Said I was his problem. He told me that he needed his freedom, wanted to be with a simple Greek girl. That he didn't understand my British ways.

I told him I'd take the baby back to England and he could have his freedom.

He went berserk. Threw me against the wall. I was so frightened I couldn't see straight. I just wanted to get away. And that's when I fell down the stairs and hit my head. I started bleeding.

He was really scared and called the ambulance.

I went to the hospital. They gave me a caesarean. But the baby boy was dead.

Oh, Damien, I am so unhappy. How can I live with myself? I had a baby in Athens – mine, not yours.

I just can't take it anymore.

Forgive me,

Laura

Well, at least she didn't sign off with love, the Voice said.

'I need a drink.'

Damien moved to the mirror and stared at his reflection with fresh eyes, scrutinising this semblance of features that didn't seem to have a soul. He looked like the ghoulish marionette with a long face and deep-sunk eyes that his father had brought him back from Prague when Damien was a boy.

No, you don't look like that. Get some perspective. She betrayed you. Shoved your adoration down the plughole. Wanted a bit of rough. You had every right to have affairs. At least you didn't pretend, like her, with her high and mighty intellectual claptrap. And look who she took to her heart. A Cretan bull... Damien, wake up. Go get straight. You're vindicated. Don't fuck it up. Tomorrow is the first day of your new life.

When Sophie returned, Damien was asleep.

She gazed tenderly at his dear face and graceful body, all curled up in his bed. The duvet cover wrapped around him, save for his fine muscled arms, long and pale, which hugged a pillow to his chest. It was hard to imagine that this beautiful man had been to the bottom of the pit, his life nearly snuffed out. His long, elegant toes were peeking out from under the cover. She touched them. They were ice cold. When she rubbed them, he giggled.

'Nurse Sophie,' he said, all silky soft, 'what a good sort you are.'

Chapter 34

*C*ome *on, Damien, go for it. Tell them your story. Everyone here is in the same boat*, the Voice said.

No, we're not, thought Damien. *The difference is, I have you yammering on at me all the time.*

He looked up and cleared his throat. 'I'm Damien and I'm an alcoholic and I'm addicted to sex and drugs.'

'Hi, Damien,' the group responded.

He paused.

Go on, Damien, imagine you're on the couch, the Voice said.

'Okay, here goes. I've been going on benders for the last twenty years, but I've always managed to keep my work separate from my leisure habits. I could drink a bottle of whisky a night chased down with half a dozen lines of coke and still get up in the morning and write. I've slept with hundreds of women and sometimes had a turnover of two a day, when I wasn't busy.

'I more or less kept things under control because of my work, until six months ago when I met a lady who played me at my own game. And the cooler she became the more I fell for her, and the more intoxicated and needy I became, the more she detested me.'

Stop. You sound like a pathetic masochist, the Voice said. *It's all so over the top.*

Damien wasn't sure what to say next. His eyes focused on the young woman who led the meeting. She had a lovely face. Wide, soft eyes and one of those mouths that turned up at the edges even when she wasn't smiling. He looked at her hand: no wedding band.

'One minute left,' she said.

'Thanks.' Her voice brought him back on track.

'Well, I certainly kept my dealer happy. I could call him any time day or night and he would supply me with coke, MDMA – and sometimes even buy me a bottle of whisky on the way to my house, if I didn't want to go out. And then, one night, I was out of my head and went to this wedding and there she was, dancing the paso doble with another man.

'I went crazy. It was a red rag to a bull. I charged him… made such a fool of myself. So finally,' Damien paused to catch his breath, 'the groom put me in a cab, and I was on my way home when I decided to take a detour. Told the cabbie to take me to the River Thames… and I jumped.

'And here's the thing: I'm only here to tell the tale because the taxi driver rescued me. He went off for a coffee but came back. I think he knew what I was going to do.

'When he pulled me out of the water, for a moment I thought he was an angel. Maybe he was. He took me, covered in mud, to the hospital, and in a strange way I felt as if I was being reborn. That was my wake-up call. So here I am. Anyway, I just want to say that I'm so happy to be alive and I really want to recover.'

He wanted them to believe him, but he wasn't sure he believed himself.

Quite good, the Voice said, *but next time inject a bit of wit.*

He held hands with the people in the circle, and prayed that he could find a way to move on.

God, grant me the serenity to accept the things I cannot change,
The courage to change the things I can,
And the wisdom to know the difference.

It wasn't easy. Twice a week, he saw a therapist who helped him stay on course. For months he kept close to home and avoided socialising, especially parties.

His day started with a meditation, then breakfast and afterwards he went back to the screenplay of *Writing in the Sand*, which was well on the way to being signed off.

Every evening he went to his AA meeting.

To his surprise, life flowed.

***

Not so with Nicholas and Kate. It was hellish in the Morley household. The kids had both gone to stay with friends in Southgate for the half-term October break, leaving Nicholas and Kate to stare at each other over takeaways and ready meals.

Yes, no, hello, goodbye, TV shows and long solo walks with the dogs seemed to work for a few days until… that Sunday night.

It started well enough. Kate was out having a drink with her best friends, Sara and Mandy, at the Bunch of Grapes.

It was her birthday. She'd said that she'd be home at 8 p.m., but Nicholas had waited until 9 p.m. and there was still no sign of her.

Not that it mattered. He was happy to be alone in the kitchen. It was his favourite place. He loved the old farmhouse table and chairs bought from a dealer in Broadstairs; the Dutch wooden dresser inherited from his beloved mother, filled with cookbooks that no one used; pretty bone china cups and saucers decorated with butterflies; the porcelain teapot, a wedding present from his Aunty Tina, that Kate had managed to crack while she was cleaning.

So there he sat with a glass of wine, munching a slice of pepperoni pizza and reading his book of haiku poems, while the dogs lay calm at his feet. Very Zen.

Moment gone. Wife home.

River stops, mind-flow shattered
The house weeps again.

'Hello, Kate,' Nicholas said when she swaggered in. His face betrayed nothing. Blank eyes and a slip of a smile.

She was drunk. Not funny drunk, but a morose, vindictive drunk.

'Come on, Nicholas, do your angry emoji,' she goaded.

'I'm not angry. Actually, I was having a very nice time.'

'Well, I'll make it even better. I want a divorce,' she snarled like a rabid dog. 'It's my birthday, in case you forgot. And that's what I want.'

'I know it's your birthday,' Nicholas said calmly. 'Don't you remember I offered to take you out this evening? You were meant to be home at eight o'clock. It's hardly my fault you've come home at eleven, sloshed.'

'Look at us.' She swayed her way to the fridge. 'Hopeless. Now then, I want to say hello to my Pinot Grigio. At least it gives me pleasure. Not like you, with your fancy-schmancy talk. I don't understand a word of it. So why would I want to listen to you rambling on at a restaurant?'

'Respect...' he said quietly. 'You don't respect me. But do you hate me?'

'Oh, there you go again. Poor Nick. Of course I don't hate you... You just make me sick.' She opened the fridge door. 'What the hell? There's nothing left.' She swung the bottle in the air. 'Who puts an empty bottle back in the fridge? I want to know, who's been at my Pinot Grigio?'

'Probably you, last night,' Nicholas replied. 'When I came home from poker, you were well and truly pissed.'

'Better than having to listen to your mumbo jumbo – the meaning of this and the meaning of that. Why don't you save it for bloody Sophie? You usually just come home for a change of clothes and off you go again. Well, soon you can have your London luvvie twenty-four seven.'

'What are you talking about?' Nicholas dunked a slice of pizza in his glass of Merlot and popped it in his mouth. 'It's all over with Sophie. I haven't seen her for months.'

'Only because she gave you the push,' Kate said with a spiteful smile. 'Anyway, it's too late. I don't give a shit who you sleep with, as long as it's not me.'

'That's enough.' Nicholas stood up from the table and took his plate over to the sink. 'It's midnight and I've got to be in London by 9 a.m. I'll sleep on the sofa.'

He'd finish with Kate. Nothing left, no sweet smiles – just a pile of bitter memories. He'd try again with Sophie.

But Sophie didn't answer when he rang. Nicholas couldn't sleep. Why should she trust him? Back and forth, back and forth, wife to lover, lover to wife.

Perhaps she'd found another man. And, if she had, it wasn't right for him to interfere. No, he must let her go…

And yet…

Chapter 35

It was the first time that Damien had attended the St John's Wood AA.

Angus McManus, who lived in Acacia Road, had invited him to lunch at the Ivy on the high street.

It made a change from the Chelsea group. Especially as he had met a woman there with whom he'd had a brief affair and, despite the fact that it was over, she'd begun to harass him.

Damien sat on a chair at the back of the room and looked around him. There were quite a few city types who wore smart shirts and expensive well-cut suits.

A sad-looking woman with bleached blonde hair and heavy make-up, sporting diamanté-studded silver sneakers, was busy texting someone on her mobile. Her hand was shaking.

He wondered what drug she was on.

But he didn't bargain for the emaciated old rocker propping up the wall behind him with straggly grey hair and dark glasses, chicken legs in skin-tight black jeans and leather pointy shoes.

Damien had seen him before, but couldn't remember where, until his brain pinged. It was Aidan, his dealer. He looked so different. Not the usual smart-ass, slicked hair and Italian designer jacket. It always struck Damien that he looked more like a hairdresser than a dealer, but now perfect cliché casting.

Aidan had spotted him and that was when the Voice chimed in.

Turn the other way. For God's sake, don't engage. People, places and things. Keep strong.

He could feel Aidan staring at him.

Do or die. Don't be a fool, the Voice continued. *He's been sent to test you. Come on, one hello and that will be it. You'll be in the shit again.*

Damien was edgy. Aidan had moved to the seat next to him. He smelt of stale cannabis and sweat.

'Hello, mate,' the dealer said. 'Good to see you.'

'Don't call me mate,' Damien said. 'Are you here because you're going straight or is it rich pickings at meetings?'

'No need to be rude. You were happy to score the coke from me any time night or day, and I gave you credit.'

'You don't have to remind me.' Damien scanned the room. 'That's why I'm moving.' He stood up and snaked his way to an empty chair in the front row.

That's it, the Voice said. *Just keep focus.*

The first share was Silver Sneakers. Husband dead two years ago. Heart attack. Now she was lonely, middle-aged and disappointed, playing the online dating game. She had met divorced men, widowed men, mostly older men, who wanted a companion. Men who'd lost their mojo long ago.

And that's when the habit set in. Prozac in the morning, a midday gin and tonic, followed by teatime vodka and apple schnapps, her husband's favourite. And in the evening when the grieving was really bad, a bottle of red and then to bed with a temazepam.

Sweet dreams, but, come the morning, numbness, burning, pain. And she started all over again. A hit of 60 mgs of Prozac to make herself feel better followed by a chaser. Until one day, she fell and broke her hip and that was it, her wake-up call.

Sam, a dapper little man with thinning hair, began his share.

'Hello, I'm Sammy and I'm an alcoholic. I have three women in my life: my mother, my wife and my mistress, in that order. The three naggers. I own a delicatessen in Golders Green called Fresser, which means glutton in Yiddish. I'm a glutton, a glutton for punishment.'

The circle laughed.

Good start, said the Voice.

'Anyway, my problem began two years ago around the time of Passover. I never liked wine, especially the kosher stuff, but things were heating up with the mistress. "Harry, I'm fed up," she says. "We can never be together on High Holy days. It's about time you left your bloody wife."

'The mistress nags me every day about this and then she sends texts and WhatsApps telling me that she's had enough. So one evening when the wife was out, the mistress calls me and says she's going to spill the beans and tell her that we've been having an affair for the last ten years. Now me, a man who didn't drink, is so upset that I go to the cupboard and take out the kosher wine. I have a glass and already I feel better, until my mother rings and says the chopped liver I brought her has made her ill and where are her sleeping pills and why didn't I come to see her today? She goes on and on. And it gets to me. And so I have another glass and then another. By the time the wife comes home, she finds me passed out on the floor with the empty bottle next to me. She wakes me up and gives me hell. And that's when I really began to hit the booze. The only way I could keep my sanity was to drink the nagging away. So then I started on the whisky and that was it. Eventually I hit rock bottom. I couldn't even get it up anymore. So the mistress found a new boyfriend and went to live with him in Ruislip.

'My son who lived in the States came to see me. "Dad," he said, "the only way to save yourself is to go to AA."

'So, I'm here. I've been coming for three years and I'm happy to say I haven't fallen off the wagon.'

Very good, said the Voice. *No self-pity and he wasn't performing... Oh dear, here comes Aidan.*

Damien glanced at the skeletal creature shuffling towards him and had a surge of guilt.

Aidan had, after all, been at his beck and call. Given him what he'd wanted.

Look, Damien, he's a bloody dealer. No sympathy for the Devil, the Voice said.

All right, no need to bang on. I'll try and steer clear.

But at the back of his mind, behind the Voice, there was a whisper.

How can you give it up, Damien? You love the drug too much.

And just as he was fighting with his thoughts Aidan grabbed him by the shoulder and swung him round.

'Hi, dude. Am I interrupting your mind talk? Come on, be a friend. Take my hand for the serenity prayer.' He reached out his palm and wiggled his spindly fingers.

'Not sure that's a good idea,' Damien said.

'Why? I'm not dealing any more.' He cocked his head to one side. 'I'm trying to recover, just like you are.' His mouth stretched into a gummy grin.

Damien could smell the putrid stench of his breath and backed away.

He's lying, said the Voice. *He's trying the friendly-bro approach. Wants you back on the books.*

'Okay, I hear you,' Damien muttered.

Look at him casing the joint for another sucker, said the Voice.

Then Aidan waved at Silver Sneakers and she waved back.

There you go, said the Voice. *Told you so.*

The prayer circle was about to start.

'Come on, Mr High and Mighty, give me your bloody hand,' Aidan said. 'I'm sure I have a better party list than you have.'

'If you don't shut up, I'll shove my fist in your face. Now get lost,' Damien hissed through clenched teeth.

That's it, you tell the little shit where to get off, said the Voice. *I don't think we should stay. I mean, heh, it's meant to be a serenity circle. Let's go.*

Chapter 36

Damien had kept the faith. Nine months clean. No drink, no drugs, day at a time. He avoided tipsy lunches and the cocktail crowd.

Stayed home most of the day. Save for his morning glory. Up at seven, shorts on, ready to run along the river path.

Out of body, out of mind, flying high, into the Zen zone, where there were no words to disturb his peaceful, painless journey. He wasn't lonely.

Writing in the Sand was a big hit. Top of the bestseller list and a critical success. Added to which, the film was in production.

Damien was ready to move on.

He looked at his face in the mirror and ran a hand across the shadow of stubble along his jaw.

Shave, Damien, said the Voice.

'On reflection, I think you're right.'

Damien enjoyed the ritual of a traditional shave. He whistled as he dipped the badger brush into the basin of warm water and swished it in a dish of rose geranium soap. Next, he swirled the suds round and round along his jawline, after which he slid the cut-throat razor in gentle upward strokes through the bristly stubble. Finally, he splashed his face with Creed Vétiver, his favourite aftershave.

He brushed his hand across his smooth skin.

Better, much better. You're getting there. Well done, Damien, well done, said the Voice.

A white shirt, navy Armani trousers and Lobb shoes. He was good to go.

Lunch today with Justin Baird at Scott's Mayfair restaurant. Excellent fish and seafood. Very sparkly, classy and a great place for gossip with the literati.

When Damien arrived, Justin was already at the desk.

'No tables outside, but anyway I'm sure you don't want the paps on your tail.'

'Why not?' Damien said. 'Come on, Justin. Nobody who's somebody comes here to dine incognito.'

'Oh well, it's cooler inside and no car fumes,' Justin said.

Damien's eyes swept across the room, clocking the clientele, as the maître d' showed them to their tables.

Who's Who artsies, money merchants, Ascot hats eating oysters and Dover sole, washed down with vintage whites and fine champagne.

The looks and whispers thrilled him.

Yes, here I am. Back after my sabbatical. Risen out of the ashes.

You show 'em, the Voice said.

'Glad you're here,' he muttered.

'What did you say?' Justin said.

'Nothing much, just talking to myself.'

The sommelier arrived.

'No wine, just tap water for me,' Damien said.

'Well, I'll be drinking for both of us, then,' said Justin. 'A glass of Dom Perignon, please.'

He smiled at Damien and opened his arms as if he were about to hug him.

'I'm so glad you're back on form again,' he said, 'but I have to admit your bullish behaviour at our wedding was terrific entertainment... I also want to say... and I really mean this...'

he grabbed Damien's arm and looked into his eyes with shining sincerity, '… it was so nice of you to introduce me to my wonderful Anna. Thank you.'

'Why?' Damien said.

'Why what?' Justin replied.

'Why did you use the word *nice*?'

'Why not?' Justin said.

'Because nice is a dull middle-class word that I find really offensive.' He winced and pressed his forehead with the back of his palm as if he were in extreme pain. 'It's a terrible word.'

Damien, what's wrong with you? He was only being nice. Why can't you be nice? said the Voice.

'Sorry, Justin. It's one of my pet hates. Words can drive me crazy.'

'You're a very difficult man,' Justin said quietly. 'Always picking away at other people's grammar. Any tiny word that doesn't match up to your high literary vocabulary you consider an insult.'

Let it go, Damien, said the Voice. *Okay. Now follow up with something friendly.*

'Do you believe there's no free will, Justin?'

That's it, Damien. Change the subject to something wanky and meaningful, said the Voice. *Not a good idea for Justin to get really rumbled and walk out.*

The waiter arrived with a plate of oysters and lobster bisque in a silver tureen.

'Look at those beauties.' Justin sighed. He picked up a shell and slurped down the oyster, chewing it twice before he swallowed it.

'Well?' Damien asked. 'What do you think?'

'No free will? You mean someone up there charting the moves?'

'Destiny, karma, kismet. Checkmate before the game's started. Winners and losers already decided.'

'It's not a question I can answer right now.' Justin swallowed his last oyster.

Damien took a spoon of soup.

'Good?' Justin asked.

'Good,' Damien replied. He ate rapidly. 'Mmmm, I didn't realise how hungry I was.' He took a slice of bread and dipped it in the bowl.

Justin looked at his friend and for a fleeting second saw the young student that he'd shared a flat with at Oxford. He remembered him eating a whole loaf of bread with cream of tomato soup. Full of hope and besotted with Laura.

'How's the love life?' Justin asked.

'*Nada.*' Damien swiped his finger round the edge of the empty bowl and sucked it.

***

Not that the AA meetings, three times weekly, which had been intrinsic to his recovery, weren't also a potential source of interesting material… He had seen quite a few attractive women, who like him were there to grasp the handle on their lives.

And then, one Sunday in June, there she was. A wisp of a woman, all legs and arms, short blonde boyish hair, a cherub face with her pillowy Cupid mouth and cooey blue eyes, looking for a spare chair. The Marylebone AA meetings were always packed.

Okay, here we go. Don't rush it with the new girl, said the Voice.

'Like mine?' said Damien.

He stood up and offered her his seat.

She looked in her late twenties and gave him a sweet little smile. 'Thanks, but I'm happy to stand at the back.'

Maybe she didn't go for the chivalrous approach? The "new school" guys were far less accommodating, and some women seemed happy not to be given special consideration.

Damien felt old. He'd try a more matey approach after the meeting.

Would she spill the beans to the group? Alcohol? Drugs? Sex?... Maybe all three?

After each share he waited for her to tell her story, but she didn't.

The last to speak was a well-built man with a smooth tan and good pecs wearing a bright white T-shirt and pale blue jeans. Best attire for a humid day, not like the city boys in their dark suits and drip-dry shirts stealing time for the midweek Marylebone meet.

'I'm Paul and I'm an alcoholic,' the man said. 'I started drinking when I found out that my wife was a gambler... I feel guilty because it was really my fault she started in the first place.'

Here we go... my fault, her fault, our fault. Got a feeling this is going to be boring, said the Voice.

'A year ago, her mother died of cancer,' the man continued, 'and not only that, around the same time, our son had been suspended for smoking weed just when he was taking GCSEs, and our thirteen-year-old daughter was being bullied at school. What with all the domestic drama going on, our sex life had dwindled to nothing. I felt like the invisible man. She hardly said hello when I came home from work.'

Stop bleating and get on with it, said the Voice. *It's all about you, you, you! How you felt, Mr Selfish.*

'Anyway, one day she caught me sending a flirtatious text to a woman I met at the gym. We had an argument... I said that I'd only had a drink with her a couple of times, but she didn't believe me. She was right... I was having an affair.'

Well, if a healthy man doesn't get his oats... said the Voice.

'One night I got plastered and told her the truth. I was fed up with our sexless life. She would make every excuse under the sun not to sleep with me. Headaches, feeling sick... Anyway, I promised not to see the woman again... I would change gyms.

But she didn't trust me anymore.' He paused and, looking down at his hand, fiddled with his wedding band.

Come on, Mr Pecs. Don't be shy. What happened next? asked the Voice.

Damien was fidgeting. He glanced behind at Blue Eyes. She looked bored. She caught his look. He winked.

'That's when she started gambling, online poker. And I really started drinking. At first, I didn't worry how much money she was spending from our joint bank account because there were only small amounts going out. Well, if she felt like a bit of a flutter, why not? It wasn't drugs… But it started to worry me when I came home after work and she'd make me dinner and then go back to her laptop. Didn't even look at me. Just stared at the screen like a zombie.

'Then she started going out alone in the evening. Tuesdays and Thursdays… dance classes, she said. But when she started staying out all night and hiding our bank statements, I knew something was up.'

Damien coughed and looked at his watch. One more minute to go.

'I didn't do online banking, didn't trust it, so I phoned the bank. There was a withdrawal for £4K. She told me it was to pay for Botox and fillers. We had terrible rows. Shouting and screaming, which only made matters worse for the kids, for everything.

'She finally admitted that she was going to casinos with friends. Every time she went out, I would get absolutely trolleyed at the thought that she was throwing away my money, bleeding me dry. I drank a bottle of whisky every night. How I managed to function in the day God only knows. But I did.

'Last week I'd finally had enough. I waited up for her till five o'clock in the morning. I was well and truly pissed and as soon as she walked through the door I hit her. I've never hit a woman in my life, and that was my wake-up call. When I sobered up, we made a pact. She would go to Gamblers Anonymous and I would go to AA.'

Well, I must say the last bit was pretty dramatic, said the Voice.

The meeting was over. Damien scouted the room for his new challenge, but she had left.

No point. She's a no-hoper. Don't get involved with someone as lost as you are. If I were you, I would steer clear of women till you get yourself sorted out, said the Voice.

'If you were me? Who else are you if not me? Anyway, probably right not to get involved.'

Ah, that's a good sign. So we have started to agree on things, the Voice said. *A meeting of two minds.*

Chapter 37

And each night Damien meditated, letting his mind float like driftwood down a river, ready to greet his dreams with a clear, light head.

One night, he was enjoying himself in Nananoonoo Land, lying on a beach with a silky dark-haired beauty, who was massaging his back with suntan oil, when Elizabeth rang.

He pulled himself out of his sleep state and snatched the phone from the bedside table.

'Hello, Damien,' she said, all friendly. Silence. 'Hello... hello... Can you hear me?'

'Yes, I can hear you,' he replied.

'How are you?'

He glanced at his alarm clock. 'It's one o'clock in the morning... a bit late for a chat.'

'Or early... depending which way you look at it... I hear you're back in the saddle again. Don't think I haven't been keeping tabs on you.'

'You sound a bit tipsy, Elizabeth.'

'Not at all. Just thought I'd call you... Obviously not a good idea. You're making me feel awkward.'

'Look, maybe we could speak later? I've an early morning meeting,' he said in a weary voice.

'There was a time when you'd have been delighted to hear from me, night or day.'

'Elizabeth...' Damien sighed. A shaft of moonlight peeped through the curtain, throwing a silvery light on his pale, solemn face.

What did she want, this woman who had caused him such pain, burnt him out? Should he cut her off? Maybe not... That would encourage her. Challenge her to win him back. No, he wasn't going to jump again.

'So, what's up?' he said.

'Well... it's Javier.'

'Yes?'

'He's left me.'

He laughed. 'I didn't know it was that serious.'

'Thank you for diminishing our relationship.'

'Just assumed you were hot lovers,' he replied. 'Come on, Elizabeth, you can't expect me to play the sympathetic confidant.'

'Of course not. Anyway... I just want to say I'm sorry.'

'For what?' Damien rolled over and switched on the bedside light. He lay back in bed and shielded his eyes.

'I was a terrible bitch to you.' Her voice sounded different, kinder.

'True.'

'Just that Javier was so difficult.' She hesitated.

'So what happened?' Damien said. 'Come on, Elizabeth. You usually have a tongue like a switchblade. Spit it out.'

'Please, stop bullying me.'

'You've phoned me to moan about your ex in the early hours of the morning. What do you expect? The spell's broken, Elizabeth. Get to the point.'

'Well, he just casually said that he was going back to Buenos Aires to marry a twenty-three-year-old Argentinian girl. Told me in bed... I think he expected me to congratulate him.'

'Maybe it's got something to do with you. Perhaps he didn't see you as wife material.'

'For God's sake, Damien, who said anything about marriage?'

'But that's the answer, isn't it? An Argentinian alpha male from a wealthy conservative Catholic family, of course he wants a wife and kids. And you, what do you want?'

'I don't know…'

'Why are you really ringing me? Dangling Javier in front of my nose. Seriously, Elizabeth. Why should I care if he's left you, after what you put me through?'

'Because I'm lonely. And I want us still to be friends. All those chess games that we played, which you mostly won and you understood so much. I didn't have to explain anything. I miss you, Damien.'

'Yes, well, it's probably just because you're not used to being hurt or alone. I'm sure you'll get over it.'

'So that's it. We can't be friends?'

Damien held the phone away from his ear.

Don't worry, I'm still here for you, the Voice said. *Now come on. Give her a wide berth. You know she'll do it again. Get you all churned up. A sweet beginning and then – BOOM – you'll be back down the rabbit hole. Don't be a schmuck… Tell her to get lost.*

'Damien… come over… now…' she whispered. 'Why sleep alone dreaming of me when we can be together?'

Yes. Why not? It would be a good litmus test. See if he could just have sex with Elizabeth without being obsessed with her.

'Come on, Damien, you know you'll love it. I'll make you so hot.'

He couldn't hear the Voice, only hers.

He had a quick shower and dressed. Jeans, a crisp white linen shirt, slip-on loafers that he wore sockless, a last look in the mirror to check his hair, and off he went.

A warm June night. And as he revved the engine of his car his other half hoped it wouldn't start.

Apart from the odd one-nighter, he'd managed to temper his sex addiction. And tonight he would fight the good fight. Take what he could without falling into the bottomless pit.

***

She stood at the door with a champagne glass in her hand, Titian-red hair tumbling on her shoulders just so, and she wore that green silk kimono, the one he'd bought her in a vintage store in Paris, loosely belted round her wasp waist.

Barefoot, sleek, graceful… That smile, almost real. But her eyes, they looked tired and red under the lamp light, and a web of fine lines round her mouth betrayed her age.

Wordless, she cupped the back of his neck with her hand and drew his mouth to hers. Just the lightest touch to tease.

And yet… Damien was surprised that she hadn't used a little more imagination, a more inventive approach, not so predictable. Maybe start with friendly, and less of the textbook seductress. What happened next? More thriller. Leave him room to flex his muscles first.

He slipped his feet into a pair of Moroccan slippers. 'Would you like a drink?' she asked.

'Wouldn't mind a cup of Horlicks,' he replied.

Elizabeth giggled. 'You're teasing me, aren't you?' She held his face between her hands. 'Are you trying to cool me down?'

'Nope, I'm serious. I'm on the wagon.'

'Well, I'm afraid I don't have any Horlicks,' she said. 'Not something that my guests have ever requested.'

Apparently, he had outwitted her. And he loved it. 'Cocoa?'

'No. I don't think so,' she said.

'Never mind, a glass of water will be fine.' He waited.

'There's a bottle by your bedside,' she replied.

Your bedside. Maybe now that Javier had gone, she wanted

him. Not just for a night with Damien Spur... but for something more.

She'd lost her metal edge. There was a softness about her that he hadn't seen before... or so it seemed.

'Well then,' she said, 'let's make up for lost time.'

Minutes later, Elizabeth, legs astride, rocked back and forth while Damien, her horse, held her heaving breasts.

Faster, faster she rode and just as he was ready to explode, she cried, 'Not yet... wait for me.'

Here we go, the Voice chipped in. *She's so controlling. What does she expect, that you're going to have a tea break while she takes her time with Kama Sutra 54, the good old Rocking Horse?*

Not that she cared what he thought. It was as if she'd forgotten he was there. He moaned just to remind her.

At last, Elizabeth reached her nirvana. 'Ah, AH, *AH*... JAVIEEEER!' She juddered, swinging her face from side to side and then with a whimper collapsed on Damien's chest.

For a moment, he said nothing. This woman whom he'd idolised – sophisticated, beautiful and difficult to know – had revealed herself in the throes of her passion as a victim, just as he'd been with her.

'That was wonderful.' She swung her leg over his torso and rolled onto her back. 'What a ride. How was it for you?'

'What an idiot I've been.' He slapped his hand on his head.

'What are you talking about? You sound so aggressive.' Elizabeth, wide-eyed, reached across him for the bottle of water.

'Leave it.' He grabbed her arm and pushed it away.

'Now then...' she sat up and crossed her arms, '...tell me why you're behaving like a rough pig.'

'Is that my role, to be Javier to you?' It was better to be angry than hurt.

'I don't understand.'

Damien grasped her shoulders and made her look at him.

'You called out *Javier*...'

'Did I? Oh… oh, I'm so sorry,' she said. 'Strange, I don't remember.'

Like hell she doesn't, the Voice said. *You're just a proxy, a fill-in… Let's go.*

She didn't move as he dressed. Just sat up in bed and watched him… a fox who had lost her prey. She would miss him… at least until she found another lover.

'Goodbye, Elizabeth. Thank you for having me.'

'The pleasure was all mine,' she replied with a sly smile.

'Just don't call me again,' he said, and left her to dream of lost love.

Chapter 38

Damien was finally free. And so was Sophie.

'Ah, there you are.' Sophie had waited for her sister by the entrance of Regent's Park… It was 9 a.m. and Anna was late.

'Sorry! Justin and I had a bit of a tiff.'

'What about?'

'Damien rang me this morning to ask whether I was interested in joining him for a literary weekend in Brighton this July mentoring young writers. I told Justin and he went crazy. He thinks I've still got a thing about him.'

'Sounds interesting,' Sophie said as they walked through the gate.

'To be honest, I'm so busy in the next few months decorating our house that I didn't want to commit.'

'Or maybe it's because you don't trust yourself. Tell the truth: you've always had a thing about Damien, haven't you?'

'Come on, don't start that one. He changed my life and for that…'

'I know, you're eternally grateful.'

They strolled past a tramp asleep on a park bench, swathed in a blanket of newspaper, a Jack Russell by his side who, like his master, looked perfectly at peace.

'The old boy's a regular,' Anna said. 'Never seen him beg for money and yet his dog always looks well fed and happy.'

'Probably just likes the outdoor life,' Sophie replied. 'Did I tell you about the woman who slept in the Hyde Park subway when I was at ballet school in Park Lane? I passed her every day. She had snow-white hair, which she wore in a bun. It looked like a huge balloon. Apparently, legend has it, that's where she hid her money, and when she ran out, she withdrew more cash from a bank account she had in the Mayfair branch of Barclays.'

Anna looked at her sister and burst out laughing. 'Sophie, stop telling porkies and let's talk about my book.'

The two women sat on a bench opposite the boating lake.

'First let me say one thing about Nicholas,' Sophie said.

'If you must,' Anna sighed, 'but you said you've moved on, so why do you still want to talk about him?'

'Well, the strange thing is that now it's over, I miss the friendship.' Sophie took a plastic bag of bread from her pocket and threw some crusts in the water. The ducks dipped and the lucky ones swam away with the crumbs in their beaks. 'It's a shame,' she continued. 'Sex got in the way. He was a terrific friend, very generous and we did have fun.'

'Please, Sophie,' Anna said, 'I don't want to hear about him any more. I'm much more interested to know whether you've started on my drawings?'

Sophie had been commissioned to illustrate her sister's next book, *Abba de Giggler*, a sci-fi tale about a boy from Earth invited to join the annual laughter conference on Planet Ha Ha.

'Not yet. Still reading the story. Don't worry, I know the deadline's end of July. It will all be done by then.'

'Please don't let me down. If your illustrations aren't up to scratch I'll be the one to blame.' Anna jabbed Sophie's chest with her index finger.

'Okay, okay… Calm down,' Sophie said, 'or you'll have a heart attack. I won't disappoint you. It's a great opportunity – thank you.'

Anna still wasn't sure she'd made the right decision. 'Tell you what, why don't you come with me to the villa? You can do the work there.' At least she could keep her sister focused.

'What a great idea... Are you sure Justin won't mind?'

'Of course not,' she replied. 'Anyway, he has to be in London this coming week. He's got a new client, Levi Stern, who lives in Vienna. He's flying in on Wednesday with his family and Justin's playing host.

'He's written an incredible biography, which I've read, about his father, Andrei Stern, who was in hiding in Nice during World War II and was arrested by the Gestapo who had occupied France. The people who ran the laundry where he took his washing had sold the names and addresses of their Jewish customers to the Gestapo for £2 per head.

'Andrei was imprisoned at a hotel with many of the other Jews who were then sent off to the concentration camps.'

'And Andrei? What happened to him?' Sophie asked.

'Luckily,' Anna continued, 'as he was waiting to be loaded into a lorry to be transported to a camp, the Allies bombed the road bridge crossing the river Var, just outside Nice, and the Jews were sent back to the hotel. Before the bridge could be rebuilt, Nice was liberated and Andrei had escaped death.'

'What a story!' Sophie said. 'It was meant to be. Andrei was literally saved by a heartbeat. It wasn't his time.'

If only it hadn't been Daniel and Mikey's, she thought to herself. 'Well then, when shall we go?'

'Tomorrow?' Anna said.

***

The south of France in June. A perfect time to stay at La Maison de Rêve with its rose-painted walls and cool marble terrace stretching out across the lush garden.

In her mind's eye, Sophie rises with the sun before her sister wakes and, taking out her inks, begins her first illustration.

266

Magenta and blue… A little boy in the dark looking out of the window at the night sky, holding his teddy… golden yellow.

An early morning swim in the pool, and later coffee and croissant on the terrace, a little more work, followed by lunch and a siesta. And then the day stretching into an evening aperitif on the terrace, heady scents of mimosa and jasmine wafting through the soft air like a beautiful woman leaving a trail of her perfume as she passes by.

Perhaps a delightful supper of a *Niçoise* salad, followed by *fraises du bois* and, afterwards, stargazing through a naval telescope inherited from Justin's grandfather.

Dream on, Sophie, dream on…

***

And Damien?

Writing in the Sand was ready to roll. The director Marc Castle had asked him to meet the actress Ariana Bianchi, whom he'd cast as Sandra, Samuel's mistress.

She had a lovely voice and wanted Damien to write the words to a song she'd composed on the guitar.

'Angus, I'm a hardcore thriller writer, not a lyricist.'

'So what,' his agent said. 'Surely it would make a change from sweating over a novel for months on end.'

'Not if it doesn't work. Writing lyrics is a huge skill. Look at Don Black. You think it's easy writing Bond themes? Who can forget "Diamonds Are Forever"?' He swung his swivel chair round and sang the first verse in his deep, throaty voice. 'Why don't Netflix ask him?'

Angus sat behind the large desk, enthroned in a wingback leather Chesterfield. 'Never knew you could sing… and now I know you can't.'

I agree, said the Voice. *Come on, show you have a sense of humour.*

Damien gave a dry laugh.

The office was more like a gentleman's study. There was a rosewood cabinet of golf trophies next to a library case of his clients' books and, on the mahogany desk, party invitations and a display of silver-framed family photos. One in particular caught Damien's eye. Angus was standing in a field of heather wearing a kilt, with a whisky flask in one hand and a gun in the other. In the background was a misty image of a large estate.

'Ah! The Laird of the Manor. Do you realise we've known each other twenty years and you've never invited me to a shoot?'

'I don't believe in mixing business with pleasure,' his agent replied.

Good thinking, said the Voice. *Don't want to get too friendly. Especially if I leave you one day.*

Damien picked up a crystal paperweight and squinted at a blue admiral butterfly captured in the centre.

'This is how I feel – trapped. Why should I write a song? It's not in my contract.'

'Why not?' Angus said. 'I would have thought you'd be delighted to try your hands at something new... and think of the royalties.'

There was a timid knock at the door.

'Come in,' Angus said crisply.

Damien flicked a glance at the pretty young woman who placed two cups of fresh coffee and some shortbread biscuits on the desk.

'Thank you,' he said. 'I haven't seen you before. You must be new. What's your name?'

He gave her that look. The one that could tease a habit off a nun.

She flushed and averted her eyes.

'Claire,' she replied. 'I started last week.'

'Well, Claire,' he said. 'Angus here usually keeps a stash of my favourite biscuits... He's obviously not informed you.'

'No problem, Damien,' his agent said. 'Claire, why don't you pop round the corner and get some custard creams for Mr Spur?'

'Thank you, Angus. Must say it's not like you to humour me.'

'Look, I know you're a creature of habit and I just want this to be a happy and productive meeting.'

***

Damien answered the door. On the front step stood Marc Castle, tall and elegant beside a diminutive young woman with a Spanish guitar casually slung across her shoulder.

Marc smiled at Damien. 'Good to see you again. This is Ariana, our leading actress.'

Damien felt that familiar stirring.

Just his type. Glamorous without trying. A real beauty.

'Hi Damien, what a pleasure to meet you.' She shook his hand. 'Well, gentlemen,' she said brushing past him, 'let's not waste time. Where are we going to work?'

'Up the stairs, first on your left; the living room.'

'Got it.' And off she flew.

Wow! She's some hot chilli pepper, said the Voice. *A Brazilian chick who kicks ass.*

***

Ariana sat on an antique mahogany piano stool with the guitar on her lap.

'I am going to play you the theme tune I've composed.'

Damien liked her style. 'Fire ahead.'

Marc laughed. 'Theme tune, Ariana? Hold on. I thought you just wanted to play your song in the last scene.'

'Yes. Sandra could strum it on the beach to Samuel before she vanishes but it should also play out the end of the movie.

A lasting memory of his great love… and we can use variations of the melody through the whole movie.'

She lifted her arms up above her head making a large arc and then brought them to rest. She gave a deep sigh.

'It's a sad composition. Just the guitar. No orchestration. Listen.'

As she strummed the minor chords, lifting the sound to a poignant crescendo, Damien's breath rose with the wave of melodic intensity. His thoughts swept away into the past. He could see his father in his mind's eye. At first playing with him on the carpet and then the funeral, sad notes.

Next, Laura appeared with her furrowed brow and sad brown eyes gazing at him as if to say "What has become of us?". His loved ones back from the dead like magic. Damien blinked back his tears.

Don't be ashamed, he heard his father say. *It's good to cry. If you can't cry, you can't feel.*

Damien didn't hide his tears.

When the music ceased, for a moment nobody spoke.

Ariana laughed and broke the spell. She glanced at Damien's tear-filled eyes. 'Ah! Always a good sign when you move the writer.' She took out a tissue from her bag and gave it to him.

He dabbed his eyes. 'Thank you, Ariana. I think you've passed my litmus test.' He turned to the director. 'So, Marc…' he said, 'I think the theme tune is hers… But of course,' he added giving him a sanguine glance, 'you're the director and you have the last word.'

'Yes, I think it works.'

Chapter 39

'Oh my God.' Damien stared at the packet of white powder in his hand. It had been dropped through his letterbox in an innocuous Manila envelope. No note, just his name and an "A" on the back.

He leant against the wall and shut his eyes.

Focus on your yogic breathing, said the Voice. *Slow your heartbeat. Calm down. Breathe in through the nose, out through the mouth.*

Damien's nostrils flared as he inhaled. He held his breath and exhaled slowly with an "ah" sound.

That's it. That's it, Damien.

'Help me,' he said to the Voice. 'I'm in agony – blocked, can't write. My mind's asleep. The powder… it'll wake me up. Don't tell me to throw it away.'

I need to think about it, said the Voice.

'That makes two of us,' said Damien.

Gone. The effortless chain of words that flowed from his mind.

Gone. His imagination that drove his stories to an end that never failed to surprise him.

All gone.

He was lying on his bed, clutching the bag of white magic to his breast, when the phone rang.

'Angus! Good to hear from you,' Damien said.

'Bullshit. Why haven't you returned my calls?'

'Because I know why you're ringing me.'

'What's wrong with you?' his agent said. 'Bloody fantastic offer, carte blanche, write what you like. Your take on *Don Quixote*. Brad Pitt and Leonardo Di Caprio. Tarantino. Who wouldn't kill for the deal?'

Angus smelt the big one. Oscar time. Lots of offers, riding with his client in style, first class.

'I'm not ready to start another project. I'm still working on the theme song for *Writing in the Sand*,' said Damien.

He was tired of his agent's nagging. Every day, Angus called to say how lucky he was, how grateful he should be. The enormous fee that he would be paid to write the hottest project in film land…

'For goodness' sake, how long does it take you to write the bloody lyrics for a simple tune?'

'Don't talk to me like that. I'm not your workhorse,' said Damien. 'I'm having problems. I just can't write at the moment. Nothing's working. The words aren't there.'

Shut it, Damien. He's not your bloody therapist, the Voice said. *Don't drop your armour.*

But he couldn't stop.

'You don't have any idea what it feels like to spend night after night searching for something that just isn't there. I've lost it, Angus.'

'Pull yourself together.' His agent hated histrionics. 'You're a professional with a deadline. Just finish the lyrics… it's not bloody Shakespeare. You're writing a few lovey-dovey words so Ariana Bianchi can show off her singing.'

Come on, Damien, the Voice said. *Bastard. Show him who's boss.*

'Fuck off, Angus. What do you understand about human frailty? You're sacked.'

He sat on the edge of his bed with his head in his hands, utterly in despair.

Damien? said the Voice.

'Yes.'

Don't sabotage yourself.

'I can't carry on like this… I'm dried up. Finished.'

He stroked the packet of white powder that would open up the gates to his creativity again.

No, Damien. I'm your best friend. Listen to me. DON'T.

That white magic dust was so close to his heart. Open sesame.

Just as he tore the corner with his teeth, the phone rang again.

'Oh, what the hell!' He picked it up.

'Hello, mate,' Aidan said. 'Did you like my gift?'

'I was about to blow it when you called,' Damien replied. 'Trying to get me hooked again, are you?'

'Well, that's not a very nice thing to say. I just wanted to cheer you up. Heard that you were having probs with your brain.'

'Who the hell told you that?'

'One of my clients. Shouldn't really welch, but as it's you…' Aidan paused. 'Come on, Damien, have a guess?'

'For fuck's sake, get on with it. Who?'

'Mrs Temazepam. You shared at an AA meeting. Said you had mind freeze, couldn't find your mojo… Anyway, if the powder keeps your brain cells jumping, I'm very happy to supply you again.'

How kind of the little shit, said the Voice. *Now take my advice. Just tell him to fuck off nicely and then, Damien, throw away the coke…*

It was 11 a.m. Damien had migrated from his bed to the sofa in the living room. He'd even made the effort to wash and dress.

She'd left two messages.

Hi, Damien, Ariana said. *How goes? I'll see you at your house at noon. Please confirm.*

Hello, Damien. Haven't heard from you... I assume you're working...

You jerk, yelled the Voice. *What are you doing? NOTHING! Just sitting there paralysed. Stop with your mental constipation. Ring her!*

Damien pressed the dial button.

'Ariana,' he said, 'I can't write the lyrics to your song. The melody is beautiful, but the words won't come. I'm sorry.'

She'll understand, said the Voice. *What's the betting she'll want to save your creative soul?*

'I'm coming over,' she said. 'Let me inspire you.'

Told you, said the Voice. *Now she understands human frailty. That's the sort of woman you need.*

Damien's nose itched. He was dying to snort a line.

'Fuck Aidan.' Damien flushed it down the toilet.

I love you, said the Voice.

***

That afternoon Ariana arrived with her guitar looking irresistibly beguiling.

She wore a tiny white vest and a red gypsy skirt that flashed her bare, tanned legs. Her feet were slipped into gold-thonged sandals.

Damien held his breath.

This could be dangerous, said the Voice. *Don't start with the compliments. I can tell it won't wash with her.*

But it was Ariana, in the spirit of the role of Sandra, who played the seductress.

She took his hand and led him upstairs to the living room. 'Let's sit together, we need to be close. This is the melody.'

She strummed her guitar and hummed a wordless song, her voice soft and warm like a cashmere blanket.

Damien closed his eyes. His mind calmed.

That's lovely, said the Voice. *Could almost put you to sleep. But don't get too cosy – remember you're working.*

'Let's improvise,' Ariana said when she'd finished playing. 'You're Samuel, I'm Sandra. Okay, let's take it from when you tell me you're going to leave. You've been separated from your wife for three years and now she's back in your life after a failed suicide attempt. You're drawn to me, but your history is with her. You grew up together. The marriage fell apart because she was always depressed. Okay, let's go,' Ariana said.

'You start,' said Damien timidly.

She moved closer, in character; Sandra, the Seductress.

'Why, Samuel, why? You said that we'd spend the rest of our lives together. Don't leave me. I love you.' Her chestnut-brown eyes fringed with curly black lashes looked so sad that even Damien wanted to cry.

Oh boy, she's really into this. I can see we're in for a heavy session, the Voice whispered. *Okay, your turn. Remember you're trying to resist her.*

'She needs me, Sandra. You're beautiful and gifted and there will always be some lucky man to adore you. My life is complicated. I have a history with my wife and I swore never to get divorced till she died. That's not fair to you.'

'I don't care if we never marry. I'll take you any way I can.'

She flung her arms round Damien's neck and hugged him to her breasts.

Mummy didn't do that! said the Voice.

'I can't hear you,' Damien mumbled. 'I'm on full charge.' He crossed his legs. 'Okay, Sandra.' Holding her face in his hands, he gave her a passionate kiss. 'I've changed my mind. I adore you – I'm staying.'

Ariana drew back.

'I'm sorry,' Damien said. 'I got carried away.'

'No. That's good! Now you're aroused, let's switch roles. You be Sandra.'

This is kinda weird, said the Voice. *A bit too gender fluid for me.*

'No, I'm sorry, I can't do it,' Damien said. His head throbbed. His throat was dry. He poured himself a glass of water. 'I'm not an actor. All this is a little bit too much for me. Too much drama.'

Go on, you tell her, said the Voice. *You're a fella and that's it.*

Ariana picked up her guitar and kissed his cheek. 'You don't trust me yet. That alpha-male armour is closed around your heart. But next time it will become easier. I'll see you tomorrow evening. Dusk on the river will be beautiful,' she said, and left.

Damien was exhausted. His mind was frayed. He didn't sleep well that night.

What the hell is she going to try next? said the Voice. *I tell you, she's a brainwasher.*

'Well, it's a new adventure.' Damien reached for his alarm clock and set it for 8 a.m. A morning run would clear his head.

'Please let me get some sleep. Give me some space. Or I'll start omming.'

Okay, said the Voice, *but it's all a bit LA to me. All this malarkey just for a few corny lines.*

'Come on. She's great. A real turn-on,' Damien said.

And she was funny. The following evening, she came dressed as a troubadour and serenaded him from the pavement.

Damien leant out of the balcony window. The night was warm. The sunset cast its gossamer orange light over the sky as it descended into dusk.

Magic can happen at any time.

Damien was in the moment, part of the cosmos. That unexpected happiness when everything comes together, as rare as a shooting star.

Even the Voice was silent.

A group of passers-by had gathered. They stood bewitched as Ariana cast her spell. When the song ended, there was a hush. And then the spell was broken as the people clapped and cheered.

Ariana looked up at Damien, her eyes glittering diamond bright.

'*This* is how love feels!' she said. 'Write with passion. Be Sandra! Leave a lasting memory for Samuel, your great love. It's okay, you can be vulnerable with me. Find your feminine energy! You know who your characters are. You understand Sandra – she's part of you.'

The onlookers clapped again.

Ariana sat on the bonnet of Damien's Jaguar and continued to talk in soothing tones as she gently strummed low chords on her guitar.

'She loves Samuel, but he's going to leave her, go back to his wife, who needs him more than she does. Sandra is a powerful woman, the darling of her generation. But to be left by the man you love is a terrible thing. Finally, through the song, she persuades him to stay. She has kept love alive. So when it is she who disappears, that is the mystery.'

Watch it, the Voice said. *She's messing with your head. But, then again, that's probably a good thing in the circumstances.*

Damien could only hear a faint whisper.

Ariana had fused his mind. He took out his notebook.

His heart beat in time with her rhythmic chords. Up, up he went, and then his pen flew.

He didn't have to think. He only had to follow.

Art, music, poetry, dance, born of the same magic.

She had kindled the flame.

You're getting there, Damien, said the Voice. *Clever Ariana.*

He wrote the first verse, tore off the page and made an aeroplane. Caught by a summer breeze, it wafted down into the palm of his muse. She put it in her pocket, blew him a kiss and walked away.

Chapter 40

Seven dresses, plus the Dolce & Gabbana poppy print, pale-blue silk palazzo pants and a silver knitted vest, six T-shirts, two pairs of shorts, four bikinis, a black swimsuit, three pairs of shoes, two sandals, a pair of trainers, not to mention the La Perla underwear (just in case), two sun hats...

Oh, and the brushes, watercolours, inks and paper, of course. A quick call to the Grants, David and Suzanna, who had a villa in St Paul de Vence.

'I'm coming to France tomorrow with Anna,' Sophie announced. 'Let's meet at the Eden Rock for cocktails on Tuesday, 7 p.m. Dinner at your villa? What a lovely suggestion. I'll tell her.'

Sophie hoped her sister would come, though Justin had fallen out with David Grant, an art dealer. Something about a ceramic Picasso bowl. Justin had been gazumped by a Russian banker.

'Sold it, Justin. Sorry,' the dealer had said when he'd called.

'But you agreed my price,' Justin replied.

'I know but Chernov offered me double what you were going to pay. How could I refuse?'

'By showing some bloody integrity.'

Justin had slammed down the phone.

Anna was sad. She liked the Grants. No more friendly dinner parties with the chic intelligentsia – artists, writers, critics – and the occasional banker or entrepreneur. No more sparky conversations that fired the guests, especially when it came to politics or sex.

On one such evening, the illustrious Russian artist, Nicolai Prokofiev, an enthusiastic advocate of polyamory, had professed to having a wife and two mistresses.

'Why not?' he said. 'No one gets bored, especially me. Natalia, my wife, is delighted to have time off after twenty years of marriage.'

Anna, who sat next to him, was fascinated. 'How does that work?' she said.

'I bed Maria on Monday and Wednesday; Davina, Tuesday and Thursday; Friday and Saturday it's my darling Natalia, and Sunday… I replenish my alpha energy. That way everyone has a part of me.'

'Well,' Anna said, 'do your women have other "friends"? Surely that's only fair.'

'No, my dear,' he said. 'I give them plenty. They don't need extra lovers.'

Anna liked him. He stroked her arm, disarmingly attentive, staring at her with a brazen intensity. She flushed.

Justin's blood was up. 'Okay, Nicolai, that's enough,' he snapped.

The red wine had coursed through his veins. He banged his fist on the table so hard that his coffee cup jumped, spraying brown liquid on his neighbour, Frances Nestor, editor of *Art World*. Justin looked flustered and apologised.

'No matter,' Frances said. 'Remember that Nicolai flirts with everyone.'

Nicolai threw back his leonine head and laughed. 'Come, let us raise a glass to love: *L'amour!*'

Justin caught his wife's eye. '*L'amour*,' he chorused with the other guests and, knowing that a jealous man can go too far, he blew her a kiss.

***

'Where's the housekeeper?' Sophie said. 'I've got a couple of things that need ironing.'

'On holiday,' Anna replied.

'Oh no! I can't iron, I'm left-handed.'

'So send it to the cleaners. Sophie, you're going to have to pull your weight here. Surely you can make your own bed.'

'Yes...'

'And we can clean the house together.'

Sophie's eyes scanned the vast expanse of marble floor. 'Can't we hire a replacement just for this week?'

'No, we can't.'

'I thought I was here to paint.'

'You are indeed,' Anna said, 'but without staff you really can't expect me to do everything? Tell you what, you cook and I'll clean.'

'But not every day? We'll be going to some restaurants, won't we? And one day we should go to the beach, just for a break... Oh, by the way, on Tuesday we've been invited...'

'Now listen, Sophie,' Anna interrupted, 'you have a week to create the illustrations. You're being paid royally and I expect you to do a fabulous job. Because, if you don't, I won't use you again, even if you are my sister. Do you understand?'

There was a steel glint in Anna's eyes that Sophie hadn't seen before. It made her anxious.

'Is that clear?' said Anna. Her voice had an unpleasant sharpness.

It set Sophie's teeth on edge like a squeaky chalk on a blackboard.

'Well, we've been invited by the Grants to have dinner at their house on Tuesday... and of course they would love you to come too,' she added, giving Anna her best smile.

'Are you mad?' Anna replied. 'Why on earth would I dine

with someone who double-crossed my husband? Have you lost your mind, Sophie?'

'Well, I'm going,' she said defiantly.

'No, you're not.'

'Yes, I am. And tell you what, if you don't like it, I'll go and stay at a hotel.' Sophie started to cry – and couldn't stop.

Anna softened. 'Okay, okay, calm down. I know it isn't easy being alone.' Anna hugged her. 'This is a great opportunity for you. You're a very gifted artist and you've been playing at it for too long. Now stop your tears and let's get something to eat.'

When Damien rang, Sophie was on the balcony, drawing.

'Shall we FaceTime, or are you still in bed?' he said.

'You must be joking. I've been up since seven, working. Go ahead.'

He flipped over from audio to visual. 'That's better. So, no fun?'

'Well, had a little trip to the art shop in Vence, but that's about it.'

'I thought you were meeting the Grants?'

'Nope. Anna went apeshit so I thought I'd better give it a miss. Anyway, how's you?'

'Just fallen in love again.'

'Oh, who?'

'With myself.'

'How are you doing, Sophie?' Anna called from the stairs. 'I'm bringing up your coffee and croissant.'

'I'd better go,' said Sophie hastily.

'Why the rush?'

'The prison guard is bringing up my tray of vittles.'

'Oh dear, is it that bad?' Damien said.

'Not great. She doesn't want me to have any distractions. Especially you.'

'But why?'

'Because she seems to think that we're having an affair.'

'So what? She's married.'

Sophie laughed. 'I really can't believe you're that naive.'

'What do you mean?'

'Can't you see? All she and Justin talk about is her career. It's more of a business arrangement. At least for Anna. Wouldn't be surprised if she tries to sleep with you again.'

'Would that upset you?'

'I'd have to think about that,' she said. 'I do feel very close to you. Anyway, let me go or she'll lock me up in solitary confinement for the rest of the week,' and Sophie hung up the phone.

It was a very luxurious house arrest, despite Sophie's protestations. She looked around her charming Provençal room – soft hues of white, cream and beige, a huge bed with a woven Berger headboard and, above it, a gold-framed mirror reflecting a fine painting of pink roses in a crystal vase.

On the dressing table, beside the French window, a little glass jar of jasmine and lavender sprigs filled the room with a fresh, clean scent.

A shaft of early morning sunlight streamed through the voile curtains and caressed her cheeks. And that pink stone terrace, overlooking the glorious bay... Yes, if only... just for a few hours... Maybe lunch at La Colombe d'Or, the fabulous hotel in St Paul with its art collection and glamorous guests, and who knows... ?

'Good morning.' Anna peeped round the door. 'Didn't you hear me knock?'

'Sorry, I was on the terrace, drawing.'

'Oh, were you? I thought I heard you laughing.' Anna spied the easel through the curtains. 'Good to work early, isn't it? I usually start writing at six. Shall I put your tray outside?'

'Yes, please,' Sophie replied.

'So, were you chatting to someone?'

'Yes, Damien rang.'

'Oh yes. And how was he?' Anna's voice had that sharp edge again. 'I really think that you should concentrate on your illustrations.'

'I am.' Sophie took the tray and put it on the bistro table by the easel.

'Can I see what you've been doing?'

'Not yet. This afternoon – when I've completed it.'

'Well, you'd better get that fire burning. You have four more days to finish the other images and you still haven't shown me the first one.'

'Okay, okay, I'll bring it out to you.'

Anna sat in the wicker chair and waited. Yes, she really needed to see the work in progress. She really needed to make sure Sophie was on the right track.

Anna clenched the arms of her chair and straightened her back as if she were about to take off into space. She must give her confidence. Do for Sophie what Damien did for her.

Ever since her affair with him, she had never felt the same about herself. Not even Justin gave her that sense of self-worth. Yes, her husband was pleased to do deals on her behalf, but Damien… Well, he had been the greatest cheerleader and an extraordinary teacher.

'Your imagination is trapped, spinning in your mind. Free it. Stop thinking. Let the words out. The night is best – no distractions. Remember, the writer Saul Bellow said, "You never have to change anything you got up in the middle of the night to write".'

He had touched her with his words. She loved him for that.

But now she was married he never picked up the phone, asked her how she was. How she envied Sophie.

'Here we are.' Her sister stepped out onto the terrace and placed the illustration on the easel. 'What do you think?'

Anna scanned the pen and ink lines of a young boy standing by the window gazing at the moon.

'Well,' she said, 'it's good. The profile of a child with a teddy bear is beautifully drawn, a universal image. However' – she hesitated – 'the children of today are used to seeing stylised images, more modern. Single lines… Have confidence. Commit yourself to the first line you draw. But I love the colourscape – magenta, blue and yellow.'

'So you want me to do it again?' Sophie asked.

'Yes.'

'Okay. It's your call.' Sophie's lips curled into a hurt pout. All that work and now she wouldn't have time for a morning swim.

'You have great talent,' Anna said. 'Serve the story. Remember it's sci-fi so you don't need all those background scratches. And the moon, it's a symbol – a fluid circle, a tint of lemon…'

'Right, then. I'd better get on with it.' Sophie whisked the drawing off the easel and clipped another sheet of paper to the board.

'Have your breakfast first.'

'Anna, it's one thing for you to make sure that I produce what you want, but please don't tell me when to eat. I am not a child.'

Anna laughed. 'Quite right,' she said. 'Sorry if I've ruined your appetite.'

***

That afternoon, Anna returned and there it was. The first image. Clean, stylish, the boy and the teddy magicked up by a swish of the pen. The sweet nose, the chin tilted to the moon.

'Sophie! That's perfect!' she said. 'Exactly what I wanted. You're a star.'

'That's good. And here,' Sophie handed her the drawing, 'is the other illustration I started this morning.'

Anna was enchanted. Abba de Giggler in all his glory, arms outstretched, a laughing Buddha.

'Yes, yes. That's my hero.'

And so the week progressed. Sophie forgot about distractions. Her drawings came first, punctuated by a swim or a meal. In the evening, she and Anna sat together listening to the cicadas.

No need to speak. They sat gazing at the night sky. Finally at peace with each other.

Chapter 41

Washed ashore by fate, Damien had so far survived his crazy life. Just when he thought he couldn't breathe anymore, the current dragging him down into the depths of his despair, fate had pulled him up again. And his Voice. Guiding him through stormy seas, always there to keep him company, give him inspiration.

Protecting him against the minefield of temptations that defined his life. Generously allowing him a few friendly affairs since Elizabeth. Pleasant interludes without expectation on either side. But there was no spark of love… until Ariana.

Don't fog the boundaries, the Voice warned. *Just keep it professional. Don't make a fool of yourself in LA. It's your song and her music. And that's it.*

***

Airports were dangerous places. So many bars, so many temptations.

Damien sat by the window in the first-class lounge, nursing a Virgin Mary.

His night flight had been delayed. The man next to him was sipping a whisky, and already had another shot lined up on the table.

He looked up and peered at Damien.

'Don't I know you?' he said with a Californian twang. 'Yes, I do! Damien Spur, the writer.'

'The very same,' Damien replied, eyeing the glass of golden liquid.

'Well, that's a coincidence.' The man took out a copy of *Writing in the Sand* from his hand luggage and waved it in the air. 'Great job, you've got me hooked from the first chapter,' he said. 'I've always been a fan of yours. *The Empress* was a phenomenal debut. And then the second, *Legends Never Die*. Fantastic. A really intriguing thriller. Couldn't work out the ending. Fabulous twist. The gardener and his wife, who'd have thought it! Can I just say one thing?'

'Pray tell,' Damien said, still distracted by the whisky.

I know the man's a bore, but don't even think about it, whispered the Voice.

'If you want my honest opinion' – the man eyeballed him – 'I don't think it's fair that the press are always bitching about your relationships.'

'Actually, I'm rather flattered,' Damien countered. 'Writers generally don't hold much attention. Unless there's some scandal that the press can find to make the headlines.'

'Well, they certainly have rich pickings with you.' The man picked up the second shot and downed it in one.

Damien licked his lips. His head throbbed... It would be so easy, just a tot, a wee dram...

'You know something, Damien,' the man moved closer, 'I have a story to tell that will blow your mind. And I think that us meeting like this was meant to be. What were the chances of me having your book in my bag and you actually sitting next to me. So...'

He's got the fix on you, the Voice said. *One, two, three... wait for it...*

The man stretched out his hand. 'My name's Steve Diamond.'

Now close down the conversation. The man's a moron, said the Voice.

'Hello, Steve.' Damien shook his hand. 'Tell you what, I've got to send a few emails, so perhaps you wouldn't mind if I get on with my work?'

'That's fine.' Steve nodded his head vigorously, his face crimson and sweaty from the liquor. 'Maybe after you've finished sending your messages, we could continue our chat? And, perhaps,' he added, 'if I'm not being too pushy, we could sit next to each other on the plane if there's a spare seat. I know the singles are usually taken, but maybe there's a double that's free.'

'No thanks. I like my own company. That's one of the pleasures of flying.'

That's it. Nip it in the bud, the Voice said.

'Okay, fine.' The man got up from his chair. 'Not a problem. Sorry to bother you, Mr Spur. But if I can say one more thing… You write a good thriller, but you're an unpleasant, arrogant son of a bitch… So that's it.' He threw the book on the table. 'I won't be reading this anymore.'

Damien could smell the alcohol on his breath. Yep, airport lounges were very dangerous places.

***

Cocooned in the first-class cabin, Damien was happy to be alone with his thoughts, mind-travelling.

Each time the bottle of Glenfiddich, his favourite tipple, glided by on the drinks trolley, the Voice whispered, *Don't even think about it. Keep your head. Tough it out.*

Damien breathed deeply, let his mind float into nothingness and fell asleep. He didn't wake till the early hours of the morning.

Chateau Marmont, with its Gothic charms, was for Damien the only place to stay in LA. The hotel's old-style glamour, famed for its notorious scandals, suited him.

Damien – white suit, shades and panama hat – sauntered through the lobby to the front desk. Even amongst the blasé guests, his languid confidence and style caused a ripple of whispers.

The Voice was amused. *Who would have thought it? There you were a year ago throwing yourself in the River Thames, and look at you now, Mr Slick. You give all the miserable bastards who are ready to jump into the fires of hell hope.*

Damien wasn't in a hurry. He had a cold shower in the art-deco-tiled bathroom of the penthouse suite and, padding across the parquet floor of the living room with a towel round his waist, went to play a few chords on the baby grand.

Maybe he'd invite Ariana to dinner. Sing her some Cole Porter songs, play her some Chopin Nocturnes. Her raw beauty and untamed passion had captivated him. Her voice rich and smooth like honey had evoked a deep-seated rush of sadness that had brought tears to his eyes. This was the soulmate he had yearned for.

Stop, the Voice said. *Grow up. You're too old to play Romeo. And more than likely she's only interested in a creative collaboration.*

Or maybe not. She seemed to be drawn to him. The way she wooed him, held him.

Damien was confused. Dizzy with anticipation. Worried that he would make the wrong impression. If people only knew that the sexy king of the intelligentsia, *Vanity Fair*'s leading man, was really a puppy dog who didn't know his ass from his elbow where women were concerned, and had lost his way years ago, barking up the wrong pair of panties.

***

Next morning the producers, Debra Peters and Seth Landry, greeted him with casual LA smiles.

At the back sat a striking young woman with short blonde hair, dressed all in black. She gave him a lazy look. He mouthed "hello".

Marc Castle appeared. He stood next to the mixing desk, his eyes fixed on the studio floor, arms crossed, propped against the wall. He seemed calm, in command, sexy. Damien wondered if he'd slept with Ariana.

Come on, why speculate? What's it to you? The Voice was back again. *She's an artist – treat her with respect.*

Ariana made her entrance like a travelling minstrel. Cradling her guitar, she drifted barefoot across the studio to sit cross-legged in the middle of the floor.

She smiled up at the control room and, placing the cans over her ears, adjusted the microphone and strummed a few chords.

'Ready when you are,' she said brightly.

***

It was different hearing Ariana sing the song in a recording studio. He missed the closeness of that wonderful week they'd spent together working late into the night.

She was the high priestess, his teacher, mother. But not his lover. Despite her beauty and sensuality, he hadn't played the seducer.

He remembered her words…

'This is how love feels, Damien. Write my passion,' she'd said. 'Be Sandra – leave a lasting memory for Samuel, your great love.'

Damien shut his eyes and let his mind drift beyond the studio walls, carried by the sound of Ariana's sensuous voice.

He mouthed the lyrics with her.

Can't you stay forever?
Do you have to leave?
There's nowhere to go,
Nowhere to hide;
Warm on the inside and cold outside.
Be my darling,
Hold me tight.
Don't let the night-time shroud the light.
Kindle the flame;
Don't blow it out.
Warm on the inside, cold outside.
Can't you stay forever?
Do you have to leave?
There's nowhere to go,
Nowhere to hide,
Warm on the inside and cold outside.
Nowhere to go,
Nowhere to hide,
Warm on the inside and cold outside.

And then the music stopped. He was back in the control room: everybody clapping, Ariana smiling.

The engineer checked the sound. Hole in one.

Damien rushed down to the studio floor. Had he finally found his soulmate? Someone to cherish for the rest of his life, who would in turn give him what he really needed? Faith in humanity. Love requited.

Ariana took the guitar and laid it gently on the floor. Her face full of love, she opened her arms. Damien was overwhelmed. She moved towards him…

At last, a communion of passion and creativity. He was so close, a heartbeat away.

When she glided past him, into the arms of the mysterious blonde woman who had sat behind him in the control room, he turned away to hide the veil of pain and disappointment in his eyes.

And the Voice said gently, with some compassion, *I told you so. Now show some good grace: go and congratulate her.*

***

'What's it all for?' Damien asked himself as he lay in bed, wide awake, jet-lagged at 5 a.m.

Now listen to me, said the Voice. *No point in searching for love. Let it come to you.*

'Could be waiting a long time. Please, no more bloody cocktail parties. Can't bear the chatterati and I hate standing. Good old Sartre got it right – hell is other people.'

Damien liked talking to himself. At least the Voice understood him.

'I'm not sure that I know what love is anymore.' He got out of bed and padded over to the balcony overlooking the illuminated pool below. Young men and women having a party, romancing, laughing, flirting in the moonlight. He thought, of all the women he'd known, only Laura had reached his soul.

She was brilliant, he thought, *a hot mind, but frozen in bed.*

Yes, and you treated her as if she were a Ming vase. Bit of a turn-off, said the Voice.

'And you'll never let me forget it, will you?'

Just identifying your weak spot, said the Voice. *Look at the patterns. Probably started with your mother. Couldn't cope with childbirth. As soon as you were born, so the story goes, she pissed off to a sanatorium in Switzerland and left Dada to change your nappies.*

'Stop that.'

And then she returned. But she kept on disappearing. So you did your best to please. 'Mummy, don't go away,' you cried. 'I promise to be good.'

'Be quiet, Damien,' she said. 'I can't stand it when you make a fuss. I'll have to leave again.'

And she did, said the Voice.

'That's enough.' Damien pulled a pillow over his head and rolled over into the foetal position.

Okay, you poor, wee bairn, so we'll skip the mum/son bit and the adolescent fumbling. Let's go straight for the biggies.

'Do we have to? Can't you let me rest in peace?'

No, we're working here, we need to know why you always fall into the same hole. The Voice was getting stronger.

'Oh, for God's sake, go away. You're giving me a headache.'

Damien sat up in bed, put his fingers in his ears and shut his eyes. 'Om shanti, shanti, shanti, om shanti, shanti,' he chanted. But chanting a mantra couldn't block out the Voice.

So let's get back to Laura. Your wife was a liar, but you married her for better or for worse. The marriage of true minds, the Voice carried on relentlessly. *But the truth was you bored her to buggery. She bided her time and, when she was ready, left you for a man's man, who gave her a good seeing to.*

Damien was in a sweat. 'Okay, that's enough,' he said.

It's never enough. We learn from our past.

Damien was spent. 'So will I ever find love?'

Well, you know who to ask, said the Voice.

Chapter 42

Claudia was proud of Damien. The lost soul who'd tried to end his life, fired by unrequited love, had come back from limbo.

However, thus far, even though he'd found his feet, it was difficult to steer him in the right direction.

He'd been scared of his past, hardly letting Claudia scratch the surface.

The questions he'd asked the cards were trivial. None that would yield answers that could illuminate his future. But this time she had a feeling that it would be different.

'Well, Damien,' Claudia said, 'what question would you like to ask first?'

'Will I find someone with whom to share my life?' he replied.

'Cut the cards and choose one,' she said.

Damien sliced the deck and with a nimble flick extended one to Claudia.

'The Page of Wands,' she said. 'It's an interesting answer. The studious youth of the pack. Court cards represent characteristics and can be any age or sex. This person could be studying or learning something.'

Ruby flashed through his mind. The stunning student he'd met at the Cheltenham Literary Festival. 'How and where shall I meet her?' he asked.

Don't count your chickens, said the Voice. *Who knows, it could be a bloke?*

'Pull another card,' Claudia said.

Damien, eyes wide and focused, hovered his index finger over the pack.

Why are you hesitating? said the Voice. *It's all written in the stars.*

He flipped a card.

'Three of Wands,' said Claudia. 'That's interesting. They may come from overseas and meet you here, or you might connect with them if you travel abroad. It's the card of the Exodus – looking further afield.'

'Well, that's a step in the right direction,' Damien said.

He thought of Ariana. He wished it could be her. She'd sent him a beautiful leather-bound notebook from America after they'd worked together, and inside, she'd written, *Write for me and I will sing for you.*

For goodness' sake, have you lost your mind? the Voice said. *Just because she's asking you to give her more material doesn't mean she loves you. Now let's get on with the reading.*

'May I ask another question?' Damien said.

'Go ahead,' Claudia replied.

'The truth is, I need to lay my relationship with Laura to rest so I can move on. Can you help me with this?'

'Yes,' she said. 'So what's the question?'

Why are you going there? You really are a masochist, said the Voice.

Damien hesitated. *No, damn the Voice, he was going to ask.*

'Okay, Claudia... The question is... did Laura really love me or was it a lie?' He pulled a card and flipped it over.

'Ah, Judgement,' Claudia said. 'The wake-up call and rebirth. Can you see the people coming out of their coffins? A new dawn. This is a great card and shows absolute clarity.'

Damien's mouth was dry. He poured himself a glass of water and took a sip. 'But I don't have clarity. There's no direct answer to my question. Laura's past is still a mystery to me, and

I can't find peace until I *know the truth*.' He spat the words into the air and banged his thigh with his fist.

Steady on, don't be so dramatic, said the Voice. *No need to frighten away the pigeons.*

Damien laughed to himself.

'Well, it should all be clear very soon. Let's move on,' Claudia said. 'Pull another card to see what happens next.'

Damien ran his hands over the deck, trying to see if one would "speak" to him.

'This is so difficult.' He sighed. 'It's like Russian roulette. Could be that I'm going to shoot myself in the head.'

Come on. Don't keep the lady waiting, ordered the Voice.

'Just pull any card,' Claudia directed. 'The right one will find you.'

Damien handed her another, face down.

'There you are,' she said, turning it over. 'The Ace of Swords. That's the card of pure truth and logic. Cutting the negativity out of your life. Clarity will come to you.'

Good, we're on the right road, said the Voice. *Don't stop now. Keep on going.*

'One more question?'

'Yes,' Claudia replied.

'How can I stop being in disastrous relationships?'

That's good, said the Voice. *Right to the point.*

'The fact that you're asking the question shows you're ready to have an honest and mutually fulfilling connection,' Claudia replied. 'Now, pull a card for your past.'

Damien drew one from the deck.

'The Devil!' she said. 'You love drama and passion. Lust and temptation. The card signals addictive behaviour and co-dependency. The sex, drugs and rock 'n' roll. Quite frankly, you've a history of sadomasochistic relationships. Now, choose a card for the present.'

He was quick to take one. Best not to dwell on the past.

Yes, that's it – let's bury the Devil, said the Voice. *Here's your chance to sort out what you really need, not just what you want.*

'Six of Cups, much healthier. Now you understand what makes you happy. What you need is loving companionship. Possibly with someone you've known for a while, or maybe a person with whom you feel a connection from a past life experience.'

'Will I be happy?' Damien asked wistfully.

Those soulful eyes searching for answers.

This Damien would melt most women, Claudia thought to herself.

'I want you to pull one last card,' she said.

Damien was ready to take what he was given. Follow the path that destiny had dealt him. For a moment, he stroked his chosen card with the tip of his finger. He turned it over.

'Ten of Pentacles. There you have it,' Claudia said. 'This is the completion of the family – roots, belonging, security and harmony. Maybe you'll find a connection with someone related to your past, extended family, that will bring you happiness and stability. This is a lovely card for meaningful relationships.'

He really didn't care who came and from where.

What he did know was that someone would bring him happiness. Claudia had shone the light. Opened up his mind, given him hope.

***

However, Damien was lonely. No one to deflect his obsession with mortality in the wee hours. Only the Voice to keep him company.

Sometimes he woke in the middle of the night, wondering whether he was dead or alive. He stretched out his arms and bent his legs, took deep breaths in from the nose, out through the mouth, placed two fingers on his wrist to check his pulse, testing the mechanics of his being.

But after the reading with Claudia, he found his anxiety had eased. He began to surrender to the night. He was ready to embrace the past, to allow himself to remember the moments that he had hitherto tried to forget.

But what if he had chosen the road not taken? What if he'd faced his demons earlier in the game?

But you didn't. Where you are now is the only place you can be, said the Voice.

'Maybe so. But I don't want to live a blind life. Let me recall my past. It's my history, my story, and I can't just tear up the pages.'

Damien got out of bed and made himself a cup of builder's tea, with a tiny smidgeon of milk and a spoonful of acacia honey.

He opened the larder door and took out the Fortnum & Mason tin. Half a shortbread biccie left. Why not? He sat at the wooden farmhouse table, popped it in his mouth and shut his eyes.

His beloved father materialised. It was Damien's sixth birthday.

The image in his mind's eye was so clear that it was almost as if his father's spirit was with him.

'Here you are.' Daddy placed a large box on the Persian carpet in the grand sitting room of the sprawling family home in Highgate. 'Let's open it together. Aren't you lucky to be born in the summer? Look at that clear blue sky.' He opened the glass doors leading onto the terrace. 'Later, we can go in the garden and have a picnic on the lawn.'

Damien beamed. Daddy kissed his cheek. 'Where's Mama?' he asked.

'She'll be down in a minute,' Daddy replied. 'Poor Mummy's got a headache. She's resting. Now let's get on with unwrapping your present.'

A fantastic train set. A big-boy's one with a remote control. The carriages in red and gold.

Daddy was smiling at him, his eyes full of tender affection. And at that moment Damien knew he was truly loved.

But then, when he was seven, something terrible happened.

Damien shook his head as the images flashed through his mind.

Yes! You wanted this, said the Voice. *You chose to visit your past, so don't block it.*

Damien remembered how he'd eaten his dinner and brushed his teeth, ready for bedtime. But where was Daddy? He usually came to read him a story and kiss him goodnight.

Sometimes, if she was feeling well, Mummy came too. But that evening he heard his parents shouting.

'Don't you tell me what to do,' Mummy said. 'If I want to go to France for the weekend with my girlfriends, I will. You don't own me and what's more I'm the one who pays the bills since you've been ill.' Her shouting became screaming. 'I'm fed up with you. I want to leave. There's nothing left except your bloody gambling debts.'

And that was when he heard Daddy cry. He wanted to go and cuddle him, but he was scared.

'Please, please, call the doctor,' he heard Daddy say. 'I'm in terrible pain. My heart hurts.'

Mummy wasn't having any stuff and nonsense. 'You always complain,' she said. 'Last time I wanted to go to Spain, you did the same thing. And, when I cancelled the trip, like magic you were better again.'

Damien hid under the sheets and, muffling his ears with a pillow, finally fell asleep.

Come the morning, Nanny woke him. 'How's Daddy?' he asked her.

'Daddy's gone away,' she told him.

'When will he be back?'

'He's on a journey to the stars.'

But Damien knew.

'Why?' he cried. 'Mummy, why did Daddy die? He wasn't ill last week. He took me to the park on Sunday to feed the ducks. He didn't have to go to hospital or anything. I heard you say he was pretending.'

'I thought he was, but this morning he didn't wake up.'

'Oh! Daddy's gone and I didn't even get to say goodbye.' Damien, drowning in his tears, gulped for air as each new wave of melancholy washed over him.

'It's God's will, Damien,' Mummy said, and gave him a hug, which surprised him. She wasn't the touchy-feely type.

He clung to her, put his arms round her neck. How he wept.

The novelty of being cuddled by his mother gave Damien such pleasure that he kept the tears flowing.

But, after a while, Mummy had had enough.

'Come on, Damien, be a big boy,' she said. 'Go and get dressed and I'll tell Nanny to make your breakfast.'

***

The funeral took place a week later, Sunday morning. Nanny stayed with him at home. Afterwards, there was a party in the garden. The guests arrived all wearing black, which looked strange on a warm summer's day.

'Poor little one,' he heard his Uncle Harry tell the vicar. 'Hard to lose a father when you're so young. And being an only child.'

Damien wanted to say that it was okay. He was a big boy now and as long as Mummy stayed to look after him he would be fine.

But it was Damien who left. Mummy sent him away to boarding school when he was eight.

'It will be good for you,' she said. 'You're too old for nannies and babysitters and I need my freedom. It's been a long time since I've enjoyed myself.'

***

When he came home for the Christmas hols, Mummy said, 'Damien darling, this is Teddy. He's going to be your new father.'

Teddy came from Scotland. Damien quite liked him. He spoke French and was very rich. So he and Mummy married and the following Christmas they all went skiing in Val d'Isère.

In truth, his life took a turn for the better. When he was thirteen, he went to Eton. It suited him. He was good at sport and clever. When he won a scholarship to Oxford, Teddy took him to Paris without Mother.

'Now,' his stepfather said, 'let's get you sorted out. None of this romantic stuff with little virgin debutantes who, as soon as you get into their knickers, expect a ring on their finger.'

They stayed at the Ritz. Henri the concierge arranged for two gorgeous women to visit their suite.

Damien was insanely happy. Anoushka, his extremely accomplished partner, led him to ecstasy without any need to reciprocate. Then, after he had gathered back his strength, she said, 'Now, sweetie, tell me truthfully, have you had a woman before?'

'No, to be honest,' he replied, 'I haven't. Only kisses with a couple of girls at school dances. And when I went on a language trip to Brittany, I stayed with a family who had a daughter the same age as me, Amélie, and we had some fun. But we didn't go the whole way. And she didn't do what you did to me.' Damien glanced at her mouth that had pleased him so.

Anoushka stroked his hair. 'Well, then, I am delighted to be your first.'

The beautiful stranger who gave him such pleasure had never been far from his mind. How could he ever forget?

The next morning, Damien and Teddy visited the Louvre, afterwards they lunched at the splendid Le Grand Véfour, next to the gardens of the Palais Royal – a Parisienne treasure that had discreetly hosted royalty, writers, artists and politicos for more than two centuries.

'Imagine, Damien,' said his stepfather as the maître d' led them through the gloriously opulent eighteenth-century dining room, 'Napoleon proposed to Joséphine here, and this is where Colette held court.' Teddy paused at a corner table and pointed to a little bronze disc engraved with her name on the burgundy velvet banquette.

'Well, my dear fellow,' he said as they settled themselves at the adjacent table, 'look at your plaque – Emile Zola, no less.'

'If only I had his genius,' Damien said. 'Perhaps he'll call me from the grave. Give me some writing tips.'

Nana the man-eater, he thought. *One of my favourite characters destroyed every man she met. But she must have been amazing in bed.*

Damien gazed around the golden room, with its mirrored walls and glass pillars painted with classical figures, at the ornate gilded empire furnishings, and for a moment imagined himself dining next to Nana, who looked surprisingly like Anoushka, her plump breasts overflowing in a red velvet bodice, one hand between his legs and the other slipping a succulent oyster into his mouth.

The waiter coughed discreetly.

'Damien,' Teddy whispered, 'wake up. What would you like to eat?'

For the starter, like his stepfather, he chose the *ravioles de foie gras*, splashed with a froth of truffle cream. To anchor the rich flavour, a small leaf of Savoy cabbage added to the sumptuous little packets of decadence, accompanied by a half-bottle of Chateau Rieussec, an elegantly sweet Sauternes.

'Ah,' Damien gasped, biting into the buttery perfection, 'my education is complete.'

Teddy raised his glass of wine. 'A toast to manhood,' he said, 'and so much better to be initiated by a professional,' he added with a rakish smile.

A few years later, Teddy and his mother were killed in a car crash, en route to Monte Carlo.

But for all the bonhomie Damien had shared with his stepfather he would have gladly swapped it for a kinder mother.

He shut his eyes again. Laura came to mind, eclipsing any happy thoughts of Paris.

Get over it, Damien, said the Voice. *Let's face it, she wanted a no-holds-barred, free sex wrestle. A tussle with muscle. And that's that. Must have, can't have. The story of your life. Always looking for someone to leave you. Just like Mummy did.*

'Okay, okay. How many times do you have to say it?' Damien said.

Until you find the mother inside yourself, said the Voice.

Chapter 43

Damien scanned the lovely woman standing next to him waiting for a table at Le Pain Quotidien. She caught his look and gave him a wide Cheshire Cat grin, her teeth shiny and even. She was almost certainly American. Mid-to late-twenties, he guessed. Her blonde hair tied back in a sleek ponytail, two diamond studs in each ear, she held her mobile in one hand and the handle of her neat designer rucksack in the other.

He paused and gave her a full-focus stare. She was wearing an edgy biker jacket and tiny mini skirt. His eyes slid down her long, sculpted legs to her foxy high-heeled ankle boots.

'Don't say a word... I bet you're a New Yorker. Tell me I'm wrong and I'll buy you a coffee,' he said.

'How did you guess?'

'It's obvious. Your smile. Open and friendly. None of that English reserve. And the way you dress. Chic Manhattan.'

He looked for a ring on her finger. There wasn't one. Good.

'Ah, there's a table. Shall we sit together?' he asked.

'Sure,' she replied. 'As long as I can pay for your coffee.'

'What do you mean?'

'You sussed I was from NYC.'

They sat by the window.

The waitress came.

'I'll have a soy cappuccino,' she said. She turned to him. 'What are you having?'

'I'll have a double espresso, please.'

He was enjoying himself. She was quirky, this fresh-faced American girl.

'Wanna try and guess my name?' she said.

'Okay.' He gave her a quizzical look. 'Well, you could be a Paula or Gemma or Helen. Or maybe an Angie, Mandy or Anna.'

Take it slow, the Voice said. *You're doing your number, piling on the patter.*

'I'm Frances,' she said, extending a hand.

'And I'm Damien,' he replied, giving her his. She had a firm grip. He liked that. 'So, Frances,' he said. 'What's your story?'

'I'm at film school.'

'Oh really? Are you at the NFTS?'

'Yes. How do you know the place? Are you in the movie business?'

'Well, I'm a novelist primarily, but my last book, *Writing in the Sand*, has just been made into a film.'

Frances narrowed her eyes and searched Damien's face. 'Oh my God, yes! You're Damien Spur.'

'I am indeed.'

'Wow, this is crazy!' Her face had suddenly changed from a sophisticated woman into an excited teenager. 'You're not gonna believe this' – she moved so close to him that he could smell the coffee on her breath – 'but I've booked to see the screening on Saturday at the Academy of Cinema Arts, especially because you're doing a Q&A after the show. Yup. I'm so interested in the discussion. "From Novel to Screenplay", isn't it?' The words tumbled out of her mouth with such intense excitement that Damien drew back. 'Oh my! Just a sec, do you mind if I tweet this?'

'Not entirely sure it's appropriate, but if you insist,' Damien replied.

'Thank you! It's such a coincidence. My followers will love it. Okay! Here we go…' She picked up her phone.

Damien watched her fingers move swiftly as she typed.

Guess what. I'm sitting next to Damien Spur, one of my favourite writers. Serendipity. I'm going to his lecture at the ACA next week, can you believe it?

'So, Mr Spur' – she slipped her phone back into her bag – 'tell me more about the talk.'

'Well, as the title suggests, the discussion is about the visual interpretation of the written word serving the story.'

'I should imagine it's quite a responsibility shifting a novel into a screenplay,' Frances said. 'Mind you, I suppose you have to be flexible. Maybe not always faithful to the novel. Especially if the producers want the changes.'

'Not if it's in your contract that as the writer you have the last word,' Damien said.

'Luckily, I don't have that problem with my script. I originally wrote it as a book, a dark thriller which was published while I was at university. We're shooting the short in a few weeks. Shall I tell you what it's about?'

'Ah, not now,' Damien replied. 'I've been so carried away chatting with you that I'm late for my meeting.'

'Are you walking? If so, we could carry on talking.'

'Actually, I am.'

She waved at the waitress. 'Great! Then let's pay the tab and go.'

Outside in the street, Damien increased his pace. His long legs covered the ground with such speed that Frances had to almost jog to keep up with him.

'I don't want to be pushy,' she panted, 'but rather than me telling you the story, maybe you could have a look at my script? I'm not sure that the transition from book to screenplay works. I'm sure you would be amazing at that.' She took a deep breath and grabbed his arm. 'It would be so great to have your masterful eye. It's not very long, only about sixty pages.'

She was cheeky. But somehow or other her raw ambition appealed to him.

Damien slowed down.

'So, Frances,' he said in a teacherly way, 'what's your course? Screenwriting?'

'No. Directing.' She paused. 'Isn't this fantastic?' She gazed at him with a wide-eyed, where-will-this-take-us look.

Damien wasn't used to such openness.

'In what way?' he said, though he knew exactly what she meant.

'Us, meeting like this. Such a random coincidence.'

'Or maybe it was always on the cards. Who knows?' he said.

Not now, Damien, said the Voice. *It's way too early in the game to start with the kismet bit.*

'Anyway, Frances… it's been good to meet you.' He shook her hand. 'Good luck with your short.'

'Thanks. I'll see you at the screening. I'd better come up with a question.'

'Good idea.'

She turned round and walked back in the other direction. He wondered if Frances could be the one. She was different from the other women who'd been in his life, particularly his miserable and frosty mother.

Frances was a happy, cup-half-full woman… She was warm.

And, as the cards foretold, she came from overseas. Was a student – post grad.

But then again… Maybe she was just a little too lively. A party, gin-and-tonic sort of girl. Not good for him.

Just hold your horses, the Voice said. *You could have anyone. You don't want a fan – you want a soulmate. What's the matter with you? Remember who you are.*

'I am Damien Spur, the famous fucked-up writer.' He hailed a taxi to take him home.

When he arrived, his agent was waiting outside the door.

'Hello, Angus.' Damien gave him a lazy smile.

'You're late,' his agent said. 'I've been here for twenty minutes. We agreed to meet at ten thirty, and it's now ten fifty!'

'Look, Angus,' Damien said, 'how many times when I was a struggling writer did you make me wait for you?'

His agent ignored him. 'Are you going to let me in or do you expect me to wedge my foot in the door like a travelling salesman?'

'Of course.' Damien ushered him through with a wave of his hand.

Angus walked past him into the sitting room and sat on the sofa. 'Well, then, how have you been?'

Damien had always been aware that Angus had only cared about his well-being in relation to his work. He was good at the cheerleader chat, flagged him on to the finishing line. He was simply his agent, not a sympathetic friend, but to his credit he was the best dealmaker in the business.

'Do you want tea or coffee?' Damien asked.

'No, I'm fine. Haven't got the time now.'

Damien sat next to him. 'Before you start, let me make something absolutely clear. I'm not accepting any of those party invites that you forwarded to me. I told you to trash them. You know that I'm not prepared to spend my time making small talk.'

'It's okay, Damien.' Angus gave him a hard glance. 'Why not be honest? You don't want to be around the booze.'

'Yup, that's right. So, if you know that, why keep on throwing the invitations in my face?'

'Because you can't spend your life hiding away.'

'Why not? It probably makes me more exciting. I'm not into courting publicity anymore. Not interested in being the pin-up addict who bleats about his recovery and how many times a week he goes to AA. How my life has changed and that I'd never touch the stuff again. The truth is I'm still dying to have a drink and a snort of coke.'

'Okay, okay,' Angus said. 'I'm not your therapist. But I'll tell you one thing, there's a lot riding on the next book and if you start backtracking and get hooked on the alcohol and drugs again, I wouldn't think that you'd be in a fit state to even write an email, judging by your last sordid performance.'

'Thanks for the pep talk, Angus.'

'It's a pleasure. Now then, let's get down to business.'

Damien poured himself a glass of water from the only bottle on the drinks table and lifted it in the air. 'To the deal!'

His agent put the contract on the table. To the sequel of *Writing in the Sand*.

Chapter 44

Tonight, Damien was ready to set sail for the Q&A "From Novel to Screenplay".

The session was to be hosted by Alan Finnigan, head of the Academy of Cinema Arts. Damien had skipped the film. Arrived at the interval. He checked the guests in the green room. A quick spin. All friendly fire. Chat, chat, chat. Juice and water on the table, no vino as agreed.

A few minutes later there was a tap on his shoulder.

Damien swivelled round.

A bespectacled female had appeared with a clipboard. 'Hi, Mr Spur,' she said. 'I'm Ranya, Alan's PA. Everything okay?'

'Fine thanks. So where's Finnigan?'

'He's waiting for you onstage. Would you like to come now?'

Okey dokey, sunshine, here we go. No more upsey downsies, the Voice trilled. *We are back! Relax, we're going to be terrific. No one else to steal our thunder, just us and Finnigan.*

Damien stepped onto the rostrum.

Finnigan, his face red and shiny under the bright light, was frantically texting on his phone.

'Hello, Alan,' said Damien. 'Alan...? Are you there?'

Finnigan looked up. He gave Damien a blank, myopic stare through his thick-lensed glasses. 'Sorry, sorry, just a spot of bother. Good to see you!'

'Where is the audience?' Damien asked.

Finnigan looked askance. 'I've shooed them away so we can prep the session.'

Oh what! Summit's up. Mr Shifty's avoiding eye contact. So why? said the Voice.

Damien scanned the room. Two video cameras to tape the show and just enough seating to create an intimate atmosphere.

Good set-up. But why were there three chairs on the stage?

'Is there another guest, Alan?' Damien said.

'Uhhhh…' Finnigan opened and closed his mouth like a fish gulping for air. 'Well…'

'We agreed. Just the two of us,' said Damien. 'Alan?'

'Yes? Sorry, Damien. But can you hold on a sec, I really had no idea. Just had the call this morning. Didn't expect him.'

'Expect who?'

'And now he's bloody late.' Finnigan thrust his hand in his pocket. He took out a tissue and dabbed his sweaty forehead. 'And he doesn't answer my texts… Where are you, Ranya?' he yelled.

The PA ran back on stage with a walkie-talkie in her hand.

'No worries, Alan,' she said quietly. 'He's five minutes away in an Uber.'

'Okay, wait at the door and bring him straight through security and onto the stage.'

'Who's five minutes away?' asked Damien.

'Well, I had a call this morning,' Finnigan replied. 'The office tried to contact you, but your mobile was switched off… I know I broke our agreement but…'

'Yes… but what? Come on, Alan. Spit it out. Who's the mystery man?'

'It's Marc Castle,' Finnigan muttered.

'What the hell!' Damien thumped his head. 'You're kidding me! You know I can't stand the man. He made a national fool of me.'

311

The audience had started to filter into the theatre.

'So what could I do?' Finnigan shrugged his shoulders. 'He invited himself at the last minute. He's just returned from shooting a film in Kenya. How could I say no to the director of the movie? We need the publicity. How do you think this place runs? Government funding only goes so far; we need our sponsors.'

'Don't give me that crap,' Damien hissed. 'You knew he was coming all along. Just didn't want to tell me in case I stood you up.'

Castle arrived. Sauntered onto the stage all fancy dapper with his blue suede loafers and velvet jacket.

'So sorry I'm late.' He patted Alan's shoulder. 'My, you look red. Where's your make-up girl?'

'This is a lecture theatre not a film set,' Finnigan said.

Damien flicked Castle an icy glance. He retaliated with a smug smile.

'Actually, come to think of it, you could do with a bit of a touch-up too,' he drawled.

Here we go, said the Voice. *Mr Lah-di-dah is pitching for another scrap.*

The two men had fallen out in a very public way and the war wasn't over.

It was the preview of *Writing in the Sand* that had been a gut punch. Castle was known for encouraging improvisation. The actors had gone rogue, Damien's words tossed aside in the climactic scene.

After the film, Damien had grabbed him by the shoulders and slammed him against the wall. It was all snapped by the paps; in the papers and online gossip blogs the next day.

Come on, Damien, let it go. It's show time, said the Voice.

Finnigan stood up and addressed the auditorium. I hope you all enjoyed the film this evening. So now let's kick off the Q&A. Please welcome our esteemed guest, the creator of *Writing in the Sand*, author and screenplay writer, Damien Spur.'

The wave of applause gave him a rush of pleasure. 'Thank you, Alan.' He nodded at Finnigan and doffed an imaginary cap.

Okay, Damien, now keep it moving, said the Voice... *and don't dilly-dally on the way.*

Damien paused. He always did before he spoke. Building the anticipation.

'Netflix is the new novel,' he began. 'If you want to sell books and you're not the master of style, my advice is to keep the sentences short and the plot tight. Truncate the wordy bits, get on with the action. Make it quick and snappy and you'll keep them reading. So, will a book with a great story and shortcuts morph into a screenplay? Not necessarily.'

He looked at the sea of rapt faces. He was back on the throne again. Nobody held a stage like Damien Spur.

Yes, that's it, said the Voice. *Keep it coming.*

'But' – Damien gave his cryptic smile – 'that's my general advice. There are always exceptions to the rule. Me, for instance, I take the long road. I like to describe the scenery, reveal private thoughts behind public faces. However, as I write my own screenplays, it's easy for me to do a literary striptease and interpret my words into visuals.

'It's also the case that many writers, no matter how brilliant they are, just can't grasp the visual shorthand of film. That's when it's best to give the baby up for adoption and leave it to a gifted screenwriter to turn the novel into a cinematic success.'

'Thank you, Damien,' Finnigan said. 'So let's have some questions from the audience.'

A man standing at the back of the room shot up his hand. He wore dark glasses and a Fedora. An assistant handed him a mike.

'Just one question for Mr Castle. Have you and Mr Spur resolved the fracas that took place after the preview of *Writing in the Sand*? It was reported that one of Mr Spur's carefully crafted scenes was replaced by the actors' improvised dialogue?'

The Voice recognised that nasal whine.

Oh no! It's that poisonous critic Jeremy Floyd who panned the film.

'In the end, it's about authenticity,' Castle said. 'Actors know their characters, sometimes better than the script, don't you think so, Damien?'

He had thrown the gauntlet down. There was a challenge in his stare.

Damien's jaw clenched, a muscle twitching in his cheek. *Don't rise to it,* said the Voice.

'It depends,' Damien replied. 'The problem with filming spontaneous improvisations is that the scene can take a wrong turn if the actor gets carried away. And that becomes difficult as the story can lose focus. No doubt the dialogue is authentic but then again, my pen is too.'

Good, Damien, said the Voice. *Now give him a jab.*

He gave Marc a flinty smile.

'I think that your earlier film, *Someone Like Us*, didn't really work for me because you let the actors free to run the dialogue. The scenes meandered. No spaces for the audience to project. Probably why it died at the box office.'

Very impressive, said the Voice.

And then Frances stood up. She looked different from the first time they'd met – more feminine. Her blonde hair fell on to her shoulders with a soft curl. Her curvy body was draped in a pillar-box-red dress that clung to her well-formed breasts. To balance her overtly sexy image, she wore stylish black-rimmed glasses.

Steady on, Damien. Concentrate on the question, the Voice said.

She held the mike in her delicate hand.

'Firstly, let me say how much I enjoyed the film, especially the love scenes.' She looked straight at Damien. 'The female character was so authentic, her love for Samuel expressed with

314

such sensitivity. Was it easy for you to think like a woman? Write such an organically female part?'

'Personally, I don't find it a problem,' Damien replied. 'The roles men and women play in society today have become more fluid. The actress Ariana Bianchi has her own extraordinary female grace, which she brought to the character of Sandra. She gave my lines the gravitas and passion that transcends gender. Ultimately, gender doesn't matter. Love is love. Women and men feel the same when the flame is lit.'

***

At the end of the Q&A Frances was waiting in the foyer.

She was standing propped against the wall, glued to her phone. Damien tapped her shoulder.

'Hello,' he said.

She looked up at him and blinked.

'Hi, won't be a sec. I'm just posting your talk.'

'There you go again, always on your phone. Don't you miss real time?'

'Not at all,' she replied. 'Making films and social networking is my thing.'

Oh dear! said the Voice. *She's a bit of a bulldozer. You'd have thought she could have at least paused her texting to say hello.*

And then Frances switched her mobile off and popped it in her pocket. 'I thought your talk was terrific,' she said, and smoochy-kissed him on the cheek.

Okay, forgiven, said the Voice.

A tall man with dark glasses and long grey hair in a ponytail had spotted him.

'Oh no! Come on, Frances, let's go,' said Damien.

'Why, what's the matter?'

'The guy coming towards us is a nutter. I don't want to get trapped into some boring chit-chat.'

'Ah, then possessive already.'

'That's right. I just want your undivided attention.' He took her arm and moved her in the direction of the door.

***

He'd booked a table at the Chelsea Arts Club. Damien liked the retro feel. The place was full of sixties hangovers, still in the same gear. Old roses and craggy faces, cocooned by past glories. Especially in the bar, which he skipped nowadays, for obvious reasons.

People, places and things, the Voice reminded him.

They went straight through to the dining room.

'This is great.' Frances scanned the dark wood furniture and paintings on the green baize walls. 'I really like the low buzz. You British definitely move at a slower pace.'

'Well, here they do,' Damien said. 'And no mobiles allowed!'

'Oh, that's a shame. It's really beautiful here. I was going to take a pic for my Instagram.'

'Absolutely not! Would you like some wine?'

They sat at a corner table.

'Yes, please. Don't mind if it's red or white. What are you having?'

Come on, Damien, tell her the truth. You might as well start now, the Voice said.

'I'm on the wagon,' he replied, 'but, please, don't mind me.'

'Thanks, I'll have a glass of Chardonnay.'

***

They ate and Damien talked.

When the bill came, he held her wrist as she dipped into her bag.

'No way,' he said.

316

'Thank you so much,' she replied.

Frances seemed to enjoy Damien's gentleman's finesse.

'I'm not used to this. In New York it's always Dutch on the first date. I think it's mainly because the guys are shit-scared to be chivalrous. They've been drilled by human resources to treat women on an equal footing. Like I have a friend who called the females in his office "girls". He really had his fingers rapped.'

'In what context?' Damien asked.

'He actually said that it would be good if there were more "girls" on the team, as there were only two and there were eight guys. So the head of HR, who was female, told him that he must call them "women", and that "girls" is patronising and chauvinistic and doesn't reflect well on the team.'

'That's a bit extreme.'

'Funny thing is that after her lecture she hit on him.'

'And how did he respond?'

'Absolutely no way was he going down that road. Her husband was the CEO of the company. Very awkward for my pal. Told her that she was an extremely attractive woman, but he had a girlfriend and was very much in love.'

'And how did she react?'

'Apparently, she took it quite well and just said that it wasn't politically correct to say girlfriend either and instead he should use the word "partner".

***

It was midnight when he drove her back to Fulham.

'Such a great evening. I do hope we meet again,' she said.

Damien liked Frances – he just wasn't sure how much.

'I'll call you,' he said. 'Maybe lunch next week?'

'Great! And next time you're my guest.'

'We'll see about that. But you can certainly choose where to eat.'

'It won't be fancy. I like a place called Mitch's. Reminds me of New York.' Frances waited. Was he going to kiss her?

Damien Spur, the sophisticated A-lister, hesitated.

Not yet, said the Voice. *You need to be sure. She's not your usual sort. There's something sweet about her. If you start all that, there's no going back with this one.*

He stroked her cheek. 'Time to go to beddy-byes. See you soon,' he said softly, and left.

***

They sat together on a shoddy red plastic bench in a booth. The chrome tables and fluorescent lighting gave the place a ghostly feel; a harsh, steely atmosphere that not even the warm rays of autumn sunlight could penetrate.

'Frances, please put your mobile away,' Damien said. 'What are you tweeting about now? It's really very rude to be on your phone while we're eating.'

'I'm not tweeting. I'm posting on Instagram.'

Why the hell did she choose this dump? the Voice said. *I think you're on to a loser. She's too young for you. So obsessed with her phone, probably doesn't notice where she is.*

Damien jabbed the grey slab of meat with his fork. 'This burger is disgusting. Cooked to buggery. Not even fit for a dog.'

Should have gone to Gauchos, said the Voice. *At least you can have a medium-rare steak there. Absolutely delicious, soft as butter, not like these dried-up cow pats that you can bet your bottom dollar taste like shit.*

'Anyway, what are you posting about this time?' he said to Frances.

'I'm a lifestyle influencer, Damien. I have 20,000 followers. I'm going to bring culture to my brand, and you are my poster boy.' She pinched his cheek and gave him a beautiful smile.

'Great.' He bit into the burger and tried to swallow. 'Ugh! I can't do this.' He spat it into a paper napkin. 'I should imagine that prison food's better. I know the soup kitchen in Brixton is.'

'How do you know?'

'Because I've cooked there at Christmas.'

'That's good of you.'

'Not really. Just relieves me of my guilt. You still haven't said what words of wisdom you are sending to your loyal followers.'

'Give us a smile.' Frances took a picture.

She showed him the photo and then typed a short message that read, *Damien Spur loves a burger, but not this one. There will be no return visit to Mitch's Diner.*

She tapped the icon with her index finger. 'There you go – you're posted on my Insta.'

'Frances, I'm a serious writer. You are trivialising my life.'

'Come on, Damien. It's the new way.'

'Well, I'm flattered that you've taken it upon yourself to promote me, but I do actually have a publicist.'

'Not that I can see,' said Frances.

'That's because you're so obsessed with social networking.'

'True. As far as I'm concerned, everything else is a side show.'

'Maybe so, but I really don't need your help.'

'You do if you want to create a platform for the next generation of readers. Look, I know you have a huge number of devotees. The video I uploaded of your academy talk on Facebook had 8,000 views, which I cross-linked with my blog, Twitter and Instagram account, which, combined, had another 20,000 views. And that was only till yesterday! Pretty impressive, I'd say. But I guess your fans are post-thirty. So, let's widen your audience to a younger demographic.'

'Really, Frances, you're obsessive.'

'Okay, but let me show you how it works.'

She sat close to Damien. Her hair smelt of roses.

'I reviewed your book this morning. So now we take a selfie.' She moved closer.

'I wish you wouldn't. The lighting's terrible here,' he said.

Frances ignored him. 'Here we go.'

'No, really, stop! I'm not some mindless idiot. I'm leaving. This is so undignified. I think you should play with someone your own age.' He called the waiter.

'Okay, okay…' Frances had lost her happy face. 'I'm sorry. I'll just post the text.' She took a deep breath. 'Please, it will only take a second.'

Lucky me chatting to Damien Spur, she typed rapidly. *His new thriller,* Writing in the Sand, *is a mind twister. Visit my blog Spreadtheword.com to read my review.*

She clicked submit. 'Now we wait for the hits.'

Damien pushed his plate away.

'Look, I know you have the best intentions, but calm down. Why don't we go to my place and you can try to convert me over a cuppa and a sandwich.'

***

Back at Cheyne Walk, Frances sat in the kitchen and continued her mission.

Damien wasn't sure what he'd let himself in for.

What's the problem? said the Voice. *Let her talk. She might say something useful.*

***

Frances couldn't stop. She was animated like a wind-up toy.

'Social networking is a digital shout that can go viral, shared by people like me. It's key to have endorsements from celebrities and some juicy gossip to boost your profile. That's how to create a trend.'

'Trends go out of fashion,' Damien said. 'Best to be a classic. Writers find their audiences through the merits of their books, not their personalities. I'm not an actor.'

'Please, Damien, this is my field. Let me show you how it works. Next time you do a talk, why don't I film it and upload it on my YouTube channel?'

Damien took a coconut biscuit and popped it in his mouth. 'Mmm, these are good. Very crunchy and naturally sweet. I made them last night. Try one?'

'No thanks – I'm on a diet.'

He broke one in half and teased her lips open.

'Really, Damien! I get the message.' She pushed his hand away. 'You're trying to stop me talking.'

'Yes.'

Frances giggled as she let him pop the biscuit in her mouth.

'Mmmm, very good,' she said crunching rapidly and swallowing hard. 'So about my channel. It's called Sassy Yankee. I do a virtual tour of London, but it's not about places of interest – it's about people. I chat to the demographic of a particular area and get their POV on a variety of topics. I ask the same question to a woman in Knightsbridge as I do to a woman in Dalston. It's interesting to see how their opinions vary.'

'Yes. Always fascinating,' Damien responded with feigned enthusiasm.

Frances had exhausted him with her relentless digital evangelism. He stifled a yawn.

Come on, Damien. Don't fall asleep, the Voice said. *The poor girl is trying her best to impress you.*

'Am I boring you?' she asked.

'No! Not at all,' he lied.

'Okay,' she said. 'So, I start by asking light questions such as, "If you could spend the night with a celebrity who would it be?". Things like that. A bit cheeky. But the advertisers like it. Pulls in the views. Then I tackle deeper issues; politics, social injustice: "Do we need the royal family?", etc. Anything that seems relevant at the time. Nothing really planned.'

'That's great,' Damien said sarcastically. 'Any little buzz that comes into your head that you can ask to random strangers. And just a few clicks away it's transmitted to your followers. Hail, Frances, Queen of Trivia.'

'That's not true. I have a deep sense of justice and empathy for people who are struggling in this difficult world and I try to educate my followers. Tell them what I have experienced. Give them my views. Bring them closer to the truth.'

'Yes, Frances. Your truth. Just so long as it brings in the sponsors.'

'Come on! You have to admit the web is a fantastic marketing tool,' Frances said taking another biscuit. 'These really are moreish. Why don't I post your recipe on my blog and we could do a little info on your hobbies as part of your bio? And I can help you set up your own Insta profile. Damien Spur, Renaissance man. I bettya you'll sell a ton more books.'

'No, no, no! Frances, stop! I don't want or need an Instagram, Facebook or Twitter account,' Damien snapped. 'Every time I publish a new novel it sells out worldwide in three months online with multiple reprints, and first editions go for hundreds of pounds. I don't need your social-media puff.'

Damien wondered why he had hooked up to a crazy American who spent her life with her head in an iCloud.

'Can I tell you something?' She leant forward and gave him one of her fixed listen-up looks.

'If you insist.'

'Whatever you say, social media is where it's at. There's no point in you hiding your head in the sand. Don't you want to pull in new blood? That's who's going to keep the fire burning!'

'Frances, I've had enough of this. You don't have to tell me how to run my professional life. And to be honest, I don't give a damn about my legacy. I couldn't care less who reads my books when I'm dead.'

'I will,' she vowed, like a bride at the altar.

Well, that came out of the blue, murmured the Voice.

Damien was touched. She had expressed her loyalty to him with such sincerity. He felt a pang of regret that he'd been so cruel, unravelling her passion and dedication to the New World.

You have to be careful, said the Voice. *This girl could be easily hurt. And if it doesn't work out, there may be trouble ahead. Never trust a blogger.*

'I think I should go now,' she said. 'I have a lot of work to do before the morning.'

'Well, thank you for a sparky afternoon.' He walked her to the door. 'See you soon,' he said.

Damien watched her leave, swinging her bag on her shoulder. For a brief moment, she looked back. He gave her a wave and shut the door.

'Okay, what shall I do?' he asked himself.

You've only known her for a few days, the Voice said. *I suggest that instead of you doing the seduction bit, let her make the moves. You play hard to get. That way, if things don't work out in bed, you won't feel guilty.*

***

Damien was quite happy to coast along without any fireworks. Play it cool. He still wasn't sure he fancied her.

By week three, Frances had decided to change the status quo. Hitherto, the dates had ended with a friendly peck on the cheek. And even though Damien insisted on paying the tab, Frances did manage to squeeze in a gift. Namely a pair of Vilebrequin swimming shorts. He had planned to stay with Justin and Anna for the weekend in Antibes and had pointed out a pair on display in the window as they passed the shop in the Burlington Arcade after a visit to the Royal Academy.

She gave them to him over lunch at La Famiglia.

'What a lovely surprise!' He took the patterned blue and yellow shorts out of the bag. He leant forward and kissed her softly, sweet on her lips. Frances held her breath. She was floating.

'Let's go back to yours and you can try them on just to make sure they fit,' she said all breezy casual, with just a tiny hint of "what if he says no?" in her eyes. 'Okay?'

'I look forward to it,' he said.

***

After they had made love, Frances traced her finger across his chest and said, 'You're such a terrific guy, I can't believe we met in such a random way. It must be in the stars.'

Ah, the Voice said. *Is this your kindred spirit? Are you finally twinned with your ever-after? Claudia's cards, the traveller from abroad?*

Damien wound a strand of her blonde hair round his finger and stroked her soft cheek. 'You're such a sweet soul, Frances, but let's not get ahead of ourselves.'

'Well then, I'd better go.' Frances pushed his arm aside. 'Don't want to rush you. Make you feel pressured.'

'Please... don't take it the wrong way.'

'Is there a right way? Let me translate. It means that you're not really interested. Well, okay, I'm going to have a shower and then I'll be off.' She got up and made her way towards the bathroom.

Damien leapt out of bed, put his arms round her waist and kissed her neck.

'It's okay.' She pulled away from him. 'My fault. I was the one who seduced you. I really don't know why I'm so angry.'

She choked back her tears and wiped her face with the back of her hand, calmed herself and after a few breaths said, 'It's just that I don't normally make the moves. But I thought this time it was going to work.'

Damien caught her arm. 'Stop, stop, stop! Frances. I can't bear to see you like this.' He swung her round to face him. 'I just get nervous because I always seem to make the wrong choices. Please stay.'

***

Ten o'clock on Sunday morning Damien was in the kitchen rustling up breakfast, while Frances, wearing his pink Turnbull and Asser shirt and nothing else, sat watching him.

'It's all to do with the pan,' he said, waving the crêpe griddle in the air. 'The eggs cook quicker in a shallow pan and I don't fold the omelette. So it's more like a tortilla.'

'It's such a turn-on when a guy cooks you breakfast,' she said, standing behind him, hands on hips.

This one could be a winner, the Voice whispered in his head. *She likes you. In and out of bed.*

Damien had placed each ingredient in little white bowls on the marble worktop.

'First, butter – more flavour than olive oil.' He gently moved her out of the way and dropped a knob into the pan.

'Sauté the tomatoes.' He tipped them in. 'And wait for them to soften. Then pour in the whisked eggs. Burford browns are the best. Deep golden yolks, and a much richer taste than the usual ones.'

He moved the mixture around in the pan, occasionally prodding the edges of the omelette with a spatula.

'Let them cook for a few minutes, covering intermittently with a lid. There,' he said, running the spatula across the surface, 'nice and firm.'

'Smells good,' Frances said.

'Now for the grated cheese.' He sprinkled the cheddar on top with a flourish, let it melt and finally added some spinach leaves.

'Lovely,' she said, 'and so simple. I'm going to buy a griddle pan and if you come to stay at mine, I'll make you one.'

Damien caught that look in her eye.

Fair warning, the Voice said, *she's very enthusiastic. Already writing the scenario and it's feature length – she's hooked.*

Chapter 45

Damien and Frances had spent many happy months together: dinners, walks in the park, a long weekend in Tuscany, working on her screenplay.

On graduation day, Damien came to the show. Held her hand in the dark.

So here he was again, Damien Spur the Svengali, sitting with a zany American whose raw ambition and enthusiasm had pulled him into her journey, just like Anna had.

He stole a glance at Frances, her eyes focused on the cinema screen.

Title up – *Lost and Found*: A short film by Frances Swift.

The opening shot – a little boy lost in a labyrinthian department store. The camera tracks him as he weaves in and out through a sea of legs and then the scene swiftly cross-cuts to a woman slumped in a chair in the manager's office.

'Please help me,' she sobs. 'It was my fault. Jamie was pulling my hand. Wanted to go to the sweet shop. And he tugged so hard that I lost my grip. The next minute he'd gone.'

The scene shifts back to the little boy.

The film swirls into a dizzying kaleidoscope of colour and sound as the little boy spins round and round, panic etched on his tear-streaked face. 'Mummy,' he sobs, his voice raw with fear. 'Where's my mummy?'

A woman materialises from the throng, her face obscured by dark glasses and a vibrant blue scarf. She clasps Jamie's hand, her grip surprisingly strong. 'Don't worry, little one,' she murmurs, her voice husky and strangely calming. 'We'll find your mummy. I know just where to look.'

Swiping a tissue from her bag she dabs his eyes. 'I think she might be searching for you outside. Shhh, no need to cry.' She puts her finger to her lips and with a predatory grasp steers him by his shoulders towards the exit.

The loud hum of voices fade into a murmur. Then, a crackle, a hiss, and a man's voice on the Tannoy cuts through the silence echoing through the store.

'Jamie Jones, stay where you are. Your mum is coming to get you.'

'Wow! That's me! I'm Jamie.' The child looks up as the crowd of shoppers circle round him.

There was a palpable intake of breath from the audience as the tension rose.

For a brief moment the camera moves in on the woman's face, her grimace swiftly masked by a forced smile.

'Looks like your mum has found you, sweetie, so you don't need me anymore.'

Jamie sees the bobbing head of his mother as she zigzags through the shoppers to meet him.

'Jamie!' she cries.

And they are in each other's arms.

'It's alright, Mum, this nice lady was looking after me.'

But when Jamie turns back the woman has gone.

Jamie's mum looks towards the exit and briefly catches the profile of a woman before she vanishes into the street, blue scarf fluttering.

The film ended in a hushed silence, then the theatre erupted in a thunderous wave of applause punctuated by whoops and cheers.

So, Damien, another of your prodigies on their way, said the Voice.

***

He was fond of Frances. She had terrific energy, she was interesting, warm, sexy... always there for the taking. When he needed a break, she would leave him alone. Very accommodating. She slipped in and out of his life without making waves. No surprises. He knew where he stood; she was an open book that was easy to read.

Yes, Frances was great, but she wasn't a soulmate. Some people live without combat, settle for a restful life. Not Damien. No compromise.

***

That evening, as they lay in bed sharing a chocolate egg and drinking peppermint tea, Frances turned to him and said, 'I love you.'

Oh no, said the Voice.

'Frances,' said Damien, 'we need to talk. You're such a gorgeous person. I'm really fond of you... but it's not going to work.'

Her face drained, chalky white.

'I don't understand?'

He looked away.

'Look at me,' she said, prodding his chest. 'I'm practically living with you! And now, in bed, you tell me it's not going to work?'

He hated himself. A damaged man. Why couldn't he love this sweet, intelligent woman?

'I want to go home,' she said.

'I'm sorry, Frances, but I can't lie to you.'

Well done, said the Voice. *There's no point in beating about the bush.*

***

Elizabeth was no ordinary shoplifter. She'd been caught in Alberto Firenze with a silk dress hidden inside her Hermès bag.

It gave the manageress a thrill to take her down a peg or two. The haughty perfumer had always been rude to the staff.

"Get me this, get me that," she'd said. Never a please or thank you, leaving the garments on the floor for the assistants to pick up.

And now, finally, Lady Elizabeth Maitland was to be hauled over the coals. A hot potato who would soon be the talk of the gossip columns.

It wasn't going to be easy to keep it under wraps. She would have to call in some favours.

Maybe the newspaper editor she'd bumped into at a naughty party in Halkin Street could help her? The one who was up and at it with two gorgeous Russkies in the middle of the sitting room, while his wife Olivia, whom she knew, was stuck in the country.

Elizabeth, who was astride the Polish ambassador, waved at him.

'Hello, Ronald!' she said. 'Good to see you. Isn't this fun?'

Maybe he could keep the paparazzi off her back.

She went down to the station and asked to phone her solicitor. Who didn't pick up.

So she called Damien.

'Elizabeth, why are you ringing?' he said. 'I told you to leave me alone.'

'I'm in a terrible fix and you're the only person I could talk to. Seeing as you've had your dramas, I knew you would understand. Please help me.'

'What have you done?'

'I've been arrested for shoplifting.'

'Where are you?'

'Shepherd's Bush police station. Chelsea is closed. Will you come and help me?'

'I'm sorry, Elizabeth. No can do. Why don't you ask your man, Chang?' And he put down the phone.

Good for you, said the Voice. *Moving on…*

***

Sophie's phone pinged with a new text message:

Evelyn: Look, darling! Look what you're missing!

Sophie clicked the link, and there he was.

Close up.

That smile. Those honest eyes. He was so confident. His deep liquid voice gave her a rush of pleasure. She'd missed him. It had been a long time. So many distractions. All those empty affairs.

She drifted. In her mind's eye, he had slipped his hand round her waist and, pulling her towards him, he held her face and kissed her. Gently at first and then the wild Damien took hold and they both fell into a passionate embrace, the kiss more intense than any she'd ever had before.

Sophie blinked. Forced herself back to reality.

A young woman in a chic red dress was on the screen. Her long, elegant fingers curled round a microphone close to her mouth.

Sophie scanned her face. She was arrestingly lovely: cherubic blue eyes, turned-up nose, kiss-me lips. She asked her question.

Damien was back onscreen. A raised eyebrow and a smile. He answered her, his reply smooth as silk.

There was an intimacy between them. They spoke to each other as if there was no one else in the auditorium.

331

Were they lovers? He hadn't mentioned her.

Maybe she would be for a few months. And then on to the next.

He was a free man. Why shouldn't he pick and choose from all those delicious women who threw themselves at him?

Who are you kidding, Sophie? she thought. *You want him. Come on. Show him that you're ready – take him.*

Chapter 46

Nine o'clock Monday morning, Angus rang. Damien was in the kitchen ironing.

He loved ironing. Sliding back and forth on the sleeve of a shirt, smoothing away the creases. It gave him time to think. Plan the day.

'Can I call you back?' Damien said. 'I'm just in the middle of doing something.'

'No, no, stay on the line, please,' Angus replied in his brisk no-nonsense voice. 'I've a meeting in ten minutes.'

'Okay, just give me a sec.' He switched the iron off and propped it upright on the board.

'Now then,' he said, seating himself on a chair by the farmhouse table, 'fire ahead.'

'Well, to cut a long story short, I've just had a very curious conversation on the phone with a young man from Athens called Theo. He said he has a very special gift for you. Says that you don't actually know him, but there's a family connection.'

'Theo who?'

'I asked him but he wouldn't tell me. Said you'd understand if you met him. Apparently, he's flown all the way from Athens to give it to you in person.'

'That's presumptuous. How did he know I'd agree to meet him?'

'That was my next question,' Angus said. 'The boy was quite cheeky. Said that he thought it less likely that you'd refuse him if he'd made the effort to come to London. Especially as he's a poor student and saved all his money for the trip.'

'That's a pretty good story. Where's he staying?'

'For the last couple of days he said with his uncle in Shepherd's Bush, but he's moving on to somewhere else.'

'I must admit the uncle bit makes him sound wholesome. That's if it's true.'

Yes, it could all be lies, said the Voice. *Maybe he's some crazy stalker…*

'Well, he was very convincing,' said Angus. 'You could meet him here at the office if you like?'

'Steady on, I haven't agreed to anything yet. Did he tell you anything about himself?'

'A little. He wants to study mathematics at university. Says his dream is to do his postgraduate studies at Cambridge and he's sporty.'

'Sounds an interesting young guy.'

'So, what would you like me to do? Shall I give him your email?'

'No,' Damien said. 'Why don't you text me his number? It's so much easier on the phone to find out if the guy's on the level.'

'Okay. Will do.' Angus rang off and Damien went back to his ironing.

Another student from abroad, he thought. *Are the cards teasing me again?* He flattened the collar of his shirt and carefully pressed the edges. Maybe this new guy would make his life as difficult as Frances had. Not that he wasn't fond of Frances. He'd tried to break it off, but she had a way of creeping back into his life. Indeed, she'd rung him last night, crying.

'I'm late,' she said.

'For what?' said Damien.

'I've missed my period. It's happened before, but I feel different this time.'

'So, have you had a test?'

'Not yet – it's too soon.'

'How many days?'

'Three.'

'Well, no point in worrying yet, then.'

'But it's unusual for me.'

'Let's not jump the gun.'

'I'll wait a week, then I'll do a test.'

Three days. She could simply be stressed. Worried that things hadn't worked out the way she'd planned and that he wasn't going to be her ever-after.

Damien went quiet.

Frances carried on her anxious chatter. Could she come and see him? She missed him so much. Didn't want to lose him as a friend.

He hadn't rung her for a week. He felt guilty, mainly because there was some satisfaction in knowing that he was the one that was loved and not the lover. But who knows? Perhaps she'd wear him down. She was both irritating and adorable. Yes, he missed her. Perhaps he'd ring her next week. Take her out for lunch.

Good. Maybe you're learning, said the Voice. *Isn't it funny? All the women who have loved you. Your huge success, everything that on the surface should have been a life well lived has ended up on the scrap heap.*

Damien had tried to push the Voice to the back of his mind, but now that there were no distractions he was stuck with his uncomfortable friend. One who didn't flatter him or pander to his ego, one who let him know the real score.

You're a good man, Damien – that we know. A 24-carat gold approval from the media. Essential reading for the gossip columns. But what about your bleeding heart? You started a fabulous journey and then Laura's lies, the love of your life, messed you up. Sent you down the manhole.

'Yes,' he said to himself. 'Laura's still here to haunt me.'

Let's face it, Damien, you're jinxed by your past. But, hey, change the patterns and you stand a chance. Dance the dance. Move yourself. Shift your mind. Human kindness. That's what really matters. Don't mistake a kick in the teeth for love.

Yes, he'd see her again.

'Bye, Frances. Go to bed. It's 1 a.m. I'll call you soon.'

But damn it. She'd ruined his schedule and he'd overslept. Missed his early morning run.

And now the stress of making a phone call with a stranger who could be a nutter. A gift? What gift? He's from Greece. Beware Greeks bearing gifts.

But perhaps he was just an enthusiastic fan. Damien's books sold well in the capital. Maybe he'd brought him halloumi or baklava.

Damien poured a handful of the finest Columbian coffee beans into the hopper of his antique grinder and cranked the handle. He loved the pleasure of opening the little wooden drawer and spooning the sandy granules into the cafetière. His favourite morning ritual.

No rush, take your time, the Voice said. *Ring him later. When you've had your espresso.*

He settled himself at his desk in the living room and picked up the landline. First, he dialled 141 to withhold his number.

'Hello, Theo… this is Damien Spur. My agent said you have a gift for me. Which is very kind, but why? I need to know more about you.'

'I can't say any more,' the young man replied. 'The gift will explain everything. Please could we meet?'

'Look, I'm just asking you a simple question. What's all this got to do with me?'

'I'm sorry, but I can't tell you on the phone. It's too risky.'

'Why?'

'Because you might not believe me and then I'll never get to see you.'

'Theo, I'm going to have a shave and I'll get back to you in a few minutes.'

***

'Well... what do you think?' Damien asked his reflection in the bathroom mirror. 'Is he a psycho?'

Don't ask me, said the Voice.

After he'd shaved, Damien rang again.

'Theo,' he said in a kinder tone, 'I admit that your mysterious behaviour has piqued my curiosity. It will be interesting to see if the big reveal is as fascinating as you've had me believe.'

'I think it will be.'

'Well, I could meet you in my agent's office or in a cafe...'

'I think if you knew what the gift was you definitely would want to meet in private. Please, I know it's kind of crazy, but this could change your life forever, and mine.'

Wow! Drama, drama. This boy's got a hell of a pitch, said the Voice.

'All right. But it's definitely against my better judgement to meet a stranger from abroad, who has a gift for me but won't say what it is and wants to meet me in private.'

'Think of it as one of your stories,' Theo said.

'If I'd written the story, the guy would definitely be a killer.'

'Too predictable.'

What a cheek, said the Voice. *Arrogant little bugger.*

'Are you telling me how to write?'

'No, but this story is much more exciting.'

He certainly takes risks, said the Voice. *You could tell him to get lost. But then again there's nothing like a good teaser.*

'Okay, you've sold it to me. I'll text you my address. I'm in Chelsea, Cheyne Walk. Come tomorrow, 11 a.m.'

***

The young man stood at the door with a satchel on his shoulder. He was a handsome lad. Tall and slender with dark curly hair and a noble face.

But those eyes. Damien knew immediately. Chestnut brown, inquisitive, intense. 'You can't be,' he whispered.

'What?' the boy said.

'You can't be Laura's son?'

'I am,' the boy said.

There was a buzzing sound in Damien's ears, which grew louder and louder. He could feel his heartbeat banging against the wall of his chest. He held on to the door as if he were going to fall.

'Are you okay?' The boy dropped his satchel and lifted Damien's arm round his shoulder. 'Hold on to me. Shall I call an ambulance?'

'No,' he panted. 'I think I'll be all right. Let's just go inside.'

Keep calm, said the Voice. *Breathe. This is not the time for a heart attack.*

Damien could hardly stand. 'Give me a minute. Sit down and make yourself comfortable.'

He sank onto the rug, legs crossed, and shut his eyes. Focused on his breathing and steadied his mind until, gradually, the pounding in his heart subsided and his body relaxed.

Theo watched, hypnotised. The colour in Damien's cheeks had returned, and his breath had stilled.

'That's better.' He sighed. 'Now then.'

He rose to his feet.

'I made fresh coffee – come.'

Theo followed him into the kitchen.

There was a storm in Damien's head. Why had Laura shrouded the existence of this lovely young man with a lie? Her son! Alive and well and sitting in front of him. Why? The falling down the stairs, the miscarriage – a lie? Why had she hidden the truth about him?

'This is for you.' Theo placed a small brown paper parcel on the table.

Damien undid the wrapping and pulled out a worn blue leather diary. His elegant fingers stroked the cover.

'I've marked the page,' Theo said.

Go on, open it, whispered the Voice. *You have to admit she was always a terrific storyteller, almost better than you are.*

11 March 2002

Oh Damien, if only you knew. Here I am in Greece. Will I ever see you again? Andreas doesn't love me, he treats me as if I am some rare exotic bird. His English toffee, he calls me. I'm a novelty. We're not right together. Too late. There's a baby on the way. I'm two months gone. If only I could have told you the truth.

I should have stayed.

That last night, our last time together. New Year's Eve, before I left for Athens.

What a night. We were so in love again. No lies. We finally made it. But it was too late. It wasn't to be. LA was waiting for you and Greece for me...

And now here I am with a man who doesn't understand me. I have to simplify everything I say. No exchange of ideas.

I'm not even sure that the baby is his. That last night, what if...?

Damien! said the Voice. *Maybe your parting shot could be a life-changer. Does this mean little Achilles here is yours?*

Damien tipped back his chair and reached for his squeeze ball. 'Well, Theo, this is certainly a turn-up for the books. Even from the grave, Laura has managed to shake up the DNA. So.'

He squeezed the ball. 'This is very stressful. Just give me a second to think.'

The young man watched as Damien shut his eyes. His mouth twisted in a grimace as if he were in pain.

'Okay,' said Damien at last. 'There are two ways to go here. Maybe it would be better to let matters rest. Close the book and let things stay as they are. Don't allow Laura's mischief to change the status quo. Don't question who's your father.'

'Or?' Theo said.

Come on, Damien, look at him, the Voice said. *There's definitely a likeness. That nose, straight and elegant, just like yours. And his height. Wouldn't it be great! There's finally someone who has come into your life that might give you some stability, responsibility. It's just what you need. Think of it, the student from abroad, just as the tarot cards predicted.*

'I don't really want to suggest the second option,' Damien said. 'Imagine going back to the man who brought you up and telling him he isn't your father.'

'That's not a problem,' Theo said.

'What do you mean?'

'My father's dead. He gave me the diary before he passed away. Told me to find you. He knew I might not be his son. Said it didn't matter, he loved me anyway.'

And then Theo wept. Just as Damien had when his own father died.

Damien held him, let him cry, until the final gasp of relief came, and he was still.

'So, Theo, shall we have a DNA test?'

'Maybe?' he said. 'But suppose you're not my father? How would that change things?'

'A difficult question,' Damien mused. 'Especially as we've only just met. Perhaps we should wait. Get to know each other first.'

Yes, good idea, said the Voice. *The poor lad looks so lost. Why don't you cook him dinner, let him spend the night? It's the least you can do after he's come all the way from Athens to meet you. And, between you and me, it's all terrific material for your next book.*

Theo was happy to stay. He sat in the kitchen watching Damien prepare a seafood pasta with courgette noodles.

'Such a wonderful alternative to spaghetti.' Damien pushed the courgette through the blades, twisting it round and round as the little green spirals slid into the bowl. 'You try.'

'My first cooking lesson,' Theo replied. 'My maybe-father couldn't even make a cup of tea. When I was little, any time my stepmother, Elvira, went to see her sister in Mykonos he would take me to the local taverna. I could have anything I liked on the menu. I usually chose fried calamari, my favourite, while I watched him play tavli. He was really good and usually won. Knew all the odds. Afterwards he would play with me, explaining the strategy and logic of the game. He was really my first maths tutor. It's thanks to him I discovered my love for mathematics.'

'Well, not a bad adventure for a young lad. I bet you had fun.'

'Yes, I did.' Theo beamed, the memory still warm. 'And now it's your turn. Tell me about Laura.'

A flicker of pain crossed Damien's eyes.

'Where do I even begin? Laura hid the truth behind so many lies.' Damien noticed Theo's feet. He was wearing sandals and had long slender toes just like his. 'She probably would have made a great spy,' Damien continued. 'Never broke her cover. But I don't want to talk badly of your mother. I was madly in love when I married her. That you should know.'

He felt comfortable talking with Theo, stirring the courgette pasta, when the doorbell rang.

'Can you answer it?' he said.

'Sure. Who's there?' he asked through the intercom.

'Frances.'

'Just a second.' He returned to the kitchen. 'It's Frances. Do I let her in?'

'No, it's okay, I'll go.'

Let her wait, said the Voice. *Turning up unannounced. What a nerve.*

Frances stood on the threshold like a soldier. Chin up, arms by her side, legs astride.

She gave Damien a tense smile.

'Hi,' she said.

'Hello, Frances, this is a surprise,' Damien replied.

'I really need to talk to you,' she said. For a moment she looked past him at the handsome young man standing by the entrance of the kitchen.

He gazed back. A blush rose from her neck to her cheeks. Something had clicked.

Oh God! This is sick! the Voice boomed in his head. *She said she was pregnant with your child! Forget Oedipus. What kind of Greek mess is this going to be? Son falls in love with Dad's pregnant girlfriend. That makes your potential offspring Theo's half-brother. You'd better put a stop to this before it starts. Ask her NOW. In front of Theo. Clear the decks, one way or the other.*

'Frances, are you pregnant?' Damien said.

'No,' she said.

'I'll check the pasta,' Theo said.

When they were alone, Frances looked at Damien and said in a quiet voice, 'I lied. I thought that if I said that I might be pregnant you would keep on seeing me.'

'And how long did you expect to keep that up?'

'I guess till I pretended to have a miscarriage. Say I'd fallen down the stairs.' She gave a huge sigh and started to cry.

'Unbelievable! This is better than anything I could have written,' he said. 'What an incredible story. You and Laura tied together by your porkies. Such a great joke!' He chuckled.

And then he roared with laughter. Wave after wave rising from his core.

'You can't imagine how relieved I am that you came clean,' he said wiping the tears of joy from his eyes.

You bet! said the Voice.

'I'm glad you think it's funny,' Frances said. 'So I guess that's it for us?'

Can you believe it? She's still pushing her luck, said the Voice.

'Romantically, yes. But who knows, with your gift for fantasy, one day we might collaborate on a screenplay together.'

'Really?'

'Please, Frances, enough.'

'Okay, okay…' She paused.

She certainly can roll with the punches. Now what? the Voice said.

'So who's the guy?' Frances asked.

She gave him a sweet little smile.

Look at that! She's ready to back another horse, said the Voice.

'It's a long story,' Damien said.

'Okay. Well, suppose I'd better go. You must think I'm terrible.'

'At least you told the truth in the end.'

He took her arm to take her down the steps. She turned to wave goodbye to Damien's mystery guest.

'I'm sorry, I don't know your name,' she called.

'Theo.'

'I hope we meet again,' she said, and gave him her broad American smile.

She said it with just enough enthusiasm to irritate Damien.

'Me too,' Theo said.

That night he slept well. Thank the Lord that Frances wasn't pregnant. He was free again. Even the Voice nodded off the moment his head hit the pillow.

Next day, Damien awoke to find Theo in the bathroom, liberally splashing himself with his Vétiver.

'Morning,' said the boy.

'You're still here?' Damien glanced at him coolly and shifted his eyes to the cologne.

That's a bit of a cheek. Help yourself, why don't you, said the Voice.

'My favourite fragrance. I can see you like it? Judging by what's left in the bottle.'

Theo blushed. 'Oh, sorry, Damien. I should have asked you first. Yes, it's lovely. Very sexy. I like your taste.'

'Well then, what are your plans today, Theo?'

'Oh, I don't know. You didn't tell me what time you wanted me to leave. So I thought that we could have breakfast together. My turn to cook.'

'I'm not sure I have the time.'

'Oh, what a shame. It's been so wonderful to meet you. And so kind of you to let me stay overnight. I really didn't expect it.'

Damien felt sorry for him. He was in two minds. He had to admit he liked him. And he knew what it was like to be lonely. No mother, father, sister, brother. If he was his son, it could make things very difficult. He'd probably want to live with him. And then what? He was definitely cougar bait. And he had drive. Who knows – he might bulldoze into his life and take advantage of Damien's sentimental generosity!

'Well then, Theo, I think it's time to say goodbye,' he said. 'I want to have a run now and I'm meeting my editor for lunch.'

'So, shall we take a DNA test?' Theo said.

Damien was in a fix.

Don't be mean, said the Voice. *You can't leave unfinished business. It's his life too.*

'Okay, we can go together.'

Theo looked at Damien and gave him a sweet smile. 'I could be calling you Papa soon.'

Damien had to admit the boy had charm. Maybe even if it didn't work out, he'd still keep in touch. Be his sponsor, help him pay his uni fees, take him to restaurants and the theatre, even go fishing together. Be like a father to him.

Chapter 47

After his usual run he returned home, had a shower, towelled himself dry with a vigorous rub and slipped on his robe.

He poured himself a cup of tea and sat down in the Chesterfield armchair by the picture window in the living room, ready for his daily Bach music fest.

'Alexa, play the *Goldberg Variations*,' he said. The achingly perfect melody flooded his being and swept away the discords in his mind. Time for a heart to heart with the Voice.

'So what am I going to do about Sophie?' he asked himself. 'How am I going to cross the bridge from friend to lover?'

Change your tune, the Voice replied. *Sophie wants muscle. It's not exactly sexy seeing you coked out of your mind like a gibbering wreck or wallowing in self-pity after that bitch Elizabeth ground you into the dust.*

'Okay, okay. There you go again. Why do you have to make me feel that I'm the only man in the world who's ever had his heart broken?'

Because it's going to be difficult to change the status quo unless you recognise your past behaviour. Being Mr Vulnerable is fine but it's not a turn-on for someone like Sophie. You need to replace those pictures in her head.

For a moment Damien was distracted by the nocturnal scream of a vixen mating. Was Sophie a screamer? he wondered.

'I really love her.' Damien took a sip of tea and settled his head on the cushion, his eyes bright with thoughts of Sophie lying on his bed. Entwined together. Her head on his shoulder, both at rest after they'd made love.

Damien? Where are you? asked the Voice. *Wake up! Would you like my advice, or not?*

'Yes! No need to shout. You're giving me a headache.' Damien massaged his temples. 'I was just having a pleasant moment.'

Okay, the Voice continued. *So show her your other side. Stop with the friendly-bro approach. Make it a date night. Dinner first and then on to a nightclub for a smooch. Fire her up. Then take her home and get that mojo working. No hesitation. When you're in the zone, there's no need to think.*

YOU NEED TO ACT.

***

The night went well. 3 a.m. A last dance at Annabelle's. So close, languidly swaying, his arms around her waist, Sophie nuzzling his neck, until there was no doubt.

And that kiss. It was as if it had always been there, hiding in the shadows.

Damien couldn't hear the Voice, only his heart beating triumphantly as Sophie responded to his warmth.

No words.

Until finally she whispered, 'Well, that's a surprise. You've melted me.'

'Let's go home,' he said taking her hand.

Synchronicity. He was ready and so was she. He carried her up the stairs to the bedroom and, laying her on the bed, lifted up her dress. She spread her legs.

He stroked her, softly at first, his fingers keeping pace with her arousal, moving faster as her breath quickened and her body grew taut; taking her to the edge, then he paused.

'Ask me,' he whispered.

'Oh my God, please, Damien, don't make me wait,' she moaned. 'I want all of you.'

And as he slowly entered her, the Voice whispered, *No need for a threesome now, I'll leave you to it.*

Acknowledgements

My long and winding road to complete Damien's journey has not been a solitary one. There have been many angels on the way.

Firstly, my editors, Charlie Mounter, who chivvied me along. Kept the pot boiling and the narrative flowing. And Sam Stanton Stewart, who encouraged me to allow Damien his vulnerability and let him ride the waves with charm and wit.

Renowned Composer Debbie Wiseman and her husband Tony. Both happy to read the extracts and ever patient Debbie kept me calm and gave me good advice.

Award-winning children's writer, Anthony McGowan, honed the synopsis and gave me some excellent tweaks.

But the perseverance prize goes to lovely actress Cherie Lunghi who painstakingly went through the final draft and spent many hours reading through the chapters with me, helping cherry-pick the good bits and discard the pips.

Other dear friends who stayed with me on the journey – radio playwright Helen Kluger; Robert Sellers, showbiz author and journalist; Julie Midwinter, Adrienne Ventura, Hedi Nedrum and Anne Ker-Lindsay.

Having completed the final draft it was time to send the sample extracts to the publishers. And that's when my son Waldo and his terrific wife Lindsay stepped in.

'Give them the teaser,' they said. 'A swift sexy pitch which leaves the reader wanting more. Cut it like a trailer.'

Samples sent. Submission requested and accepted by The Book Guild. An excellent team of players who have released Damien Spur out of my fantasy into the real world.